C000185174

DON

Diana Stainfor
West before p
Bird of Paradise. She is also the
Indiscretion, Friends and Other Enemies and *The Wilder Side of Life.* Having lived in Italy for some years, she is now based in London where she writes full time.

By the same author

BIRD OF PARADISE
THE INDISCRETION
FRIENDS AND OTHER ENEMIES
THE WILDER SIDE OF LIFE

DON'T LOOK BACK

Diana Stainforth

Published by Arrow Books in 1995

1 3 5 7 9 10 8 6 4 2

© Diana Stainforth 1994

Diana Stainforth has asserted her right under the Copyright, Designs and Patents Act, 1988 to be identified as the author of this work

This book is sold subject to the condition that it shall not, by way of trade or otherwise, be lent, resold, hired out, or otherwise circulated without the publisher's prior consent in any form of binding or cover other than that in which it is published and without a similar condition including this condition being imposed on the subsequent purchaser

First published in the United Kingdom by Century in 1994

Arrow Books Limited
20 Vauxhall Bridge Road, London, SW1V 2SA

Random House Australia (Pty) Limited
20 Alfred Street, Milsons Point, Sydney,
New South Wales 2061, Australia

Random House New Zealand Limited
18 Poland Road, Glenfield
Auckland 10, New Zealand

Random House, South Africa (Pty) Limited
PO Box 337, Bergvlei, South Africa

A CIP catalogue record for this book is available from the British Library

Random House UK Limited Reg. No. 954009

Papers used by Random House UK are natural, recyclable products made from wood grown in sustainable forests. The manufacturing processes conform to the environmental regulations of the country of origin.

ISBN 0 09 9256711

Printed and bound in the United Kingdom by
BPC Paperbacks Ltd, a member of The British Printing Company Ltd

Acknowledgements

Many people gave up their time to help me research this book. Their expertise and experiences have given credibility to my story and I am most grateful to them.

I am indebted to John Page and Julia Schulze at Lloyds and Peter Clark of C. Claims for their insights into the world of marine insurance.

I thank John Pennefather, David Stancomb, Bill Dineen of Southern Motorboats, and Peter Raymond for sharing their love and knowledge of boats and sailing.

I am grateful to Constable Ian Hill, Marine Intelligence Officer, for the information concerning marine crime.

My thanks are also due to Hilary Peake, my guide to Melbourne; my Rhode Island guides, Mark Schubin and Karen McLaughlin; Sue Brown, my Isle of Wight guide; Moyra McGhie for her insights into the housing market; Tanja Klijn, press officer at the Rotterdam Hilton; and Raymond Levine for his 'Belworth' hospitality.

Also I thank Judith Baldwin for her good-humoured typing.

Finally, I am indebted to my agent, Gill Coleridge, for her continued support and encouragement – and for her sailing expertise.

Diana Stainforth
London
4th January 1994

I

London – June 1988

RIGHT UP UNTIL the day when they bought the house on Ladbroke Hill, Anna was afraid that Charlie would change his mind about it. Even that morning, in the taxi on the way to the solicitor, he'd begun to talk of Melbourne with the touch of homesickness which she'd always translated as his way of telling her that he was free to return to Australia whenever he chose.

Anna stood on the far side of the square, looking across at their new house: their first home. She wished Charlie had come with her, but he'd hurried back to work, saying they'd no time to waste, especially now that they had such a large mortgage to pay. He'd called her sentimental: they'd seen the house yesterday, they'd see it again this evening, and at the weekend. But Anna had wanted to visit it this morning, because only now was it their own.

Ladbroke Hill was an oasis of quiet, a few minutes' walk from the busy, wide sweep of Ladbroke Grove. More of a triangle than a square, there were just fifteen houses built around a small garden containing two creamy, flowering horse-chestnut trees and a wooden bench. All the houses were in pairs except for theirs, which stood alone above the brightly-painted houses which curved down the hill towards Portobello and the bustling street market. As soon as Anna had seen the house she'd been drawn to it. She'd been reminded of Cliff Cottage, and the toing and froing of people in the market had recalled the ebb and flow of the tide on the beach below at Belworth Cove. But it wasn't just nostalgia for a house once loved which had attracted her. Ladbroke Hill had evoked memories of a time when she'd felt happy and safe – before everything went wrong.

The sun was hot; it beat down on Anna's head. She could feel it on her scalp where her hair parted, slightly to the right of her crown. Her hair was doing what she called its curtain act, when it hung, thick and soft and straight to her shoulder, with every vestige of the curl she had tonged into it that morning long since disappeared. Tucking it behind her ears, she crossed the road.

Even on a bright June morning there was something deliciously secretive about this house. Built during the last century, alongside the racecourse which had bordered the Notting Barn and Portobello Farms, it was hidden from passers-by by a high wall covered in ivy and an ancient yew tree whose top branch had snapped in the hurricane of the previous October. Although in desperate need of repair, the building retained its classical beauty with curved – though badly worn – steps leading up to a high, arched portico and fan-topped windows, tall and elegant in spite of the cracked panes.

She picked her way up the half-moon drive, tripping over the fronds of ivy which rampaged across the gravel, and when she reached the steps she stopped to scrape the mud from her high heels. As she did so, she overbalanced and rubbed the sleeve of her smart white linen suit on the dirty stonework. Charlie was right. She'd been silly to come.

Now that she was here, she couldn't leave without going inside. Her key grated in the lock, and she had to put her shoulder against the door to heave it open. There were no carpets or furniture, just a pile of junk mail on the unvarnished boards of the hall floor and particles of dust dancing up and down in the warm, stale air, but even in its dilapidated state, Anna found the house beautiful.

The rooms on both sides were identical, with a central cantilever staircase curling up to the attic, and exquisite mouldings surrounding every doorway and window. In her imagination she saw it painted and furnished, and she pictured herself sweeping down the stairs in a low-cut evening dress whilst Charlie, in a dinner-jacket, paced up and down, tapping his watch because for once she would have kept him waiting.

Anna opened the door on her right to what had once been a study, with panelled double doors leading to a dining-room. From it, French windows led out on to a wrought-iron balcony which looked down on a jungle of a garden in which honeysuckle and ivy fought for sunlight. Beyond the dining-room, at the top of the garden steps, there was a pretty, circular morning room – or rather there had been until Miss Elismore, the arthritic old lady who'd owned the house for the past thirty years, had partitioned it into a bathroom and kitchen when necessity forced her to rent out the top two floors.

Anna couldn't wait to restore the house to its early glory. Xavier Benites-Macdonald, their architect, had quoted them a hundred thousand pounds, after which they'd have a home to be proud of. She was already proud of it.

As she opened the balcony doors, she heard Glenn Miller's *Chattanooga Choo-Choo* drifting up from the basement. She knew the tune well; it was one of her grandmother's favourites. Stepping forward, she peered over the railings, and found herself looking down into the small, hostile eyes of Mr Shufflebuck, their sitting tenant. He was stretched out on a green and white striped deck-chair, his slight body encased in white flannels, and looked as though he were posing for an advertisement for a cruise. On a chair next to him was an enormous marmalade cat.

'I suppose you won't allow me to sit in the garden, as Miss Elismore did,' he said, pursing his lips like an aged, angry pixie.

In spite of his unfriendliness, Anna couldn't help feeling sorry for him. 'We're having some work done on the house and won't be living here for a few months, so you're welcome to use the garden for the time being,' she said politely.

'It's so unfair.' He sat up. 'Miss Elismore told her nephew that I was to live here, undisturbed, for the rest of my life. She didn't put it in her will, because she trusted him.' He rose abruptly and disappeared into the basement.

Anna sighed. Charlie was right, the sooner they bought out Mr Shufflebuck the better, even if it did mean increasing their loan.

Taking her compact from her bag, she checked her make-up. Her face was what some people called heart-shaped and others called square. Today it looked heart-shaped because she was happy. She drew the mirror closer and picked a speck of dust from one of her long eyelashes. Then she retouched her mascara, with a hint of turquoise to emphasise the colour in her eyes. They were her best feature – at least Charlie said so. It was the first compliment he'd paid her. He'd walked into her office on his first day at Marinecover, and said in his drawling Australian accent that her eyes made him homesick for the sea off Wilson's Promontory.

Suddenly, Anna noticed the time. She'd been at the house for an hour and she'd only intended to stay five minutes. She hurried out and set off down the drive, sensing Mr Shufflebuck watching her from behind his net curtains.

'You can't force me out,' he shouted, opening his front door. 'I know my rights.'

She stopped, then walked back towards him. 'I'm sorry you're upset, but if we hadn't bought the house someone else would have.'

'This isn't just a house, it's my home.' He raised his hands to his face so that she couldn't see his tears.

His distress took Anna back to Cliff Cottage, to the day when the new owners had moved in. She wanted to tell him that she understood because she too had once cried 'This is my home', but he went inside and closed his door.

She turned and walked back down the drive.

2

BY THE TIME Anna stepped from her taxi and into the gleaming glass and chrome Marinecover building, she'd put Mr Shufflebuck to the back of her mind and was thinking of the work piled in her in-tray.

'No need to check your identification, Miss Tobias,' said Mr Hawthorn, the uniformed commissionaire.

'I should think not, I'll have been here seven years next week.' She smiled at him as she headed for the lift.

It took her to the tenth floor, where she stepped out into the smart navy blue reception area. Gordon Routlish, managing director of the entire Marinecover Group and Anna's direct boss, believed that navy was the only colour for a marine broker's office because it reminded employees that they were dealing with the sea, that most uncontrollable of risks.

Judy, the petite, auburn-haired receptionist, was seated at her oval desk, simultaneously signing for a parcel, calling up information on her computer screen, and answering a telephone query. 'Messages!' she called to Anna as she finished the call, pointing at one of the clips on the front of her desk.

'Didn't Elaine take them?'

Judy rolled her big brown eyes.

'Don't tell me she arrived late again?'

'At eleven.'

The phone rang. Judy answered with, 'Marinecover. Good morning. Could you hold the line a minute?' She covered the mouthpiece and said to Anna, 'She's a liberty-taker; she knew you were out, dealing with your new house.'

Anna sighed. 'Thanks for warning me. I hate to put someone out of work but I'll have to speak to Delia about her when she gets back from holiday.'

Scanning her messages, Anna crossed the crowded open-plan central office where the secretaries, typists and clerks keyed into computers beneath harsh strip lighting. The place buzzed with people, voices, phones and quotes. It was that buzz which Anna loved.

Marinecover was a medium-sized brokerage house, divided into four departments: Hulls, Cargoes, Liabilities and Yachts. A broker's job was to take the client's request for insurance coverage and find an underwriter – or several – willing to take on that risk. The broker was the link between the client and the underwriter. He or she was the agent of the client, taking a commission from the client's premium before passing on the balance to the underwriter who underwrote the risk. The higher the premium, the more the broking house earned. At the same time, the broker had to get the best quote – or the client would go elsewhere.

Marinecover's largest department was Hulls. Its director, Harold, a keen mountaineer, controlled a team of ten senior brokers, each backed up by a junior and a secretary, with various clerks as support. It was a tough department. Their clients were the big shipping lines, and they had to battle for business against the giant broking houses such as Merchant & Leisure.

As a junior Anna had worked in every section. She'd found Cargoes to be the dullest. There was nothing evocative about a missing load of coffee beans, whereas a yacht, however small, had a certain romance. Yachts appealed to the sailor in her, and she'd been thrilled when Gordon had promoted her to head of that department. She ran it with the help of an assistant, a secretary, two clerks and sixteen sub-agents spread throughout Britain and the Mediterranean. She didn't mind that it was the smallest section, or that in many broking houses yacht insurance was considered a backwater, a shunt sideways for well-connected employees who'd never quite make the big time. The department was Anna's baby and since she'd been in charge, promoting their complete yachting package which she'd named Yachtcover, turnover had doubled.

In the far corner of the open-plan office, Chris, her assistant, was at his desk, talking rapidly on the telephone. He was a blond, baby-faced East-Ender with cherubic curls, an angelic smile and an insatiable hunger for money. 'New client,' he mouthed at Anna. 'Greek island flotilla.'

Anna gave him the thumbs up.

Beyond Chris, Elaine, her secretary, sat hunched over her keyboard, gazing at the flickering screen as she whispered into the telephone. She was a tall, graceful girl with dark mahogany skin and an unruly mop of black curly hair hiding what could have been a very pretty face, but now she looked tired and resentful. She'd worked for Anna less than a month and at her interview she'd been bright and tidy, with her hair plaited on top and wearing a neat red suit. Today she was in a pale blue cotton dress, so creased it appeared as though she'd slept in it.

When Elaine saw Anna approach, she said all too obviously into the receiver, 'I must get on with my work. Thanks for calling.' Then she gave Anna a guilty smile. 'Did you get the house?'

'Yes, thank you.' Anna gave her a knowing look. She went into her office, tossed her bag and briefcase on to the desk, and decided to deal with Elaine later.

Her room was small – they all were – but it had a spectacular view over the roof-tops towards the new, grey, tubular Lloyd's building, not that Anna had time to gaze out of the window. Arranging her messages on her desk in order of importance, she placed Vincent Ellerby-Creswell at the top. He was a successful second-hand car dealer and one of her best clients, who'd been plain Vince Creswell of Brixton until he made his fortune, moved to Ascot, and married his third wife, Monique. At the bottom of the pile she put her elder sister, Rosamund. There was no point in calling Roz now; she always played tennis on Wednesdays.

Before telephoning Vince, Anna walked up the corridor and through the first of many doors marked 'Hulls'.

Charlie was lolling back in his chair, the telephone hooked under his chin, his long legs stretched out before him, a lock of his golden-blond hair flopping in his very blue eyes. He gave her his lazy, handsome smile and covered the mouthpiece. 'House still standing?'

She smiled. 'Of course.'

'Didn't I say it was a waste of time to go there this morning?'

'I wanted to see it.' She perched on the edge of his desk, dangling her legs in front of him, allowing her straight white skirt to ride up her thighs. She enjoyed watching Charlie negotiate a deal, she liked to see his eyes dance as he bettered his opponent, she even relished his voice. She'd never liked Australian accents in the past, but now if she heard one as she walked along the street she would turn to listen, as people do if they walk past an open window and hear a song which brings back memories, happy or otherwise.

For the first time in months she wasn't afraid of losing Charlie. By buying the house he was committed to her, even if he didn't like to think so. She picked up a paper clip, twisted it around her engagement finger and waved it in front of his eyes, something which a few months earlier she wouldn't have dared do for fear of frightening him away. He looked startled, and stopped talking. She could hear the man at the other end shouting, 'Charlie? Hell, we've been cut off.'

'No we haven't.' Charlie carried on. 'What I was saying, Bill, is that premiums are up. It's a fact of life.'

Anna pulled off the paper clip and tossed it in the waste paper basket. As she swung her legs off Charlie's desk, he grabbed her ankle. She kicked at him playfully, but he held her tight until he'd finished his telephone call. Then he kissed the soft inside of her knee and released her with a laugh.

'Did you see the old pansy?' he asked as she stood up.

'Yes. He's very upset, so I told him he could use the garden whilst we're not living there.' She opened the door, adding, 'I'd better get back to work. I've booked a table for tonight at L'Artiste Assoiffé – a celebration, my treat.'

His face lit up. 'I'd love that.'

She flushed with pleasure. 'And we have your favourite table.'

'Even better.' He motioned her to close the door, then lowered his voice. 'But I can't make it till nine, because I'm meeting a couple of guys from Merchant & Leisure after work. One of their top brokers has had a breakdown and there could be a brilliant opening for me.'

Anna stared at him in disbelief. 'But . . . Charlie . . . we've just bought an incredibly expensive house on Marinecover's cheap staff loan.'

'Merchant & Leisure would offer the same deal.'

'Then why move?'

'Because my promotion here is blocked. When Harold retires, Stuart Porterill, the dreaded, hood-eyed Cobra, will become departmental director.'

'What . . . what about Cargoes?'

'Don't be stupid! Jeremy's already there and he's barely forty. Liabilities aren't my strength and Yachts is your niche. Everyone knows you're Gordon's blue-eyed girl.' He held up his hands to silence her protests. 'I don't resent it, sweetie, you know I don't, but if I want to get on, I have to get out. You were here first.'

'And I'm three years older than you?'

'Come here, my older lover.' He laughed in his carefree way, reaching up to run his fingers through her silky fair hair, unaware of how he'd hurt her by calling her stupid. 'Brokers peak in their mid-thirties, we all know that, and by forty-five they're washed-up, tired, drained – unless they're first-rate. I want to be a director, so I need to get into position now. If Marinecover can't offer me the works, I have to move.'

She didn't argue, because he was right. 'Marinecover's been our daytime home,' she said sadly. 'We met here. It won't be the same if we don't work together.'

He chuckled. 'Anna, you're so sentimental. We'll be living together, we'll see each other every night.'

'I suppose you're right.' She forced a smile and gave him a quick peck on the cheek, then stood back, her head erect, her shoulders straight. 'I'll see you at nine. Don't keep me waiting!'

He blew her a kiss. 'I won't this time, I promise.'

Back in her office, with the door closed, Anna stood in the centre of the room taking slow, deep breaths. She told herself that Charlie was right to seek advancement, but she couldn't prevent the fears of her childhood from flooding in, of her mother saying, 'I know you hate moving, Anna, but we have to go. It's your father's job; army postings only last two years.' So they'd moved, over and over again, until the day he'd left them, so violently, so abruptly, without warning.

Taking a mirror from her desk, Anna combed her hair back off her face into what Charlie called her 'ice-maiden' look. He preferred to see it fluffed around her face as she wore it at the weekends. She wondered what he'd say if he knew that the fairest streaks came from a bottle. Smoothing down her eyebrows, she frowned at the tiny worry lines forming between her eyes, which accentuated them even more. She seemed to have had them all her life, and she wished she could be like Charlie and not fret about things, living only for today and tomorrow, with no past to pull her backwards into terrors she thought she'd conquered.

Memories swept over her, of the intense beauty of summer evenings at Belworth when she'd hurry through her homework, then run from the cottage down to the gate at the bottom of the lane. There she'd wait, swinging on the top bar, hoping her father would come home early enough to take out the *Little Auk*; to sail across the sunset sea, lost in the stillness of the golden evening. She remembered the lap of the waves and his voice, strangely light for such a tall man.

'I've had a new idea, Annie, it's going to make our fortune. I'll leave the army and we'll buy all the land around Cliff Cottage. It's a secret, but I'll tell you. I've invented a plastic egg-timer.'

'But Daddy, there already is one. Old Mr Holdsworthy's sister brought one back from America.'

'Not as good as mine. You'll see, Annie, you'll soon be the daughter of Jeffrey Tobias, the famous inventor.'

They'd sail on, laughing, talking, convinced that this time, unlike all the other times, his invention would make them rich. On land Jeffrey Tobias had been a mild-mannered dreamer, a passed-over major who'd only joined the army because his father had wanted him to, but at sea he'd been the captain of the *Little Auk*, an inventor and a discoverer, Christopher Columbus and Galileo wrapped in one.

The intercom brought Anna back to the present. It was Gordon, her boss. 'Join me for sandwiches and coffee in the board room,' he said.

'I'm on my way.'

The board room at Marinecover was acknowledged to be one of the most impressive among broking houses. It boasted two magnificent Waterford crystal chandeliers and a valuable collection of marine oil paintings. Gordon was seated at the far end of the oval, mahogany table, surrounded by his usual piles of papers. He was a suave, silver-haired man whose eyebrows and eyelashes had been permanently burned away in a schoolboy prank in the chemistry lab. This gave him an eerie, featureless appearance.

'I've bought another picture.' He pointed at a painting of two tea clippers riding the Atlantic waves.

She examined it quietly. 'I like it.'

'Thought you would. Buy the house?' Gordon wasted as few words as possible when speaking of anything other than Marine-cover.

'This morning.'

'Have to work hard to pay for it.'

'I always do.'

'Should hope so on the huge salary we pay you.'

Anna smiled. 'Gordon, I earn it.'

He chuckled. 'You've made a great success out of Yachts, the only person apart from myself ever to do so. Clients like you, Anna. You're a sailor, and you speak their language.' He waved his hand towards a tray of sandwiches and coffee. 'Help yourself. Then tell me how you plan to prevent Barry Limehouse from poaching your clients?' Barry Limehouse was Merchant & Leisure's new yacht broker.

It was typical of Gordon not to give her time to think. He'd once met Charlie in Harrods during the sale and grilled him about hull premiums over the discounted cashmere sweaters. 'I'll make sure my clients get the best quotes, and I'll increase my social contacts with them,' she replied, sounding breezy and confident because that was how Gordon liked his team. 'Barry can't compete. He's a thug and most of my people wouldn't trust him in their homes. He's even nicknamed the Thug.'

'He'll try to persuade old Isaac Finestein to give him a binding authority – which is what you should have.'

Anna put down her sandwich. 'Isaac doesn't trust any broker with his syndicate's money. I asked him to allow me to underwrite small amounts of up to fifty thousand without reference to him, but he gave me a flat "no".'

'I thought he liked you.'

'He does and I like him. I've met his family, I've dined at his home, and I went to his daughter's twenty-first birthday party. But that's social, Gordon, this is business. Isaac's the best yacht underwriter. He doesn't need to give binding authorities to brokers, and he doesn't want to.'

'At least if he won't give you permission, he's not likely to give it to Merchant & Leisure.'

'He'd damned well better not.'

Gordon smiled. 'You realise that Barry Limehouse will fight you for the Costa del Sol market?'

'He can have the crooks with pleasure.'

'You're right. Dishonest business is a waste of everyone's time. Paul Sheldon has just rejected another claim. The stupid client had sunk the boat himself by drilling the holes from the inside of the hull. Even the worst loss adjuster would discover that ruse – and Sheldon is the best.'

Anna felt the beginning of a blush and she bent to stir her coffee. 'Personally, I prefer Giles Humphreys.'

'I thought you and Sheldon were friends.'

'Oh . . . I hardly know him.'

'He's an amusing character and a brilliant sailor. Popular with women too, I gather.'

'He's a bounty hunter; all loss adjusters are.'

'Sheldon's a bounty hunter with a conscience – unlike most.'

'Come on, Gordon, they all feed off crime and disaster.'

'He'd argue that we brokers feed off people's fear of crime and disaster.'

She rose, laughing. 'Then I'd better get back to my terrified clients before the Thug consumes them.'

Talking to Gordon always made Anna feel punchy and capable. She'd originally come to Marinecover for one month as a temporary secretary, when Miss Thin, Gordon's dedicated assistant, had broken her arm. On the day before she was due to leave, Gordon called her into the boardroom, and said, 'You're a mediocre typist but you'd make a good broker. Stay, and we'll train you.' It was the challenge Anna had been waiting for.

She walked back to her office. The building was relatively quiet, since most people were at lunch. Only Elaine typed furiously, her head down, her shoulders hunched. She didn't look up as Anna walked past her and into her room. Anna closed the door and began to work through her messages. Many of the people she called, including Vince Ellerby-Creswell, were at lunch. She couldn't even phone Roz who would be on her way to collect Oliver and Phoebe, her two youngest, from school. It was frustrating. Anna liked to deal with things, tick them off and not have them hang around her desk in piles beneath her paperweights.

She sorted through the letters which had accumulated over the past days when her mind had been on Ladbroke Hill. There was an optimistic report from her sub-agent in Lymington, a number of requests for reinsurance from old clients, several demands for world-wide cover instead of the normal UK, Continent and Mediterranean, and one enquiry about transatlantic insurance from a wealthy couple who wanted to sail their very expensive yacht to the Caribbean. Anna keyed into each file, switched on her dictaphone and dictated her replies. Many only needed an endorsement for a minor adjustment to their coverage, but Anna always included a personal note: her clients appreciated that.

Her phone rang. It was Vince. 'Buy the house with your Antipodean lover?' he bellowed.

'This morning, thank you. How's work progressing on *Le Nouveau Monde*? She must be nearly ready for you to take possession.'

'Oh, she is, and she's the most beautiful cruiser you'll ever see, Annie, the best boat I'll own; and I want you to insure her because you're my favourite broker and you're the prettiest.'

'And you're my favourite client, Vince.'

'But I ain't the prettiest!'

They both laughed. He was five feet high, five feet wide, with a face like a naughty monkey – the cunning kind of ape which always fiddles with its bottom in front of nuns and little girls.

'I expect a good price,' he said.

'Don't I always get you one?' Anna reached for her notepad. 'How much is she worth?'

'A million and a half, with all the refitting.'

'She must be a stunner. That's twice what you paid for your last cruiser. Do you have the invoices?'

'I've a drawerful, mostly from Ribble's of Hamble. My old mate Fred Ribble shipped her over from the States and all the work has been done in his yard. You wait till you see the master cabin, draped in wishy-washy silk which my wife and that poncey Parisian interior designer call "*peau-de-pêche*".' Vince exaggerated the designer's lisping tones, making Anna giggle.

'Since she's a new vessel and Ribble will have fitted her out to classification, the underwriter won't need a survey,' said Anna. 'Do you want coverage for UK, Continent and Mediterranean only, or transatlantic as well?'

'Transatlantic later. She couldn't carry enough fuel to cross the ocean without adjustment, and for the time being I just want to enjoy my new toy.'

Anna questioned him about the crew, the moorings, the security and the fire alarms. When she finished Vince said, 'We're having a launch party on Bank Holiday Sunday. You can bring the Antipodean, if you have to break a middle-aged man's heart.'

Anna longed to spend her free time at Ladbroke Hill, but Vince was her best client. 'We'd love to come,' she replied. 'But as for breaking your heart, you're all talk, Vince. You're devoted to Monique.'

He laughed. 'See you at the party. In the meantime, fax me some figures. Fred Ribble tells me there's a lot of theft on the rivers, even from the marinas, and I don't want to risk my boat.'

'I'll see to it right away.' Anna wrote out the details and took the file to Elaine to type the slip.

To kill the minutes Anna tapped out Roz's number. With a bit of luck she'd catch her between collecting Phoebe and Oliver and taking Luke to his violin lesson. Or was it his piano lesson today? The whole of Roz's family seemed to revolve around Luke's musical talents and Anna couldn't help feeling sorry for the other children, even for Melissa, the eldest and the least endearing.

Roz's telephone rang and rang. Anna imagined the sound echoing through the rambling, stone-floored fenland farmhouse. She pictured Roz in the large-beamed kitchen, pursing her lips with irritation as she hurriedly dried her hands and rushed to answer. As the phone continued to ring, she imagined the noise bursting out through the open windows and across the terrace and the lawn to the rose garden, the vegetable patch and beyond that to the lines of cabbages and beetroot which covered her brother-in-law's land. She saw Roz straighten up from her weeding, sigh deeply and hurry across the grass, bending to wipe the earth from her hands as she went. Even in the garden Roz would hear the telephone because none of the windows at Lower Gossip Fen closed properly. For that reason Charlie refused to stay there except in summer. On his first visit he'd woken to find icicles on the inside of their bedroom window.

Roz didn't answer and Anna gave up, deciding that next Christmas she'd give Roz an answering machine.

Picking up her briefcase she left her office. 'Is the slip ready?' she asked Elaine.

Elaine nodded and passed over the file.

Anna read through the details. As usual, there was not a single error in Elaine's typing. 'This is perfect,' she said. 'You'll find a tape and some letters on the chair in my office. Please do them by the end of the day. If anyone phones, I'm at Lloyd's.'

'I'm . . . I'm sorry I was late this morning.' Elaine twisted her hands together nervously.

Anna looked at her. 'It's the third time in a week.'

'I know, but . . . my little boy isn't well, so I couldn't take him to the child-minder and I had to wait for my mum to arrive to look after him.'

'I didn't know you had a child,' Anna said, surprised.

Elaine looked embarrassed. 'When Delia interviewed me, she just asked if I was married or planning to get married, she didn't ask if I already had children.'

'And you didn't tell her?'

'I was desperate for work.' Elaine raised her chin and met Anna squarely. 'Daniel's father pays me nothing. When I started job-hunting I was honest about Danny, but as soon as my interviewers realised that I was a single mother living on my own, they turned me down, so I had no alternative but to hide my son.' She lowered her eyes and added quietly, 'I won't be late again, I promise.'

'That's what you said yesterday, and last Friday. Even when you are here, you're on the phone all day.'

'He's my baby. He's sick. I'm worried.'

Anna took a deep breath. 'I'm sorry, but I can't run my department unless everyone in my team is totally reliable. Delia comes back on Monday and I intend to speak to her.' Unable to bear the bleakness in Elaine's face, Anna added a quick 'Goodnight', and walked briskly through the building to the lifts. Elaine wasn't her problem. Elaine's child wasn't her concern. She thumped the call button and waited. Above her the floor numbers lit up. There was a ping and the doors opened. Anna took a step forward, hesitated, then crossed to Judy's desk, picked up the internal phone and tapped out Elaine's extension number.

She answered. 'Miss Tobias's office.'

'Elaine, this is Anna. One more chance. Don't you dare let me down.'

'I won't, I promise.' There was a catch in Elaine's voice. 'Oh, thank you.'

As Anna replaced the receiver, Judy shook her head and mouthed, 'Softie!'

3

THE MARINECOVER BUILDING was in a narrow street just a few minutes' walk from Lloyd's. No brokers had offices in the Lloyd's building, which annoyed Charlie because he liked to be at the centre of life, but Anna preferred the detachment. In the time it took her to walk through the old Leadenhall market, with its open stalls and traders shouting wares beneath the ornate Victorian arches, she frequently found the solution to some problem which had been puzzling her.

In any case she didn't like the new Lloyd's building. It was too grey, too tubular, and looked as though it had been turned inside out, with all its drains and amenities on show instead of hidden. Charlie swore she didn't like it because, according to him, like all Brits, she was marooned in the last century and couldn't appreciate a building unless it was falling apart.

Anna was uncomfortably hot as she hurried up Lime Street. The sun bounced off the glass sides of the modern buildings, casting deep, sharp shadows across the narrow twisting lane; the smell of exhaust fumes hung heavy on the summer air. She thought longingly of the garden at Ladbroke Hill, and of the romantic evenings when she and Charlie would dine outside, surrounded by a bower of jasmine and honeysuckle.

She muttered to herself about Elaine. Maybe she shouldn't have given the girl another chance, maybe she was too soft. She blushed as she realised she'd been talking out loud and wondered if she was going mad. It wouldn't be surprising if she did crack up one day – she knew many who had – what with the pressure of work, the hassles over the house, and her fear that Charlie would go back to Melbourne and abandon her. At times she'd wondered if her greatest fear was the thought of having to start again with someone new. Or the thought that she might not meet anyone at all, and become like Sandra in Cargoes who'd been dumped so many times that she'd given up on men and now lived in Ealing with two cats.

But it wasn't just insecurity which united Anna to Charlie. She loved him for having qualities which she often lacked, and which her parents had lacked. He was unreservedly affectionate, he was confident, he was always fun and he never fretted about money. He neither analysed the past nor feared the future, and he never hovered on the outside of a circle, afraid that people wouldn't like him. In the winter, when he'd hurt her with his I-want-to-be-free attitude, Anna had longed for him to become ill so she could show him how much he needed her. She'd even bought a book of invalid recipes, though she pretended it was a present for her grandmother.

She entered Lloyd's by the subterranean concourse, showed her pass at the security desk and headed for the escalators. The Underwriting Room – or The Room, as it was known – was on the first floor. In the centre was a marble-floored atrium where the Lutine Bell hung inside a tall wooden rostrum. In the old days the bell had been rung every time a ship was overdue. It was still rung on occasions: twice for good news, once for bad.

In front of the rostrum, in an oasis of relative calm, underwriters and brokers gathered to talk or to study the *Lloyd's List* of shipping movements and the bulletins on the casualty notice-boards. Skirting several groups of people, Anna crossed the floor, her high heels clicking on the marble. It was the only place where her heels made a noise, the rest of The Room being carpeted against sound.

Three hundred years earlier Edward Lloyd's Coffee House in Tower Street had been a meeting place where the owner of a trading ship could seek out a wealthy merchant – or several – prepared to share in the risk of a proposed voyage. In the twentieth century the owner instructed a broker to find him the best quote, and the rich man formed a syndicate with other rich men – and more recently the not so rich – and together they appointed an underwriting agent who in turn appointed underwriters who specialised in differing fields of insurance.

On each side of the atrium sat rows of underwriters, two to a desk – or box, as they were called – like pairs of children in old-fashioned wooden school desks. The Room always made Anna think of a very noisy library. Isaac Finestein specialised in yachts, and Anna made her way to his box. He was already deep in conversation with one broker, and waiting to talk to him was Barry Limehouse, the Thug. Limehouse was a sturdy, stocky karate fanatic with a flat face, piggy eyes and a crew-cut. If Anna had had to conjure up a playground bully, it would have been him.

Nicknames were common in Lloyd's; Isaac was known as the Midget. He was very short, with huge black eyes, a beak of a nose, and deep furrows across his forehead. Born in Leipzig in the early thirties, he had moved to England as a young child when his far-sighted father had taken his family out of Germany, leaving behind uncles and cousins who refused to forsake their comfortable homes. None had survived the Holocaust, and every year Isaac went to Israel and said *Kaddish* for them at the Wailing Wall.

Anna knew about Isaac's past from his wife Sybil. At their daughter Rebecca's twenty-first birthday party, Sybil, a motherly silver-blonde, had confided to Anna as they combed their hair in the ladies' cloakroom. 'I wish Rebecca would find a nice man, a good man, like my Isaac. We named her after his favourite cousin, one of those who . . . stayed behind. My Isaac never forgets how lucky he is to be alive.' Sybil had patted Anna on the arm. 'You should marry soon. It's a shame you're not Jewish or you'd have done nicely for one of my boys.'

Anna was nudged out of her thoughts by Barry Limehouse. 'How are your jet-set clients, Anne?' he asked.

'Fine thanks, Larry.'

'The name's Barry!'

She smiled sweetly. 'Mine is Anna.'

He bent his unpleasant face towards her. 'I can never remember girls' names, so I call 'em all darling.' He looked her up and down. 'Women enjoy a bit of rough, especially snooty ones like you.'

Anna's smile became even more sugary. 'I'm not a snob, Larry, I merely don't like you.'

Someone nearby laughed aloud, and before Barry could think of a retort, Isaac said 'Next!', and he was forced to give his attention to the underwriter.

A hand squeezed Anna's elbow and she turned to find Charlie standing behind her. 'Well done.' He smiled proudly.

'I don't know why he attacked me so viciously.'

'He was down on the Hamble on Sunday, trying to entice Ellerby-Creswell away from you. The Cobra overheard him.'

'Oh, Charlie, why didn't you warn me? Vince is my top client.'

'Because I know Vince is devoted to you.' Charlie gave her elbow another squeeze and moved away, adding, 'See you later.'

Anna was perturbed, but she decided to say no more about it. She couldn't forget how her mother's softly insidious dissatisfaction had driven her father to strive for what was beyond his capabilities – until he couldn't stand it any longer.

The Thug finished his business with Isaac and walked off without so much as a glance in Anna's direction. 'How's Sybil?' she asked, stepping up to Isaac's box.

'Cross with you. She says you ought to have more sense than to live with a man before he marries you.'

Anna laughed. 'Charlie and I are happy as we are, Isaac. What difference would a piece of paper make?'

'All the difference in the world in my wife's eyes.' He patted her hand. 'I'm glad to see you happy.'

'Thank you.' Anna opened the Ellerby-Creswell file and laid the detailed slip in front of him, saying, 'This is my perfect client, he's never made one claim, and *Le Nouveau Monde* is his fifth boat. She's an eighty-foot cruiser, value one and a half million.'

'Some vessel!' Isaac read through the details. 'Gold cherub-shaped taps in the bathroom! Whatever next?'

Anna giggled. 'Venus panels in the bedroom. Now, what about a quote? I have to fax my client tonight.'

'What percentage are you taking?'

'Twenty.'

'That's greedy, Annie.'

'He's my best client. I worked hard at keeping him sweet, I'm giving up Bank Holiday Sunday to go to his party, I earn my cut.'

Isaac sighed and did some calculations in his tiny, spidery writing. 'Roughly – and I'm talking rough figures – we're looking at a premium of fifteen thousand pounds.'

'One per cent!'

'With the first six thousand of any claim paid by the insured.'

'Isaac, my client will have apoplexy.'

'Annie, premiums are up. Look at all the disasters we've had recently: hurricanes, droughts, oil spills, the car ferry at Zeebrugge, the tankers bombed in the Gulf, not to speak of the rising rate of boat theft. An expensive boat like this is a risk. If she sinks, we lose badly. If she's stolen . . .'

'*Le Nouveau Monde* is eighty foot long; she'd be hard to hide.'

'She's a production-line model, not a one-off, so she's not impossible to steal. There's a big market for these craft among South American drug-runners. With fuel adjustments, she could reach the Caribbean and be resold.'

'My client is going to be furious, and I don't want to lose him. The Thug's already sniffing.' She waited for Isaac to reduce the premium, but he said nothing. So she took a deep breath. 'I'll cut our comission to seventeen per cent.'

Isaac recalculated. 'Fourteen thousand, and your client pays the first five thousand of any claim.'

'That's still a hell of a lot.'

'It's the best I can do. What's more, my syndicate won't take more than fifty per cent of the risk. You'll have to spread the rest through the market.'

'Isaac, if you lead, the others will follow.'

'Flatterer!'

'You don't deserve it, not after that quote.' She picked up the Ellerby-Creswell file. 'I'll come back to you.'

She went straight to Kevin Kitterick's box. In any other section of marine insurance she could have gathered a number of quotes for comparison, but in yachting she was limited. Chat was part of her job so she wasted precious minutes asking Kevin about his golfing holiday before handing him Vince's slip. 'Isaac will take fifty per cent,' she said.

Kevin barely glanced at the details. 'Oh, if the Midget's in for fifty, I'll take thirty.'

She checked with two other underwriters. Since the Midget and Kevin were in for eighty per cent, they were more than ready to pick up the balance of the risk.

Anna spent the remainder of the afternoon in Lloyd's. There were people to see, to meet for tea in the Captain's Room, to gossip with and glean gossip from. Contacts were an essential part of being a broker.

By the time she left, the stalls in Leadenhall market had closed.

At one end a refuse lorry was collecting the day's rubbish, at the other someone was hosing down the cobbled surface of the road.

'Smile!' one of the refuse-men shouted at her. 'Life ain't that bad.'

Anna laughed. 'It ain't bad at all,' she replied, thinking of the house on Ladbroke Hill.

Most employees had already gone home when she reached Marinecover. The night security guard had taken over from old Hawthorn and the evening receptionist had replaced Judy. The offices were empty, except for Chris who was on the telephone. Elaine's chair was vacant, but on Anna's desk there was a pile of neatly-typed letters and a note saying, 'I won't let you down.'

She spent the next couple of hours faxing Vince with the figures, answering more letters and making phone calls. Between work calls she tried to reach Roz but the farmhouse line was busy.

Finally she put away her work, took out her mirror and retouched her make-up. She would have liked to go home, to shower and change into a floaty, feminine summer dress and make herself pretty for Charlie, but she had no time.

The two brightly-coloured parrots were chattering in their cages when Anna arrived at the restaurant. To her surprise, she found Charlie already at their table, on the platform beside the carousel, with a view over all the other diners. He smiled when he saw her, his face brimming with excitement.

She kissed him on the cheek, and the waiter held her chair. 'So you got the job,' she said, telling herself that it wasn't the end of the world if he left Marinecover.

'Oh, it's in the bag but they don't need me to start till the autumn and naturally they want to consider terms.' He reached across and squeezed her hand. 'You're not still upset with me?'

'Of course not.' She put on a brave face. 'What are they offering?'

'They didn't, so I asked for eighty thousand basic, plus profits and a new car every two years.'

'Eighty! Charlie, that's twice what you get now!'

'I'm worth it, I earn a fortune in commission. I'm just as good with clients as you.'

That wasn't always true, sometimes he was too impatient, but she said, 'I didn't say you weren't, but I don't earn eighty thousand. I make my money on profits.'

He was all smiles again. 'You deserve a better deal, we both do. Your car is four years old. That's no perk. I just want the best for both of us, sweetie.' He ordered a bottle of Dom Perignon, telling the waiter to charge it separately, and when their glasses were filled, he raised his to Anna. 'To our success! To our new house! To us!'

She smiled. 'To our house! To us!'

'You ought to leave Marinecover as well,' he went on, smiling at her. 'They're not big enough for people like us.' She started to protest, but he held up his hand. 'No, Anna, please hear me out. Once I'm at Merchant & Leisure I'll insist they offer you a job. Then we'll be working together again.'

He was so enthusiastic that Anna allowed herself to be swept along, his optimism wrapped around her like a life-jacket, although in reality the idea of leaving Marinecover was almost as unnerving to her as moving house.

It was well after midnight when they left the restaurant. Anna would have liked to visit Ladbroke Hill, but it was too late. They took a cab back to Victoria, to the modern block where he rented a serviced apartment. He'd barely used it in the eighteen months since he and Anna had been together; they'd spent most of their time at her small, cosy Fulham cottage because his apartment was depressingly characterless. Now it was stacked with Anna's clothes. Her furniture was in store.

'Sorry about the mess,' she said, opening a large suitcase and digging through layers of underwear.

'It doesn't worry me.' Charlie threw his jacket on to the sofa, kicked off his shoes and headed for the shower.

That was another quality Anna loved in Charlie. He was so easy-going. She thought of her mother who could barely allow anyone to sit on the sofa for fear that they would crease the cushions.

Charlie was nearly asleep by the time she had laid out her clothes for tomorrow and had had a shower. She slid in beside him, under the sheet, naked and deliciously cool.

'You always take such an age coming to bed,' he mumbled, nuzzling up against her.

'I like to sort everything out.'

He slipped his arm around her bare waist. 'You could have done it in the morning.'

She stroked his fingers. 'You know how I hate to get up early.'

He buried his face in her hair. 'You smell nice, very nice.' He blew on her neck. 'Contented now we've bought Ladbroke Hill?'

She kissed him tenderly on the corner of his mouth. 'You know I am.'

'Such a lot of fuss about a house,' he said, teasing.

'Not just any house, Charlie, a special house.'

'For a special lady.' Still half asleep, he rolled on top of her, framing her face with his hands. 'A very special lady.' He kissed the tip of her nose, then her eyes, and finally her mouth, running his fingers through her hair, then down the back of her neck, caressing her body with his own.

She wrapped her arms around him and held him close, drawing him into her so that she possessed him and he could not escape. They made love gently, slowly, tenderly. In all the months they'd known each other Anna had only felt completely sure of Charlie if they were making love, until today when they'd bought the house on Ladbroke Hill. Now she felt safe. They would create a home, a haven from the outside world, and they would put down roots, so deep into the ground that nothing could ever loosen them.

4

VINCE ELLERBY-CRESWELL WAS already on the phone to her when Anna arrived at work. 'Fourteen thousand pounds!' he screeched down the line. 'Jesus Christ, Annie, that's nearly one per cent!'

'I'm sorry, Vince, but that's the best quote in the market. Premiums are up. There have been numerous big yacht claims from the UK storms last winter and those oil tankers bombed in the Gulf last week don't help.'

'What the hell has a tanker on the Gulf got to do with my yacht on the Hamble? Nothing. The trouble is, you people are too fuckin' greedy. We're in the boom of the century, but that ain't enough for you. Blood-suckers!' He slammed down the receiver.

Anna sat back in her chair and took a deep breath. Then she rose and went next door to Charlie. 'We won't be going to Vince's party,' she told him, crestfallen. 'He blew me out on the price.'

'Oh, sweetie, you don't deserve that.' He gave her a sympathetic smile. 'The guy's a multi-millionaire. I'd never have thought him tight-fisted.'

'He's careful, that's why he's a millionaire.'

The door opened and Gordon appeared, looking like thunder. 'Judy tells me that Ellerby-Creswell bawled her out. You haven't lost him, have you?'

Anna nodded miserably. 'I'm afraid so. He blew at the premium. Vince is a client but he's also a friend, so it's hard not to take it personally when he calls me a blood-sucker, even if it is business.'

They waited for Gordon to explode, but he merely shrugged. 'You've the right attitude. Keep plugging at him.'

After Gordon had left, Charlie shook his head in disbelief.

'You're the only person at Marinecover who could lose a major client and not get fired. Gordon must be in love with you.'

She gave a light laugh, her great barricade to keep emotion in, or maybe it was to keep it out, and returned to her office. Only with the door closed did she crumple into her chair.

There was a tap and Elaine came in carrying a cup of coffee. 'Milk, no sugar. That's right, isn't it?'

'Yes, thanks.' Anna paused, then added, 'How's your little boy?'

Elaine's face brightened. 'Oh, he's much better, thank you. He's with my mum today. She's staying over till I sort myself out.' She hesitated, then added tentatively, still nervous of Anna, 'I'm sorry you've lost your client but I'm sure he'll come back. Everyone here says you're the best yacht broker.'

'Do they really?'

Elaine nodded.

Anna smiled. 'Thank you for telling me. It makes me feel less . . . of a failure.'

'You! A failure!' Elaine backed out of the room as though Anna were mad.

Anna tried to put Vince from her mind and concentrate on other work but it was difficult. Calling Chris into her office, she allocated him the smaller, single craft insurance requests while she dealt with the multiples: a flotilla of holiday dinghies moored in Crete and a new sailing school off the coast of Yugoslavia, but they were small fry compared to Vince's *Le Nouveau Monde*.

At lunchtime she telephoned Roz. 'Sorry I haven't caught you before,' she said.

'You never do,' complained Roz. 'I always have to ring you. Tom gets furious because our phone bill's enormous.'

'I tried several times, but you were out. I'd have left a message but you don't have an answering machine.' Anna tried not to let her temper rise, as it had during her childhood battles when they'd shared a bedroom with a strict demarcation line down the middle, Roz's half practical and tidy, Anna's scattered with dried flowers and pebbles from the beach.

'We can't afford one.'

'Then let me give you one for your birthday.'

'Anna, you're my little sister. I don't want expensive presents from you when I can't afford to give you expensive ones back.' Roz sighed, and a moment later she said, contritely, 'I'm sorry, but you've caught me in a foul mood.'

Anna softened. 'What's wrong? Can I help?'

'Oh no, it's just the usual. The farm's not doing well and what little money we make goes on machinery; I've given up smoking again and I'm dying for a cigarette; and the children are driving me insane, particularly Melissa. She spent all weekend lying on her bed listening to rock music.'

'Like I used to?'

'Yes.' Roz let out a sudden shout of laughter. 'How's the new house?'

'Wonderful, but I wish I could spend more time there. Mother's coming to see it on Saturday. I hope she likes it.'

'Of course she will,' Roz reassured her, slotting back into her habitual role of comforter.

'Father would have loved it,' Anna said sadly, 'but one never knows what Mother really thinks. You know what she's like, she'd say a box was Buckingham Palace if she thought that would please everyone. She never admits the truth . . . even about Dad.'

There was an intimate silence as they each thought back to their rootless childhood which Roz had weathered so much better than Anna, not only because she was older and had left home before they lost Cliff Cottage, but also because she'd never shared Anna's closeness to their father, so she had not been as wounded by his death.

Anna heard nothing from Vince, but she gathered on the Lloyd's grapevine that he'd approached the Thug for a quote, which infuriated her. She wished that Delia was back from her holiday so that she could sound off about Vince, which she couldn't do to Charlie, since he'd heard it already and was becoming bored, or to anyone else in the office, because to have done so would be to admit her waning confidence.

The week passed without Anna and Charlie having time to visit Ladbroke Hill. Each evening they were either too busy or it was too late. Anna had completed her insurance exams the previous summer but Charlie had more to sit; he attended classes two nights a week. Whilst he was out, she spent many happy hours studying the ideas for the house put forward by Xavier, their smooth and incredibly expensive Scottish-Spanish architect.

On Saturday morning, whilst Charlie played squash, Anna raced over to Ladbroke Hill to rake the drive, brush the steps and open the windows to let in fresh air because her mother loathed stuffy houses. More junk mail had collected during that week and she threw most of it straight in the bin. Amongst the pile was a well-worn envelope on which was written in elaborate, lacy writing, 'P. Shufflebuck, rent for week – £20.'

She stuffed it in her jeans pocket. Twenty pounds was nothing for a two-room flat in Notting Hill, even one in a dilapidated condition, but they couldn't increase the rent because he was a sitting tenant; their only option was to try to buy him out.

Deciding to have one more attempt at being friendly, Anna went down the stone steps to his front door. Written on a card next to the bell was 'Mr Marilyn (P Shufflebuck)'. She stifled a giggle as she envisaged Charlie's reaction, and rang the bell.

'Yes?' came a muffled answer.

'Thank you for the rent, Mr . . . umm . . . Marilyn.'

'Only my friends call me Mr Marilyn. To you I am Mr Shufflebuck.'

Anna didn't reply. She thumped back up the steps. He was an obstinate old pansy and there was no point in wasting precious time on him.

She found an old pair of shears in the coal shed and chopped back the worst of the ivy from the drive. She was raking it into a pile when her mother drove in, slowly negotiating the gateway in her eight-year-old Ford Fiesta.

Anna dropped her rake. 'Hello,' she called out, hurrying to open the car door. 'Did you have a good journey? Did you find it easily? I'm afraid the house is a mess. I wanted to clean it up before you saw it, but . . .'

'Darling!' Her mother smiled sweetly up at her. Her face was eternally heart-shaped, as Anna's was when she was happy. 'Darling, don't talk so much. Give me time to recover. I've been driving round in circles.'

'Sorry.' Anna jumped away, wondering why she could get things right with other people, but seldom with her mother.

Veronica Tobias stepped from the car, smoothed her silver-blonde hair back into its bun, and gazed up at the house. 'Oh, but it's enormous!' she exclaimed. 'It's beautiful. But it must have cost a fortune.'

'It did, but we love it.' Anna hesitated, and added tentatively, 'I think Dad would have liked it, don't you?'

Her mother stiffened. 'It's exactly the kind of house he longed to buy, if only one of his inventions had succeeded. Dear Jeffrey!' She linked an arm through Anna's. 'I tried to pretend that I was content in that dreary little house in Leatherbridge, I really did. There was no point in us all mourning the loss of Cliff Cottage.' She stepped away, and hurried towards the front steps.

Anna followed. 'Mum, I'm sorry, I know you don't like talking about him but sometimes I . . . want to speak of him, so that he doesn't disappear from me, from my life, from us.'

'It's been fifteen years since his . . . accident, and I still find it hard to accept he won't come back,' said her mother, picking a piece of loose plaster off the portico. 'I half believe he'll come ambling round the corner any minute, wearing that dreadful old grey cardigan.'

Anna laughed, but she was very touched, and in that moment she loved her mother unreservedly, even if she couldn't face what had really happened. 'You mean the one you wanted to give to a jumble sale and he wouldn't let you?'

'Yes. I was so ashamed when our new neighbours saw him dressed so scruffily. But I wouldn't part with it now. I'll never throw it out, it's far too precious.' Her mother straightened her shoulders and smiled bravely, much as Anna often did. 'Now, show me the lovely house. I promised Granny Tobias I'd be home in time to give her tea and you know how cross she gets if she's kept waiting.'

After looking over the house, they met Charlie for an early lunch, and then they drove in convoy with her mother to the North Circular, pointing her in the direction of home so that she didn't get lost.

Anna would have liked to tell Charlie about her father's old cardigan, but she was afraid he wouldn't understand the significance of her mother retaining it. He came from an extremely wealthy family who'd always lived in the most expensive area of Melbourne, and she felt sure that his mother did not berate his father for shaming them by dressing like a tramp.

5

WHEN ANNA ARRIVED at work on Monday she was delighted to hear Delia's familiar bossy voice echoing down the corridor from the Personnel Department. 'Welcome home!' she said, sticking her head around Delia's door. 'How was Canada?'

'Fun, but I'm glad to be back. Come in and sit down.' Delia was bustling around her office, dictating a memo to her secretary. She was very tall and thin, with a gamine face, short, black fluffy hair and dramatic dark eyes. She wore sharp suits and high heels, which made her seem even taller. When Anna and Charlie made up a foursome with Delia and her married lover, Russell, Delia swayed above the lot of them but she didn't give a damn. Anna admired that.

Delia finished the memo and her secretary left the room. 'It was great to get away,' she said, settling her long limbs into her chair and sipping a cup of cold mint tea. 'My cousins are nice, but two weeks is a long time to be a guest, especially when you're used to living on your own. Now tell me what's been happening here. Chris says you want me to replace Elaine.'

'I did, but not any more. She's improved tremendously.' Anna leaned forward. 'I had a helluva week, I lost Vince Ellerby-Creswell. He blew at the premium for his new cruiser.'

'Oh no! What did Gordon say?'

'He was remarkably calm about it. I was sure I'd be kicked out, which is the last thing I need with a new house.'

'How is the love nest?'

Anna turned pink with pleasure. 'Wonderful.'

'When's the wedding?'

'Oh, I'm not fussed about getting married any more. Buying the house has changed things. Charlie's committed himself, whether he likes it or not. You must come and see it. Bring Russell.'

'If I'm still seeing him! Mother has been nagging me to give him up. She keeps banging on about married men using lonely, single women for sex.'

'But you always say you wouldn't marry Russell, even if he were free.'

'Too right I wouldn't!' Delia fluffed up her dark hair. 'The sex is great, but he's even more selfish than my ex-husband.'

Anna laughed. 'I'd better get on with my work.' She rose. 'I missed you, Dee, I had to pretend not to care too much about losing Vince.'

'Or they'd have called you a weepy woman?'

'Exactly!'

They smiled at each other, friends and allies in what was still predominantly a man's world.

On her desk Anna found a pile of telephone messages. Before dealing with them she called Chris to her office. 'I've told Personnel that I'm perfectly satisfied with Elaine,' she informed him in a voice which invited no discussion.

He turned slightly pink. 'Yes, of course.'

Anna was so busy all week that she had little time to brood over the loss of Vince Ellerby-Creswell. Nevertheless, because she'd lost Vince, winning him back became more important than all her other business. She sent him a fax wishing him many happy cruises on *Le Nouveau Monde*. It was a long shot, but she was convinced he wouldn't be able to resist it. But she was wrong; she heard nothing.

Unable to keep up the pretence with Isaac, she invited him to lunch at the Captain's Room. 'I've lost Creswell,' she admitted as they sat down.

'I know.' He slid his small knees under the table.

She smiled brightly and beckoned the waiter. 'Not that he matters. Business is soaring. People who once lived in rented flats now own two houses, three cars and a yacht.'

'All mortgaged to the hilt,' Isaac grumbled, ordering asparagus, followed by poached salmon.

'What's wrong with that, Mr Pessimist?'

'Booms don't last.' He tucked his napkin under his chin. 'Lloyd's has nearly four hundred syndicates, thirty-six hundred members – or Names, as we call them – with more clamouring to get in and all because by being a Name their money will earn interest twice over, once in their building society, or wherever they choose to invest it, and once pledged to Lloyd's.'

'But Lloyd's needs more members so as to take on bigger business,' Anna protested. 'You're an underwriter, Isaac. I'd have thought you'd be pleased.'

'I'm also a working Name, as are all underwriters, so I have a stake and I can assure you, my dear Miss Innocence, that I wouldn't put my money in some of these high-risk syndicates – but then I'm an old man and a careful one.'

Anna didn't like to contradict him but she thought he was making a fuss. 'No one's lost out yet,' she said.

He smiled thinly. 'In 1960 a Name had to have seventy-five thousand pounds in liquid assets, the current equivalent being a million pounds. Today a Name only has to have a quarter of a million – and I wonder how many could realise it in cash if they had to, and how many fully understand what is meant by unlimited liability.'

'Isaac, they're warned when they join.'

'But we all only hear what we want to hear, don't we, my dear Anna?'

'You may be right, so in the meantime let's enjoy the years of plenty.' She ordered the most expensive wine on the list.

Anna and Charlie spent Saturday at Ladbroke Hill with their architect. They agreed on a plan to keep five of the eight bedrooms and transform the other three into luxurious bathrooms, each with the high-pressure showers to which Charlie was addicted. The upstairs kitchenettes, installed when the house was rented, would become spacious walk-in closets. The current small bathroom would be a sauna. Before the interior work could begin, the roof, gutters and brickwork needed repair. It was a massive job, but Xavier promised that by the autumn Charlie and Anna would be living in splendour. Their only hindrance was that their planned basement kitchen would have to wait until Mr Shufflebuck could be persuaded to move.

'We need a new phone line,' Anna said as they were leaving the house. 'Miss Elismore shared her number with the basement.'

'Better get two. You know how I like to talk.' Charlie draped an arm around her shoulders and they walked down the steps to his car.

The following week Charlie was in Liverpool for a series of sales strategy meetings at Marinecover's northern offices, and Anna drove down to Weymouth to interview a new sub-agent for the Dorset office. Michelle was an amusing, gutsy divorcée with a West Country accent and a love of the sea. They lunched in the Sea Cow bistro on the quayside and discussed ways of attracting new business, whilst rain lashed the fishing boats and battered the people who fought to cross the bridge which divided the estuary from the inner, more sheltered harbour.

In the afternoon Anna headed back to Lymington and her Hampshire sub-agent. Although the A31 would have been quicker, she took the road across the Isle of Purbeck towards the chain ferry because she couldn't bear to pass so near to Belworth without visiting it.

The lane which led down to the cove was even narrower and more overgrown than she remembered. On either side the banks leaned inwards, long grasses caressing her car as she passed. It had stopped raining and the sun shone, sparkling on the hedgerows and on the drops of water which hung like diamond necklaces between the leaves. Through gateways Anna caught brief glimpses of rolling green countryside and, in the distance, the scrubland which belonged to the Ministry of Defence where her father had once worked.

At a certain point, and Anna knew it so well, the lane rose above the grassy bank, up on to the summit of a small hill and there, before her, the land fell away to the village of Belworth nestling in a fissure in the cliffs. Beyond the village was the sea, stretching away into the soft haze of the horizon.

She stopped and rested her chin on the steering wheel. The view hadn't changed, it never did, that was why she loved Belworth. Its constancy gave her strength.

She'd come once for a weekend, on her own, desperate to escape the empty vacuum that had become her life: the succession of temporary jobs, so tedious that she was often convinced her watch had broken because time passed so slowly; the flat she shared with three other girls, each of whom was about to buy her own home, whilst Anna couldn't afford to; a love affair which was going nowhere, and which she didn't want to go anywhere, with a man she wasn't even sure she liked. Belworth had reminded her of all that was precious in life. She'd returned to London refreshed, and a month later she'd started work at Marinecover.

She wound down her window so that she could smell the sea and drove on, slowly, following the steep, twisted lane until it met the stream which ran down through the centre of the village to the sea. Belworth consisted of a dozen grey stone cottages, most with thatched roofs, an old pub, a shop which sold everything from potatoes to newspapers, and the bus stop from where Anna had taken the bus to school. She parked her car and walked down the path between the stream and the cottage gardens of rambling roses and hollyhocks.

The cove was sheltered, protected by high cliffs, with a narrow entrance. It wasn't as large as neighbouring Lulworth but it was easier to sail in and out. Standing on the beach, Anna breathed in the air, the salt and spray, and the smell of tar from the fishermen's nets. In the sound of the waves she heard her father's voice saying, 'Come on, Annie, into the boat,' and she remembered how cold the water always was, except in high summer, when they wheeled the dinghy down the slipway and waded out to launch it. Often she'd had to clench her teeth to prevent them from chattering but she'd never complained: she'd been too afraid he'd leave her behind.

There were several fishing boats pulled up on the beach and lobster pots piled at the top of the slipway. A grizzled old man was sitting on the end of an upturned boat, chewing tobacco as he mended his nets. Anna recognised him as old Mr Holdsworthy, whose granddaughter Margaret ran the bed and breakfast where Anna had once stayed. She smiled when he glanced her way and was surprised that he responded with no more than a nod.

She started to climb up the steps which led from the beach to Cliff Cottage.

'That's private property, Miss,' he called after her.

'I know, I used to live there. Don't you recognise me, Mr Holdsworthy? I'm Anna Tobias.'

'Good heavens, how elegant you've become.'

'Thank you.' Anna had told him on her last visit that her father had died, but not the circumstances, and he asked after her mother and Roz.

'Margaret didn't tell me you were staying,' he said.

'Oh, I'm just passing through. I was nearby and I couldn't resist coming down to see the cove and Cliff Cottage.'

'Oh, it'll be shut. The owners only come in August, sometimes not even then. It was a shame you had to leave, the place hasn't been treated proper since.'

'Thanks for warning me. It's good to see you again, Mr Holdsworthy. Send my best wishes to Margaret.' Anna hurried on up the steps, deciding that next time she came here she'd bring Charlie. Now that they were a definite couple, she could risk sharing Belworth with him.

The cottage was built on a levelled area some thirty yards back from the end of the cliff. It was neither beautiful nor spacious, just a grey stone cottage, cleverly extended by a circular drawing-room from whose curved window seat there was a spectacular view of the rugged Dorset coastline. This position gave Cliff Cottage a grandeur which no other house in Belworth possessed. At every hour of the day the light changed, and every day it was different. Sometimes it was pale gold, sometimes deep blue, and at other times glorious turquoise. Even in the rain, the light had beauty. It existed in the shadows of the sea mist and in the reflection of the sun on the water. It caught the cottage sideways, illuminating the curve of the sitting-room windows. As a child Anna had loved to walk across the front terrace and watch her giant shadow caress the waters of the adjacent cove.

Standing on the terrace, Anna watched the gulls circle above her head, dipping and diving, their cries carrying on the wind. Behind her the cottage looked sad, the garden was unkempt, the windows were shuttered and every shutter needed re-painting. She walked around the outside, past the kitchen and under the archway into the back yard, to the old shed where her father had worked on his experiments. She tried the door but it was locked, so she wiped the dust and sand from the pane and peered inside. The shed was empty, except for the wooden bench where her father had spent hours poring over designs which never reached production.

Staring into the little room where her father had been so content, Anna was choked by the thought of his last day, when he'd left the house at Leatherbridge at the usual hour and taken the morning train to London, using up his season ticket on its final day, pretending to them that he was going to the office, with never a hint that he'd lost his job, yet again, a month earlier.

She stepped away from the hut and sat down on the old stone bench outside the kitchen door, resting her chin on her hands. How could he have killed himself? How could he have left them – left her – with this anger, this bereftness? How could he have failed them so – and they him? What were his thoughts as he placed his briefcase on the platform and stepped into the path of the oncoming train?

Suddenly, the wall became uncomfortable and the bench cold. Anna rose and hurried back down the steps. Mr Holdsworthy had disappeared and she was glad – she didn't want to talk to him again. She almost ran up the street to the car park, jumped into her car and drove away. Only when she was reaching the top of the hill did she draw into a gateway and stop.

She sat in the car, her eyes closed tightly, her knuckles white where she gripped the steering wheel. The stone bench had brought back a memory from wherever she had pushed it nearly twenty years earlier. It was her thirteenth birthday and she'd come home from school early, excused hockey because she had a stomach ache, a 'growing-up' pain. Feeling precious and adult, she'd sat down on the bench outside the back door. Inside, her mother was on the telephone and Anna had waited because she suspected that her mother had baked her a surprise birthday cake and she didn't want to spoil the gift. She'd leaned back against the wall and listened to her mother's voice drift out through the open kitchen wndow as she confided in some person unknown. 'We haven't told Anna yet, but we'll have to sell Cliff Cottage. Jeffrey's been made redundant.' Her mother had started to cry.

Anna had remained outside, frozen by fear to the stone bench. Even now, after all these years, she could remember the terrifying helplessness of listening to her mother cry, and when she thought back to that afternoon, it often seemed that her father had died then, although it was another three years before he killed himself.

6

ALTHOUGH VINCE'S REJECTION of Anna's proposals continued to niggle her, Anna consoled herself that she'd never taken on so much new business. The owners of the Greek flotilla had recommended her to a dozen other companies; Michelle, her new Weymouth agent, had fifty clients already; and Stephen, her Isle of Wight contact, faxed her so many times with requests to quote that her fax machine overheated.

Charlie was also riding high. He received an unofficial nod from Merchant & Leisure that their vacancy would be his, and he celebrated by ordering the latest, most powerful BMW on the market, although Marinecover provided him with an adequate, if tamer, model. On the evening it was delivered, they roared up the M40 to Oxford, to Le Manoir aux Quat' Saisons for a wildly expensive dinner. On the way home Charlie was stopped by the police for speeding but even that couldn't dampen their high spirits. They were still laughing when they reached his flat, and fell into bed.

'We have fun, don't we?' he said, nuzzling up to her.

'We have a wonderful time.' She kissed him tenderly, and wondered if he were about to ask her to marry him.

'I will miss you when we don't work together,' he admitted, smoothing her hair back from her face and kissing her with hunger.

She was so pleased that he had told her, it meant a great deal. She slid her arms around his neck. He ran his hands down her body and buried his face in the warmth of her breasts, as she moved beneath him, gently, insidiously. They made love slowly, languorously, enjoying each other's body. They kissed and caressed, and for once he did not hurry her but took her gently, carrying her with him, so that when he thrust deep inside her, she was with him and wanting more.

When Anna arrived at work next morning she was still glowing from their lovemaking. Not even a long-winded letter of complaint from a Mr Cargill, a client who had not yet been compensated for a yacht stolen at Easter, could dampen her high spirits. She chased up his claim with Bridget, the claims adjuster employed by Isaac's syndicate – they were known as Bridget and the Midget, because she was as tall and serene as he was small and bustling.

'We haven't settled because one of Paul Sheldon's agents found Cargill's outboard motor on a stolen boat in Cowes,' Bridget explained.

'Oh come on, Bridget! Don't use delaying tactics on me. My client reported his boat was stolen. What's the problem?'

'Why would anyone remove the motor from a new yacht, and if they have, where's the yacht?'

'With some other thief, I imagine.'

'Sheldon wants to talk to Cargill again.'

'Don't tell me you suspect him of making a false claim? He's a shy little man. I asked him to call me Anna, but he's so timid he still calls me Miss Tobias. He wouldn't even have the courage to steal a pint of milk off someone else's doorstep.'

Bridget chuckled. 'You'd defend Barbarossa.'

'I would if he were my client.' Anna replaced the receiver. She hoped that Cargill hadn't been involved in something fishy. Most loss adjusters would merely prove a wrongful claim, advise the syndicate not to pay out and submit an invoice for their time, leaving the moral issue of attempted fraud to someone else's conscience. But not Paul Sheldon. He would inform the police: that was what Gordon had meant by a bounty hunter with a social conscience.

It was late on Thursday afternoon when Elaine entered Anna's office bearing a lavish bouquet of pink and white orchids.

'Are you sure they're for me?' asked Anna, surprised that Charlie would send her flowers when he was in his office less than twenty yards away.

'The envelope says "Miss Tobias".'

Anna slit it open and removed the card. 'Listen to this!' she exclaimed. ' "My apologies for being rude. I accept your quote. See you at the party. Vincent Ellerby-Creswell." '

A moment later her fax machine confirmed Vince's acceptance of her terms.

Anna reached for the phone and tapped out Isaac's number. 'Midget,' she crowed triumphantly, 'I haven't lost Creswell.'

He chuckled. 'I never believed you had.'

With a broad smile at Elaine, she picked up the flowers and walked through to the board room where Gordon was working in his usual place. 'Look what I've received.' She waved the bouquet at him. 'Ellerby-Creswell's accepted – and apologised.'

Gordon's featureless face broke into a grin, or at least the nearest he could manage. 'Well done.'

Charlie was happy to go to Vince's party, because it gave him an opportunity to show off his new car. They roared down the motorway so fast that they were among the first guests to arrive.

Fred Ribble's boatyard was on the river Hamble. It consisted of four large hangars set back from the water, and a marina full of luxury cruisers. For the launch party, *Le Nouveau Monde* was suspended above one of the slipways, and the river bank had been transformed into a replica of Henley Regatta, with a candy-striped marquee and giant urns of pink geraniums. 'I feel underdressed,' Anna whispered to Charlie when an exotic redhead swanned past, swathed from head to foot in gold lamé. She was followed by an elderly gentleman and even older lady in bright orange chiffon, her wrinkled bosom glittery with diamonds, her bleached hair teased up like white candy floss.

'You look perfect.' Charlie touched her simple scarlet silk shift. 'I hate gaudy clothes and I hate dyed hair.'

Anna smiled enigmatically and changed the subject.

'How's my favourite yacht broker?' cried Vince as Anna approached. He was short and tubby and weathered, like a Cox's apple left on the tree all year.

'Delighted to be with my favourite client,' she replied, bending so that he could kiss her on both cheeks.

'I was sure you'd weaken and come back to me with a better price,' he added with a chuckle.

'I'd already given you my best price, Vince.'

'I know, I checked elsewhere.'

'I know you checked elsewhere.'

He gave a shout of laughter. 'What a girl you are! And this is lover boy?' He held out his hand to Charlie. 'Welcome to the Ellerby-Creswells'.' He lowered his voice conspiratorially. 'As Anna knows, the name's really Creswell but Monique likes a bit of class, so I added my mum's maiden name, Ellerby.'

'Vince! You're fibbing, it was your idea.' Monique stepped forward. She was an elegant sun-streaked blonde of indeterminate years. 'Hello, Anna.' She kissed her on both cheeks. 'Ah, and this is the new bloke? So glad you could make it.' She spoke perfect English with a strong French accent, made more amusing by the slang she'd picked up from Vince.

Charlie and Anna joined the other guests and found themselves next to a couple who kept a yacht in Puerto Banus. When the man discovered that Anna had insured *Le Nouveau Monde*, he asked for her business card. 'You're not Australian too, are you?' he said, nodding towards Charlie.

She smiled and shook her head.

'It's a fine country. I know it well, particularly Melbourne,' he went on.

'Charlie comes from Melbourne.'

'Which part?'

'Toorak. His father is a well-known surgeon.'

'Ah, the rich! I had a girlfriend who came from Toorak but her parents didn't think much of me.' His eyes twinkled. 'I was poor in those days.'

Anna didn't confess that she'd never been to Australia because to do so would be to admit that Charlie had never invited her.

Other guests arrived and soon there were well over two hundred people, talking and laughing in the sunshine. Charlie chatted effortlessly to everyone. Being with him, Anna found it easy to join in, although conversation was a skill which she'd had to conquer. Charlie was naturally sociable. They lunched on lobster, followed by strawberries and cream, and as they finished, Vince produced a brass bell, smaller than but similar to the Lutine Bell in Lloyd's, and rang it loudly.

'Friends,' he called out, his round face creased in smiles, '*Le Nouveau Monde* is the best boat I'll ever own. I want to thank you for coming to her launch.' He put his arms around Monique. 'This is a very special day for us.'

Monique picked up a bottle of champagne which was tied to the boat by a pink ribbon. She held it aloft, then let it drop. As it smashed against the hull, they all cheered and raised their glasses, and the eighty-foot cruiser slid slowly down the slipway into the water.

Vince was the first up the gangway. 'Line up for the tour of inspection,' he shouted, ringing the bell again like a small and bossy school prefect.

'Anyone would think we were at Butlins,' grumbled the gushing redhead in gold lamé.

'Keep your voice down,' hissed the man who knew Melbourne. 'This is Vince's big day. He's come a long way and he deserves to be proud.'

They trooped up the gangway and into the main saloon, which was decorated in gold leaf and festooned with luxuriant peach and cream satin curtains, with life-size photographs of Monique, all shot through a soft-focus lens to make her look twenty years younger. It was not to Anna's taste but she admired it loudly for Vince's sake. The master cabin was similarly excessive, with a heart-shaped Jacuzzi surrounded by a curved panel depicting Botticelli's *The Birth of Venus* – except that the face of Venus had been superimposed with a portrait of Monique. Anna didn't dare catch Charlie's eye in case he made her giggle.

At the end of the tour Vince presented each guest with a gift – a gold tiepin inscribed with *Le Nouveau Monde* for the men, a gold link bracelet similarly inscribed for the women.

'We've had a wonderful day,' Anna told him. 'Thank you again for those glorious orchids.'

'Ah, so they came from you,' Charlie said with mock jealousy.

Vince was chuffed to be thought of as a rival. 'Look after my favourite girl,' he told Charlie. 'You must both come out to Puerto Banus when the boat's there. We'll have fun, that's what life's about, eh?' He hugged Anna and slapped Charlie on the back, and waved them goodbye.

Out of earshot, Charlie asked, 'Did he mean those flowers you gave to your secretary?'

'Yes, I should have warned you, thank goodness you didn't tell Vince.' Anna linked her arm through his, and smiled as she recalled the pleasure on Elaine's face when she'd handed her Vince's bouquet.

*

Anna was at Isaac's box, discussing the insurance of a recently restored Dutch barge, when the news came through that the bank rate had risen by half a percentage point.

She groaned. 'Oh no! Our mortgage.'

Calmly, Isaac scratched his initials on the bottom of the slip. 'We have to keep inflation down. I told you, people must stop buying on credit.'

'But you can't buy a house without borrowing,' Anna replied, irritated by his complacencey.

Returning to Marinecover she found Charlie at his desk, keying data into his computer. 'The interest rate's gone up,' she told him, irrational panic rising in her.

'Don't worry, sweetie, we can afford it. We have a cheap mortgage.' He gave her a reassuring smile and returned to his work.

Anna went into her office, took a deep breath and counted to twenty. Charlie was right. They had nothing to fear. They had good, secure jobs, they were both earning – and Charlie was not her father. He would not easily be crushed.

Four days later the rate was increased by another half point, and Charlie grumbled, 'There's nothing wrong with the economy, it's the gloom-and-doom journalists predicting a recession who are causing people to panic.'

Anna said nothing, because she didn't want him to think that she lacked confidence, but that night she dreamed of the rented house in Leatherbridge.

Xavier's quote for the exterior building work at Ladbroke Hill was two thousand pounds more than his verbal estimate. Anna wanted to argue it, but Charlie refused. If it had been work he'd have fought to get the price down, but in private he never quibbled over money because he considered it was demeaning; he paid Xavier's deposit without query.

The bank rate rose again and lack of confidence hit the stock market, causing share prices to tumble. There were long faces in the offices and wine bars of the City as people recalled the previous October's Black Monday and wondered if it had been a foretaste of worse to come. Two of Anna's clients who'd been about to buy new yachts decided to wait, whilst another informed her that Barry Limehouse was offering better incentives.

'What kind of incentives?' she asked.

'Well . . . er . . . you know.'

'You mean sex?'

The client was silent.

Anna thumped down the receiver and called to Elaine, 'The Thug is fixing them up with hookers! He makes me sick!'

Depressed and worried about the sudden downturn in her figures, Anna redoubled her efforts to increase her business, but everywhere she went – to the fashionable south coast marinas, the boatyards and the yacht charterers – the Thug followed, undercutting her quotes.

Work was proceeding on Ladbroke Hill almost faster than they could afford. The chimney was strengthened, the roof and windows were renewed, and the unsafe interior floorboards were replaced, the new wood standing out sharply against the old. Xavier called on them with catalogues for baths and bathroom fittings and, swept along by his enthusiasm, they selected the most expensive.

Charlie was in Newcastle when Anna received the bill. Horrified, she phoned Xavier to ask him to hold the order but he was out, so she took a cab over to the house, hoping to catch him on site. There was no one around, the builders were at lunch, and the only sign of life was Mr Shufflebuck's cat patrolling the garden wall. Anna raced upstairs to check the bathrooms. The baths and basins were already plumbed in and the custom-made brass units were firmly in place. There was nothing to be done; they'd have to pay.

She returned to work and was in the board room, discussing her sales strategy with Gordon, when Miss Thin gave them the news of the Piper Alpha oil rig explosion.

'There'll be one hell of a claim,' Gordon said glumly. 'Thank God we're not underwriters. What with the hurricane, then this, there'll be some very unhappy people in Lloyd's.'

When Charlie arrived home, Anna was watching the latest news on the oil rig, but it wasn't until they climbed into bed, which wasn't the ideal time, that she had a chance to talk to him about the house, because he'd been on the telephone all evening. 'I really think we should give up this flat,' she said. 'It's crazy to keep paying rent if we can live on the top floor of Ladbroke Hill.'

With a groan, he sank into the pillows. 'I'm not living on a building site with all my clothes thick with plaster dust.'

'Charlie, the top floor is habitable. It only needs decorating.'

'Anna, please, I've had a long, hard day. Let's talk about something cheerful, such as our house-warming party. I say we should have it in September.' He kissed the tip of her nose. 'And as a concession to your meanness, we'll have ordinary champagne instead of vintage.'

She linked her arms around his neck. 'Charlie, I'm not mean, I'm careful. I learned to be when I was a child, and old habits die hard.'

'But we're rich, Anna, and we're going to be richer. You don't need to be so scared of spending money.' He smiled at her. 'Don't you trust me?'

'Of course I do.' She kissed him.

He went on to talk about the party. They didn't make love – often they didn't. Charlie wasn't the sexual person Anna had first thought him to be, but he was a truly affectionate man and that was a quality she loved in him.

She thought back to his first day at Marinecover, when he'd walked into her office and made it clear that he liked her, without worrying if other people noticed. Anna had found that both flattering and unnerving, because she was too cautious to neglect the fact that if she had an affair with a colleague and it ended she'd be left looking a fool. So, for a month, they fenced around each other, meeting in the corridor at the coffee machine or for after-work drinks in City wine bars.

Finally, on the pretence of collecting a file, Charlie had come to her cottage in Fulham. She opened her front door and stood back to let him pass because the hall was narrow. He brushed against her, and she could still remember the frisson as his sweater touched the skin on the back of her hand. She led him into the sitting-room which had just been repainted, and he joked, 'I like your new scent,' and they laughed nervously.

She'd gone into the kitchen and he followed, circling around her as she unsuccessfully tried to uncork a bottle of wine. Then he took the bottle and the corkscrew from her and said, very softly, 'Shall we drink it in the bedroom?'

Those early days of their lovemaking had been spiced by secrecy. They spent every evening together, making love until dawn, then separated to grab an hour's sleep and arrive at work at different times and from opposite directions. During the day, if they met, they'd talked in stilted voices and gone to great lengths not to touch each other, which was as erotic as a passionate embrace because it contained all the impatience of desire and the knowledge that that desire would be fulfilled. One evening, unable to control themselves, they'd made love on the deep-piled navy carpet in the board room. Lying beside Charlie now, Anna tingled with the memory of that moment of pure, raw sex.

Charlie didn't get the job with Merchant & Leisure. Their letter was waiting for him on Saturday morning when he and Anna returned from their big, fortnightly shop at Sainsbury's. 'I feel such a failure,' he told her, crumpling the letter into a ball.

She put her arms around him to comfort him. 'It's only a setback, Charlie, you'll find something else, if you want to.'

'Yes . . . but I told Russell and . . . oh, I can't remember who that I'd been offered the job, and now I'll look a fool.'

She kissed him on the chin. 'Everyone knows that you're one of Marinecover's bright stars and they'll think Merchant & Leisure are idiots not to take you.' She smiled at him and said, 'What would you like to do today? You choose.'

She expected him to shrug off his disappointment and say that he wanted to see Batman, because he'd been going on about it, but to her surprise he sighed and buried his face in her neck, mumbling, 'Oh, I don't care. I just want that job.'

Anna held him close. She felt needed by him in a way she hadn't done before, and it was a strange sensation, for until that moment she'd believed him to be the protector and herself the one in need.

He was still subdued on Sunday, when they were to drive up to Lower Gossip Fen for her grandmother's birthday lunch. Anna asked him if he preferred to stay at home but he shook his head, watching glum and silent as she tied a silk bow around the champagne which they'd bought as a present.

It took them an hour to get clear of the suburbs of north London and a further hour to reach Lower Gossip Fen. The farm was named after the crossroads where, according to local history, women on their way to market used to meet and talk, although Tom claimed it had been specially named for his wife. He'd inherited the land and the house just before they'd married. It had been badly run down, having belonged to an elderly widowed uncle, and all the money Tom made from his endless rows of cabbages and beetroot was ploughed back into modernising the machinery.

The old farmhouse was built on the only raised ground in the area. It was a sprawling, grey stone building with low-beamed ceilings and flagstone floors, lovely in summer when the garden became a sun-trap but freezing in winter because Tom and Roz could not afford to heat it properly. From late autumn to early spring, the house was battered by the north-east wind which drove the mist in from the Wash and up the canals, known locally as drains.

The first Christmas after Tom and Roz married, a lorry carrying sheep had got lost in the fog, missed the narrow road which passed the farm gates, and tipped into the drain. Those animals which hadn't drowned had escaped in panic to rush around the farmyard. Four had broken into the kitchen and hidden under the table, dripping with mud and defecating with fear. Anna remembered her father offering to buy them from the lorry driver to save them from the slaughter-house, although heaven only knew where he thought four sheep could live at Leatherbridge. But she had loved him for trying, and the memory of his efforts was especially poignant, for within a few months he had killed himself and none of them had been able to save him, for unlike the sheep he had hidden his fear.

By the time Charlie and Anna arrived, her mother and her grandmother were already seated at the dining-room table. 'Sorry we're late,' said Anna breezily. 'The traffic was terrible. Hello, Mum . . . Happy birthday, Granny.' She bent to kiss her grandmother's aged cheek.

'It's rude to be late, Anna,' said her grandmother, a straight-backed woman with grey hair and piercing eyes.

'I'm sorry, Granny.'

'In my day young people never kept their elders waiting.'

'Yes, Granny.' Anna moved around the table, kissed her mother briefly on the cheek, then, leaving Charlie to make the polite conversation he was so good at, she escaped to the large, beamed kitchen where she found Roz and Tom organising the children's chores.

Roz took after Granny Tobias and their father's side of the family. She had a handsome, angular face, broad cheekbones and a mass of curly reddish-brown hair. Tom had the same colouring as his wife, so much so that people often took them for brother and sister, but he was very different in character. Where she was bright, bossy and easily irritated, he was placid and patient with a constantly benign smile.

'Sorry I'm late,' Anna announced, then she added, so that they did not question him, 'Charlie may be a bit quiet, he's had a disappointment.'

'Nothing serious?' asked Roz.

'He applied for another job and didn't get it.'

'Sounds like Dad.'

'Oh, no! He's quite different.' Anna was shocked at the suggestion. She picked up a pile of plates. 'Shall I carry these in?'

'No thanks, Melissa will.'

'I'm stacking the machine!' snapped Melissa from behind a curtain of lank dark hair.

Roz mouthed 'Teenagers!' and raised her eyes heavenward. Then she called to Luke, the red-headed musical genius, and chubby, freckly Oliver to take over from Melissa. Only Phoebe, aged five and dainty like a tiny golden flower, was excused kitchen duties. She sat at the table next to Anna's mother.

At lunch Anna was placed between Oliver and Tom with her mother opposite. Charlie was down the far end, next to Melissa.

'Thank you for the champagne,' said Roz. 'Granny, Anna and Charlie bought a bottle of champagne. We'll have it with the cheese. I know that's when you prefer to drink it.'

'I do love champagne.' Anna's mother smiled across the table.

'I know,' said Anna. 'And we'll have some on your birthday too.'

The old beamed dining-room glowed with their contentment as they ate and drank and talked and laughed. Charlie was listening patiently as Melissa unburdened her frustrations. He caught Anna's eye and winked, and she wanted to kiss him for putting aside his own thwarted hopes.

'I went to Belworth the other day,' she told her mother tentatively, wondering if she should, but feeling it was furtive not to do so. 'I saw Mr Holdsworthy and he said that Cliff Cottage is only used in August. I climbed up there. It was so neglected.'

Her mother looked so sad that Anna wished she'd kept quiet. 'One day I'll go back to Belworth, but not yet,' she said, quietly, so that Granny Tobias could not hear. 'I'm far too busy looking after you-know-who. I couldn't leave her, not even for one night.'

She spoke in a way which begged for agreement and Anna hurried to assure her. 'You're right, Mum, she couldn't cope without you.'

Melissa brought in the cheese and Tom poured the champagne, but as they raised their glasses to Granny Tobias, she fixed Charlie with her steely gaze. 'The next time I drink champagne I hope it will be when you marry my granddaughter,' she said firmly. 'I don't approve of people living together outside wedlock.'

Anna turned scarlet. 'Granny! Please!'

'I'm eighty-six and I'll say what I like.' She pointed a bony finger at Charlie. 'Well, young man, what answer have you?'

Charlie blushed like a naughty schoolboy caught with his hand in the sweet tin. He hesitated, then replied, 'Anna has yet to meet my family, but I plan to invite her to Australia for Christmas.'

With a shriek of delight Anna shot out of her place, ran around the table, and hugged him.

7

BECAUSE ANNA WAS happy her worries evaporated, and because she was no longer anxious, Charlie was in a good mood, which in turn made her happier. Although he hadn't said so, she was convinced that in Australia he planned to ask her to marry him. In her day-dreams they came home engaged – or rather they came home and Charlie formally asked her mother's permission to marry her, because Tom had spoken to her father when he'd wanted to marry Roz, and if Charlie didn't do similar, Anna knew she'd never hear the end of it from her grandmother.

As she hurried to and from work she planned their wedding. It would be early next June; she'd have chosen May but it was considered unlucky and April could be very cold. She'd have liked to marry in the little church at Belworth but that would have distressed her mother, so she'd opt for the old stone fenland church at Lower Gossip, where the vicar was amenable, and Roz's garden would be beautiful in June. Charlie would probably think a church ceremony was sentimental, but she could pretend it was for her mother's sake, although in reality Anna herself wanted a traditional wedding.

Over the following weeks she plotted all the details: her dress, her bouquet, the guest list. Often she'd be lying in bed, next to Charlie, and he'd be talking about their house-warming party, whilst she smiled and nodded and wondered whether her dress should be ivory or cream.

When Xavier sent his next bill Anna paid it without protest, telling herself that since Ladbroke Hill was to be their marital home it needed to be perfect. When the bank rate rose for the seventh time in three months she forced herself not to panic, and on the day that rising inflation figures caused alarm in the money markets, she went late-night shopping in Bond Street and spent a fortune on a red silk dress by Giorgio Armani.

At work, Anna brimmed with energy. Gloomy predictions of an impending recession no longer troubled her, and her confidence was contagious. She won back the client who'd abandoned her for the Thug and persuaded another to order a cruiser from Fred Ribble. After she and Charlie spent a weekend with Vince and Monique aboard *Le Nouveau Monde* in Puerto Banus, she returned home with the names of six prospective clients tucked inside her vanity case. Back at her desk Anna found a grateful letter from Mr Cargill, informing her that his claim had been settled in full. She rang Isaac and said, 'I told you Cargill was honest.'

He chuckled. 'So you were right this time.'

'Don't you dare incorporate Sheldon's fee in Cargill's next premium.'

'Anna, my name's Isaac Finestein. Others might do that, I don't.'

'I know, I was only joking.'

He changed the subject. 'A little bird tells me you're off to meet Charlie's family.'

'At Christmas – and I can't wait.'

'You must bring him to our *Shabbat* dinner one Friday, if he wouldn't be bored.'

'Of course he wouldn't. We'd love to come.'

They fixed a date. When she told Charlie he groaned as she'd feared he would, but on the evening he was charming, as she'd known he would be.

To Anna's frustration work on the house had ground to a halt because the builder, the only one whom Xavier trusted, was on holiday. Although the bedrooms and bathrooms were ready for plastering, the kitchenettes had yet to be dismantled, the sauna hadn't been installed and, because Mr Shufflebuck hadn't accepted their offer, the morning room was still partitioned into a kitchen and bathroom.

Charlie loved to discuss the party but he had no patience for the details, so in odd moments during the day, Anna snatched time off work to arrange it. She booked the caterers, the champagne, a florist and a steel band. Secretly, she considered this organisation a rehearsal for her wedding and for all the entertaining which she and Charlie never had time to do, but which she pictured them doing once they were married.

On the day she posted the invitations she returned to the flat to find Charlie reading a letter from Xavier. 'The front steps have to be replaced.' He gave a loud groan. 'Why the hell didn't Xavier discover that earlier? This house is costing us a fortune.'

'We'll spend some of the funds set aside for carpeting,' Anna said calmly, determined to have no more money arguments.

'But what about our party?'

'We'll dance on the bare boards; it'll save us hiring a floor.'

He was all smiles as he hugged her. 'Oh, you're so wonderfully practical, you're just like my mother.'

Anna didn't know whether to be pleased or not. She'd seen a photo of Charlie's mother and she looked like a large blonde horse.

Between work and the party Anna had little time to gossip with Delia, so they set aside an evening and met after work in a wine bar, choosing a secluded table where they could talk uninterrupted.

'Here's your invitation,' said Anna, handing Delia a white envelope.

Delia slit it open with her long scarlet thumbnail. 'Dancing to the Blue Steel Band! It sounds fabulous. I shall buy a new dress.'

Anna laughed. 'I already have, and I'm nearly bankrupt paying for it.' She took another invitation from her briefcase. 'I did a separate one for Russell. I know he has a flat in town and his wife never leaves the country, but I didn't like to post it in case she found it. Can you give it to him?'

Delia looked flustered. 'He . . . er . . . might not be able to come.'

'You mean, you don't want him to? Dee, have you two split up?'

'I've been thinking about what Mother said.' Delia fiddled with the stem of her wine glass. 'I went to the theatre last week and sat next to an empty seat – Russell's seat – but he was at his son's school play. I spent last weekend on my own, and the one before. I know he'll stay in town for something special but he won't stay just to do nothing – to read the Sunday papers, watch TV, the kind of weekends you spend with Charlie.'

'I agree with you,' said Anna. 'Have you told him?'

'No, but I intend to.' Delia's cheeks turned pink. 'You see, there is someone else I'd prefer to bring.'

'You cagey woman, who is he?'

'I haven't been out with him yet but I've always liked him and I think he likes me, though I'm not sure in what capacity – he's one of those men who give nothing away. But if I invite him to your party, I'll soon discover if I'm wasting my time.'

'Is he someone I know?'

'Paul Sheldon.'

'Oh no! Not Sheldon. He's so arrogant.'

'Anna, I thought you liked him. You spoke to no one else at the Christmas party. In fact, I was so sure you fancied him that I kept quiet, but now that you and Charlie are . . . well . . . you know, why shouldn't I have a crack at Paul?'

'Delia, he's married, you don't want that again.'

'His wife's dead. She was killed in a car crash.'

Anna stared at Delia. 'When?'

'January, I think.' Delia sat back in her chair and studied Anna's face. 'Why are you looking so solemn? Did you have sex with Paul? Is that why you don't want me to bring him?'

'Delia!'

'So what if you did? Charlie was in Australia, he hadn't phoned and you seemed convinced he planned to dump you – and you were very drunk when Paul drove you home.' Delia paused, but when Anna didn't speak she went on. 'I like Paul and it would be a perfect opportunity for me to get to know him better – and don't tell me Charlie would be cross for Russell's sake, because Charlie doesn't give a damn about anyone, except you.'

Anna took a deep breath. 'If you promise to keep it secret, Dee, I'll tell you what happened. No one else knows, and certainly not Charlie.' She leaned forward so as not to be overheard. 'I didn't have sex with Paul Sheldon, but I might have done if I hadn't been so drunk. On the other hand, if I hadn't been drunk I wouldn't have gone home with him.' She pulled a face, which turned into a remorseful grin. 'We left the party but I can't remember the drive. At some point he must have asked me to go home with him, and I suppose I said yes. I remember he had a studio somewhere off the King's Road, with a spiral staircase leading up to a galleried bedroom. I know that much because I remember clinging on to the hand-rail as I walked up the stairs. I can't even recall kissing him, I was that drunk, but I do remember that one moment I was upright and the next I was leaning over the gallery being violently sick, straight down on to the Persian carpet fifteen feet below.'

Delia gave a howl of laughter. 'Oh Anna! What did he say?'

'He was very kind, considering how abrupt he sometimes is. He cleaned it all up, whilst I lay in the bath and cried and wanted to drown myself. Then I told him that I thought Charlie didn't love me, and he told me that his marriage was in trouble. He was having a trial separation, though he didn't say why, I think he was too loyal. I remember him bringing me a mug of tea and that I got out of the bath, wrapped myself in a towel, and sat on the end of his bed to drink it.'

'What happened next?'

'Oh . . . nothing. I burst into tears again, I just couldn't stop crying, but by that time Paul had had enough of my tears, and I don't blame him. He went to sleep in the spare room, whilst I lay on his bed, stifling my sobs in his duvet. After an hour, when I was sure he must be asleep, I crept out, grabbed a cab, and went home.'

'And you haven't seen him since?'

'I left a message on his answering machine offering to pay for the cleaning of the carpet but he never called back. So I rang him at work, and he told me that he and his wife were together again. He was very cool, as though I were chasing him. You know what I mean, the man-doesn't-phone-girl syndrome. He made me feel an idiot, and before I could get my own back by telling him that I only went home with him because I was drunk and upset about Charlie, he said he had a call waiting and he cut me off. Now you understand why I don't want him at my party.'

They didn't talk of Paul Sheldon any more, but gossiped about work. It was late when they parted, taking separate taxis. As Anna watched the night streets of London flash by, she began to wish that she hadn't told Delia about Paul Sheldon.

On the day of their house-warming party Anna woke with a streaming cold and a sore throat. She lay in bed, sneezing and sipping hot tea, whilst Charlie searched for his squash racket and sang *Rudolph the Red-Nosed Reindeer*.

'Don't!' she begged him, laughing and sneezing again.

He leaned over and kissed her forehead. 'At least your nose will match your dress.'

She took a swipe at him but he ducked away and left the flat, calling over his shoulder, 'See you later. Stay in bed.'

'I can't,' she wailed. 'I'm needed at the house.'

'No, you're not. The caterers know exactly what to do, you told me so last night.'

He went out, and she sank back against the pillows and slept until it was time for her hair appointment. Forcing herself out of bed, she pulled on a track suit, swallowed two paracetamols and called a taxi. Three hours later she was back in bed, trying not to squash her softly-curled, newly-streaked hair, or chip her freshly varnished nails.

Charlie came home at five. 'You'll have to stay in bed,' he said on feeling her burning forehead.

'I'm not missing a party when I've spent as much as I did on a dress.'

'Then you'd better have a brandy.' He poured her a stiff one, and had one himself.

The drink and a shower made Anna feel better. She fixed her make-up, except for her lipstick, and slipped the red dress over her head. Short, smart and clinging, but not being too tight, it accentuated those curves which she liked and not those she'd spent a lifetime battling to reduce.

'What do you think?' she asked Charlie, sliding the skirt up to reveal the lacy tops of her stockings.

'I love it. Will you promise to wear that dress in Australia?'

'If you'd like me to.' She came to him and kissed the corner of his mouth.

He ran his hands down her back, pulling her close to him, feeling for the hem of her dress. 'We haven't made love for two weeks,' he said, his fingers touching her suspenders.

She bit the lobe of his ear. 'We're always too busy or too tired.'

'We've time now.' He buried his face in her rippling hair and whispered, 'Take the dress off. Please! I can't wait till after the party. I want you now.'

He slipped the dress over her head and laid it carefully on a chair, then he took her in his arms and kissed her bare neck and her arms. They fell back on to the bed, and looked into each other's eyes and smiled.

'I thought you were ill,' he said, kissing the tip of her nose.

'I was – but you've cured me.'

They took time to touch and feel, to caress and titillate. He stroked her back and her buttocks, sliding his fingers inside her lacy underwear. She kissed his chest, she buried her face in his stomach, and he ran his fingers through her hair, twisting its silky blondeness as he gave a low moan. She gave him pleasure, and he returned it. He pulled her on to him and held her above him, and they made love. Then he rolled her over and they loved again. She wanted it to last for ever, and yet nothing could have held her back. She clung to him, wrapping her silky stocking-covered legs around him, and relished the feeling of him deep inside her.

Afterwards, they lay close and talked about Australia until Anna glanced at the clock-radio and wailed, 'Seven-thirty!'

They shot out of bed, giggling with panic, as their taxi driver rang their bell. With no time to wash away Charlie's love-making, Anna pulled on her dress, grabbed her high heels and her coat, and followed him out of the flat. In the lift she doused herself with scent; in the taxi she combed her tangled hair; at the traffic lights she retouched her lips.

Tom and Roz were already on the doorstep when Charlie and Anna arrived full of apologies and excuses about the extra-ordinary number of cars on the road, although their shining eyes told another story.

Anna had agreed decorations with the florist, but she was rapt in wonder by the clever transformation of the house. Rich folds of green and white moiré were draped across every window, with just a touch of scarlet to add warmth. Fans of flowers hid the worst of the builder's eyesores, and the banisters, stripped of paint but not yet varnished, were woven through with honeysuckle and cream roses. In the double dining-room, where the buffet was laid out on tables along one wall, a strategically placed weeping fig covered a section of damp plaster, and in the drawing-room, where the steel band played by the open garden window, large mirrors deflected the eye from the unpainted walls underneath.

'It's fabulous.' Charlie hugged Anna. 'You are clever.'

Anna was pink with pleasure and fever.

'It's a palace!' Roz exclaimed in admiration. 'Mother told me your house was big but I'd no idea it was so grand. It must have cost a fortune.'

Charlie laughed. 'It still does.'

The guests arrived, the band played, the waiters circulated with canapés and champagne. There was a commotion near the front door and Vince Ellerby-Creswell burst in, followed by a sun-tanned, sun-streaked Monique and half a dozen of their friends from Puerto Banus.

'You thought I wouldn't come, didn't you?' he said, wrapping Anna in a bear hug. 'We flew up especially, just for the night.'

'Vince, I'm flattered.'

She was surprised to see Russell. 'Is Delia here?' he asked.

'Oh . . . er . . . didn't she come with you?' Anna couldn't think of anything else to say.

'We haven't spoken for a month. It was Charlie who told me about the party – yesterday.' Russell was offended not to have received an invitation, but Anna could hardly tell him the reason without betraying Delia, so she hurriedly introduced him to Roz and Tom and escaped to the kitchen.

Her sore throat was coming back with a vengeance, exacerbated by talking and by the smoky atmosphere. She checked the dining-room where some of the guests were already tucking into the cold buffet, then she joined the spectators around the dance floor. Gordon was deep in conversation with an earnest brunette; short, tubby Vince was teaching tall, serene Bridget to jive, and Isaac and Sybil Finestein were executing a perfect foxtrot to the admiration of the onlookers. Anna searched for Delia but couldn't see her.

'Great party, Anna,' said Kevin Kitterick, leading a blonde in a transparent dress on to the dance floor.

'Thanks Kevin.' She giggled as she remembered Charlie once telling her that Kevin listed his sexual conquests in the back of his Filofax.

There was a break in the music. Some people left the dance floor, others joined in. Charlie took Anna by the hand. 'This one's ours,' he said, drawing her into his arms.

'Charlie, I ought to check that the caterers don't need anything.'

'No, you don't!' He held her tighter. 'Everything's perfect.'

'Are you sure?'

He smiled at her self-doubt. 'It's a brilliant party. Now relax and enjoy yourself.'

It was after eleven when Anna walked into the back kitchen

where the caterer was discreetly clearing away the buffet. 'Any problems?' she asked.

'Your tenant's in a rage. He's been up twice to complain about the noise.'

Anna raised her eyebrows. 'Oh dear!'

She made her way back to the front of the house. As she reached the hall, the front door opened and Delia stepped inside, dressed from head to toe in bright white which accentuated her black hair.

'Sorry we're late.' Delia fluttered forward like an excited white moth and, as she did so, Anna caught sight of Paul Sheldon.

He was standing on the threshold, taller than Anna remembered, or perhaps he appeared so because she felt awkward in front of him. He filled the door frame, not because he was big, but because his presence dominated. But he looked different; his normally unruly dark hair was neatly swept back and he wore a dinner-jacket which made him look older and more sophisticated, whereas she recalled him as being rugged and almost boyish. And there was a reticence, a hollowness around his thoughtful grey eyes, which was new.

'Hello, Anna,' he said in a pleasant, detached voice, as though they had scarcely met.

'Hello.' She was furious with Delia but she couldn't show it in front of Paul, so she waved her hand towards the dining-room, saying, 'You'll find plenty to drink but I'm afraid most of the buffet has been eaten,' and she turned on her heel and walked up the stairs, past three guests waiting to use the first-floor loo, and on up to the solitude of the top floor.

A moment later, Delia followed. 'I'm sorry,' she began, 'I know you told me not to bring Paul.'

'Dee, couldn't you have seen him another night?'

'When? I had to have something to invite him to, I couldn't just ring him, even I don't have the nerve to do that.' She paused. 'Anna, please, don't be cross. Paul is the first unattached, attractive man of the right age whom I've dated since my divorce. I'm thirty-nine and . . .'

'You're thirty-six.'

'I'm thirty-nine and I lie about my age because I don't want everyone to know that next year I'll be forty.'

Seeing Delia so vulnerable, Anna's anger evaporated. 'If he were any other man I'd have welcomed him with open arms,' she said.

'But what's wrong with Paul? So you threw up on his rug and burst into tears – that's embarrassing, but no more.'

'Because . . . things went a little further.'

'You had sex with him?' Delia asked in her usual, direct way.

'I burst into tears in the middle of it, when he was actually . . .'

'Why didn't you tell me that before?' Delia was offended and baffled. 'Anna, we're friends, best friends, and I always tell you everything. You're so secretive.'

She thought of her father's death, which even after all these years her mother refused to call suicide. 'I was brought up to suppress unpleasant truths.'

'Well it isn't normal, you know.' Delia flounced down the stairs to look for Paul.

Anna followed unhappily. She was exhausted and her throat hurt and she longed to go to bed. Unable to face the gaiety in the drawing-room, she slipped through the dining-room and out on to the balcony which overlooked the garden. It was cold and the air had the first frosty nip of autumn. She gripped the railing and stared up at the full moon. It had a bright white hazy edge, almost an October moon.

'Anna!'

She turned sharply to find Paul Sheldon standing just inside the dining-room.

He stepped out on to the balcony. 'I apologise for gatecrashing your party but Delia assured me that I'd be welcome.'

Anna blushed. 'I . . . er . . . didn't mean to be rude.' She hesitated and, although she wasn't sure if she should – it was so difficult to gauge other people's grief – she added, 'I'm sorry about your wife, I only heard recently or I'd have written.'

He stared out at the garden. 'Thank you.'

There was an awkward silence, he made a move to leave, then he stopped. 'I like this house,' he said softly, his voice suddenly gentle. 'It reminds me of my godfather's house in Rhode Island where I spent the summer after my father was killed.'

'I'm . . . er . . . sorry.'

'Oh no, you've misunderstood, I loved that house.' He smiled. 'That first summer I spent at Whaler's Rock was magical.' He paused. 'You see, that's where I learned to sail.'

She whispered, partly because her throat was dry and partly because there was an intimacy on the balcony which she feared to break, 'I too learned to sail from a house I loved.'

He touched her shoulder, so briefly that she wasn't sure if he had done so or if his fingers had skimmed past her and she had imagined his touch. 'Then you understand magic,' he said.

If Anna had not known Paul as she did, she would have asked to hear more about Whaler's Rock and perhaps even shared some memories of Cliff Cottage with him, but she was paralysed by the embarrassment of their brief, inglorious passion.

Because she didn't answer him, Paul said, 'I'd better make sure that Delia is enjoying herself,' and he disappeared into the house.

Only then did Anna realise how anti-social her silence must have seemed, but it was too late. Paul had been swallowed by the crowd and she felt too tired and unwell to search for him.

The party ended at four, by which time Charlie had passed out on the sofa. From experience Anna knew it was hopeless to try to wake him, so she covered him with his jacket and made a bed of sofa cushions for herself on the floor, taking off her beautiful red dress before covering herself with three damask table-cloths. It was cold and uncomfortable, and she longed for the warmth of their duvet and the softness of real pillows.

She was awakened next morning by Mr Shufflebuck calling, 'Errol Flynn! Come home! Come on boy!'

Anna's throat was parched and sore and she reached for her glass of water, sipping it gratefully. On the far side of the room Charlie slept, lying on his back, snoring. Anna heard Mr Shufflebuck climb the garden steps and open the kitchen door which had been left unlocked. A moment later he stepped into the room.

He was wearing a full-length green satin dressing-gown, and his eyes were red-rimmed from crying. When he saw Anna lying on the cushions, he gave a gasp of fright and averted his eyes from her naked shoulders. 'I'm looking for my cat,' he said. 'Your noise frightened him and he's run away.'

She tried to say 'I'm sorry', but no words came out.

'Decent people would have warned me about the party,' he went on. 'They wouldn't have broken my pot-plant, my favourite, with the pink geranium.'

'We'll replace it,' she croaked.

'I'm talking about manners not money, but people like you wouldn't know the difference.' Pursing his lips, he stalked out of the room.

Anna dragged herself off the cushions, washed, dressed, and swallowed two paracetamols with the last of the orange juice. From the kitchen window she saw Mr Shufflebuck searching for his cat in the street below the garden. He was proffering an open tin of cat-food as he peered under parked cars.

Taking Charlie's coat because it was warmer than her own, Anna left the house. Out in the street she hailed a cab. As she climbed into it Mr Shufflebuck walked past, his shoulders hunched dejectedly. He didn't even look at her.

She had to go all the way to Chelsea before she could find a garden centre which sold terracotta pots already planted with pale pink geraniums. Asking the cab to wait she selected one which looked similar to Mr Shufflebuck's, except that it was larger and it contained two plants. Back at the house she paid the taxi driver. As it drove away she saw a flash of marmalade fur disappear under a parked car. Putting the geraniums down on the pavement Anna looked under the car. Errol Flynn stared back at her. 'Come on!' she said, clicking her fingers.

He yawned and licked himself.

'Good boy! Come here!'

He didn't move.

'All right, stay there.' She straightened up.

Immediately the cat strolled out from underneath the car and rubbed himself against Anna's legs.

'You are a contrary creature.' She bent, tentatively, to stroke him. She'd never touched him before and was afraid that he might bite or scratch her, but he purred contentedly, so she slipped her hands under his chest and lifted him on to her shoulder, picked up the pot of geraniums and walked back towards the house.

'Mr Shufflebuck! I've found your cat,' she called, staggering down the steps to the basement under the weight of the cat and the terracotta pot.

He opened his door. 'Oh you naughty boy!' he cried, holding out his arms. 'Where have you been?'

'I found him under a car,' said Anna.

'And he let you pick him up? Good heavens! He doesn't usually like strangers.'

She smiled. 'He's lovely but very heavy.'

Mr Shufflebuck's face softened. 'I've had him since he was a kitten. I found him hiding in a dustbin just off the Portobello Road. He was so small and so frightened, and now look at him! The King of Ladbroke Hill.'

'I'm sorry about last night,' Anna said contritely, holding out the pot of geraniums. 'I bought you this as a replacement.'

Mr Shufflebuck stared doubtfully at the two large flowering plants. 'Mine had only one plant.'

For a moment Anna was nonplussed, then she replied, 'Please accept the second one as our apology.'

'But I don't want it. You people think that money counts instead of feelings, but you're wrong.' He stepped back inside his flat and closed the door.

Anna was so irritated that she nearly hurled the pot straight through his sitting-room window, but instead she placed it right outside his front door so that he could not ignore it.

8

ANNA ARRIVED AT work on Monday, still suffering from flu, to find her telephone ringing. As soon as she pressed 'Answer', Vince's voice came over the squawkbox and echoed around her office. 'Annie! *Le Nouveau Monde*'s been stolen!'

'What?' She switched the telephone back to 'Receiver Only'.

'She went whilst we were in London. My beautiful boat! Some bastard's taken her.' There was a choke in his voice.

Anna could hear Vince crying and her heart went out to him. She searched for a pen and notepad and waited a few moments for him to recover before saying, as gently as possible, 'I need some details. Sorry to ask you now, Vince, but we must file a claim. What happened?'

'I gave the crew the weekend off because we were coming to London, to your party. I always give 'em weekends if we don't need 'em – except for the deckhand who ain't allowed to leave the boat unguarded. But this stupid bastard fell for some tart who just happened to walk along the quay. He didn't dare invite her on board – that's one of my rules – so they went down to the beach, drank some wine, smoked some dope, and screwed their fuckin' brains out. Sorry to be coarse, Annie, but I could murder him.'

'It's all right, Vince, I understand. What happened next?'

'He woke up on the beach next morning to find the girl gone, and when he arrived back at the harbour my beautiful boat had gone too.'

'You've told the police and the harbour-master?'

'I've told everyone.'

'What do they say?'

'That it was a set-up job and the girl was part of it. She's disappeared – of course.'

'Vince, *Le Nouveau Monde*'s a big boat; she'll not be easy to dispose of.'

'Unless she's taken to the Caribbean and sold to a drug runner,' he said bitterly.

'To cross the Atlantic she'd need her engine modified and fuel capacity enlarged. My bet is she's still in the Mediterranean. Sooner or later she'll have to dock to take on fuel and that's when we'll catch her. I'll fax you a claim form and warn the underwriter. If there's any news, let me know.'

'I'll be heart-broken if I don't get her back,' he said. 'I wish I hadn't come to London.'

'You're making me feel guilty.'

'I'm sorry, I didn't mean to. You're a sweetheart. I'll be in touch.'

Anna took a slug of cough medicine, then she buzzed Bridget. '*Le Nouveau Monde*'s been stolen in Spain.'

'That big cruiser! I don't believe it!'

'Bridget, you're not going to wriggle out of this one. It was stolen on Saturday whilst my client was in London, at our party – and you danced with him . . . Yes, the tubby little man with the blonde-streaked French wife.'

'Anna, I'm sure your client's honest, but this is a big claim and we'll have to ask Sheldon to investigate before we pay out.'

'Vince won't mind, he has nothing to hide, he just wants his boat back. If Sheldon can trace his boat he'll be over the moon.'

Anna made herself some Lemsip and went to inform Gordon. He was in the board room, morosely studying Marinecover's August figures. 'It's your worst month this year, Anna,' he said, pointing to Yachts' column.

'Only because all the other months were brilliant.'

'You've lost five old clients.'

'Little clients, Gordon, who've sold their small yachts to pay their higher mortgages. I haven't lost a major client.' She was angry and defensive, made worse by her thumping headache. 'I came to tell you that *Le Nouveau Monde*'s been stolen.'

'Good God!'

'Vince is devastated.'

'What do Isaac's lot say?'

'They're getting Sheldon to investigate, but I'm sure Vince is on the level.' She sneezed violently. 'I'm going home to bed, I'll be in tomorrow.'

She expected Gordon's usual, inattentive sympathy but he frowned. 'I know you have a new house and you've been organising your party and you're off to meet Charlie's folks but we're heading for hard times, Anna, and this isn't the moment to take time off.'

Anna sneezed again. 'Gordon, I'm ill.'

'You can't afford to be unwell, Anna. You do a good job but the yacht market's shrinking and you must hold on to your share.'

'Gordon, I've made a fortune for Marinecover this year.' She held up her hand to stop his interrupting. 'Yes, I've done well for myself too, but I don't intend to die at my desk.' She walked out of the board room, collected her coat and briefcase, and went home.

Charlie was up north all week, drumming up new business, so she couldn't tell him what Gordon had said, not that he'd have wanted to hear bad news.

That evening Anna telephoned Delia. 'Oh, Anna,' Delia said, 'I was about to ring you. The party was terrific, everyone loved it.' She paused, then added pointedly, 'I must say for two people who are meant to be indifferent to each other, you and Paul seemed to be very cosy on the balcony.'

'Oh . . . we were just talking about sailing.'

'He told me.'

Anna wondered what else Paul had told Delia, and if they planned to meet again, but she didn't like to ask. Delia was right, she had Charlie. Nevertheless she felt proprietorial towards Paul because they had been intimate, and she had not had so many lovers.

Her first boyfriend was Sebastian. They'd met when she was seventeen and he was twenty, at a tennis party given by Jacynthia Peabody, the first friend her mother made after they went to live with Granny Tobias, in her bungalow on the outskirts of a small village not far from Northampton. Anna didn't want to go to the party, she was shy in gatherings where she knew no one, but she'd agreed, to please her mother who was terribly lonely since her father's death. She remembered cycling up to the Peabodys' very grand house to find the drive full of expensive cars. Embarrassed by her old bicycle, she'd hidden it in the rhododendrons. As she walked nervously towards the tennis court where a dozen or so people were gathered, all strangers, a very tall, aristocratic-looking, fair-haired young man had stopped speaking to his companions and given her a friendly smile. 'Here comes my partner,' he'd called out, waving his racquet at Anna.

That evening Sebastian had driven her home in his red MG sports car. Anna didn't tell him about her bicycle hidden in the bushes, and by the time she returned the following morning it had been stolen.

Sebastian had been about to start an army commissioning course at Sandhurst, in order to become an officer, and he'd spent his last weeks of freedom with Anna. They played tennis, swam, danced and kissed, but they did not make love, not yet. Anna had been due to sit her A levels that year – she'd planned to go to university – but her distress and shock over her father's death and her sudden change to a new school at such a crucial time took their toll. Now, she had Sebastian – dependable, practical, unflinching, the opposite of her father. Modern History and English Literature seemed sterile compared to his long letters, and instead of studying she day-dreamed, instead of attending a lecture, she slipped off to the Family Planning Clinic.

At New Year, she'd stayed with Sebastian at his parents' house in Cumbria and after everyone else had gone to bed, he'd crept along the creaking corridor to her bedroom. Even now she could recall his expression, a mixture of lust and fear.

They'd made love quickly, fumbling, terrified his parents would hear. She hadn't enjoyed it much, although she'd pretended to, but after he'd crept back to his room, she stood naked in front of the mirror and wondered if she looked different and if the next day people would know she'd done IT.

That first love affair had lasted three years. Having fluffed her A levels, Anna couldn't go to university, so she'd drifted into a typing course and a series of dreary jobs, living at home when she wasn't with Sebastian, often bored but afraid to make a change. Then, he confessed that he'd had a fling in Germany whilst on manoeuvres.

Hurt and humiliated, Anna had screamed at him never to contact her again. She returned all his letters and presents, and shut herself in her room to cry – until her mother had forced her way in. 'Sebastian would have made you miserable, darling,' she'd said gently. 'He's in the army, and remember how you hated moving. You always wanted to plant trees which would take years to sprout.'

'I thought if I could plant a tree, then we'd have to stay to see it grow.'

'I hated moving too,' her mother confided.

'Did you?' Anna stopped crying. 'I never realised.'

'I loathed it, but I tried not to let your father see.'

'You should have told me, Mum. You shouldn't have hidden it, and then maybe he would have . . . confided in us.'

Her mother's face closed in. 'Come on, get up!' she said, hurrying towards the door. 'We'll pretend that Sebastian never happened. That's the best way.'

A week later Anna had moved to London, driven as much by the desire to escape from her mother's self-deception as the need for a new life. She signed on at a temporary secretarial agency and joined three other girls in a rented flat. Her next lover was a flatmate's cousin. He made it clear that he didn't want commitment and, although Anna wasn't in love with him, she was offended. She moved on, wised up, toughened up – at least she appeared to, but in reality she was terrified that anyone she cared for would leave her. Sometimes she had a regular boyfriend, but more often than not she didn't. Frequently she'd backed away from love before giving it a chance, because she couldn't bear the thought of the pain should it go wrong. Charlie hadn't allowed her to back away.

All that week Anna suffered from flu. Each morning she dragged herself into the office and every evening she went straight home to bed. Charlie returned disheartened having failed to win a big new account. His dejection was exacerbated when Gordon sent round a memo saying that expenses had to be reduced and lavish entertaining halted.

Vince faxed Anna daily. There was no sign of *Le Nouveau Monde* but the police were still holding the deckhand. As an afterthought he wrote on one fax, 'How soon before they pay out my claim?'

She faxed back: 'Expect visit from Paul Sheldon.'

The gloomy economic climate was unnerving her clients. Of the six she'd met in Puerto Banus, three had decided to sell their boats, one had gone bankrupt and only two – the least profitable – reinsured through her. Their premiums weren't high but they helped her September figures, which scraped in lower than last year's, though not as bad as she'd feared.

Her South Coast agents, who a few months earlier had had more business than they could cope with, were as shocked as Anna by the sudden economic reversal. She visited them to rally their spirits. She didn't need to tell them that if their figures didn't improve, she'd have to let some of them go. The fear of redundancy was already in their eyes and she couldn't help sympathising. She knew the shame suffered by a father when forced to confess, 'I've lost my job.'

Arriving back in London in the early evening, Anna stopped at Ladbroke Hill. No one had been to the house for some days; the builder had moved out and they were waiting for the plasterer to finish a previous job. In the drive fallen leaves had congregated in piles of gold and red and rust. She kicked them off the front steps and unlocked the door. As she stepped inside, she glanced down into the basement. Next to Mr Shufflebuck's front door was her terracotta pot with its two pink geraniums, beautifully tended.

She'd arranged to meet Charlie at his favourite Indian restaurant. He arrived late, still dispirited by Gordon's cut-backs. To cheer him up, Anna ordered all his favourite dishes, even the ones she didn't particularly like, and by the end of dinner he was more cheerful.

'I have a surprise for you,' he told her, reaching into his jacket pocket with such an air of secrecy that she thought he was going to give her an engagement ring. But he produced an air ticket.

She opened it and read aloud: 'Miss A. Tobias, London Heathrow to Hong Kong Kai Tak to Melbourne. Oh Charlie! I'm really going.' She leaned across the table and kissed him. The engagement ring would come next.

9

VINCE WAS HOUNDING Anna for payment. When she tried to explain that Paul Sheldon was still checking the Mediterranean ports, he threatened to move all future business to Merchant & Leisure. It was frustrating for Anna because she didn't want to lose Vince – she'd already lost Cargill, who couldn't afford another boat – but there was nothing she could do to hurry Vince's claim.

In the heady days of the summer she'd invited her mother and Roz to lunch at L'Escargot on her mother's birthday, which coincided with the day on which she had to submit her November figures to Gordon. At the time she'd thought nothing of it. Now, things were different. If she'd been meeting with anyone else she'd have cancelled them, but neither her mother nor Roz could afford L'Escargot, and Anna knew that if she pulled out they'd make do with a sandwich and a cup of coffee in John Lewis.

'Our figures are rock-bottom and Gordon's sure to want me,' she confided to Elaine, 'so I'll wait till I'm sure Mother and Roz are seated, then I'll tell L'Escargot that I've been held up but they're to charge me.'

Chris looked up from his desk. 'No need to disappoint your mum. Gordon's out this afternoon.'

'Are you sure?'

'I heard him tell Miss Thin.'

'Then I'll go.' Anna grabbed her bag and hurried out.

She arrived, breathless, at the restaurant to find her mother and Roz in the pale green upstairs dining-room, discussing every dish on the menu with a patient waiter.

'Oh, there you are!' her mother called out gaily. 'We were afraid you'd forgotten. We're having such fun, aren't we, Roz? Do take the rest of the day off, Anna. Roz has to catch an early train, but you and I could go shopping.'

'I wish I could,' said Anna, thinking how pleasant it would be, 'but things aren't easy at work.' She glanced at the menu and decided that her mother would be too hurt if she merely ate one course, and left.

'You'll need some new clothes for Australia,' her mother persisted. 'Charlie's family sound very grand.'

'I know, but I can't take the time off when business is plunging.'

'I'm not asking for the moon, just a few extra hours with my daughter.'

'Mum, please don't make me feel guilty.'

Her mother spread her white damask napkin on her lap. 'I can't see the joy in having a high-flying career if you're not able to have one afternoon free.'

Anna sighed; her mother was right, but there was nothing she could do about it.

She was away from her office for longer than she'd intended, because it began to rain hard as they left the restaurant. She couldn't find a separate taxi to take her mother to the station, so they shared one, which meant she didn't reach Marinecover until nearly four o'clock.

Gordon was pacing up and down in the reception area when she stepped from the lift. 'What the hell do you mean by going to lunch with your mother when you've handed in such appalling figures?' he demanded.

Aware that everyone nearby was listening, Anna turned scarlet. 'It was her birthday, but I wouldn't have gone had I known you were here.'

'What are you talking about? I've been here all day.'

'You told Miss Thin you'd be out.'

'How could I? Miss Thin's on holiday. Come to the board room.'

He stalked down the corridor. Anna scuttled after him, wondering if she'd misunderstood Chris but knowing that in truth she hadn't; he'd knifed her in the back.

Gordon took his usual seat and Anna pulled up a chair opposite. 'I'm sorry I was out . . .' she began.

He didn't give her time to finish. 'You were needed here. I've had Isaac Finestein on my back because he couldn't find you. Ellerby-Creswell sank *Le Nouveau Monde* himself.'

'I don't believe it. Vince loved that boat.'

'Sheldon has proof. He has photographs of *Le Nouveau Monde* on the Hamble with her ski boat in place, and of that same ski boat in Majorca last week.'

'That's no proof Vince is involved. Anyone could have taken the ski boat.'

'The man with the ski boat has confessed to the police that Creswell paid him and two accomplices ten thousand dollars each to scuttle *Le Nouveau Monde*. Attending your party was Creswell's alibi. He left the stupidest deckhand on board, one whom he knew would not resist the girl, and as soon as she'd enticed him away three men boarded *Le Nouveau Monde*, sailed her out into the Med and pulled the stopcocks. The plan would have worked if one of the men hadn't kept the ski boat.'

Having heard the facts, Anna had no alternative but to accept that Vince was guilty. 'To think how he bullied me for payment,' she said indignantly. 'Why the hell did he do it? He's loaded.'

'Not any more, I gather from Sheldon, and he won't see a penny from this, in fact I shouldn't be surprised if he goes to prison.'

'So he should! He's a crook and a con man.'

'He probably planned it from the outset,' Gordon interjected with his customary cynicism.

'How he must have laughed when we argued over the premium. Oh, I could kill him! All that "Annie, this is the best boat I'll ever own. Annie, you're my favourite broker." ' Anna caught sight of Yachts' figures on the table in front of Gordon, and added, 'I apologise for November, but I'm doing my best in an uphill struggle. Clients are scared by the rising interest rates and all this talk of recession.'

Gordon shuffled his papers and cleared his throat. 'I'm warning all heads of departments that there are to be redundancies. I hate to put people out of work but I have no alternative.'

Anna thought of Chris, and she started to tell Gordon that she could manage without an assistant but, in spite of what Chris had done to her, she couldn't bring herself to cause someone to lose their job. 'If that's everything, I'll get back to work,' she said.

'Yes, that's all – for now.'

As Anna passed Chris's desk on her way to her office, his neck turned bright red. She didn't say anything, but she couldn't help feeling sad that, whereas once they'd fought their competitors for business, now fear of unemployment was driving them to turn on each other.

The Ellerby-Creswell attempted fraud was the gossip of the office that afternoon, but for Anna it cut much deeper. Vince had deceived her and she was both angry and hurt. Of course, she wasn't so naive as to think that Vince had always followed the letter of the law. He was a man who'd made his fortune in a cut-throat business. She knew that, for tax purposes, he claimed Monique as his secretary and all his houses were paid for by his business. She'd seen wads of cash in his pocket and heard him say that he paid the taxman and the vatman just enough to keep them at bay. He avoided – and possibly evaded.

This was different. To sink *Le Nouveau Monde* he'd had to plot and execute his crime; he'd booked his flights to London knowing that whilst he hugged her and swore that he couldn't bear to miss her party, *Le Nouveau Monde* was being steered out to sea, to her watery grave. Anna couldn't imagine being driven to such a point. Even her father, bowed down by debts and shame, had not resorted to crime.

That evening, she recounted the full story to Charlie. Initially he was very sympathetic but at midnight, when she started hacking obsessively through every detail for the third time, he fell asleep. So she lay beside him all night, trying not to fidget as she burned with anger and the need to express it.

At dawn, whilst Charlie slept, she slipped out of bed, collected up her jeans, a sweater and her boots and crept through to the kitchen where she washed in the sink, cleaned her teeth and dressed as quietly as she could. She didn't make coffee because the machine gurgled loudly. Instead, she drank some fresh orange juice straight from the carton, and left the flat.

It was a cold, damp December morning and she'd forgotten to bring a coat but she couldn't go back to the flat in case she woke Charlie. So she gritted her teeth, climbed into her car and set off. The first of the rush-hour traffic was already pouring into London as she headed west, down the M3. It didn't take her long to reach the Ascot exit.

Anna had been to Vince's house on several occasions, but always in summer when the lawns surrounding the house were manicured to velvet and the cultivated woodland which shielded the property from the road was an impenetrable thicket of glorious green, dotted with pink and white rhododendrons. The house was a sprawl of Hollywood mock-Tudor, with so many false black beams that it resembled a chessboard. In summer the woods had given it a soft frame. Now it looked stark and garish.

Too angry to be afraid, Anna left her car in the middle of the drive and marched up to the house. She was about to ring the bell when she noticed another vehicle parked beside the kitchen door. It was a Renault estate, not the kind of model Vince favoured. Its tailgate was open and its seats were piled high with suitcases and boxes.

Vince walked out, carrying a suitcase. He turned pale when he saw Anna.

'Yes. It's me,' she said.

'What . . . what are you doing here?'

'Catching you trying to escape.' She stepped towards him. 'You deceived me, Vince, you hassled me for payment when all the time you'd sunk your own fucking boat.' She slapped him as hard as she could across his face, shouting, 'You bloody crook!'

He was so stunned that he dropped his case and backed away, clasping his cheek across which the shape of Anna's fingers showed red and angry. 'I don't know what you're talking about,' he spluttered.

'Vince, don't lie to me again.'

He hesitated, then genuine shame flooded into his face. 'I'm sorry, Annie, I really am. I'll tell you the truth, I don't know why I should, except that I like you. I didn't want to sink *Le Nouveau Monde*. I loved her, you know that, but I needed money. I backed a bum business deal and I had to pay up.'

'Vince, I trusted you, I assured the underwriter that yours was a genuine claim.'

'I hated to do it to you.' He picked up his case and placed it in the car with the others.

'If you needed money, why didn't you sell the boat?'

'If I'd advertised her and couldn't find a buyer, it would have looked damned fishy if she'd sunk.'

'So you planned it months ago?'

'Annie, I wouldn't have done it unless my back was against the wall. I could go to prison for this. The police may be waiting for me when I try to board the ferry at Portsmouth. I sent Monique on ahead, just in case.' He wrung his chubby hands together in anxiety. The smooth operator who'd wheeled and dealed his way up from the streets of Brixton had been replaced by a frightened middle-aged man in need of a shave. 'You wouldn't swap cars with me, I suppose?' he asked.

'And help you get away? You're joking! I should call the police.'

He gave a resigned shrug. 'I thought you'd say that, but it was worth a try.' He opened the driver's door and Anna noticed the brass bell from *Le Nouveau Monde* on the front seat. He saw her looking at it and pulled a face, trying unsuccessfully to hide the emotion which sprang into his eyes. 'I had to keep a memento,' he confessed. 'I know I'm a sentimental fool, but that boat meant the world to me.'

'That's why I couldn't believe you'd sunk her.'

'You've no idea what you'll do when you're desperate.'

'I wouldn't steal.' She walked to her car and drove away, still sufficiently angry that when she met another car coming up the drive, she refused to give way and eventually it was forced to back down all the way to the main road.

Confronting Vince made her feel better, not just because she hadn't allowed him to walk all over her without protest, but also because she knew that he regretted sinking *Le Nouveau Monde*, and that made her feel less foolish for having trusted him.

She returned home, showered, changed and went to Lloyd's, where she chatted to various people before lunching with Bridget.

On her arrival at Marinecover, Judy beckoned her to the desk. 'The police are here with Gordon,' she whispered. 'You're to go straight to the board room.'

'Good heavens! Why?'

'Creswell, I think.'

Anna smoothed down her skirt, removed a hair from the sleeve of her black jacket, and knocked on the board room door.

'Come in!' shouted Gordon.

She stepped inside. At the far end of the long mahogany table sat Gordon, two plain-clothes detectives and Paul Sheldon. Except for Paul, who smiled at her, they all looked extremely serious.

'Good afternoon,' she said brightly. 'I believe you want to see me.'

'Too right they do,' Gordon snapped. 'What the hell did you mean by going to warn Creswell this morning?'

'I didn't warn him, I lambasted him.'

'The house was under surveillance, Miss Tobias,' explained the senior detective. 'We were on the point of arresting Creswell when you blocked the drive and he escaped through the paddock.'

She recalled the car which she'd forced to back down. 'Oh, I'm sorry. I didn't realise that was yours. It was unmarked.' She turned to Paul. 'If they'd warned me, I wouldn't have gone.'

Before he could speak, the detective cut in. 'How were we to know that you planned a showdown with Creswell? Most of you young City types couldn't give a damn about right and wrong.'

'Well, I do care. Vince used my party as an alibi. He bullied me when we didn't pay out, I've every right to reproach him.'

Paul raised an eyebrow. 'And hit him?'

Their eyes met and she laughed, and for a moment it was as if they were back on the balcony. 'And hit him,' she repeated his words.

The senior policeman rose. 'I'm satisfied that the young lady is not involved in anything of a fraudulent nature.'

'You don't mean that you suspected me too?' said Anna, horrified.

'Mr Sheldon didn't, but we suspect everyone.'

'Then I'm delighted to have been able to prove my innocence.'

'They already knew.' Paul closed his briefcase. 'The car was bugged.'

'Mine or Vince's?'

'Creswell's – though next time you decide to administer rough justice to fraudulent claimants, perhaps I'd better wire yours too in case you need to call for help. You could have been hurt.'

'I had to confront him.'

His eyes twinkled. 'I'd have done the same.' He walked out of the board room with the detectives following.

As soon as they closed the door, Gordon turned on Anna. 'How could you be so unwise? You laid yourself open to suspect motives. What a mess you got us into. We can't afford to waste all this time, you know.'

'I'm sorry, it won't happen again. But look on the bright side, Gordon. Our cut of Vince's premium gave Yachts its best ever monthly figures. Isaac's syndicate doesn't have to pay out because Vince's claim is fraudulent. We haven't lost, Vince has. He has neither the boat nor the money.' She turned to leave.

He cleared his throat. 'Er . . . Anna . . . can you stay a minute?'

She smiled. 'Yes.'

'You remember that I told you that we have to reduce staff?'

'Of course.' She hoped he didn't mean Elaine.

Gordon pretended to rub at a mark on the table. 'This is not easy for me to say, Anna, but . . . er . . . I'm very sorry to tell you that you are to be made redundant.'

The air dispelled from her lungs as though she had been punched below the rib cage. Blood drained from her face and congealed around her heart as rejection rolled over her, up her, into her every pore. She tried to speak but couldn't, she wanted to scream 'No!' but the word wouldn't come.

Gordon talked quickly to fill the awkwardness. 'We're amalgamating Yachts with Hulls until things pick up. You're preoccupied with your new house and your visit to Charlie's parents.'

'That's . . . that's not true, I've worked as hard as anyone.'

'Anna, please, you're making this more difficult.'

'How do you think I feel? I've lost my job.' She took a deep breath. 'What about all my clients?'

'Chris will handle them.'

'You're keeping him, but making me redundant?'

'Anna, he earns less than half your salary. I have to economise.'

'I've been here seven years, Gordon. I've been loyal, you owe me loyalty.'

'I'm sorry, I really am, and if it's any consolation, nineteen other people are being made redundant at this moment.' He paused. 'Including Charlie.'

She was reeling with shock. She stood up and began to walk slowly towards the door, putting one foot carefully in front of the other as though afraid that the floor would disintegrate beneath her tread.

'Don't take it personally, Anna,' Gordon called after her. 'I'll give you a first class reference; I'll do my best to find you another position.'

'It's because of the Creswell case, isn't it?'

'No, I promise. The redundancies were mooted last week.'

'I don't believe you, Gordon.' She walked on, out of the board room and, with her head held high, she crossed the open office to her own room. Only inside, with the door firmly closed, did her façade slip. She slumped into her chair, buried her face in her hands, and cried.

The door opened and Charlie swaggered in, smiling broadly. 'We're going out to celebrate,' he said.

'Charlie, we're unemployed.'

'A good thing too!' He laughed aloud. 'Marinecover's a shitty little broking house and there are much better jobs around. Better pay, better clients. Hurry up and clear your desk.' He produced a black plastic sack, opened the top drawer of her desk and started to remove the contents.

'Don't,' she cried, grabbing a pile of notes. 'I have to ring my clients, I can't just leave them.'

'Let Chris sort it out.'

'I owe them an explanation.'

'For God's sake, Anna! Marinecover have kicked us out. You owe nothing to your clients.' He took her jacket from its hook.

'Charlie, please, I can't leave so quickly, I want to say goodbye.'

He pulled her to her feet. 'Your friends are waiting for you in the wine bar. Who cares about the rest? They stabbed us in the back. Come on!'

'I must phone Delia.'

'She's already at the wine bar.'

'I want to say goodbye to Isaac.'

'Speak to him tomorrow.'

'I want a few minutes in here, alone. I want to say goodbye to my office.'

Charlie took her face in his hands and looked into her eyes. 'Anna, you're finished here. Don't waste your sentiment. You'll get a better job with nicer people; we both will.' He kissed her gently on the lips. 'Believe me, this is all for the best.'

She looked up at his handsome face, wanting so much to believe him, but when they took the lift down for the last time she experienced the same aching sense of banishment as on the day when they had moved out of Cliff Cottage.

They went to a wine bar not far from Fenchurch Street station, and the rest of Anna's day was blurred by the quantity of champagne she drank. When Delia said she was sorry that Marinecover couldn't be very generous with redundancy pay, but Gordon wanted Anna to keep her car, she replied confidently that it didn't matter because she'd soon have a new job. When she met Elaine in the ladies' cloakroom she told her, 'If you need a reference, I'll be glad to give you one.'

Elaine looked embarrassed. 'I'm . . . er . . . staying at Marinecover.'

'You're not going to work for Chris?'

'I can't afford to leave, I have Danny to support.'

Anna nearly blurted out, 'So much for loyalty,' but she knew that would be unfair, and she said, 'Elaine, I understand.'

The reality of losing her job suddenly hit Anna. Tomorrow Chris would be in her office, at her desk, and Elaine would sit opposite, taking dictation. It would be as though she had never existed.

She wondered if this was how her father had felt when he'd been made redundant by the army, and the insurance company, and all the other jobs at which he'd seldom survived his trial period – except the last job, where he'd been for nearly a year, long enough for him to feel secure, so that when they called him to the office and handed him his cards, he'd been unprepared, which had made it much worse. Not that he'd shown his distress for, as the personnel officer explained to Anna's mother after his death, all he'd asked for was to keep his season ticket.

Anna slipped through the crowded bar and out into the street, staggering in the cold air. There was a taxi rank outside Fenchurch Street station but as she was about to hail the first cab, she realised that she'd left her bag in the wine bar. Not wanting to go back inside and needing to sober up, she wandered along Fenchurch Street to Fen Court, a small, secluded square, sandwiched between tall buildings, where she sat down on a bench next to one of the ancient tombs. Above her the branches of the trees rustled, silhouetted like spiders against the evening sky. Around her the fallen leaves and litter swirled into piles, to be swept up in the morning. She leaned forward and rested her forehead on the tomb, the cold stone welcome against her hot skin.

A hand touched her shoulder and she cried with fright.

'It's only me,' said Elaine. 'I brought your bag.' She sat down beside Anna. 'I'll feel a traitor working for Chris.'

'You mustn't. It's a good job.'

'He stabbed you in the back.'

'I know, the bastard!'

'I won't forget what you did for me.' Elaine had a choke in her voice. 'I hope you find something soon.'

Anna smiled. 'Thanks. You've been a great help.'

They shook hands in the small, deserted courtyard, holding on to each other for a moment longer than necessary in an act of mutual encouragement. Then Elaine walked away, down to Monument station for her long train ride out to the suburbs, and Anna returned to the wine bar and Charlie.

She found him lolling on a bench near the taxi rank. He didn't ask her where she'd been, he was too drunk. They climbed into a taxi and set off for home, but when they reached the Embankment, he said, 'Let's get out, let's walk,' and he banged on the glass partition separating them from the driver.

They wandered along the pavement beside the river wall. The air was damp but it felt good on their hot faces. The jagged pinnacles of the Palace of Westminster rose up before them into the orange evening sky and the lights from the far side of the Thames danced on the oily black surface of the river. It had stopped drizzling but the pavement was still wet and the street lights reflected in the puddles which had collected in the well-worn paving stones.

Charlie reached for Anna's hand. 'Let's change our flights and leave for Australia on Saturday. Let's have a real holiday, a whole month in the sun.'

She hesitated, thinking of Ladbroke Hill, their mortgage and the money they'd spend which they ought not to spend.

'Oh come on, Anna! Please! I'll give notice at the flat and we'll move all our stuff to Ladbroke Hill before we go. When we come back we can live in the attic. It'll be ready by then. That's what you've wanted to do for months, isn't it?' He drew her closer, smiling at her like a little boy pleading for a treat.

Suddenly she was overwhelmed with a longing to escape, to walk in the sunshine, to live in the suspended animation of a holiday, to postpone the future. Why should she worry? They'd find other jobs, better jobs. Charlie was right. 'Let's go,' she replied, reaching up to kiss him.

He hugged her fiercely. 'This time next week we'll be there. Oh, I can't wait!' He paused. 'I'd prefer not to tell my parents we've lost our jobs.'

Anna agreed. 'They'd only worry, and so would my mother. She'd be terrified, she'd keep remembering Father. I'm not even going to tell her I've left Marinecover until I have a new post.'

He kissed the tip of her nose. 'We'll say we're taking an extended holiday instead of a bonus.'

She smiled at him. Sometimes he was thoughtless, but on other occasions, such as this, he was so considerate.

'You'll love Australia.' He slipped an arm around her waist and danced her up the wide pavement, singing *Waltzing Matilda*.

A passing taxi driver wound down his window and shouted, 'Getting married?'

'Maybe,' Charlie replied, waltzing Anna in and out of the street lights.

She looked up at him and felt secure and safe.

10

Melbourne

AN EMERGENCY LANDING by another plane at Tullamarine airport forced Charlie and Anna's aeroplane to circle, and from the window she caught distant views of Melbourne – a gentle and undramatic city built on a grid of streets, stretching away through interminable suburbs to a far-off mountain range. She saw the brown curl of the Yarra river and the blue curve of Port Phillip Bay, and over it all a warm silk haze which reflected both the blue of the sea and the purple-green of the mountains.

Charlie's parents were waiting at the airport. As Anna followed him across the arrivals hall to meet them, she put on her best future-daughter-in-law smile, wishing that she'd had time to change out of her creased travelling clothes. In London she'd seen photographs of his parents and decided that his mother looked haughty and bossy, but in the flesh they both seemed much more homely.

Phyllis Blythely was a large, sun-baked Nordic blonde with a long but friendly face. Donald was a handsome grey-haired man, as slim and neat as his wife was ample. Charlie had inherited his perfect features from his father and his blond colouring from his mother.

'It's a treat to see you.' His mother threw her arms around Charlie and kissed him on both cheeks. 'And it's good to meet you at last, Anna.' She embraced Anna so fiercely that she nearly knocked her over.

'Thank you, Mrs Blythely.'

'Oh call me Phyllis, everyone does.'

'And you're to call me Donald.' Charlie's father squeezed her hand. 'Welcome to Melbourne, Anna.'

'Thank you.' It no longer seemed to matter that her clothes were creased.

Charlie walked ahead with his mother, pushing the luggage trolley. Anna followed with his father. 'First visit to Melbourne?' he asked.

'The first time in Australia,' she replied as they stepped out of the terminal and into the warm sunshine which stirred the bluish leaves of the gum trees in the airport car park.

'We're having a barbie tonight – a barbecue. I told Phyllis you'd be tired but she can't wait to show you to the relatives. Vivianne, Charlie's sister, is coming, so is Ingrid, Phyllis's sister, so's my mother. She's a tricky old woman and we have to humour her. Naturally, we've invited all Charlie's cousins. I'm sure he's already told you everything about his family.'

Anna smiled and nodded, and hoped this kindly man never discovered that whenever Charlie spoke of Melbourne he talked of weekends at fashionable Portsea with the twins, Josh and Matt, his closest friends from Melbourne Grammar, or of the grand houses in Toorak where they all lived, or the smart clubs where he'd learned to sail. He'd never mentioned any cousins.

They drove into town along the freeway, Phyllis at the wheel, with Charlie beside her.

'How did you manage to secure five weeks' holiday?' Anna heard her ask Charlie.

'Oh, we took the extra time instead of a bonus.'

'Good heavens, you must be doing well!' Phyllis glanced at Anna in the driving mirror.

'We are.' Anna smiled brightly.

They went on talking and Anna heard Charlie use words like 'promotion' and 'profits', and she hoped he wasn't getting too carried away. She stopped listening because she didn't want to think about work or Marinecover or job-hunting, or any of the problems which faced them on their return to England. Instead, she watched the flat, unfamiliar countryside give way to small bungalows, then to the tighter confines of the city where stately Victorian civic buildings rubbed shoulders with glass and steel high-rises and the traditional green trams rattled furiously along wide tree-lined boulevards.

South of the city they turned along a bustling street of fashionable boutiques and pricey restaurants.

'This is Toorak Road. Toorak's our most expensive district,' Donald explained to Anna.

She studied it eagerly. 'Charlie told me.'

They stopped in a side street of old houses which had balconies of delicate cast-iron tracery. Anna reached for the door handle.

'You're not home yet,' said Donald. 'My clinic's near here and I have to get back to work.'

'Are you operating today?'

'Me? Oh, I shouldn't think so. A corn or a boil perhaps, nothing more. Most of my patients are suffering from sunburn at this time of year.' He stepped from the car and waved them goodbye.

Anna felt a fool. She was sure Charlie had said that his father was a surgeon.

They drove on, past magnificent houses set amid manicured lawns, and surrounded by billowing trees and security fences. In the driveways Anna saw expensive cars parked in front of imposing entrances, and through gaps in hedges she glimpsed enormous swimming pools and tennis courts. She waited expectantly for the Blythelys' house.

They crossed a busy road – she saw that its name was Glenferrie – and almost immediately the houses became smaller. They were comfortable, but not grand, with less land and smaller pools.

'This is Malvern,' said Phyllis, turning into the driveway of a pleasant red-brick house, one storey except for the centre section which had a second floor for a master bedroom suite.

It was similar to the better houses in Leatherbridge, though not the most expensive, but it was nothing like the mansion which Charlie had intimated. Not that Anna minded, except that it made her uneasy to recall how he'd led her to believe otherwise.

With his face turned away from Anna, Charlie turned to collect their luggage from the boot but she could see that his neck was scarlet with embarrassment. She longed to tell him that she still loved him and didn't care if his parents weren't millionaires but she was concerned about his exaggerating, only she couldn't speak of it in front of his mother.

'Come inside, dear,' Phyllis said, noticing that Anna looked very pale. 'You must be tired. Charlie will bring in your suitcase.'

Charlie glanced up and met Anna's gaze, and was afraid. She smiled to reassure him, and he became sheepish, and she realised with some shock that he shared the trait of delusion with her own mother. When her parents had moved to Leatherbridge, her mother had inserted 'Weybridge' into their address because she thought it sounded smarter, until Granny Tobias announced that Weybridge was full of new money. Whereupon her mother changed their address to Leatherhead. The result confused the post office to such an extent that the Tobiases received no mail for six weeks. It unnerved Anna to think that Charlie might have done the same.

The Blythelys' house was modern and open-plan, with big squashy sofas which Phyllis called 'lounges', and chintzy curtains. It was homely, just like Phyllis, and set in a neat, colourful garden with a patio and a small swimming pool to one side.

Phyllis showed Anna to a single room on the ground floor, overlooking the pool. 'This used to be Vivianne's room,' she said. 'Viv now shares a flat in St Kilda with two other nurses, but she'll be here tonight for the barbie. That's Charlie's room.' Phyllis pointed to a door opposite. 'I know you two live together in London but Donald's mother doesn't approve and she's liable to drop in any time, the old busybody, so you have to have separate rooms or I'll never hear the end of it.'

Anna blushed and stammered, 'I quite understand.'

'Of course, I don't give a damn,' Phyllis went on in her endearingly direct way, 'but if you plan to have kids, you should get married for their sakes. That's all I say. Now you get some sleep, dear, and I'll wake you later.' She went out and closed the door. Anna remained in her room, sensing that Phyllis wanted Charlie to herself, recognising in Phyllis that intense mother love for a son which Roz had for Luke.

It was early evening when Phyllis woke Anna with a cup of tea. She was wearing bright turquoise shorts and a shocking pink halterneck, which on a woman her size and her age, particularly one whose arms and chest were baked to leather, looked terrible, but because Phyllis didn't care, it somehow didn't matter. 'Charlie's outside and Vivianne's arrived,' she told Anna, unselfconsciously adjusting a bra strap. 'Come out when you're ready.'

Anna sat up. 'You're very kind.'

'I'm glad to meet you. Charlie hasn't brought home a girl since Serena.' Phyllis paused when she saw Anna's blank expression. 'He must have told you about Serena?'

'You mean Matt and Josh's sister?'

'The romance didn't break up Charlie's friendship with the twins, I'm glad to say, but it could have.' Phyllis left the room, calling over her shoulder, 'We're by the pool; we'll be eating soon.'

Anna felt nauseous with uncertainty. Charlie had exaggerated everything – the house, his father's occupation, but amongst it all he had never mentioned Serena, except as Matt and Josh's younger sister. She rose, showered, and prepared to be charming to Charlie's relations, although her one desire was to question him and get to the bottom of all this.

She dug through the layers of smart clothes in her suitcase, discarding her exotic designer outfits. Her peach silk trouser-suit would look ridiculous next to Phyllis's shorts; her white silk Italian-knit shift could be ruined for ever by one splash of barbecue sauce; one spark from the barbecue on her red Armani dress would consign a fortune to the rubbish bin. Charlie had watched her pack all these unsuitable garments and said nothing to warn her. If her own family had been glitz and riches, she could have understood his fears. As it was, she couldn't.

Selecting a pair of orange shorts and matching T-shirt, Anna walked out on to the patio looking far more confident than she felt. Immediately a dozen sun-tanned faces around the barbecue surged forward to meet her.

'I'm Vivianne,' said a young woman whom Anna had identified as Charlie's sister because she shared their mother's long face and ample blondeness. 'Charlie's on the phone. As I'm sure you know, my brother was born with a receiver attached to his ear.'

'I do indeed.'

They all laughed, and Vivianne clasped both of Anna's hands. 'Welcome to the Blythelys'. Now, meet the rest of the family.' She introduced Anna to her paternal grandmother, a fierce octogenarian in an upright chair. 'This is Charlie's English girlfriend, Granny,' she shouted. Then she whispered to Anna, 'She's not deaf, she has selective hearing.'

Anna thought of Granny Tobias with affection. 'Just like my grandmother.'

Charlie's aunt Ingrid, a smaller version of his mother, offered her a glass of wine or a can of beer – she chose the wine – and Vivianne introduced her to more cousins: an androgynous fifteen-year-old named Pippa; an intense biology student with horn-rimmed spectacles; a dull young couple who lived in Sydney; and many others, all of whom said confidently, 'Of course Charlie's told you all about me.'

How could Anna hurt them with the truth?

She was exhausted by the time the party ended, far too tired to interrogate Charlie, and the following day they spent with Vivianne, so Anna had no chance to find out why he had misled her. The next day they visited friends, and the next, and it was not until Charlie hired a car and they drove down to Portsea that they had time alone. Then it was such a glorious day that Anna was loath to mar it by grilling him about a past girlfriend, or arguing over what – she tried to assure herself – was just a bit of exaggeration.

The week passed in a haze of new people and new places. Anna would have preferred to take things gently, to laze by the pool and get to know Charlie's family, but he couldn't bear to stay at the house. Matt and Josh were in the States until Christmas, so they raced around meeting all his other friends as though they'd have no time for them once the twins were back. In London, Anna and Charlie were always out. In Melbourne, she'd expected life to be quieter, but Charlie was even more social because he knew more people.

'I haven't met Serena,' Anna said as casually as possible one morning after breakfast.

'Oh, you will.'

A hoot from outside cut short their conversation. More friends had come to show Anna around St Kilda, the arty, bohemian seaside of Melbourne where Vivianne shared a flat. On the sea front Anna bought postcards for her family and Delia, Judy and Elaine.

'Just think of those poor sods battling to work through the London rain,' said Charlie, stretching out his arms to the sun's rays.

'You must be doing well to take such a long leave,' said one of his friends admiringly.

'We are.' Charlie smiled at Anna and for a moment she had an awful feeling that he'd started to believe the lie.

On all these trips they ate out, and on nearly every occasion Charlie insisted on paying for everyone.

'We must be more economical,' Anna said one evening after they treated six people to an expensive dinner.

'Oh, sweetie, don't be so mean! My friends are showing you the sights. Buying them dinner's the least we can do.'

'I know, and they're very kind, but we're out of work, we must choose less costly restaurants.'

He took a beer from the fridge and drank it straight from the can. 'Aren't you enjoying yourself?' he asked in an uncertain voice, as if suddenly remembering how he had exaggerated.

'I'm having a wonderful time.' She put her arms around him to reassure him. 'I love your family and your friends, they couldn't be nicer.'

'Then please don't spoil our holiday by worrying about money. We're clever, we're winners, we'll find good jobs.' He drew her close. 'What happened to your father is not going to happen to us.'

'I know, but I'm nervous, I can't help it. I've suffered too many changes to take luck for granted.' She kissed his lower lip and tasted beer. 'Let's be more careful.'

'If it makes you happier.' He nuzzled her and she pressed against him, seeking the protection of his arms. He kissed her face, her eyes, her forehead, whispering, 'I want to make love to you in the pool.'

She giggled, partly with relief because she'd made her point and he'd consented, albeit reluctantly. 'What about your parents?'

'They're asleep.'

They went out into the warm night, to the pool where the water still held the heat from the day. In the shadows near the house they undressed and slipped into that side of the water where a large tree shielded them from the moonlight. They swam together, Charlie on his back and Anna on top of him, her body caressing him, her hair fanning out around her. He ran his hands down her back until he gripped her buttocks. They kissed deeply, fiercely. She floated away from him, teasing, then back to him and finally on to him, wrapping her legs about his waist and her arms around his neck as they made love in the bubbles of the swimming pool.

Afterwards, they lay naked on warm surrounding tiles. Anna longed to ask Charlie about Serena but she didn't want to break the magic.

*

The days drifted one into another. Anna enjoyed staying at the Blythelys'. With Phyllis clucking around her like a giant blonde hen she could almost forget the pain of redundancy.

She didn't meet Serena, and there never seemed to be an appropriate moment to question Charlie. Nor did they visit Wilson's Promontory as he had promised in London. When she mentioned it to Charlie, he replied that it would be more fun to go with Matt and Josh and, although Anna pretended to agree with him, she was disappointed. She wondered how he would ever ask her to marry him if they never had a minute to themselves.

At Christmas they invited his parents and Vivianne to dinner at Stephanie's, one of Melbourne's best known restaurants. It was in an old Edwardian house, the interior divided into rooms with a number of tables in each. At the last minute Charlie extended the party to include Ingrid. The meal was delicious and the evening was a great success, but when the bill came Anna caught sight of it and paled. Not that she blamed Charlie for wanting to entertain his family – they'd often treated her mother – and it was unlikely that Ingrid could afford to come to England for their wedding.

One morning Anna remained at the house whilst Charlie visited his grandmother. Donning her bikini, she took her breakfast out to the pool and stretched out on a sun-lounger. She pictured Delia and Elaine and the bustling office at Marinecover; she imagined Gordon in the board room and Isaac in his box at Lloyd's – and she wondered if they thought of her. With the heat of the sun on her bare limbs and the pool lapping beside her, she couldn't claim to envy them the artificial lighting and the winter cold, but at the same time she couldn't forget the people who'd been her daytime family.

She heard footsteps. 'At last I've caught you here,' said Vivianne, flip-flopping across the patio in a pair of turquoise rubber sandals and a crumpled pink sun-dress. 'Every time I come, you're out.'

Anna smiled. She liked Vivianne, who reminded her of Roz. 'Charlie wants to see all his friends.'

'My brother knows the whole of Melbourne – or rather the so-called beautiful people.' Vivianne stripped off her dress to reveal a clashing red bikini.

'You mean Matt and Josh and Serena?'

'Yes, all that Toorak crowd who went to Melbourne Grammar.'

Anna kept her voice casual. 'Of course Charlie told me about Serena but he never said how long they were together.'

'A couple of years, until he left for England.'

'I suppose she's a lot younger.'

'She was sixteen when it began. Far too young, that's the shame.'

Anna longed to ask whether Vivianne meant it was a shame because Serena would have been the rich society wife whom Charlie needed, or because he'd realised too late that he loved her, but they were interrupted.

'Josh and Matt are back,' Charlie called excitedly from the kitchen window. 'Come on! We're meeting them by the river. Want to come, Sis?'

'No thanks. I'm on duty soon.' Vivianne smiled at Anna. 'Don't worry about Serena, she got married last month.'

Now Anna was concerned that Charlie carried a candle for a married woman.

They drove up to the Yarra river, a wide sludgy ribbon of water flanked by gentle green parkland. Anna kept silent until he parked the car, then she asked, 'Charlie, are you still in love with Serena?'

'Don't be silly!' He waved to two men sculling on the river. 'Josh! Matt!'

Anna persisted. 'You never told me she'd been your girlfriend.'

He reached for her hand. 'Serena's in the past.'

'Did you love her?'

'She was too young.' He stepped from the car as Josh and Matt drew into the river bank, leaving Anna as confused and uncertain as before.

Josh and Matt were identical twins. Tall and dark, they were pleasant-looking but lacked Charlie's carefree spirit, and it was clear to Anna that they idolised his charm as much as he envied them their riches.

On the way home in the car, Charlie told Anna, 'They like you,' and she sensed that she had passed an important test.

They arranged to meet Josh and Matt that evening in a popular French bistro, whose walls were papered with copies of *France Soir*, and they arrived to find them sitting with a large group of friends crowded around three tables. The men were all sun-tanned and sporty, the girls were mostly blonde. They flirted with their sun-kissed hair, flicking it from side to side as they spoke. Only one girl, at the far table, was different. She had a delicate Victorian face, the kind which gazes mournfully from old sepia photographs, and her straight brown hair was tucked behind her ears as Anna often wore hers.

When Anna was introduced to her the table fell silent. 'This is Serena,' Charlie said, without any embarrassment.

A pale, cool hand stretched across the table towards Anna and a tight voice said, 'How do you do? I don't think you've met my husband, Howard.' She introduced a man who looked like an insipid version of Charlie.

'Hello.' Anna tried to smile as though Serena were just another of Charlie's friends, but it came out as a grimace.

Whether by design or chance, a place had been reserved for Anna at the opposite end of the table. People asked her questions and laughed in response to her replies, although half the time they couldn't hear her. They leaned forward to speak to her, which saved Anna from having to look at Serena.

'Melbourne's the best city in Australia,' they told her. 'Forget Sydney. It's pushy.'

She quoted, 'Melbourne creates art and Sydney sells it.'

They all laughed. 'Where did you learn that?'

'Charlie taught me.' She smiled at him across the table.

At the end of the meal, Anna went to the ladies' loo. She was in the cubicle when two girls came in to retouch their make-up.

'Charlie's a shit,' said one, not realising that they weren't alone. 'Did you see Serena's face? He should have warned her that he was bringing the English girl.'

'Josh and Matt could have told her.'

'No, it was up to Charlie. Men are such cowards. Don't you remember last Christmas when he dated Serena every night and she thought – we all thought – that he was planning to ask her to marry him? Then he told her on the last evening that he'd met a girl in London.'

'At least Serena had Howard to turn to.'

There was a click as one of the girls closed her bag.

'She'd divorce Howard in a flash if Charlie came back.'

'He won't return; he's a success in London. Here, he was always in debt. Matt and Josh often used to pay for him.'

They went out of the cloakroom. Anna listened for their retreating footsteps before she stepped out to the mirror. What they'd said about Charlie being in debt was overwhelmed by her relief that he wasn't still in love with Serena, although she was hurt to hear that they had been lovers the previous Christmas, whilst she had sat in London waiting for his call. It wounded her to discover this, even a year later, but she'd have to put it behind her. In any case, there was her own fiasco with Paul Sheldon.

On her return to the table she found that Serena and her husband had left, and Charlie was waving his gold card at the waiter, ignoring the protests from his friends, as he shouted, 'Dinner's on me.'

Anna could do nothing, except smile thinly and hope that Charlie would now feel he'd discharged his debt.

They moved on to the Metro, a huge discothèque in an old theatre, which Josh told Anna was the 'in' place that year. Anyone with fifteen dollars could gain entrance but only those in the know, like Josh and Matt, could go upstairs. The music was loud and pulsating, and Anna danced with Charlie, with Josh and Matt. Someone ordered a magnum of champagne and they toasted the coming year.

It was late when the party split up. As the waiter arrived with their bill, Charlie grabbed it.

'No, Charlie, you treated us all to dinner,' Josh protested. 'That's more than generous. Not even Matt and I stand everyone to a whole evening.'

The others voiced their agreement and reached for their wallets. To Anna's relief, they persuaded Charlie to relinquish the bill, but now she suspected that he wasn't merely repaying Matt and Josh, he was trying to outdo them.

She was subdued on the journey home.

'Tired?' Charlie asked, nuzzling her.

She shrugged.

'They all love you.' He nibbled her ear. 'I knew they would.'

When they reached the house she said, 'Charlie, we need to talk.'

'Oh, save it for tomorrow.' He smiled and ruffled her hair. 'I'm whacked.' He tottered down the corridor into his room and passed out, fully clothed, on his bed.

Anna went out on to the patio and stood alone beneath the eucalyptus trees, with the warm night air all about her and the rustling leaves above. She was too agitated to sleep. Marinecover had paid her three months' notice and the minimum redundancy of a week for every year she'd worked. Charlie had no redundancy because he hadn't worked there long enough. He only had his salary, his commission, and his holiday pay – and he'd spent that in the first week.

It was dawn before she fell asleep. She dreamed of the house on Ladbroke Hill, its rooms empty to the night, the only sound the mincing footsteps of Mr Shufflebuck as he danced to the *Chattanooga Choo-Choo*. She saw herself standing on the balcony, only it wasn't the market below her but Belworth Cove. Then Mr Shufflebuck's footsteps became the slap of the waves against the side of the dinghy and the music became her father's voice, promising, 'One day we'll be rich, Annie. We'll own all the land near to Cliff Cottage, and we'll buy a sixty-footer and sail around the world.'

In her dream, Anna heard herself scream at him that he'd never owned a sixty-footer, or even a forty-footer; that the largest boat he'd possessed was the *Little Auk*, a sixteen-foot dinghy, and the furthest they'd sailed was from Belworth to Bosham. As for owning all the land around Cliff Cottage, he hadn't even managed to retain the house. He'd gone, leaving her without saying goodbye, without explaining why, without giving her a chance to help him.

II

ANNA WAITED UNTIL Charlie had finished his breakfast before she spoke to him. 'I know you hate to discuss money but last night was terribly expensive,' she said, as he turned slightly pink. 'At the end of January, Marinecover will terminate our cheap mortgage and if we don't have another employer offering the same perk, we'll have to find a bank or a building society to take on our loan – at the full rate.'

'We can always sell the house.'

'No!' She was stunned by his suggestion.

'Anna, I'm not living like a pauper for the sake of bricks and mortar.' He picked up his car keys and walked out, shouting over his shoulder, 'I'm going to see Matt and Josh.' He didn't invite her to go with him, and she didn't volunteer.

She went out to the pool and slumped down on a sun-lounger. She wished she was at home, where she would feel less helpless, instead of with Charlie's parents, in front of whom she was obliged to keep up a façade of all being well.

A hand touched her shoulder. She looked around, expecting Charlie, but it was Vivianne. 'Don't worry,' she said, 'his rages soon pass.'

Anna was embarrassed that they'd been overheard. 'I'm . . . umm . . . afraid this is serious.'

Vivianne drew up the second sun-lounger. 'Anything I can do to help?'

Anna hesitated. 'Can you keep a secret? I promised Charlie I wouldn't tell anyone, but I have to talk to somebody, I'm so worried. You see, we're out of work, we lost our jobs in November.'

'You mean . . . you've been retrenched?'

Anna nodded miserably. 'The firm was losing money and they

axed twenty people. It happened after we'd booked to come here, so we agreed not to tell your parents because Charlie didn't want to worry them, I haven't told my mother either. The problem is he's spending money like water, and we have a huge mortgage.' She swallowed hard. 'I love our house, I couldn't bear to lose it.'

Vivianne looked concerned but not surprised. 'Charlie has always been extravagant – Dad was frequently having to bail him out. He doesn't mean to get into debt, it's more that he feels he has to impress. Underneath all the charm, I think my brother is quite insecure. He was out of work for a spell here, and I guess to be retrenched again must seem like a recurring nightmare – but I don't imagine he dared tell you that.'

Anna shook her head. She thought of her father who had hidden his failures from her mother, and wondered if she also, insidiously, pushed too hard.

Charlie returned within the hour and called her into the house. 'Sorry about this morning.' He reached for her hands.

She linked her fingers through his. 'We're both under pressure.'

'You're right, it's the strain.' He smiled, relieved because she'd supplied a reason which meant that he was not entirely to blame. 'We should get away, on our own. I still haven't taken you to Wilson's Promontory. Why don't we go today? Now! Just the two of us.'

'Oh, Charlie, I'd love to.'

'You pack us a bag, whilst I book a lodge on Tidal River. I'll ask Mum for steak and beers and we'll stop to buy the rest.' He slid his hand up the soft inside of her thigh and whispered, 'We'll have our own private barbecue as we watch the sun go down.' He kissed her gently on the mouth. 'No wonder we argue, we're never alone, but that's my fault. I'm sorry.'

She loved him for being honest enough to admit when he was wrong.

They left Melbourne within the hour and drove down the rugged coast road to Wilson's Promontory, the national park at the most southerly tip of the Australian mainland, where lush forests cover the lower slopes of the mountains and brightly-coloured birds flit from tree to tree. Anna watched them with delight.

As they neared their destination, they saw the lighthouse

perched on a granite headland polished smooth by the wind and rain, and below it the beautiful beaches of white sand washed pristine by the blue-green sea.

'Didn't I tell you that the sea was the same colour as your eyes?' said Charlie.

'You did.' She leaned across and kissed him, and rested her hand on his thigh, her fingers gently circling.

The car bounced along the narrow road, throwing her hand higher. 'Could you stop that?' he pleaded.

'No.' She laughed and moved her fingers even higher.

'Then you've only yourself to blame.'

She chuckled. 'That's what I'm hoping.'

They collected the key to their lodge. It was a simple wooden bungalow in the shade of two eucalyptus trees with a covered wood veranda at the front on which there was a table and chairs. Inside was a living area, a tiny kitchen and a bedroom dominated by a double bed.

'Want to swim?' asked Charlie, carrying in their bags.

'No.' Anna closed the lodge door and pushed him backwards into the bedroom.

It was weeks since they had made love without fear of his parents overhearing. Now they fell on to the bed and on to each other, passionately, furiously, driving away their problems and their arguments by the physical strength of their lovemaking. Afterwards they threw on their swimsuits and raced hand in hand down to the beach, to play in the surf, laughing and splashing each other like children. They kissed with the salt water on their lips and floated with their arms and their legs entwined. This was the closeness for which Anna craved and she felt that nothing could separate them.

In the late afternoon they went for a walk along one of the many wooded trails which clung to the lower slopes of the mountains. At one point they came out beside a huge granite rock which dominated a tiny cove in which there was a beautiful pool, so clear that when they peered into it their faces stared back at them.

'I want to ask you something,' Charlie said stiffly.

'Yes.' The word came out in a whisper as her heart began to thud.

'Oh, Dad, look!' squealed a child's voice, and before Charlie could say any more a small boy raced out of the woods and jumped into the pool, splashing water over them. He was followed by three other children and two adults.

Charlie and Anna looked at each other, grinned and walked on. She didn't mind the interruption. In fact it was a bit of a relief although she wasn't sure why. Charlie had been about to ask her to marry him, and now he'd ask her later and she'd accept. It was what she wanted, it was what she'd dreamed of, but for some inexplicable reason, with her future mapped out ahead, and the security she'd always longed for within her grasp, she was filled with doubts – not just about Charlie and his extravagance, but about what she wanted from life.

They came to a beach of white sand which squeaked beneath their feet. 'It's quartz,' he told her. 'Come on! Let's swim.' He grabbed her hand and pulled her with him across the beach and into the waves.

In the water he stripped off his clothes and tossed them on to the beach, hiding his nakedness in the surf. 'Join me,' he said.

'We'll be arrested.'

He laughed. 'Who cares?'

She unzipped her shorts and threw them on to the sand. Then she slipped off her bikini and knelt beside him, naked. He drew her on to him and held her close, so that the pull of the waves could not separate them, and by the time they left the beach Anna's doubts had retreated.

That evening they cooked the steaks which Phyllis had provided, baked the potatoes they'd bought at the little store, and tossed the salad in Phyllis's dressing of oil, vinegar and garlic. They ate outside, sitting at the rough wooden table, with the cries of the forest birds and the sound of the sea in their senses, and the warm evening air on their sun-kissed limbs.

Charlie reached for Anna's hand. 'We've never talked about children,' he said.

'No, but I've thought about it.'

He looked surprised. 'Have you?'

She blushed prettily. 'Charlie, of course I have. I love you and I want at least three.'

'Then we'd better hurry up, hadn't we?' He watched her in the lamplight, and again Anna's heart began to race. 'I'm sorry I didn't tell you about Serena,' he went on. 'It was silly of me to think you wouldn't find out, but I never loved her as I love you.'

Anna leaned across the table and kissed him full on the mouth. 'I know that now.'

He smiled. 'You're the best thing that's ever happened to me. You're brave and honest and you face up to problems, where I try to pretend they don't exist.'

'I prefer to face adversity than have it creep up on me.'

He reached for her hand and kissed the tips of her fingers. 'We must never have secrets. We must always tell each other everything.'

'You're right.' She looked away from him, hesitated and said, 'There is something I ought to tell you, it's been preying on my mind.'

He kissed her fingers again. 'I'm sure it's nothing. Tell me.'

'Well . . . umm . . . this morning, after you went out, I was very upset and Vivianne found me and I . . . um . . . told her that we'd been made redundant.'

Charlie released her hand. 'What the hell did you do that for?'

'I was worried, you know I was.'

'So you babbled to my family after promising you wouldn't,' he shouted.

'Charlie, she won't tell anyone, I asked her not to.'

'They'll find out, people always do.' He pushed back his chair and went inside, into the bedroom, where he slumped dejectedly on to the bed.

Anna followed him. 'Charlie! Please!' She touched his shoulder. 'I'm sorry. I shouldn't have said anything, but your extravagance terrifies me.'

He buried his face in his hands. 'I can't stand everyone knowing I've been retrenched again. Matt . . . Josh . . . all my friends.'

'Viv won't tell them.' Anna sat down beside him. 'And we go back to England next week. By the time you see Matt and Josh again, you'll have a new job.'

He sighed. 'You're right. I'm sorry I yelled at you.'

She put her arms around him, rocking him, comforting. She didn't mind so much that he'd raised his voice, it was the way he'd turned angry and accusatory which disturbed her.

They remained at Wilson's Promontory for a further night but although Charlie went out of his way to make amends, that magical moment on the veranda when they'd spoken of children did not return.

Back in Melbourne they were met at the front door by Phyllis, smiling expectantly, but she tactfully masked her disappointment when Charlie made no announcement. That evening, over dinner, Anna chatted brightly about Wilson's Promontory, the beautiful scenery, the forest and the parrots. When she stopped talking, she received a sympathetic smile from Phyllis.

During the last days of their holiday, Charlie was very quiet. He barely left the house, he didn't even see Matt and Josh, and they spent every evening with his parents. He was affectionate and considerate to Anna, but he showed no desire to make love to her. She was glad; she needed time to think. In England, Charlie had seemed charmingly boyish. Here, with his family he became childish. And yet she did not hold that against him, for she still harboured immensely wounded anger towards her father, and her feelings for her mother had always been a volatile cocktail.

On their last day, whilst Anna was packing, she glanced out of her window and saw him standing beside the swimming pool, his shoulders hunched and his hands dug deep into the pockets of his shorts. He looked so vulnerable and sad that she left her suitcases and went outside.

'We're going to be all right,' she said, putting her arms around him.

'Thank God I've got you.' He hugged her fiercely, and she knew that somehow the balance of their relationship had altered in this past month. Charlie now needed her just as much as she needed him – as her father had needed her mother.

12

January 1989

ANNA WAS VERY pleased to be home. The house on Ladbroke Hill sparkled in the winter sunshine and the drifts of fallen leaves shone like dark, wet gold. There were more leaves on the front steps, and the front door had swollen through lack of use. Charlie had to put his shoulder against it to heave it open, staggering inside on top of the mountain of letters and junk mail which had accumulated during their absence. He cursed as he kicked aside a newspaper and hurried to switch on the central heating. It roared into life and he turned to Anna, looking more cheerful than he had for days. 'We'll go back for another holiday when we're in work, when we're riding high.'

'Of course we will.' She smiled, relieved to see the old, optimistic Charlie return.

They gathered up their mail, a mixture of Christmas cards and bills. 'No need to depress ourselves looking at those today.' Charlie put the bills on one side and opened a card. 'Oh good! Russell and Delia back together. We must meet them for dinner next week.'

Amongst Anna's cards, she received a motorbiking reindeer from Elaine and Danny, a kitten in a Christmas stocking from Judy, a religious message from Miss Thin, and a note from Isaac and Sybil. Their gestures gave her a warm glow; she'd been wrong to fear that they'd forget her. She slit open the large, ostentatious envelope bearing a Spanish stamp and read aloud, ' "Merry Christmas from Vince and Monique Ellerby-Creswell".'

'What a cheek,' said Charlie.

Anna laid their card on the table. 'I could murder Vince, but he does make me laugh. He has such *chutzpah*.' She opened her last envelope and spluttered furiously, 'Hypocrite! Listen to this: "Dear Anna, Do keep in touch. Let me know if you need any assistance, Gordon." That's one person's help I don't want.'

She opened the door to the dining-room and gagged on the smell of paint. 'This room's been painted,' she said, surprised. Hurrying to the balcony she pushed aside her makeshift curtains and opened the doors. As the light poured in she saw that the dining-room, the old kitchen and the unmodernised bathroom with its ancient clawfoot bath had been meticulously decorated in the buttermilk destined for the top floor. 'Oh, Charlie, they've done the wrong rooms.'

He checked the drawing-room and discovered all their furniture stacked inside, instead of in the attic. Anna ran upstairs and found that their intended bedroom had been replastered but not lined or painted. The other rooms were untouched, with faded floral wallpaper still hanging in strips from the walls.

'We're not paying for this, not bloody likely,' she raged. 'In fact they owe us for the wasted paint.' All her accumulated anger became focused on Xavier, and she went down the stairs three at a time, retrieved the phone from under a pile of cushions, and started to tap out his number.

'Anna, don't call Xavier!'

'Why not?'

'Because we owe him two thousand pounds and I promised to pay him when we got back.'

'Charlie, we've paid him. Don't you remember? You used most of your last month's salary!'

He flushed and looked away. 'I used that money for the last instalment on my car. If I'd defaulted, it would have been repossessed.'

Trying to keep calm, Anna lowered the receiver. 'I thought you bought the car outright.'

'I have now.' He put his arms around her. 'Don't be angry, please! I'll sell the car if we need the money, I promise, but I'd be selling at far less than the price I paid, so there's no point in taking a loss unless we're desperate, and we won't be, we'll be in work before the end of the month.'

She was about to remind him that they'd agreed never to have secrets, but she was too tired from their long journey to say more than: 'Another time, please tell me.'

'Of course I will.' He held her tighter and she leaned against him, relishing the warmth of him which came through his jacket, to her coat, and then to her. He had a point, she told herself, why sell the car at a loss unless they had to?

Since the top floor hadn't been decorated, they decided to use the dining-room as their bedroom, so they dragged the double bed in from the drawing-room, by which time they were too weary to make up the bed, so they threw a blanket over the mattress and collapsed on top, fully clothed. Charlie went straight to sleep, but Anna couldn't. Her mind began to race, churning with all the things she ought to do: clean the house, write letters, phone Roz, phone her mother, revamp her curriculum vitae, find a job. Her sense of urgency was as acute as if she only had this one day, and was due back at work in the morning.

Unable to lie still, she crept from the bed and into the drawing-room where she began to clean, washing the grime from each crevice of the ornate white marble mantelpiece, and from the long windows and skirting-boards. Then she got down on her hands and knees, and scrubbed the floorboards. Finally she arranged the furniture, grouping the sofa and armchairs around the fireplace and placing her long refectory-dining table at the garden end. She pulled the pieces one way then the other, trying to make as little noise as possible, until she was satisfied with the look of the room.

Charlie's flat had been furnished by the landlords, so most of the furniture was hers. It had filled the cottage in Fulham, but at Ladbroke Hill it vanished into the huge rooms, leaving acres of bare floor between each piece. They had no carpets because that money had been spent on building work, and their only floor-covering was her precious red and green Turkish rug left to her by Grandpa Tobias. She laid it in front of the fireplace, and stood back to admire her handiwork.

It was years since she'd scrubbed a floor – she'd had a cleaner, so had Charlie – and the rub on her knees on the wet boards and the ache in her arm took her back to her childhood and the endless moves from one army house to another. She recalled how they would spend the morning scrubbing the old house and the afternoon scrubbing the new one, because however clean it had been left, her mother didn't trust another woman's housework.

Charlie appeared in the doorway. He surveyed the bare floor

and her curtains, which were too short for the floor-to-ceiling windows. Once he might have compared the room unfavourably to his parents' house, but now he joked, 'At least we have time to decide on a colour scheme.'

She laughed. 'We certainly have!'

They drove to the nearest supermarket, and whilst Charlie pushed the trolley Anna stacked it with pasta, salad, rice, milk, eggs, mince and potatoes, anything which was easy to cook and inexpensive. Passing the cool shelf Charlie reached inside for a packet of smoked salmon but Anna prised it from his fingers and put it back. He grinned sheepishly.

That evening Anna telephoned her mother. It was hard to keep up a jolly pretence about Marinecover, and when she spoke to Roz later, she admitted the truth.

On Saturday they woke to find Mr Shufflebuck's rent envelope on their front door mat.

'I never thought we'd need this,' said Anna, tipping out the carefully folded notes.

'Twenty quid a week for a flat in Ladbroke Hill? Can't we increase it?'

'The solicitor said no. He's been here years – and he's a sitting tenant. Thank goodness he never accepted our offer or we'd have increased our mortgage.' She linked her arm through Charlie's. 'Let's go to the market. We've never been, we've never had time.'

They strode down the hill with their identical leather jackets buttoned up tight against the cold air and their jeans tucked into expensive leather boots bought in Harrods when they had money. They passed stalls selling antique silver, ancient leather suitcases, prints of London and bric-à-brac.

'It's fun, isn't it?' Anna said as they eased their way through the jostling crowd of collectors, tourists, shoppers and pickpockets. 'Look at that.' She pointed at a stall whose overhead bar was hung with brass trumpets and horns. 'I'll buy you a trumpet from my first pay packet.'

Charlie laughed and pointed at a stall which sold period velvet coats and silk dresses. 'I'm certainly not buying any of that rubbish,' he said, louder than he intended.

The stall-holder, a striking woman with an angular freckled face, a mop of hennaed curls and sleepy sensuality gave Charlie a filthy look. 'I wouldn't sell my clothes to an ignorant arsehole like you,' she shouted at him.

Charlie turned scarlet, but before he could retaliate, Anna dragged him on down the lane, saying, 'Leave her! Forget it!'

They spent Mr Shufflebuck's rent on fruit and vegetables, a bunch of daffodils and bread from Ceres, where the smell of baking made them salivate with hunger. They bought a large pizza for lunch and half way home their hunger got the better of them and they ripped open the bag, tore off hot, cheesy chunks and stuffed it into their mouths as they walked up the street. With tomato dripping down their chins, they laughed aloud to think what their colleagues at Marinecover would say if they could see them now.

The Monday post brought Anna and Charlie down to earth with an official letter from Delia, enquiring what arrangements they had made to transfer their mortgage to another lender. She added in her own writing, 'Sorry to have to send you this.' They put the letter to one side; they had until the end of January.

They had ordered *Lloyd's List International* on Tuesdays and Thursdays when it published vacancies, so they spent the day preparing their CVs – Charlie at the refectory dining table in the drawing-room, Anna at Grandpa Tobias's old oak desk under the front window of their bedroom. The following morning Anna raced down to the newsagents whilst Charlie shuffled sleepily around the kitchen, making coffee. She ran all the way home, clutching the *Lloyd's List*, and spread it out on the table, open at page seven. Side by side they studied each vacancy.

'Nothing.' Anna stepped away, flattened.

'They'll have more on Thursday,' Charlie said confidently. 'Let's go out for the day.'

'Charlie, we can't waste time, we must try the headhunters and the personnel departments.'

He sighed. 'Oh, all right, but I have to go to the bank first.'

Anna made the bed, tidied the kitchen and poured herself another cup of coffee. Although she tried not to, she kept thinking about Marinecover; picturing the office and all the people in it. She missed them, even those she'd disliked.

Charlie returned an hour later, carrying a word processor – not an expensive one, but nevertheless Anna was aghast. 'We can't afford it,' she protested. 'Are you crazy?'

'We need it for our letters of application and our CVs. We can't write them out by hand.' He placed it on the refectory table. 'It's a shop model. I got it for half-price. Oh, Anna, don't be cross, everyone has a home computer.'

'Not everyone is out of work!'

He didn't reply, but plugged in the machine and settled down eagerly in front of the flickering green screen. Anna retired to their bedroom and sat down at her desk. She started to list all the suitable headhunters and brokerage houses, but she was too agitated to concentrate properly.

That evening she ate scrambled eggs in their bedroom, whilst Charlie had a take-away curry in front of the word processor. When he came to bed she pretended to be asleep, but he slipped his arms around her and whispered, 'Don't be upset. Please!'

'I'm worried.' She nestled against him, she couldn't be angry for long, they needed each other too much.

There were no suitable vacancies in the *Lloyd's List* that Thursday but Charlie remained optimistic. He perfected his CV and his covering letter, spending hours at the word processor until he was satisfied with the layout. Anna drafted hers by hand and left it on her desk while she prepared supper.

'What do you think?' he asked, coming into the kitchen whilst she was chopping onions for the bolognese sauce, and proudly waving her beautifully-typed CV under her nose.

She read it through streaming eyes. 'It's terrific. Thanks. I was wrong about the word processor. It is worth having.'

He stood behind her and drew her close, pressing himself against her and kissing the back of her neck, under her hair. When she responded he broke away, opened the fridge and reached inside for a can of beer.

Anna pretended not to mind but she couldn't help being aware that they hadn't made love since his outburst at Wilson's Promontory. At first she had not wanted to. Now, she wondered if he no longer found her attractive; or was it that being out of work had sapped his libido? She carried on chopping the onions and said nothing. So much of life had become stacked against them recently that she couldn't bear to face the fact that something else might be going wrong.

Charlie was called for an interview by the first headhunter to whom he sent his CV, and Anna waved him off from the door step, calling, 'Good luck!'

He grinned and gave her the thumbs-up.

She went back into the house and settled down with the telephone and her own list of headhunters, but as she reached for the receiver she was suddenly paralysed by fear. The world of Lloyd's and Marinecover had rejected her, and she had no reason to suppose it would welcome her back.

Her phone rang. She jumped with fright and answered, stuttering, 'Hello?'

'Not keeping in touch with old friends?'

'Isaac! Oh, how lovely to hear from you.'

'Gordon says he hasn't heard from you.'

'He's the last person I want to speak to.'

'Anna, don't bear a grudge; making you redundant wasn't personal – it was business, and he could be helpful. Have you found another job?'

'I was about to phone Keifer & Bell, the headhunters.'

'If you need a reference, I'll be glad to give you one.'

'Do you really mean that?'

'Ellerby-Creswell wasn't your fault. He's a plausible rogue and if I'd been in your shoes I'd have thumped him too. Come to lunch with me soon.'

'I will, Isaac. Thanks for everything.'

'For what?'

'Oh, it would be too difficult to explain.'

She had tears of gratitude in her eyes as they said goodbye. Isaac believed in her, and the paralysing fear lifted. She phoned Keifer & Bell, her rediscovered confidence enabling her to convince Mr Keifer to cancel another appointment in order to see her the following afternoon. When she replaced the receiver she gave a yelp of excitement: she was no longer on the scrap heap, Keifer & Bell wanted her.

Charlie came home with a grin nine miles wide because he had an interview with Hull & Steel that Friday. 'Fifty thousand plus profits!' he crowed. 'Better than Marinecover – and we're in a recession.'

'That's brilliant!' Anna hugged him.

'Let's celebrate.' He began to look up the number for L'Artiste Assoiffé.

Laughing, Anna removed the book from his hands. 'No, Charlie, that's the treat for when we get our jobs; tonight we'll go somewhere cheaper.'

They went to Geales, an inexpensive fish restaurant behind Notting Hill, where they sat upstairs at a table near the window and ate fish and chips and mushy peas.

'One day we'll look back on all this and laugh,' said Charlie.

Anna didn't answer, she had her mouth full.

They walked home, hand in hand, through the elegant tree-lined crescents, and when they reached the house Charlie drew Anna to him and they made love and she realised how silly she had been to look for disaster where it didn't exist.

The offices of Keifer & Bell were in a modern office block not far from St Paul's Cathedral. Mr Keifer, a large, bald man, was a former personnel manager with a major insurance company. His experienced eye noted Anna's smart black jacket and short – but not too short – skirt. 'Ah, Miss Tobias, it's good of you to come in so quickly.' He crushed her fingers when he shook her hand. 'I'm sure we'll be able to help you.'

He waved her to a sofa near the window and took the armchair opposite. Anna opened her briefcase and handed him a copy of her beautifully-typed CV. He read it whilst a secretary brought in tea in dainty porcelain cups. When he reached the last line, he looked up, smiling. 'I can think of one vacancy already, but they won't match your previous salary.'

She thought of Charlie's fifty-thousand offer. 'I was hoping for an increase.'

'With so many redundancies and the economy heading for recession, you must be realistic.'

'What about perks?'

'My dear Miss Tobias, companies only offer cheap-rate mortgages and smart cars when they need to attract employees. In the past three months I've had fifty applicants chasing every position.'

She hesitated, but she couldn't afford to be too choosy. 'I'll apply,' she said. 'After all, if I prove myself they'll pay me more.'

'That's the right spirit. Now you go home and by the time you arrive, I'll have fixed up an appointment.'

He was true to his word. As Anna walked into the house he telephoned with the details of her first interview, with Boatsure, a small broking house off Houndsditch.

She went into the drawing-room to tell Charlie, who was sitting at the word processor. 'Didn't I say we'd win through?' he asked her, smiling.

'The salary's less than Marinecover,' she confessed, feeling a failure when she compared her prospects to his. 'It's only twenty thousand with profits, but no perks.'

He turned off the word processor. 'Hull & Steel are only offering thirty basic. The stupid headhunter made a mistake and included last year's profits.'

'What about a cheap mortgage?'

He shook his head.

'Oh, Charlie, we'll lose the house.'

He reached for her hand. 'Anna, sweetie. I think we should sell it. What's the point of owning a mansion if we live on bare boards in two rooms?'

'No! Please! We'll manage.' She smiled brightly, trying to exude enough confidence for both of them, but underneath, behind the façade, she was shaking.

After Marinecover, Boatsure seemed small and shabby. Their offices, on the top floor of a building soon to be demolished, smelled of damp and desolation. Anna couldn't imagine that there would be any profits. She was interviewed by an elderly personnel manager who doubled as the managing director's secretary. 'You'll definitely be hearing from us, Miss Tobias,' said the woman when Anna rose to leave.

Anna nodded and fled, gasping with relief when she stepped out into the fresh air. From a call-box she telephoned Mr Keifer.

As soon as he heard her voice he enthused, 'They think you're perfect, Miss Tobias. Well done!'

'Mr Keifer, the job won't pay enough to meet my commitments. I have to keep looking.'

'Well . . . if that's what you want, although I must say in these difficult times . . .'

'Mr Keifer, I have to do better. I'll phone you on Monday to see if you've had any more vacancies. Have a nice weekend. Goodbye.'

Taking a firm stand made Anna feel in control of her life, and she walked down Lime Street, past Lloyd's, smiling at people she knew, outwardly her old, breezy self.

'Anna!' Kevin Kitterick bounded across the road to greet her.

'Hello, Kevin, how's the golf?'

'Marvellous! I've just got back from Florida.' He went on to describe every tee and green and each ball he'd hit and which iron he'd used, whilst Anna tried to appear interested. Finally he said, 'Marinecover were insane to let you go. Chris isn't half as good.'

'It's kind of you to say so.' She forgave him for boring her.

'It's the truth. Chris doesn't have your touch with the clients. He attracts the kind of idiot who spends twenty grand on a boat but is too mean to pay marina fees, ties it up on a swinging mooring in the middle of a deserted river, leaves the papers and spare key on board, and wonders why it is stolen.'

Anna laughed aloud.

Kevin looked pleased and warmed to his theme. 'One of Chris's clients had a boat stolen, was paid out by us, then he bought the same boat from a small ad in a yachting magazine without realising it was his own, because he didn't have the vessel's papers properly checked. Buyers are so gullible. That's why these river pirates get away with it.' He leaned towards Anna, and she remembered his Filofax, and for an embarrassing moment thought he intended to proposition her, but he whispered, 'Confidential. Merchant & Leisure are planning to dump the Thug. Phone Prue Longman, and say I told you to.'

Anna was overwhelmed with gratitude. 'Kevin, I don't know how to thank you.'

'Give me your business when you're back in the market.'

'Oh, of course.' She thought of her unspoken allegiance to Isaac, then told herself she'd deal with that dilemma when she reached it.

Prue was delighted to hear from Anna, which gave her confidence a further boost. They fixed to meet the following week in the bar of the Tower Hotel overlooking St Katherine's Dock, not at the office because, as Prue explained, Barry wasn't yet aware that his job was under review.

Charlie came home brimming with satisfaction. He'd been shortlisted for the Hull & Steel job. To celebrate they ordered a giant pizza and opened their only expensive bottle of wine. As they finished eating Delia and Russell telephoned and – although Anna and Charlie couldn't divulge the details of their job prospects – hearing good news they hurried over with another bottle. It was the first time that the four of them had met since Anna and Charlie had been made redundant and, sitting in front of the drawing-room fire, wine glasses in their hands, they laughed and joked as if nothing had changed.

It was well after midnight when Delia and Russell left and as they were saying goodbye, Delia asked, 'Have you found a new lender to take on your mortgage?'

Charlie flushed. 'We will.'

'You only have ten more days,' she persisted, oblivious to everyone's discomfort. 'I really think you should sign on with the DSS. They'd pay half your mortgage interest.'

'Delia,' Anna said firmly, 'we don't want to talk about it tonight.'

'I'm only trying to help!' Perplexed and upset, Delia stumbled across the gravel to Russell's car.

Anna and Charlie went into the house and closed the front door. 'We don't need hand-outs!' He exploded in fury.

'She doesn't mean any harm, she's just tactless.'

'She's jealous of you, she always has been. You're prettier than her, cleverer than her, and you earned more than her. If she was such a good friend why didn't she warn you that you were going to lose your job?'

'Charlie, she couldn't, she had to be professional.'

'She could have alerted you to beware of Chris.'

'I know,' said Anna sadly, 'but she didn't.'

On Sunday they drove up to visit her mother and grandmother. Charlie didn't want to go, she suspected he dreaded her grandmother's probing, but Anna said they couldn't put it off any longer without hurting her mother's feelings. They arrived at noon and exchanged belated Christmas presents, and talked cheerfully about Australia.

To Anna's relief, her grandmother didn't ask why they hadn't come back engaged, although after lunch, when Anna and her mother were alone in the kitchen, her mother whispered, 'I wish you'd brought some photographs, I wanted to see the Blythelys' mansion. Are they frightfully wealthy?'

Anna thought of the pictures on her dining-room table which she had purposely left behind, not for her own sake but for Charlie's. 'They're comfortable.' She picked up a dishcloth to dry the cutlery.

'No more than that?'

Anna glanced at the half-open sitting-room door beyond which Charlie was reading the newspaper headlines to her grandmother, who'd mislaid her spectacles. 'No, but they're very nice.'

Her mother lowered her voice further. 'Is . . . something wrong, Anna?' she asked, anxiously, her face suddenly lined with worry.

'No, of course not.'

'I had rather hoped that you and Charlie would come home . . .'

'Mum, please, not now!'

'Sorry.' She squeezed Anna's hand. 'It's your life, you must do as you wish.'

With her mother beside her, Anna found it hard not to confide. At the same time, seeing the disquiet flood her mother's face, she was driven by a desire to protect her.

Anna dressed carefully for her meeting with Prue Longman, choosing a business-like charcoal-grey suit. Prue, a large efficient woman, was already seated at a secluded table when Anna arrived at the hotel. 'Gordon and Isaac sing your praises,' she said, giving Anna a firm handshake.

'Thank you.' Anna took the chair opposite Prue.

'So does Paul Sheldon.'

Anna looked surprised.

'He says you fight for your clients, even when they don't deserve it. I assume he's referring to that rogue Ellerby-Creswell, whom I fear is still at large and drinking pink gin on Costa del Crime.'

Anna sighed. 'The Vinces of this world always get away with it.'

'Because they're seasoned crooks.' Prue wasted no more time on chit-chat, but explained the set-up at Merchant & Leisure, a brokerage house considerably larger than Marinecover. 'We'd be offering a basic of fifty thousand, with the usual perks,' she said. 'That's probably less than you earned before but in this present climate we have to keep salaries down.'

It was the same deal as Marinecover, but Anna didn't say so.

'You appreciate that this is a preliminary discussion,' Prue went on, 'but I can tell you, Anna, that you're our first choice.'

'Thank you.' Anna relaxed into her chair. It was wonderful to be wanted.

'We're seeing Barry on Friday morning, so I'll call you in the afternoon. We'd want you to start in a fortnight.'

Anna wished it could be sooner because they needed to transfer the mortgage, but she didn't say so.

She arrived home, still buoyed up by the success of the interview, to find a message from Gordon on the answering machine. 'I may have something for you,' he said. 'Get in touch.' She erased the tape, she didn't need him now.

Delia rang as Anna was pouring herself a celebratory glass of wine. 'I'm sorry about the other night.'

'Oh, don't worry,' Anna answered gaily, taking a slurp of wine. 'I'm celebrating, I have a terrific new job, I can't tell you where, but it'll be confirmed on Friday.'

'That's wonderful. How about lunch tomorrow?'

Anna only hesitated for a moment. 'See you then.'

Charlie came home even more confident about Hull & Steel. He longed to rejoice with an expensive dinner but Anna insisted on somewhere reasonable, so they compromised on a pasta restaurant where they drank two bottles of wine, followed by three sambucas. Then they staggered home and fell into bed and made love with such energy that Charlie knocked his bedside lamp off its table. It shattered on the floor but they barely noticed.

Delia was already at their favourite table when Anna arrived at their usual wine bar. 'You've had some night,' she teased when she saw the dark rings under Anna's eyes.

'You can say that again!' Anna collapsed on to a chair and laughed aloud, tossing her hair back off her face as they surveyed the babble at the bar. Friendly faces turned her way. People shouted, 'Good to see you back.'

She smiled and waved and wondered why she'd felt so unwanted.

*

On Friday, as soon as the post dropped through the letterbox, Charlie shot out of bed and ran naked to the front door. He returned with a smartly-typed white envelope. 'This is it,' he crowed, waving it in front of Anna.

She sat up, the duvet huddled around her, and watched as he slit open the envelope.

There was silence as his eyes sped over the words. Then he looked at her, his eyes stricken, his naked body shrunk and vulnerable. 'They've taken the other applicant.' He crunched the letter into a tight ball, hurled it across the room and ran upstairs.

Anna longed to comfort him, but she sensed that he needed to be alone, so she went into the bathroom to take a shower. Whilst she was cleaning her teeth, she heard his footsteps on the stairs but when she came out, his clothes had gone from the chair and he had disappeared.

Imagining that he'd gone out for a walk and would come back, still disappointed but resigned to try elsewhere, she washed up from the previous night, telephoned all the headhunters on her list, and wrote a couple of letters. At midday, Charlie was still not back and Anna kept thinking of her father, shamed beyond the brink of despair by her mother's expectations.

She hurried out to buy an *Evening Standard*, not wanting to go far in case Charlie returned or she missed Prue Longman's call. Arriving home, she heard the telephone ring. She raced up the steps and as she unlocked the front door she caught Prue's voice on the answering machine. 'Anna, I'm sorry to have wasted your time, but we've decided to extend Barry's trial period until the autumn. Good luck with your job-hunting.' There was a click, and the machine rewound.

Anna couldn't think or cry. She stumbled into the bedroom and sank to the floor, hugging her knees against her chest, her face buried in her arms.

She was still there when Charlie returned. As he came into the bedroom, she reached up her hand to him, desperate for comfort, but he walked straight past her to their bed and fell diagonally across it, drunk. He hadn't even seen her and by the time he sobered up, Anna had turned in on herself. She still loved him, at least she thought she did, but the lover who had once been so decisive and optimistic was disintegrating in the face of adversity, and she realised then that she could no longer depend on him.

13

ANNA AND CHARLIE had to approach eighteen banks and building societies before they could find one prepared to consider their mortgage application whilst they were unemployed. During this time they were deluged with letters and telephone calls from Marinecover demanding to know the name of their new lender.

The East Metro Bank, whose head office was in a soulless building not far from Holborn, had a reputation for tough dealing and high rates. The loans manager, Mr Hyde, was a portly man with heavy-rimmed glasses which gave him the appearance of a disgruntled owl awoken from its slumbers.

He called them for an interview and scarcely gave them time to sit down before saying, 'We've valued your property at three hundred and fifty thousand pounds.' He held up his hand to silence their protests. 'I know that's less than you paid for it and that you've spent seventy thousand on repairs, but the market's falling, the house is undecorated, and you still have a sitting tenant. No, Mr Blythely, please don't interrupt me! Your previous mortgage was for two hundred and thirty thousand, but East Metro's policy is not to lend more than sixty per cent of the value when borrowers are unemployed to allow for our costs if we have to repossess. So you'll have to reduce your request by twenty thousand pounds.'

'How are we to find twenty thousand pounds when we're out of work?' asked Anna in despair.

'Sell something. What car do you drive?'

'A BMW, but it's nearly five years old. I'd be lucky to get five thousand for it in this economic climate.'

'Redundancy?'

'I've only two thousand left and we owe the builder a thousand.'

He turned to Charlie. 'What do you drive, Mr Blythely?'

'A BMW – and I'm not selling it.' Charlie pushed back his chair. 'Come on, Anna, we're not going to sit here and be insulted.'

She laid her hand on his sleeve. 'Charlie, please, we'll lose the house.'

'Anna, I've told you already we ought to sell it.'

'I love our home.'

'Then you can sell your car, but I'm not sacrificing mine.' He rose and walked out of Mr Hyde's office, calling for someone to let him through the security door.

Anna took several deep breaths, and when she looked up she found Mr Hyde watching her with a mixture of embarrassment and sympathy. 'I'm sorry, it's the pressure,' she said. 'The strain of it all.'

'He's right, you should sell.'

She pictured the iron balcony from where she could watch the world without it seeing her. 'Ladbroke Hill is my haven. I feel secure there. I seem to have lost so much in my life, I can't bear to lose this as well.' Her eyes filled with tears. Angrily, she brushed them away. 'I'm sorry,' she repeated, and she hurried from his office.

Charlie was out when she arrived home, and she was glad. She lay down on their bed, pulled the duvet over her head, and closed out the world.

He returned in the early evening, bursting into the room without turning on the light and tripping over her shoes. 'Here's your damned money.' He tossed wads of twenty-pound notes on to the bed.

Switching on the bedside light, Anna gasped in horror. 'You haven't robbed a bank, have you?'

He laughed loudly, maniacally. 'A bank? I should have thought of that. No, I sold my car to keep your precious house.'

She reached up to him and took him in her arms, drawing him down to her, cradling his head, as she whispered, 'Thank you.'

He nestled against her and closed his eyes. 'Next time, the house goes.'

She didn't reply, because she knew that what he said was absolutely logical.

*

By selling both their cars and using much of Anna's redundancy money they reduced their loan request, and the East Metro Bank took over their mortgage on the understanding that until they could make monthly payments their debt would accrue at a full per cent above the normal rate. The situation was to be reviewed in three months, with the bank reserving the right to repossess. These were tough terms, but Charlie and Anna had no alternative. They couldn't afford to pay Xavier as well; he arrived in silent fury and stripped out the expensive shower fittings.

The reality of being unemployed began to bite. It eroded their energy and sapped their confidence; they dreaded weekday mornings and the sight of people walking purposefully towards the Underground station. They had to force themselves to go on searching, dragging up reserves of courage to telephone head-hunters, braving interviews, and trying to mask their anxiety. Each Tuesday and Thursday they studied the *Lloyd's List* and pursued every vacancy, even the ones outside their fields, but at every interview there were more and more applicants, all qualified, all desperate.

Shielding her mother from their predicament became an increasing strain on Anna, and when she discussed it with her sister, Roz was very sympathetic. 'I wish we could help, but all we earn goes into the farm or on the children.'

'Roz! Please! I haven't confided in you because I want money, I just needed to hear a friendly voice, that's all. We'll be all right, don't worry, something will turn up for one of us.' Anna changed the subject to ask after the children.

When Anna and Charlie had been working they'd dined in restaurants every evening. Now they seldom went out, even to a pub because two drinks each meant spending a fiver. Instead they watched television and ate pasta in every shape and size, or tucked into the giant stew which Anna made on Saturdays, buying the ingredients with Mr Shufflebuck's rent.

Lack of money isolated them. They couldn't meet Delia and Russell because they couldn't afford to pay their way, they didn't visit Roz and Tom because the rail fare was expensive, and they didn't see Anna's mother and grandmother so as to avoid the inevitable questions about why they no longer owned a car. In moments of desperation they lay on their bed, silent and uncommunicating, Charlie watching television, Anna wondering what was going to happen to them. But at other times they shared intense closeness; when they huddled together and whispered their fears, and made love and comforted each other.

Bills started to arrive: gas, electricity, telephone. They paid the phone because without it they'd never find work, and they paid the electricity because they couldn't live without light, but they left the gas, believing it to be more difficult for the Gas Board to cut the supply.

With the approach of spring the days grew longer and the weather became marginally warmer. Bright green buds covered the trees and out in the garden daffodils and crocuses pushed eagerly up through the wet clay.

'I've set the heating to go off in the daytime,' Anna told Charlie one morning.

'I know, I've overridden the clock.'

'Charlie, we can't afford it.'

'I refuse to freeze – on top of everything else.' He pulled the duvet up over his head and went back to sleep.

Stung by his tone, Anna retreated to the kitchen, where she opened the garden door and sat down on the stone steps. She wondered if she was being appallingly selfish by refusing to sell the house, if this was how her mother had been towards her father, but even as she resolved to agree that Ladbroke Hill must go, she couldn't bear to sacrifice it just yet.

Delia left several messages on the answering machine but Anna didn't return them because she couldn't stand to hear the pity in Delia's voice. Charlie said it wasn't pity, it was satisfaction, but Anna preferred to believe the best. Her lifeline was Roz, to whom she spoke in the evenings after six o'clock when it was less expensive. Anna, who'd never bothered about these things, was learning fast.

Isaac wrote, inviting them to dinner. When Anna telephoned to refuse, he said, 'Why not? Because you're out of work? I know that. Do you think that means we don't want to see you?'

She felt humbly grateful. 'We'd love to come.'

But at the last minute Charlie refused to accompany her, saying he was too ashamed at being unemployed, and as it was too late to cancel, she had to go alone, on the Underground all the way up to Highgate, where the Finesteins enveloped her with their warmth, their Jewish humour and their chicken soup. The evening flew by and suddenly Anna realised that it was nearly midnight.

She shot out of her seat. 'I must go.'

Sybil Finestein reached for her hand. 'Not yet, dear, have some more coffee.'

'No.' Anna didn't mean to be so abrupt but she was terrified of missing the last tube train. 'It's been lovely. Thank you.' She rushed out into the hall, grabbed her coat and ran from the house.

'I'll walk you to your car,' offered Isaac, perplexed.

'No! Please! I'm fine. Goodbye.' She was half-way down the drive.

He followed her. 'But I insist.'

'My car's just here.' She pointed to a small black BMW.

'Anna, what are you saying? That's my daughter's car.'

'Oh, how silly of me, I made a mistake, mine's up there. Goodbye. Thank you.' She waved and hurried on. As soon as she was out of sight she ran, arriving at the tube station with one minute to spare.

She had to change trains twice, and at one point she found herself on a deserted platform with three drunken men. They walked towards her, swaying and laughing, and her heart started to pound. She felt sick with fear, she wanted to escape, but she could hear the train coming and it was the last one that night. One of the men held out his hand and for a terrifying moment she thought he was going to hurl her into the path of the oncoming train. She had a vision of herself, straddled across the electrified rails, the train bearing down on her, braking hard but unable to stop, cutting off her legs and arms but leaving her alive and screaming under its wheels.

But the men didn't touch her. They laughed at her fear and walked on.

Anna was still shaking when she got out at Holland Park. Clutching her coat around her she hurried up Ladbroke Grove, a solitary, frightened figure, half-running beneath the eerie, leprous branches of the plane trees.

Charlie was lying on their bed, fully clothed and fast asleep. She wanted to hit him, punch him, kick him, for being so weak, but she was too tired even to say his name. She flopped down on her side of the bed and slept.

In the morning he mumbled, 'Did you have fun?' but Anna feigned sleep because she was still angry.

They received a letter from Mr Hyde demanding to know when they would start to repay their loan. Anna swallowed her pride and signed on at their local unemployment office. Charlie refused to go with her but that didn't affect her claim, and for the next sixteen weeks half the interest on their mortgage would be paid. As their monthly payments were still entirely made up of interest, they'd receive a thousand pounds a month; they still had to find the other thousand.

'After sixteen weeks we'd usually pay all the interest,' the woman at the DSS office told Anna. 'But with such a large sum, we can't promise. If taxpayers discovered we were using their money to keep people in mansions, they'd be rightly furious.'

'I paid tax too,' said Anna. 'Tens of thousands of pounds.'

The woman shrugged and beckoned to the next applicant.

Anna was glad Charlie wasn't with her because he'd have made a scene and she was too drained to deal with his anger: she had enough of her own. She returned home by way of the market, buying a pizza in Ceres, not one of the exotic pizzas which she and Charlie used to buy but the smallest, cheapest pizza on offer. Walking home up the hill she passed the second-hand clothes stall. The girl with the freckled face and tobacco hair was pouring herself a mug of coffee from a Thermos. She glanced at Anna and her eyes flicked with recognition. Anna turned her head away and hurried on. She was in no mood for confrontation.

Having braved the DSS, Anna humbled herself and telephoned Gordon.

'Why didn't you return my calls?' he asked her.

'Why do you think?'

'Pride?'

'Something like that.'

'Are you working?'

'No, that's why I'm phoning. You said you knew of a vacancy.'

'Anna, that post was filled weeks ago. You should have come back to me earlier. I wish I knew of another, but I don't, every brokerage house is laying off staff. We've had to close Yachts and dismiss Chris – but I expect Delia has kept you up to date.'

'Oh . . . er . . . we haven't spoken recently.'

'I'm sorry to hear that, but friendships are a casualty of these dog-eat-dog times. Come to lunch in early May. Fix it with Miss Thin. I'm away till then.'

'I will, once I have a job, Gordon.'

'You have to show your face, Anna. Believe me, I know what I'm talking about. I was made redundant in the early seventies and I can still remember the shock. Even when I found another job, the fear of losing it haunted me for years. I expect you for lunch when I get back.'

She wished him goodbye, wondering if she would ever understand him. Since he cared for her enough to keep in touch, how could he have thrown her out, knowing the pain that would cause her?

She redoubled her search for work, revisiting every headhunter and telephoning each personnel manager, but she was hampered by rail and Underground strikes. Not able to afford a taxi, she missed interviews because she could not get to them.

Charlie went out less and less. His renewed optimism had evaporated and frequently he didn't leave the house all day, but lay on their bed watching mindless quiz games on the television. He became so absorbed in the world inside the set that if the phone rang he wouldn't answer it in case he missed a clue. When his mother telephoned, he refused to speak to her. If Vivianne rang, he turned up the volume on the television so as to drown her voice on the answering machine.

When Anna returned from job-hunting, she longed to talk, to share her trials and disappointments, but she was aware of Charlie's interest returning to his programme, so gradually she gave up telling him whom she'd seen, and sat alone in the drawing-room, sometimes even eating on her own to escape the constant babble from the set. They were drifting apart, which made her sad, but after battling all day to find work, she was in no mood to come home and compete with the television for his attention.

During the first hot spell that summer, Anna returned home by tube after another fruitless interview. It was the rush hour and people pushed and shoved, sweat pouring down their winter-white faces. By the time she reached Holland Park her cream jacket stuck to her back and her hair hung in limp strands down her face. As she walked up the hill, limping in her high heels, she thought of her father frantically searching for work and, suddenly, she was no longer angry with him. She asked herself how they could have been so blind to his despair.

At the grocery shop she stopped to buy bread. It was next door to a popular pub, The Admiral Vernon – known locally as the Vernon – named after the admiral who in 1739 captured Porto Bello from the Spanish, after which the original farm of Portobello took its name. As Anna came out of the shop she noticed a sign in the pub window. 'Weekend bar staff required. Apply Gerry Simcock, manager'.

She started up the hill towards the house but when she reached the first crossroad she stopped, hesitated, then took off her jacket, folded it into her carrier bag, undid two buttons on her blouse, sprayed some scent on her throat and wrists, and rolled over the waist-band of her skirt to raise the hem. Finally she ran her fingers through her hair to fluff it out, retouched her lipstick, and walked back down the hill to the pub.

The interior was old, beamed and dark, with rickety tables and chairs, bare floor boards, and walls covered in black and white photographs of Portobello in days gone by. On one side there was a public bar where four men played darts. On the other was the saloon bar where two old men perched on high wooden stools. At a table near them a younger man of about Anna's age was doing the *Guardian* crossword. He had the refined face of a Renaissance poet and brown hair drawn back into a ponytail.

Anna approached the bar where a man with a swarthy complexion was pulling pints.

'I'd like to see Gerry Simcock,' she said.

'You're looking at 'im, luv.'

'Oh . . . umm . . . it's about the job.'

He stared at her. 'You're a bit smart for a barmaid. Got any experience?'

'No, but I can learn.'

'Sorry, luv, I ain't got time to teach you.' He picked up four pints, two in each hand, and carried them through to the public bar. Anna waited. Beside her the old men whispered.

When the manager returned and saw her he said, 'You still 'ere?'

'I'll work for less money whilst I'm learning.'

'You don't give up, do you?'

'I need a job.'

'All right. Two-fifty an hour, six till midnight. Thursday, Friday, Saturday, occasional Sundays. Three pounds once you know the ropes. You wash up, clean up, and you don't leave till the place is ready for the next day. You're not late, you don't get drunk, you use your own till, and if it's short more than once a week I take it out of your wages. When you can pull a pint as fast as me, I'll pay you more. Any questions?'

'If my till's over, presumably that's offset against future losses?'

The old men laughed as Gerry's jaw dropped and he spluttered, 'Yeah . . . er . . . of course.'

'Thanks. You won't regret this.' She walked towards the door.

'Why are you so happy?' Gerry called after her. 'I'm only offering you fifteen pounds a night. That ain't no fortune.'

'It is when you're broke,' she answered with a big smile.

14

WHEN ANNA TOLD Charlie that she was going to work at The Admiral Vernon he stared at her in consternation.

'Maybe you could find a temporary job too,' she suggested, kicking off her high heels.

'In a pub? Sweetie, I haven't come halfway round the world in order to work behind a bar.'

She said, as calmly as she could, 'Charlie, we have to pay the bills or we'll be cut off.'

'Anna, I've paid them, so stop worrying.'

She wanted to question him as to what he'd paid with, but that was the kind of thing her mother would have done, so she limped into the kitchen and switched on the kettle. Whilst she waited for the water to boil, she leaned her forehead on the window pane and looked down on the garden and tried not to dwell on all the hopes and dreams she'd had when they'd first bought the house. Mr Shufflebuck came out of the basement to water his pot plants. Anna wondered if he realised that they no longer had money. If so, he must be gloating at their misfortune and she couldn't blame him.

She wished Charlie would put his arms around her and say he was grateful to her for working in the evenings. No, grateful was the wrong word. She just wanted reassurance that they were a team pulling in the same direction, instead of this resentment that she felt emanating from him, as if she were his mother and she'd reduced his pocket money.

For her first night at the pub, she wore a denim skirt, a white T-shirt, and flat canvas shoes. She'd intended to ask Charlie to collect her, but he went out whilst she was having a shower – he always seemed to disappear when she needed his support – so she wrote him a note: 'I finish at midnight. Please meet me.'

It was a hot, sultry evening and The Admiral Vernon was very busy. People sat two to a chair or swarmed over the pavement, drinking in raucous groups. They blocked the doorways, those going in refusing to give way to those coming out. At the bar they were six deep, pushing and shoving and yelling their orders.

'Come 'ere and take over!' shouted Gerry as soon as he saw Anna.

She slipped around the end of the bar to join him. 'You'll have to show me what to do.'

'It's simple.' He pointed to the rows of glasses and bottles. 'Those are pints, those are half-pints, these are for wine; gin and whisky are one measure, a double is two.' He waved his arms wildly towards the public bar. 'I'm needed next door.'

'You can't leave me yet,' protested Anna as the sea of faces pushed up to the bar, waving money and shouting their orders.

'I'll help her,' offered the pale young man with the ponytail whom she'd seen the previous day.

Gerry slapped him on the shoulder. 'Thanks, Dominic, 'ave a drink on the house.'

Dominic slipped around to Anna's side of the bar. He was tall and very slim with long, artistic fingers and a slow smile. Dressed in faded jeans and a loose embroidered shirt, he looked too much of a dreamer to move fast, but as soon as he started to work he went into overdrive.

'You take that and I'll take this,' he said. 'Your first customer wants two pints of bitter.' He tapped one of the handles. 'This one! Remember to tip the glass or you'll give him too much froth.'

Anna reached up for two pint mugs, tipped one glass under the nozzle and pulled the brass handle.

'Pull again,' Dominic shouted above the babble. 'That's right. Now put that glass down and let the froth settle whilst you start the next pint.'

Dominic was on to his third customer in the time it took Anna to fill two pints. 'One-fifty each,' he called to her, returning to show her how to use the till.

She took the money, rang up the amount and, terrified of making a mistake, carefully counted the change into the customer's outstretched hand. Instantly she was besieged by other thirsty drinkers. She pulled another pint and slopped froth all over her canvas shoes. She poured a gin and tonic, and knew she'd given too much gin. She poured a glass of wine and a piece of cork dropped into it. Luckily, the customer was too drunk to notice. Beside the till was a list of prices but Anna had no time to give more than a cursory glance as she rang up charges and handed out change, praying that the float would not be short.

It was stifling behind the bar and her hair stuck to her face and her T-shirt clung like a second skin. The beer-soaked canvas of her shoes rubbed her toes and the smoke stung her eyes. Customers leaned on the bar and puffed cigarettes in her face. They breathed out alcohol and onion-flavoured crisps, and made silly jokes which she pretended to find funny, when in reality she was gagging on the smell.

By the time Gerry rang the bell and called last orders she was exhausted.

'Doing all right, girl?' he asked, returning from the public bar.

She nodded, too tired to reply.

'Anna's done fine.' Dominic tapped some tobacco into a double Rizla and rolled himself a cigarette.

She gave him a grateful nod. There were times lately when the kindness of strangers made her want to cry.

Anna wiped the beer rings from the tables, whilst Gerry checked her till.

'Well I never!' he exclaimed.

'Anything wrong?' she asked fearfully.

'Just twenty pence over. That's a miracle for a beginner.'

'Thank you.' She glanced at her watch. It was nearly midnight and she wondered what had happened to Charlie.

'You did well.' Gerry counted out her fifteen pounds.

'It was all thanks to Dominic.' She turned to where he sat in a corner of the pub, smoking his rolled cigarette. 'Some of this should be yours,' she said, holding out a five pound note.

He shrugged. 'If you insist,' and to her shock, he pocketed her hard-earned cash.

Anna had to force herself to smile. It had never occurred to her that he would accept her money.

There was a noise outside in the street. 'That'll be for me,' she said. 'See you tomorrow. Good night.' She picked up her bag and denim jacket, and hurried out so that they couldn't see how devastated she was to lose five pounds.

But there was no sign of Charlie, just an old tramp urinating in the gutter. Angry and disappointed, she crossed the road and ran home.

He was stretched out on their bed, watching a late-night horror film.

'You weak bastard!' she screamed, switching off the set as the monster filled the screen. 'I was working in a filthy pub so that we can live, and you can't even be bothered to fetch me.'

'You didn't have to go.' He pressed the remote control and the monster returned.

Anna yanked the plug from the socket and the screen went blank. 'You do nothing . . . nothing to help. You're pathetic; you're not a man, you're a baby.' She sank down on the bed and cried from deep disappointment in Charlie, in herself and in their life.

He sat, frozen, his face flushed as if she'd slapped it. Then he whispered, 'I'm sorry, Anna. I know I let you down, but I can't stand not having a job and money. I feel so useless.' He reached for her hand, anxiously entwining his fingers through hers. 'I'm sorry, I'm a failure and you'd be better off without me.'

Those were the exact words which her father had written in the note he'd left inside the briefcase he'd placed on the platform – before he stepped into the path of the train.

Anna had a sudden vision of Charlie, stepping off the platform at Holland Park, and she put an arm around him. 'No, I wouldn't,' she hurried to reassure him. 'But I get upset when you won't speak to me. We used to share our problems.'

'I don't know what to say to you; I feel so helpless. You keep trying to find work but I can't even bear to do that, not any more. I haven't got your guts, Anna.'

'I'm not brave, Charlie, I just don't want to lose the house.'

He kissed her and she let him, although she felt no desire, just a longing to be held. 'Don't leave me,' he pleaded.

She wondered if her father had ever feared that her mother would desert him.

'I'll try harder, I promise,' he said, smoothing her hair back from her face. 'I won't let you down again. I love you; I couldn't survive without you.' He slid her jacket from her shoulders and threw it to one side. Then he began to unbutton her T-shirt, kissing her neck and shoulders, murmuring, 'I need you. I need you.'

Anna responded because she couldn't bear to wound him further, but she felt no passion, just sorrow and exhaustion. Where once his touch had made her body throb with desire, it now craved only comfort. Because he had disappointed her as a protector, Charlie did everything he could to satisfy her as a lover. He kissed, caressed, and thrust. He was gentle and tender, he was rough and passionate, but he could not touch her. Because Anna knew the fragility of his confidence, she faked an orgasm. Only then was he reassured.

Afterwards she lay beside him, listening to his breathing, wondering if she was unfair to him. She'd never needed his protection when they had money, when they were successful, and it wasn't his fault that he couldn't adjust. But because he couldn't adapt, she knew that she was stronger than him and that even if they found new jobs, and earned high salaries again, their relationship would not turn back.

The following evening Dominic offered to help Anna again but she firmly turned him down. It was a quiet night in the Vernon and, blissfully oblivious to how annoyed Anna was with him, Dominic sat at the bar talking to her about his music. He was a session musician; Anna assumed not a financially successful one. As midnight approached she sensed that he was plucking up courage to ask if he could walk her home, when Charlie appeared.

'Ready?' he enquired, giving Dominic a suspicious glance.

She collected her bag and followed him out, calling 'Good night.'

'Who's that long-haired git?' asked Charlie as they set off up the hill.

'Oh, just a friend of the manager.'

'I think he fancies you.'

Anna shrugged. She was so tired that she could barely put one foot in front of the other.

They passed a brand new, gleaming VW Golf.

'Look!' Charlie seized her by the arm and pointed excitedly. 'The keys have been left in the door. The owner must have forgotten them. Why don't we go for a ride?'

Smiling, Anna pulled him away.

He shook off her hand and took a step towards the car. 'Anna, I'm serious. Why don't we take it and sell it? We'd get at least eight grand and, hell, we need the money.'

It dawned on her that he really wasn't joking. 'We can't steal,' she said, horrified.

'Why not?' He took the keys from the door. 'We're desperate.'

'Not that desperate!' She grabbed them from him, opened the car door, and tossed them inside, on the floor. Then she walked on, up the hill.

After a moment Charlie caught up with her and slipped his arm through hers. 'I was only joking, sweetie,' he said, kissing her on the cheek.

She smiled, she wanted so much to believe him.

It had been Anna's intention to continue to look for a job, but working at the pub drained her energy. The heat, the smoke and the smell of drink made her queasy. It permeated her clothes and her hair, so that in the morning she could still smell the pub and it made her nauseous.

She didn't see Dominic for some time, then he drifted into the Vernon one quiet evening, pulled up a stool, and asked, 'Why didn't you tell me you had a boyfriend?'

'You didn't ask.'

'You don't look very happy together.'

'We used to be,' she said, sadly. Then, embarrassed, she moved to the far end of the bar.

One evening when she'd been serving non-stop behind the bar and the sweat was pouring down her face, she looked up to find Mr Shufflebuck standing opposite her. 'Do . . . you sell matches?' he stammered.

She reached for a packet. 'Twenty pence.'

He counted out the coins. 'I didn't know you worked here, Miss Tobias, or I wouldn't have come in,' he said, and he picked up the matches and slipped out through the crowded bar.

'That old boy's a real character,' said Gerry, joining Anna behind the bar. 'He used to be a choreographer in Hollywood, and he's known as Mr Marilyn because he once danced with Marilyn Monroe. He's very kind to the lonely old ladies around here. Poor Mr Marilyn – he's having a hell of a time. A rich young couple bought the house where he's lived for years and they're trying to drive him out. It ain't fair, not at his age.'

To Anna's relief a customer demanded her attention, but she couldn't help wondering how long it would be before Gerry discovered her identity.

Delia telephoned on Friday afternoon when Anna was unloading the washing machine and Charlie had gone out. 'Hi there! So glad about tomorrow.'

'What about tomorrow?' asked Anna.

'The rugger at Twickenham, the Middlesex Sevens. Russell and I assumed you two wouldn't be going this year, but we met Charlie for a drink last night and he said he'd already bought the tickets.'

'He has?' Anna grew cold as she thought of the money.

'We'll pay for ourselves, of course, but Charlie's right, Anna, being out of work doesn't mean you can't have fun. You should have come last night. Charlie seemed so depressed, we're very worried about him. He told Russell that you never go out together any more. Anna, you need to see friends more than ever now.'

'I was busy last night,' Anna hissed through gritted teeth, as she recalled the drunk who'd tried to grope her behind the bar.

'Charlie said you were at home. Oh well, it's not my business. See you tomorrow. We'll pick you up at noon.' Delia rang off.

Anna slammed the washing machine door shut, picked up the basket of damp clothes and walked down into the garden, to the washing line behind the old apple tree. How could she go out at night when they had no money and she had to work? How could she be fun when she was so tired? As she pegged Charlie's jeans on to the line, she wondered if he'd also told Russell that they hadn't made love for weeks.

Anna wasn't happy with Charlie, she admitted that, and she couldn't see them staying together, not for ever, but she felt very protective towards him. She returned to the house and studied her face in the bathroom mirror. There were dark rings under her eyes and her skin had a greyish pallor. Digging inside her make-up bag she found some dark foundation. By mixing it with water in the palm of her hand she managed to create a light suntan. With rouge and a large fluffy brush she gave her cheeks a pinkish glow. Gloss in the centre of her lower lip gave an illusion of sensuous vitality.

When she arrived at the Vernon, Dominic was leaning against

the bar talking to Gerry. 'You look happy,' he said. 'Boyfriend problems sorted out?'

Anna smiled and pretended that he'd guessed right.

Charlie collected her at midnight, and as they walked home she linked her arm through his and said, 'I'm glad we're going to Twickenham.'

'You're not angry? I thought you would be.'

She drew closer to him. 'We deserve a break.'

He kissed her full on the mouth. 'I'll look for bar work too – next week. I promise.'

She slid her arms around his neck and he kissed her again, edging her back against the nearest wall. She felt sudden and acute desire. It rolled up her body and down each arm, tingling the nerves beneath the surface of her skin, making the hairs on her arms stand upright, driving away the recent weeks when they had existed without affection or communication. She held him tighter, wrapping her arms around him, wanting him to blot out the houses, the lamp light, the world. He ran his hand up her thigh and lifted the hem of her skirt. She moved her body against his, pressing into him, wanting him to take her then and there, to be masterful and daring and unafraid. She wanted him to hurt her, to be rough and powerful, to show himself in charge.

He stepped away. 'We'll be arrested.'

She tried not to show her disappointment.

At home she showered the smell of the pub from her hair and her body. She felt deliciously fresh and cool when she joined Charlie in bed. He took her in his arms and drew her close, cupping her face in his hands as he kissed her again and again. He kissed her throat and her breasts, his mouth running down her soft, cool skin. He kissed the back of her neck, where her hair was damp, then ran his tongue down her spine, licking each vertebra. But the rush of acute desire which Anna had experienced in the street did not return; in its place there was a soft longing, a tenderness.

They caressed and kissed, drew close, and moved away, then drew close again, teasing and titillating. They stroked and whispered, their fingers gently circling; they paused and looked into each other's eyes, and smiled; they didn't speak because there was no need. The change in their relationship did not spoil their lovemaking, but it altered it. When Charlie enveloped Anna in his long limbs, he shut out a frightening world, a world frightening to both of them, but even more so to him.

Afterwards Anna fell asleep in his arms, something she hadn't done for months, and in the morning she woke to find him in the kitchen, spreading butter on to thin slices of brown bread. She joined him, wrapped her arms around him and kissed the stubble on his chin, and froze. Next to the fridge, in a transparent cool-bag, were three bottles of champagne and some cans of beer. Next to them were two pounds of smoked salmon and a pile of uncooked sausages.

'Where did that champagne come from?' Anna demanded.

'From Russell.' Charlie carried on spreading the butter.

'And the smoked salmon?'

'Delia. We're providing the bread, the sausages, and we're making the picnic. I decided to start the preparations and let you sleep.'

She was ashamed that she'd suspected him of wasting their money.

'Russell and Delia don't know you're working in a pub, and I think we should keep it that way,' he said, reaching for another slice of bread.

'Oh, Charlie, I'd prefer to tell them the truth because they're bound to wonder why I have to be back by six.'

'We'll pretend you're meeting Roz.' He smiled, tentatively. 'Please?'

'All right.' She was reminded of the first occasion when her father had lost his job after they moved to Leatherbridge, and how her mother would drive him to the library at nine every morning so that their neighbours wouldn't realise he was unemployed.

There was already a large crowd of revellers in the grassy car park at Twickenham when they arrived in Russell's brand new Range Rover. He parked in their favourite place, close to the footbridge leading to the stadium, and alongside some friends they'd made in the past two years, since Charlie had organised their first visit. Whilst Russell and Charlie set up the tables and chairs, Delia and Anna arranged the food, spreading a white damask tablecloth over the table and laying out the dishes of smoked salmon and sausages. Delia had also brought cheeses and salads.

'I'm sorry you've had to do it all,' Anna told her, taking the clingfilm off a whole Brie.

'You've done enough.' Delia gave Anna a quick hug. 'I'm so glad you came.'

Anna responded with a warmer hug. 'I'm glad too. What you said on the phone was right, we need our friends.'

For the first time in months, she felt attractive and fun, and not downtrodden. She didn't mind that her navy jacket had seen better days, whereas Delia's crimson trouser-suit was brand new. Russell and Delia were friends, even when she and Charlie couldn't pay their own way, and that made Anna especially happy, because everything else in their life was equated to money – or rather, to their lack of it.

Russell opened a bottle of champagne and poured four glasses. 'A toast to Anna and Charlie,' he said.

They clinked glasses and Anna smiled at Charlie. She knew he dreaded the prospect of working in a pub, but the fact that he was prepared to do so gave her genuine hope for their relationship.

There was roar from the stadium as the first team came on to the pitch, and the tournament began. The teams of seven came primarily from rugger clubs in Middlesex, with a number of overseas visitors. By the end of the day two teams would have battled their way into the final.

Friends from previous years joined the party at Russell's Range Rover. The men talked rugger and money markets, the women tried not to look bored. More champagne appeared, more people dropped by, and soon there was a large group, with Charlie in his element in the centre. Anna caught his eye and he winked.

After lunch they crossed the footbridge and made their way into the oval stadium, scrambling over other people to reach their seats.

'How's Elaine?' Anna asked Delia.

'She's been promoted to Miss Thin's assistant.'

'Oh, good. Send her my best wishes. What about everyone else?'

'Hawthorn's retiring next week; Gordon's been on holiday.'

'I know. He asked me to have lunch on his return.'

'He did? That's great.' Delia paused. 'But I'm not sure he'll be able to offer you a job. We've had to make more redundancies.' Delia held out her hand. 'It's starting to rain. Rugger's boring enough without getting wet. Let's go back to the car.' She rose and sidled along the row to the aisle.

Anna followed. 'Who's been made redundant?'

'Stuart, "The Cobra".'

'I never liked him, he was such a chauvinist.'

'And Judy.'

'Oh no! Poor Judy! How did she take it?'

'She tried to touch me for a loan, only a hundred pounds to pay her gas bill, so I lent her fifty. She was so grateful. She paid me back, of course, but I was stunned that Judy had no pride.'

'Perhaps she was desperate.'

'She shouldn't have asked, it was embarrassing.'

If Anna had had a knife she'd have stuck it into Delia's back, but they walked on in silence, Delia unaware that anything was wrong. At the Range Rover there were other people for Delia to talk to, whilst Anna cleared away the lunch in order not to have to talk to anyone.

She was growing anxious about getting back to the Vernon when Charlie and Russell appeared. 'Anna has to meet her sister at the house at six,' Charlie explained.

'We'll run you back, but first we'll settle up.' Russell took a roll of twenty-pound notes from his pocket. 'Charlie, we're paying for the tickets.'

'No.' Charlie held up his hands. 'They're on me.'

'But you've paid for most of the food and drink.'

'No we didn't,' said Anna. 'You did.'

'No,' said Delia. 'We only bought the cheese and salad.'

Anna turned to Charlie to back her up, but he flushed and looked away, and the truth hit her. She felt sick as she stared at the three empty bottles of champagne and the remnants of the smoked salmon. 'You mean . . .' she began.

Charlie cut her short. 'This is our treat. It was last year and the year before.'

'We were working then,' said Anna.

'So what?' He glared at her like a defiant child. 'Because we're out of work, it doesn't mean we can't afford to see our friends.'

There was an awkward silence and Russell fiddled with his glass whilst Delia looked at her watch. Anna picked up her bag and walked towards the footbridge, pushing through the oncoming crowd as she crossed over the stream. On the far side she made her way along the back of the stadium, heading for the exit nearest the train station.

As she reached the turnstiles, deserted now but for two policemen and an alsatian, she heard Delia shout, 'Anna! Wait!'

'What for?'

Delia came stumbling across the tarmac, gasping for breath, her face the same deep crimson as her trouser-suit. She held out Russell's forty pounds. 'Take the money.'

'I don't want it.' Anna walked on.

'Then for God's sake stop being so hard on Charlie. He didn't mean any harm, he hates being out of work just as much as you. Please come back.'

They had reached the main road and had to stop for traffic. 'I can't come back,' Anna shouted above the roar of the cars. 'I have to take a train, I start work at six, in a pub. I do it because we're broke – and that idiot Charlie, who hasn't yet dirtied his own hands, wastes my hard-earned wages on champagne!' Words and emotion choked Anna. Heedless of the danger, she took a step into the traffic.

Delia grabbed her arm. 'Why didn't you tell us you were broke? How were we to know?' She pushed Russell's money into Anna's hand, saying, 'Take it, please!'

Anna hesitated.

'Come on, you need it more than we do. You can pay us back from your dole money; you are on the dole, aren't you? If you're not you should be. I told you that before, but you wouldn't listen to me.'

If Delia hadn't added that, Anna might have accepted the money, but she remembered what Delia had said about Judy. She pictured Delia arriving at Marinecover on Monday morning and telling everyone how poor Anna had grovelled for forty pounds.

'No, thanks,' she said, tucking the notes into Delia's jacket pocket. 'We may be out of work but we're not fucking beggars.' She ran across the dual carriageway, dodging in between the cars, and when she reached the far side, she didn't look back.

15

CHARLIE DIDN'T COLLECT Anna from the pub that evening, not that she'd expected him, but if he had come her rage might have abated, whereas his absence gave it fuel.

She found the house in darkness, although the front door was unlocked. Intent on confronting Charlie, even if she had to wake him, she opened their bedroom door and switched on the light. He was in bed, asleep, his blond head on the pillow, his face serene. Anna stared at him, exasperated by his ability to sleep in all situations – then she froze. On the far pillow, *her* pillow, was a mop of bleached blonde hair.

It took a moment for the reality to sink in, and when it did Anna staggered as though she'd been punched in the stomach. She felt faint as blood rushed from her limbs, and her hands and feet turned to ice. At the same time she was filled with murderous rage. She crossed to the bed and kicked it hard.

Charlie woke to find Anna standing over him. 'Oh . . . um . . . hello,' he mumbled drunkenly.

'You bastard!' She punched him in the face.

He put his hands up to defend himself. 'Anna! Please!'

'I hate you!'.

The bleached blonde sat up, clutching the duvet around her naked shoulders. 'What's going on?' she demanded.

'Get out of my bed!' shouted Anna.

'Yes, go.' Charlie didn't look at the girl. 'Please go!'

'You're a bloody liar, you told me you didn't have a girlfriend.' The girl slid naked from the bed; thin, pallid and slightly grubby. Retrieving her clothes she disappeared into the bathroom to dress.

Charlie glanced shamefacedly at Anna. 'I know I shouldn't have done it, but I was angry with you.'

'You're disgusting.'

'Don't worry, I used a condom.'

'That's not the point. You betrayed me. Whilst I was slaving to earn enough to feed us, you were humping some tart in our bed! In our house! On my pillow!' She walked out of the room and slammed the door, crashed across the hall into the drawing-room, and threw herself down on the sofa. She was cut deep inside by his infidelity, by his weakness, by his treachery. She wasn't so much jealous of the girl, it went far beyond that, to the very depths of disappointment.

In the hall she heard the girl hiss, 'I want my taxi fare. It's the least you can do.'

Charlie replied, 'I've only got ten pounds.' Anna heard him slit open Mr Shufflebuck's rent envelope.

The girl left the house, stomping angrily across the gravel drive. Charlie opened the drawing-room door and whispered, 'Anna!'

She didn't answer. She lay perfectly still, with her eyes closed, pretending to be asleep. If Charlie had stepped nearer, he would have seen the glisten of tears on her cheeks, but he crept away.

Anna scarcely slept all night. She kept thinking of Charlie sneaking another woman into their house, into their bed, pretending that he lived alone, kissing her, making love to her, entering that other woman's body. Of course they'd had their problems recently, they'd had so much stacked against them – but in the past couple of weeks, since her outburst when he hadn't fetched her from the pub, they had grown close again. That's why his disloyalty and his lying hurt her even more.

Early next morning she telephoned Roz to invite herself to Lower Gossip Fen.

'Of course,' said Roz. 'When?'

'Today. Now.'

'Anna, why are you whispering? Is something wrong?'

'I'll tell you later.'

'Is Charlie coming too?'

'Definitely not!'

'I'll meet you in Ely. There's a train from King's Cross at ten; if you hurry you'll catch it.'

Anna slipped upstairs to the master bedroom where their suitcases were stacked along one wall. She selected an overnight bag, packed her toiletries from the bathroom and crept into their bedroom to fetch her shorts, a couple of T-shirts, a pair of jeans and a pink sun-dress. Charlie was sprawled across the bed, fast asleep. He didn't even stir.

On the hall table she left a note: 'I need a break. I've gone away. I'll be back on Tuesday. Anna.' She didn't write 'love, Anna', because at that moment she loathed him.

Roz was waiting by the ticket barrier when Anna arrived at Ely. 'You look frightful,' she said, giving Anna a brief hug. 'Are you ill?'

'No, it's Charlie, he's . . .' Anna's face crumpled.

'I'm afraid you'll have to tell me later,' said Roz, ushering her through the ticket office. 'I've had to bring Oliver and Phoebe because Tom's taken Luke to hear the Cathedral choir, Melissa's in a sulk and refused to leave her room, and Granny Tobias can't control them. Did I tell you she's here? No? Oh, I forgot. Mother brought her over for the night whilst she helps Jacynthia Peabody with a charity bazaar.'

Oliver was sitting in the front of Roz's battered estate car. He stuck his freckled face out of the window, and shouted, 'Phoebe pinched me.'

'I don't care,' replied Roz. 'Get in the back. And don't argue!' She pushed him back between the seats to join Phoebe and Augustus, their huge black, slobbering labrador. As Oliver sat down he reached across and tweaked one of Phoebe's blonde pigtails. She screamed and burst into tears.

Anna fastened her seat belt. 'Thanks for letting me come at such short notice.'

'Oh, one more makes no difference. No, I don't mean it like that, you know I don't, I'm pleased to see you.'

They drove through the fenland on the narrow straight road between the deep drains whose water had dried to a green sludge in the recent drought. All the land around Lower Gossip Fen was baked and cracked, and in the fields Tom's cabbages wilted in their rows like soldiers fainting on parade.

The children fought in the back seat, Augustus dribbled down Anna's neck, but Roz barely noticed the commotion. She merely raised her voice. 'We have ten to lunch,' she yelled. 'All bores, I'm afraid.'

'Would you mind if I missed it?' Anna had to scream to make herself heard. 'I've had an awful three days and I'd just like to rest.'

'I'll send Melissa up with a tray.'

'I'm not hungry, I feel a bit sick.'

Roz glanced in the mirror to check that Oliver and Phoebe weren't listening. 'You must appear to eat whilst you're with us. Tom says I fuss but I'm terrified Melissa's becoming anorexic. She starves for days, then binges. Of course, she won't listen to anything I say because I'm just her mother, but she admires you, she thinks you're glamorous and interesting.'

Anna pulled a face. 'I hardly look it now.'

'No, you don't,' replied Roz, with her usual honesty. She turned into the farmyard and a cloud of dust mushroomed up over the car.

'You don't know what a relief it is to get away from London,' said Anna.

Roz nodded, but her mind was elsewhere. 'I must do lunch. You're in the attic bedroom.' She hurried towards the kitchen, shouting at Melissa because she hadn't laid the table.

Anna followed slowly, her bag hooked over her shoulder. She wished that she could have Roz to herself, even for ten minutes, just to hear her bossy, reassuring voice say that everything would be all right. But Roz was busy, and it was unreasonable to expect otherwise – except that Anna was too unhappy to be reasonable.

The old stone farmhouse was cool and dark, most of the windows being too deeply set to let in much light. Through the hatch which opened into the dining-room Anna could see Melissa sullenly laying the table. Beyond the dining-room the drawing-room was suffused in sun which poured in through the French windows. Anna imagined herself living at Lower Gossip Fen, cooking lunch every Sunday, knowing exactly what she'd be doing each Monday, and at that moment she envied Roz the safety – even the tedium.

In no mood to make conversation, she avoided Granny Tobias and crept up the back stairs, the squeak of the floorboards drowned by the gut-thud of rock music which Melissa had left on in her bedroom. The attic was Anna's preferred room because, like Cliff Cottage and Ladbroke Hill, it was a world of its own. Tucked under the rafters, with a door which opened on to the roof, on a clear day she could see Ely Cathedral.

She waited until Roz banged the gong for lunch before she slipped down to the bathroom for a shower. As she turned on the tap there was a deep gurgle, then the pipes shook and a torrent of water cascaded over her. It had a brackish taste which came from the good, clean fenland earth. It drove away the grime of the city, the smell of the pub and the discovery of Charlie. Just thinking about him in bed with another woman, made Anna feel nauseous.

Returning to the attic, she discovered a plate of sandwiches next to her bed. For Roz's sake, she ate them.

She was so exhausted that she fell into a deep, numbing sleep, not waking until the late afternoon, when the slamming of car doors and voices shouting 'Goodbye' woke her. Even then she didn't get up, but lay on her bed and thought of Charlie. She was not only deeply hurt but angry. Did he think she enjoyed being short of money? Did he imagine she wanted to work in a pub, pouring drinks for hours on end? Of course she didn't, but she hadn't minded the hardships so long as they were together. Now it enraged her to think how protective she'd felt towards him, how she'd been afraid to push him as her mother had driven her father.

She heard Roz shout at Melissa to make the tea, and she rose and slipped on her pink sun-dress. Her hair, which had been wet when she'd fallen asleep, had dried crumpled like heavily creased silk curtains. She was forcing a comb through its tangles when Roz came up the stairs.

'You look better already,' Roz said brightly.

'I feel it – though I still don't know what I'm going to do. I came home and found Charlie . . .'

'Tell me tonight. I have to give Granny her tea.'

'Yes, of course.' Anna tried not to mind that Roz had no time to listen.

They went down to the garden, where their grandmother was dozing in a deck-chair beneath the weeping branches of an old birch tree. Anna did her best to appear cheerful, pretending that she was merely taking a short break from her busy job and happy life but, inside, she was breaking.

It wasn't possible for her to talk to Roz that evening either, because at supper Melissa announced that she refused to return to her weekly boarding school.

'Don't be silly,' said Roz. 'You have to go, we've paid the fees.'

'I hate it.' Melissa pushed her heavy, dark hair back off her face and stood up. She was tall for her age and, because she'd grown quickly, she tended to stoop, which made her look plump when she wasn't.

'You can't leave school at fifteen, 'Lissa.' Tom used his pet name for her.

'I don't have any friends. The other girls don't like me.'

Anna escaped into the kitchen to start the dishwasher. Melissa was her least favourite of Roz's children, but she couldn't help sympathising with her, although to have intervened would have infuriated Roz. She remembered the endless new schools of her own childhood and the eternal feeling of being an outsider, standing on the edge of a gaggle of girls, trying to pluck up the courage to push herself forward.

The argument was still raging in the dining-room when Anna called 'Good night' and went up to bed. As soon as her head hit the pillow she fell into the same deep, anaesthetising sleep and woke only when she heard Roz shout, 'Hurry up, Melissa! You're going to be late.'

Anna listened to the children being bundled into the car for school, then she drifted off into a silent argument with herself over Charlie, wondering sadly what had gone so wrong and if she were partly to blame – then, alternately, angrily convincing herself that they were finished, that he disgusted her, and that she could not bear him touching her again.

A noise on the stairs brought her back to reality. Phoebe was standing in the door to her bedroom, wearing pink pyjamas decorated with Easter bunnies. 'I'm ill,' she said, wrinkling up her pert little nose. 'No, I'm not really sick, but I didn't want to go today so Daddy said I needn't.' She stepped into the centre of the room and pirouetted in front of Anna, her blonde plaits flying round her head.

Anna yawned. 'Does Daddy often let you stay at home?'

'If he doesn't, I cry.' Phoebe giggled and executed a dainty curtsey. Then she cocked her head on one side and listened. 'Mummy's back!' she whispered, and she scampered down the stairs to her own bedroom.

Roz was busy all day, ferrying Luke to his music lesson, collecting Oliver from Scouts, and driving their grandmother home. Anna would have accompanied them, but she knew that her mother would sense something was wrong and she felt too vulnerable to parry the inevitable questions. So she offered to remain at the house with Phoebe and in the afternoon, when the sun grew warm, she put on her bikini and stretched out on a rug, just below Phoebe's bedroom window. Above her, faint fingers of cloud drifted across the pale blue sky. Near her, bees fed on the sweetly-scented nicotiana plants. Charlie seemed far away, on another planet, in another life. She decided not to telephone him, not yet, because she wanted to savour this oasis of calm, this escapism, knowing that once she heard his voice her angry wounds would reopen.

Roz came home later than she'd intended and was too rushed to chat. Anna went to bed early, feeling sun-kissed and stronger, but in the morning she was nauseous. She hurried down the stairs and only just reached the bathroom before she was sick. It took her some time to recover, leaning on the basin as she swilled water around her mouth and splashed it on her face. When she opened the bathroom door she found Roz waiting for her.

'Anna, you're pregnant.'

'I'm not, I'm on the Pill.'

'When did you last have a period?'

'Roz, you're like a school matron. I had one at Easter. Well . . . maybe a little longer ago than that. Yes, it was two weeks before I started work at the pub, and that was at the beginning of April.'

'Seven weeks.' Roz reached up to the top shelf of her medicine cabinet and handed Anna a small box. 'Pregnancy-testing kit. Use it tomorrow morning.'

'Roz, believe me, I'm not pregnant. Things have been very difficult and I've been under great stress. We're out of work, we're broke and I found Charlie in bed with . . . another woman.'

'Oh, no!' Roz put her arms around Anna. 'What a bastard! I'm so sorry.'

Roz's sympathy brought tears to Anna's eyes. 'I feel so . . . let down,' she said.

The doorbell interrupted them. Roz patted Anna on the shoulder. 'That's the sweep. I must go, we'll talk later.' She started down the stairs, adding, 'George, our neighbour, is coming to dinner. He's a rich, widowed farmer.'

Anna grimaced. 'Isn't it a bit late for a blind date?' she asked, waving the pregnancy kit.

'Oh, George wouldn't mind, he's a kind old thing.'

'I don't want a kind old thing!'

Roz smiled. 'There. I've made you laugh.' She went out to speak to the sweep.

Anna returned to the bathroom and stood on the scales. She'd lost a stone since Christmas. She wasn't pregnant. It was nerves, worry, stress, tension; all the things which she'd once coped with – even thrived on – which now combined to crush her. She put the pregnancy-testing kit back on top of the cabinet.

George wasn't so decrepit and bumbling as Roz had made out, and it occurred to Anna that she'd done this on purpose. He was a good fifteen years older than her – but then so was Tom – and he was stocky, with greying hair and very thick eyebrows. But he had kind, shy brown eyes and the air of a man who longed to be looked after and who would be so grateful. His navy blazer was short of two buttons, and when he sat down Anna noticed that he wore one black sock and one navy.

'Do you like our fenland?' he asked Anna when Tom was busy carving and Roz was in the kitchen.

'I love it in the summer. When the sun shines, like today, I wonder how I'll ever be able to make myself go back to the city.'

'Then why leave?'

'Oh . . .' She blushed and laughed. 'The bright lights, I suppose. And I had a good job – before I was made redundant.'

'That must have been horrible.' He spoke with genuine sympathy.

'It was. I felt so . . . rejected.'

George glanced at Tom, who was pretending not to listen. 'Perhaps you'd like to see my water garden. My wife designed it before she died. The lilies are just coming into flower.'

She thought of Gerry, who was expecting her to work on Thursday. 'Unfortunately, I need to go back to London tomorrow.'

'You can't go,' Roz shouted through the kitchen hatch. 'There's a rail and tube strike.'

'Then you've no excuse.' George gave Anna his shy smile and she thought what a nice man he was, though definitely not for her.

Roz woke Anna next morning. 'Use it now,' she said, dropping the pregnancy-testing kit on to the bed.

Anna sat up. 'I'm fine today.'

'You're pregnant – I know, I've had four children. You have that "heifer" look in your eyes.'

'All right. Give me the kit.' Anna got out of bed, put on her dressing-gown and padded downstairs to the bathroom. Roz followed. Anna closed the door in her face, shouting, 'Don't wait outside.' Then she opened the box and read the instructions.

A short while later she stepped out of the bathroom, her face drained of all colour.

Roz was sitting on the stairs. 'I'm right, aren't I?'

Anna nodded and swayed against the wall. She felt faint, and it wasn't just with nausea, it was with fear and disbelief. She buried her face in her hands. 'Oh God. This is all I need. What am I going to do?'

'Have it or get rid of it,' said Roz in her typically blunt way. 'You must be practical, Anna. Children cost money and they require constant attention, especially babies.'

'I'll have to go back today. I must talk to Charlie.'

'Are you going to marry him?'

Anna gave a helpless shrug, and began to shake. 'I don't know what I'm going to do now. I'd pretty much decided to tell him we were finished, though God knows how we'd separate when neither of us can afford to move. But after this, I don't know. I can't face it alone – and why should I? We're both responsible. I'd better telephone him.' She started down the stairs. Yesterday she hadn't wanted to speak to him, today was different – but then today and from now on, until she – or they – decided what to do, everything else was in limbo, and she felt so much more vulnerable.

'You're not going to tell him on the phone?' Roz called, aghast.

'Of course not, but I want him to be home when I arrive. And I want him to be alone.'

'What about the strike?' Roz asked.

'There must be a bus from Ely.' Anna dialled the Ladbroke Hill number. As it rang, she pictured Charlie reaching sleepily for the receiver.

It rang five times, then the machine cut in. 'This is Charlie

Blythely and Anna Tobias. Sorry we're not available. Please leave your name, number and any message.'

Thinking he must be in the bathroom, Anna waited a minute and redialled. Again, the machine answered. This time she spoke. 'Charlie, I'm coming back today. I should be there by four. Please be home.'

Roz had found a bus timetable. 'There's one at noon from Cambridge,' she said. 'We'd better leave soon. It's bound to be crowded. You pack whilst I make you some breakfast.' She started for the kitchen.

Anna stopped her with a big hug. 'Roz, you're an old bossy-boots, but you're a brick and I don't know what I'd do without you.'

'Just phone to say you're all right, because I'm going to be worried sick.' With an anxious frown, Roz hurried into the kitchen.

Anna went upstairs to pack. The prospect of a long, hot bus ride made her feel queasy and her meeting with Charlie filled her with apprehension, but she had to see him today. Whatever had happened before, whatever they decided for the future, she was pregnant with his child and she needed his support.

16

BECAUSE THE UNDERGROUND was on strike and half the buses were out in sympathy, Anna had to walk all the way from the Victoria coach station, up through Knightsbridge to Hyde Park, her feet drumming on the hot pavements until they felt as if they had been bastinado'd. The park had been transformed into a temporary car park, with rows of cars baking in the sun and weary drivers wandering up and down, trying to recall where they'd left their vehicles.

Once on the grass Anna took off her shoes. As she walked across the park, she rehearsed her conversation with Charlie, improvising his replies, the confrontation growing angrier as she became more tired. But when she reached Ladbroke Hill and saw the house bathed in the gold light of late afternoon, the trees bursting in new bud, her spirits lifted. She pictured herself, more forgiving than she believed herself capable, coming home from hospital, the baby in her arms, with Charlie, her now working and completely transformed husband, beside her.

The front door was latched but not double-locked. She entered, calling out, 'I'm home.'

There was no answer.

She called again, 'Charlie!' her voice echoing up the stairwell, but there was still no reply.

Afraid of what she might find, she gingerly opened their bedroom door and peered inside. The room was a mess, but empty. The bed was unmade and the duvet lay on the floor amid piles of newspapers and an empty bottle of wine, but for once Anna wasn't annoyed; she was too relieved at not finding him with another woman.

Feeling dizzy from the heat and the lack of fresh air, she opened the balcony doors and went into the kitchen. In the sink was a pile of washing up. In the fridge was a carton of milk turned sour, a loaf of bread whose slices had curled at the edges, and yogurt past its sell-by date. But in the drawing-room, to her surprise, the whirlwind of papers which usually covered the dining-table had been stacked neatly beside the word processor, with the note she'd left for Charlie lying on top. She turned it over in case he'd written on the back, but he hadn't. Then she opened the drawers of the chest where he'd intended to keep his papers. Inside were two packets of envelopes and some loose stamps, nothing more.

The answering machine registered three calls. The first was from her mother; the second was from Vivianne – 'Charlie, call me when you get in'; the third was her own message to him.

To kill time until he returned, Anna washed the dishes, threw out the rubbish, and changed the bedclothes. Then she refreshed herself with a cool shower and slipped on a sun-dress. There was still no sign of Charlie, but the house smelt clean and that made her feel less queasy.

After tidying away the last of her belongings, Anna carried her overnight bag upstairs to store it with their other suitcases. Switching on the light she started across the room. Then she stopped dead. Against the far wall stood her four matching cases and a jumble of other bags she'd collected over the years, but Charlie's suitcases had gone.

For a second she couldn't believe what she saw. She was transfixed, frozen inside and out. Then she gave a small cry and ran down the stairs into their bedroom, and opened the drawers which Charlie had used. They were empty. She opened the cupboard where his suits always hung, but the hangers swung free. She went to the bathroom and saw what she'd failed to notice earlier, that his white towelling dressing-gown had gone from behind the door and his shaving kit was no longer inside the cabinet.

She clutched at the bathroom wall as the floor seemed to buckle beneath her feet. She'd never thought he'd walk out, not without warning. Staggering to the telephone, she tapped out Delia's number. 'Is Charlie there?' she cried.

'No. Why should he be?'

'Delia, I have to talk to him, please put him on.'

'He's not here. We haven't seen him since Saturday.

You remember Saturday? The day when you were so rude to me?'

'Dee, he's taken all his clothes, and I need to know where he's gone. It's very important.'

'Oh, he'll come back. Russell removes his shaving kit every time we row and sometimes we don't speak for weeks.'

'But Charlie's never done this before. He hasn't even left a note. There's nothing.' Anna's voice started to shake.

Delia was still babbling on about Russell when Anna replaced her receiver.

Anna went into the bedroom and stood at the end of their bed, her hands clasped to her face. She didn't know what to do; she couldn't think where he'd gone. Had the girl meant something to him? Was he with her? Did he suspect she was pregnant? Was that why he'd run? No, he couldn't possibly realise.

Suddenly she thought of the word processor. Perhaps he'd left a message in the machine. That would be typical Charlie. Hadn't Vivianne said he was childish? She hurried to the machine, switched it on and slipped in the disc. As the menu came up on the screen, the telephone rang. She grabbed it. 'Yes.'

'Anna, it's me.'

She wanted to scream at him but she stopped herself, because arguing wouldn't solve anything. 'I've been so worried.' She spoke as calmly as she could. 'I found all your clothes gone, I . . .' Her voice quavered. She stopped and took a deep breath. 'Charlie, we need to talk.'

There was silence, then he said, 'I'm in Melbourne.'

She couldn't speak for shock.

'I arrived this morning. I couldn't stand it any longer. I couldn't bear living in that house with no money, no carpets, no car, nothing.'

'You mean you've gone back to Australia without seeing me?'

'I couldn't face you. I'm so sorry, I loved you and we could have been happy if we hadn't lost our jobs. You keep the house. You were the one who wanted it.'

'Charlie, I'm pregnant.'

He gasped audibly.

'I found out today. I came back to tell you.'

'Oh God! I'm sorry. I'd never have left if I'd known.'

Tears filled her eyes. 'We have to decide what to do.'

'I can't come back.'

'You have to! We're both responsible.'

'I'd send you some money, but I don't have any – you know that. I had to borrow off Viv for my fare home.'

'Charlie, I'm having a baby. Your baby!' She started to cry, deep gut sobs of fear and abandonment.

'Anna! Calm down! We can't talk if you cry.'

But she couldn't stop. Cradling the receiver in her arms, she sank to the ground and buried her face in her knees.

'Anna, I have to go now,' Charlie was shouting. 'I'll think of something, don't worry, I'll call you later.' There was a click as he replaced the receiver.

She was left with a hollow echo on the line, which seemed to emphasise the distance between them. She'd known Charlie was weak – she'd witnessed that months ago, but she hadn't wanted to face it – but she'd never have believed he'd disappear to the other side of the world without telling her. He had run away, he was a coward, and she despised him – as she'd once hated her father for deserting them. But with her father, she'd grown to understand, to sympathise, and to feel terrible guilt. Charlie she'd never forgive, and she certainly didn't want his child.

It was some time before she had the strength to stand up. She went to the bathroom to wash her face and caught sight of herself sideways in the long mirror. Soothing the material of her dress tightly over her stomach, she examined it to see if she could detect a bulge but there was nothing. She laid her hands flat and thought of the life inside her. Was it a girl or a boy? Did it look like her or Charlie?

Dropping her dress, she turned away from the mirror. She mustn't think about the baby as a person. The only solution was to get rid of it. She saw herself checking into a clinic having made what Roz would describe as a 'practical decision', except that Roz herself would never do it. But Roz's situation was different; she had a husband. Anna recalled Elaine struggling to bring up Danny on her own.

She felt hungry with a hollow emptiness although the idea of eating made her sick. In any case there was no food. She opened a can of Coke and drank the contents straight from the tin, then she lay down on their bed with the duvet pulled up tightly around her, shivering in spite of the warmth of the night.

The telephone was on the bedside table. Anna had no doubt that Charlie would ring her, and she ran over what she would say to him. He must send money, she didn't care where he borrowed it, if necessary he must ask his parents. She'd sort out the rest – somehow – somewhere. She'd seen advertisements on the Underground for pregnancy advice agencies. But even as she worked out the practicalities, she had a sudden picture of Charlie, out on the town with Josh and Matt, and imagined him saying, 'Anna? Oh no, that's all over now,' and she fought back her tears. The cruelty of Charlie's weakness cut as deeply as any hurt she had known.

The phone rang. She seized it. 'Yes?'

'Anna, it's me, Roz. What happened? You were meant to phone me when you arrived. Are you all right? I've been so worried.'

'Can I call you back? I'm waiting for Charlie to phone.'

'What do you mean? Isn't he there?'

'He's . . . in Australia. He'd gone before I got back.'

'What? Why? Does he know you're pregnant?'

'He does now. Roz, I'll tell you everything later.'

Anna replaced the receiver and waited. The minutes ticked by; then the hours. She slept fitfully, waking every so often to lift the receiver to check that the telephone was in working order – until she made herself desist in case Charlie was trying to get through.

In the morning she felt terribly sick. In her rush to reach the bathroom, she tripped over the cord of her bedside light which smashed on the floor. On her way back to bed she trod on the broken porcelain and cut her foot. She dripped blood all over the duvet until she realised what had happened. Not long afterwards she heard the milk float turn in to the drive to deliver Mr Shufflebuck's solitary pint. Staggering out of bed she grabbed her dressing-gown and hobbled around, trying to find her purse, but by the time she located it the milkman had gone. Crying with frustration, she made herself a cup of milkless tea and returned to bed.

She was sure that Charlie would ring in the morning, which would be late evening in Melbourne, but he didn't. In the afternoon she excused his silence because that would be the middle of the night. In the evening, his morning, she waited expectantly.

Nine o'clock would be his seven, too early for Charlie. Midnight was his ten o'clock. She waited. The minutes ticked by, then one hour, two hours. A terrible, gripping loneliness came over her when she realised that he was not going to help. It numbed her face and her limbs. She couldn't even cry. She felt totally abandoned by him, as if her pregnancy had nothing to do with him and he did not care what became of her, and had never cared. Every rejection she'd ever suffered rose up before her. She'd lost her father, Cliff Cottage, Charlie, Marinecover, and in that moment if Anna had had the right pills, she'd have taken them.

In her half-sleep Anna heard the front door open and footsteps in the hall.

'Charlie!' she croaked. 'Oh, thank God you're back.'

'Miss Tobias?'

She tried to sit up. 'Who's there?'

'It's me, Mr Shufflebuck. Your sister telephoned me. Your line is out of order and she's worried about you.' He paused. 'Are you all right?'

Anna tried to speak but she couldn't; all she could think of was that Charlie hadn't been able to telephone her. It wasn't that he hadn't tried.

Mr Shufflebuck peered into her room, his small bright eyes widening in dismay when he saw Anna slumped against the pillows like a broken doll.

'You're ill,' he said. 'Oh, dear me. Have you seen a doctor?'

She shook her head.

'Have you eaten?'

She shook her head again.

'That's very silly.' He hurried away.

Anna closed her eyes. Mr Shufflebuck had left her to die, not that she blamed him after the way they'd treated him.

A few minutes later she heard his footsteps and she opened her eyes to find him standing beside her bed, holding a glass of milk. He was wearing an aubergine velvet suit and a black fedora hat, and if Anna hadn't felt so ill she'd have laughed. 'You must drink this,' he said, pursing his lips like a disapproving matron to a disobedient patient. 'I was going to give it to Errol Flynn, but he won't mind. I'll buy him some more.'

'It'll make me sick,' Anna whispered.

'Milk's good for you.' He held the glass closer to her.

The sight of the milk, thick, white and creamy, made her gorge rise. She rolled off the bed and ran to the bathroom.

When she had recovered she became aware of china clattering in the kitchen. Opening the door she found Mr Shufflebuck, still wearing his black fedora, meticulously washing her teacup and saucer. 'Oh, please don't worry about that,' she said. 'It's very kind of you but I'll be fine now. I'm not really ill, just . . . a bit off colour.'

He flushed, and it was clear to Anna that he thought she was referring to period pains. 'You should lie down with a hot water bottle on your stomach, that's what the chorus girls used to do.'

'Mr Shufflebuck, I'm all right. Really.' She forced a smile. 'Thank you.'

'It's frightening to be unwell when you're on your own,' he said with feeling.

'How did you know I was . . . alone?'

'I saw Mr Blythely go out with his suitcases.'

'I see. Yes, well, he has gone.'

Mr Shufflebuck left and Anna returned to bed. Since Charlie couldn't telephone her even if he wanted to, she slept peacefully for the first time since she'd discovered he'd gone. She was woken by Mr Shufflebuck carrying a tray with a bowl of chicken soup and two pieces of thinly-sliced bread, carefully spread with butter and with the crusts removed. At the sight of food, Anna was suddenly ravenous.

'I've bought you some groceries.' He laid the bill on her bed. 'Of course my rent isn't due till Saturday, but I don't mind advancing it this once.'

'Thank you, you're very kind.' She tried not to wolf her food.

'Your sister rang again. She's reported your telephone to British Telecom but they say it's not a fault, it's been disconnected.'

'But Charlie paid the bill last month.'

'Oh well, maybe they've mixed you up with someone else, it happens all the time nowadays. It's these silly computers, there's no substitute for the human touch.' He went into her kitchen and stacked her provisions neatly in the cupboard and in the fridge. When he reappeared, he was carrying a dustpan and brush.

'Oh, don't worry, please, I can manage,' protested Anna.

'No, you can't.' He swept up the shattered bedside lamp.

She thanked him again and sank back into the pillows. It was wonderful to be looked after, to put the future on hold and be a child again, if only for one day.

That night Anna dreamed that Charlie came back and that everything had been a misunderstanding; she wasn't really pregnant but had appendicitis; he hadn't gone to Australia but to Liverpool. She saw herself in hospital, coming round from the appendectomy to find Charlie dressed in a doctor's white coat, telling her that he loved her as he slipped a diamond ring on to the third finger of her left hand. But when she reached up to kiss him he stepped away, and only then did she realise that he was teetering on the edge of a platform and that the train bearing down on him was headed for Ladbroke Hill.

She woke trembling, her cheeks wet, her heart pounding as if it had been for real, and for the remainder of the night she stared into the darkness and wondered if her obsession with the house had driven Charlie away, or if he would have let her down anyhow, sooner or later.

As well as the morning sickness, Anna had picked up a germ and she ran a slight temperature which made her feel dizzy and weak. Until she was well enough to go out, Mr Shufflebuck did her shopping and brought her a bowl of chicken soup each noon. Sometimes he stayed for a short chat, but never more than a few minutes, scuttling away to his basement or hurrying to meet his aged partners at a *thé dansant* in a hotel in Shepherd's Bush.

For Anna, the evening hours were the bleakest. She couldn't telephone Roz or Delia and they couldn't speak to her. She hoped that Delia would visit her, but she didn't. No one called. She tried to watch television but none of the programmes could hold her attention. She opened a book but the words swam before her eyes. From time to time she heard music from the basement, Glenn Miller's trombone or Marilyn Monroe singing *Diamonds Are A Girl's Best Friend.*

The days were warm and the evenings sultry, and people sat outside until late, their voices drifting up from the pubs along Portobello. The sound of others enjoying themselves made Anna feel even more isolated. She didn't want Charlie back, she never wanted to see him again, but they'd been together for more than two years and she ached with loneliness. She grieved for company, she mourned the absence of a friend, a lover, another being. She missed a body touching hers in bed, and someone to talk to as she dozed off, even if he was usually already asleep. She mourned her hopes, however fragile their base had ultimately become.

She received an anxious note from Roz, asking, 'What's happened? Call me collect', together with a registered letter from East Metro. She opened it and read: 'As you have failed to respond to our two previous registered letters (copies attached), we have no alternative but to put this matter into the hands of our solicitors.'

Anna turned the page. There were two copy letters, the first was a reply to her letter advising East Metro that the DSS would pay half the interest, the second gave them fourteen days to make an appointment to discuss their accruing debt. She'd never seen either before.

Clutching the letters in one hand and some coins in the other, she hurried to the call box half way down the hill. She was put straight through to Mr Hyde who informed her icily, 'We take a very poor view of borrowers who don't reply to letters, Miss Tobias.'

'We never received your previous letters, Mr Hyde.'

'That's impossible. They were registered.'

'It's the truth. I wouldn't forget a letter which threatens my home, I can promise you.'

He sighed. 'Oh very well, I'll check but it'll take time. Please hold on.'

Not wanting to waste money, Anna replaced the receiver, retrieved twenty pence, and waited ten minutes before redialling East Metro. 'Oh, Mr Hyde, we were cut off,' she lied from necessity. 'It's all this computerisation.'

'Miss Tobias, I tried to ring you but your home phone has been disconnected.'

'That's what I mean. Our number's constantly out of order, so are those of our neighbours.'

'Er . . . how unfortunate. Well, my assistant has checked and both letters were signed for by Mr Blythely.'

Anna reeled against the side of the phone box. 'I never saw those letters until today and I need time to sort this out.'

'Miss Tobias, we can't allow you any longer. The DSS pays only half your interest and you are months behind with the other half.'

'Mr Hyde, if I were going to abscond, I wouldn't have telephoned you today, would I? Give me a week. Please!'

He hesitated. 'Oh very well, though it's against East Metro's policy. A week, and not one day longer.'

Anna could find no letters from East Metro in the neat pile of Charlie's papers next to the word processor. Nor were there any in his bedside table or in any of the bedroom cupboards he'd used. The drawers in the chest where he'd kept his stationery were empty, except for the top two. Nevertheless, she pulled them out, one by one. As she was removing the third drawer, a wad of paper fell down. It was a folded, brown envelope and inside were half a dozen unopened letters, including the two from East Metro.

Horrified, Anna slumped into a chair. Apart from East Metro there was a final demand for the telephone, another for the electricity, a gas bill and a statement from their joint household account into which she had paid ten pounds a week from her pub money. Last Monday, whilst she was at Lower Gossip, Charlie had withdrawn the lot.

She picked up her purse and walked down to the telephone box, stuffed handfuls of coins into the machine and tapped out his Melbourne number.

Vivianne answered. 'Anna, Charlie's been so worried about you.'

'Put him on the line. Quickly!'

He took the receiver. 'Anna, I tried to call you but your number's out of order. I've been thinking about us and I don't consider it's the right moment to have a baby, but if you really insist on keeping it then I suppose . . .'

'Charlie, you lied. You didn't pay the bills, you hid them. What's more, you stole my pub money. You took my earnings from our account.'

'I needed it for my travel expenses.'

'You took my wages. You're a liar and a thief.'

'Anna, don't get upset. You must think of the baby. Viv's sure that if I pick the right moment to tell Mum and Dad they'll come up with some money.'

'Charlie, I don't want your baby. I'm getting rid of it. I don't

want any part of you – and I never want to hear from you again.'
She walked back up the hill to sort out the muddle of her life.

17

ONCE ANNA HAD made up her mind to have an abortion, she wanted it done instantly. She contacted several pregnancy advice agencies and discovered that to have it carried out immediately she'd probably have to pay. Although she only had a quarter of the necessary money, she made an appointment with the least expensive agency. Then she put on some make-up, combed her hair, and went down to The Admiral Vernon to ask Gerry to advance her a month's wages.

He was leaning morosely on the bar, talking to Dominic who was rolling a cigarette. 'You're a sly one,' he said when Anna appeared. 'Mr Marilyn dropped by to say you were ill. Funny how you kept it quiet that it was you who was harassin' the old boy.'

Anna turned crimson. 'I've apologised to him.'

'Sorry ain't good enough. I don't want you here; and don't go bleatin' to Mr Marilyn that I sacked you. I don't want him upset again, do you understand?'

'Of course I won't tell him.' She backed out of the pub.

Driven by the desperate need for money, Anna took her red Armani dress, the one she'd bought for the party, to a second-hand dress shop. They put it in the window at three hundred pounds; she'd get half, but only if it sold. Then she took Vince's gold bracelet, the one engraved with *Le Nouveau Monde*, to a jeweller. They gave her sixty pounds. She knew it was worth more but she was in no position to argue. Finally, she went into a second-hand electrical store and arranged for them to buy Charlie's word processor and expensive hi-fi equipment. On the way home, she stopped at the flower stall near the Electric cinema, where Charlie had once bought her daffodils, and purchased a dozen creamy roses for Mr Shufflebuck.

The pregnancy advice agency was an efficient, clinical operation with pleasant business-like staff. Although Anna's mind was made up to have a termination, the agency insisted that she saw a counsellor, which cost her another thirty pounds. The woman talked of guilt and regret, neither of which Anna wanted to hear about, before she agreed to refer her to the two doctors necessary to sign the special form. Throughout it all Anna was completely calm. It was as though she'd taken temporary possession of someone else's body, to the extent that when offered a cup of tea she said she took sugar, which she didn't.

By the late afternoon everything was arranged. Her appointment was for the following week, at a private nursing home in north London. She walked out of the agency feeling like a robot, which was exactly the unthinking being she needed to be. But everything conspired to remind her of the baby. Going home on the bus she sat next to a pregnant woman; each time they stopped they did so outside a branch of Mothercare; in the supermarket she found herself squeezed between a man with a toddler and a woman with twins; and as she walked along the pavement women with prams came at her from every direction.

Mr Shufflebuck was watering the pink geraniums outside his front door when Anna reached the house. She guessed he'd been to his *thé dansant* because he was wearing his colonial, tropical white linen suit and a panama hat. A pair of cream kid gloves were tucked into his top pocket.

'I shall fetch you from that tavern tonight.' He emphasised the word 'tavern'. 'It isn't nice for a young lady to walk home alone.'

'Thank you, but I'm . . . er . . . not working there any more.'

'I'm glad to hear it.' He bent to remove a dead leaf, his aged pixie face almost touching the fresh pink blooms.

Anna sat down on the basement steps. 'You've been very kind.'

He glanced up at her. 'Let me stay here.'

'Mr Shufflebuck, you can remain as long as I do, I promise. But I may have to sell the house. The bank want their money and I have only a week to come up with a solution.'

He gave her a shy smile. 'You may call me Mr Marilyn – all my friends do. You see, I once danced with Marilyn Monroe.'

Anna didn't reveal that she already knew, because that would have ruined his story. Instead, she gave him an encouraging smile.

'I don't know how I dared approach Miss Monroe,' he began, 'but the music started . . .'

'The *Chattanooga Choo-Choo*?'

He nodded. 'I looked at Miss Monroe and she smiled at me – that funny, sweet, girlish smile – and she gave me courage. She was wearing a red satin dress, like the one she wore in *Gentlemen Prefer Blondes*. She was a lovely girl, Miss Tobias, and I cried when I heard she'd passed away. Of course, by then I'd left Hollywood. Oh, I do miss it!' He glanced inside his basement home. 'One shouldn't live in the past, but it's very tempting when the present is so uncertain.'

'Don't worry, Mr . . . umm . . . Marilyn.' Anna found it strange to call him by a new name. 'I won't sell the house unless I'm forced to. I've had an idea to earn some money; I don't know why we didn't think of it before. If I rent out the top two floors that should almost cover the mortgage.'

'Tenants?' Mr Marilyn looked worried. 'Miss Elismore let rooms to students and they were very rowdy.'

'I shall let suites, not rooms.' Anna walked down the steps to him and placed her hand on his arm, the first time she'd intentionally touched him. 'I don't want to do it, but I have no option if I want to keep the house.'

'Then I suppose you'll have to,' he replied stiffly, and he withdrew into his flat.

Exasperated by his prickliness, Anna went upstairs.

She spent the weekend calculating the cost of renting out the top floors. Because the tenants would have to share two kitchens, she decided it was unfeasible to have more than four. Pacing the barren upstairs rooms, she divided them into four flatlets, two on each floor, each with a bedroom, a sitting-room and a bathroom or shower. To estimate the decorating, she gauged the price of paint at the nearest discount store and scanned the local paper for the cheapest carpets. In the back of the *Evening Standard* she checked the rents of comparable properties and made appointments to see two. One was luxurious at a thousand pounds a month, the other was a hell hole for two hundred. Anna priced her flatlets at five hundred a month on the first floor where the rooms were more spacious, and four hundred in the attic. If she added Mr Marilyn's rent, her mortgage deficit would be reduced to a hundred pounds a month. Once she'd spent that on lunch.

All this activity helped to keep her mind occupied, but she could not prevent the crushing emptiness which descended upon her when she fell into bed, late at night, and automatically reached out for Charlie. Then, she felt sliced by his desertion.

She tried not to think about the baby, telling herself that it was just another obstacle to be overcome. In a week it would all be behind her and she'd ring up Delia to arrange to meet for a drink, pretending not to have noticed that Delia hadn't contacted her. She pictured herself in their usual wine bar, full glass in hand, saying over-brightly, 'Charlie? Oh, he's in Australia. We're having a break. Me? Oh, I'm doing up the house. Such fun!' But just occasionally she forgot her resolution and laid her hands on her stomach and wondered if the baby was a boy or a girl.

She pre-empted Mr Hyde's next demand by asking to see him, and he fitted her in on the following afternoon, two days before her abortion. She dressed in her grey business suit, with her fair hair tucked neatly behind her ears. Mr Hyde had a new pair of spectacles, dark tortoiseshell-rimmed ones which made him look even more like a disgruntled owl.

'I've come up with a way to repay my loan,' she told him, laying her neatly-written calculations on his desk. 'I shall let out all the rooms which I'm not using. See here.' She tapped the page with her finger. 'The rent nearly covers the monthly payments and I shall earn the rest.' She gave him what she hoped was her most endearing smile. 'Under the terms of our loan, I need your permission to take in tenants.'

His glasses steamed up. 'It's out of the question, Miss Tobias. If we repossess it will be unpleasant enough to make you homeless, it would be a nightmare to make four other people homeless too.'

'If I rent out the rooms you won't need to repossess.'

'The DSS won't pay your mortgage interest if you let the house.'

'I don't plan to live on state benefits, I'm going to work.'

'What does Mr Blythely say?'

'He's gone back to Australia.' She took a deep breath. 'He's left me and he wants nothing more to do with the house.'

'Oh dear, I'm sorry. How awkward, Miss Tobias. Supposing you can't find a job?'

'I'll live in one room and let the rest of the ground floor.'

Mr Hyde hesitated, and for a moment she thought she'd won, but he shook his head. 'I'm sorry.'

Anna played her last, desperate card. 'House prices are falling. If you repossess mine in the state it's in you'll be lucky to get your money back – if you can find a buyer, which is unlikely. As you keep pointing out, I still have a sitting tenant. So you'll be responsible for a huge, semi-vacant, vandalised property. Squatters will move in and you'll have to go to court to get them out. That'll cost you money. When they go they'll leave the place in a mess and it'll be worth even less. My scheme is your best investment.'

'Miss Tobias, it's against bank policy.'

'Mr Hyde, if you give me this chance and I fall behind with my payments, I'll go without further argument. That I promise.' She held out her hand. 'Have we a deal?'

With a groan of defeat the loans manager shook her hand. 'Very well, but I shall review the situation constantly, so all your tenants must be on one month's notice – no longer.'

'You won't regret this.' Anna gave him a big smile. 'One more thing.'

'No! Nothing else! I absolutely refuse.'

'Will you come to tea at the house when it's ready? It really is very beautiful.'

Mr Hyde took off his spectacles. 'You're an unusual young woman, Miss Tobias. I should be delighted to accept.' He rose and gave her a small, neat bow.

On the last morning before her abortion, Anna felt sicker than ever. When she recovered enough to go out into the garden, she found Mr Marilyn hovering outside. 'You must see a doctor,' he told her firmly. 'I shall phone one immediately.'

'I'm not ill, I'm . . . pregnant.'

'You're going to have a baby?' He smiled hesitantly. 'How exciting! Congratulations!'

Anna wished she'd kept silent. 'I'm not . . . keeping it,' she said.

'You're not going to . . . get rid of it?'

'Mr Marilyn, Charlie's left me, I'm out of work, and I can't face bringing up a child on my own. And I don't want to. I don't want a baby.'

'I'll help you.'

'Don't! Please! I've made up my mind. I should never have said anything to you. By tomorrow it'll all be over, and I can start the rest of my life.' She went into the house and remained there all day so as not to have to face him.

That evening she discovered his rent envelope pushed under the front door. Inside were twenty-five pounds. She took it down to the basement and knocked on his front door.

He unlocked it slowly. 'Yes, Miss Tobias?'

'You've paid me five pounds too much.'

'I did it on purpose.'

'Mr Marilyn, it's very kind of you, but I'll still have to let the house.'

'I didn't do it for the house, I did it for the baby.'

A lump formed in her throat. 'I can't keep the baby,' she almost screamed at him. 'Don't you understand? I couldn't cope, not at the moment.' She pushed the extra five pounds into his hand and ran back up the stairs, away from his sorrowful eyes.

In the morning she sensed him peering through his net curtains as she left the house, clutching her overnight bag.

It was the rush hour and the tube from Holland Park was packed. Anna couldn't find a seat and had to strap-hang with her face squashed against a man's shoulder. It was hot and she felt nauseous, but gritted her teeth. At Oxford Circus she had to change trains. As she stepped on to the escalator she was followed by a young mother struggling with a baby in a pushchair.

'Can I help?' asked Anna, not looking at the baby.

'That's very kind. It's so difficult travelling with a child.'

Anna steadied the pushchair until they were safely at the bottom, then she hurried away before the mother could thank her.

In north London she had a short walk from the station to the clinic. She passed a small park where a boy was playing with a puppy, rolling a ball along the grass for the little dog to chase. Anna stopped to watch. It was a glorious May morning, fresh and green and full of hope. Last night's dew still clung to the daisies beneath the flowering cherry trees. When the ball rolled in among the fallen blossom, the puppy chased it, scattering the pink petals as if they were confetti.

If it had been raining everything would have been different.

There'd have been no boy, no puppy, no sparkling dew or fluttering blossom. Anna would have hurried past the park without a glance, head bent against the drizzle, and rushed up the steps of the clinic where even now the receptionist was waiting to book her in. But the beauty of that day changed everything. She slid her hand under her T-shirt and stroked her stomach. She didn't want a baby, not at the moment – and she didn't want Charlie's baby ever – but she couldn't bring herself to violate such a day. She began to understand what the counsellor had meant by regret and knew that for the rest of her life every glorious May morning would possess a secret sadness.

She walked back to the station. 'I haven't changed my mind, bump.' She patted her stomach. 'I'm just postponing it, that's all.' But even as she spoke, she knew it wasn't true.

18

MR MARILYN WAS ecstatic when Anna told him that she hadn't gone through with the abortion. He rushed up to the Notting Hill public library and borrowed every baby book he could find.

'You're meant to rest,' he wailed when he discovered Anna carrying a dozen rolls of lining paper up to the attic. 'It says so.' He read aloud: 'A mother should be careful not to strain herself.'

She replied over the banisters. 'Mr Marilyn, I have to decorate the rooms.'

'Baby won't like it.'

'Baby will prefer it to being homeless.' She went on up to the attic and set about reading the instructions which accompanied the rolls. It took her all morning and many botched attempts to line one wall, by which time she was exhausted and covered in glue, but she persevered – she had no alternative – and by the end of that week she'd lined the whole attic.

Now that Anna had decided to keep the baby, she minded her nausea less because there was a point to it. Nevertheless, she had to push herself to rise early and scour the market for bargains, swaying as the crowds jostled her and hoping she wouldn't faint or be sick, or both. On a hardware stall she found a job lot of pale lemon paint. It wasn't a shade she'd have chosen, but at half-price she couldn't afford to be fussy. On another stall she bought a roller. To save money she dispensed with purchasing the handle and used the wooden pole from the garden rake. On the way home she passed a skip. In it were some aluminium steps. They were paint-splattered but perfectly usable, and she dragged them back to Ladbroke Hill.

That afternoon she pulled on her glue-encrusted jeans and T-shirt, scraped her hair up under an old baseball cap and started to paint. Gagging on the smell, she pushed the roller backwards and forwards across the ceiling. As she worked she thought of Charlie and Delia and Russell; of Marinecover, Gordon, Isaac, and of all the people who had meant so much to her. Once, she wouldn't have believed she could survive without them. Yet, she had.

At teatime Mr Marilyn appeared, carrying a beautifully laid tray, with a cup of Earl Grey tea, an exquisitely cut cress sandwich, and a multi-vitamin pill on its own small saucer.

'Did you remember to phone your doctor?' he asked, fussing around her.

'Yes, but he won't see me, he only has private patients and I am no longer covered by Marinecover's health insurance.'

'But you must have a doctor.'

'I'll register with a National Health one.' She sank to the floor and rested her aching back against the wall.

Mr Marilyn watched her eat the sandwich and drink the tea. 'You ought to stop painting now,' he said, distressed to see her so tired.

'I will, when I've finished the ceiling.' She picked up the roller.

'But the baby book says . . .'

'Damn the baby book! I have to earn a living.'

He hurried downstairs, shaking his head.

She called after him. 'I'm sorry, I know you mean well.'

He didn't reply and she was too weary to pursue him.

By nightfall Anna was so exhausted that she could barely walk. With no energy to cook she ate some cereal and fell into bed. In the morning she bullied herself back to work, almost as though she were two people, the master and the slave, the mind giving orders to the reluctant body. That evening she finished the first bedroom. Even Mr Marilyn grudgingly admired her handiwork.

To escape his chivvying, Anna took a morning off decorating to sign on with a nearby National Health doctor, a pleasant but overworked Scotsman who was visibly relieved when she elected to have all her check-ups at the hospital. Returning home she found a typed envelope among the junk mail on the hall floor. Fearing another unpaid and unpayable bill she sat down to open it, but to her delight she found a cheque: her red Armani dress had been sold. With a whoop of excitement she ran downstairs to share her good news with Mr Marilyn.

The prospect of telling her mother about the baby had filled

Anna with apprehension, not because she was ashamed to be pregnant but because she dreaded her mother's disappointment. It wasn't just the baby she'd have to disclose but the whole spiral of failure: no job, no Charlie, no money. She couldn't forget her mother, ashen with anxiety as the hours ticked by when her father, who always caught the same train home, had not returned. Then the relief when they'd heard the footsteps on the path, followed by a tentative ring on the bell. Anna could still picture her mother, hurrying out of the cramped little kitchen to the rather dark front door, her mouth already open to berate him for being late, for going out without a coat, for forgetting his key yet again, for worrying them. Only now, years later, Anna understood that her mother's nagging was her way of showing that she cared. The trouble was, they weren't her father's footsteps. It was two policewomen come to tell them that her father was dead.

To forestall a visit from her mother and to stop her from telephoning Marinecover, Anna sent her a card to say that she would be away on business for a few weeks, after which the Notting Hill telephone exchange was to be renewed so her line might be out of order. She didn't like to tell such blatant lies, but she could think of no other excuse for her silence.

There were many days when Anna spoke to no one except Mr Marilyn. Her world belonged to the attic and the radio, and she became so involved in the news items that they became her reality. The Chinese students in Tiananmen Square existed in her attic. She heard their voices, listened to their protest, and cried for them as the tanks rolled in. She knew the temperature in Washington, the share prices on Wall Street, and if Milan's Malpensa airport was closed by fog. She heard the traffic updates and knew far better than when she'd worked – when it had been relevant – which streets were blocked and which trains were cancelled. And yet, for the two hundred guests who'd drunk her champagne and danced at her house-warming party, she no longer existed.

She was particularly hurt by Delia's silence. 'She was my closest friend,' she confided to Mr Marilyn one Sunday morning. 'She must know I'm here, on my own. I can't believe she's still offended because I shouted at her.'

'Perhaps she's tried to telephone. If she can't get through, she may think you've gone to Australia.'

'Maybe you're right.' Anna picked up her purse and hurried down the road to the call box and tapped out the familiar number.

'Hi there,' Delia answered in a brisk tone.

'Dee, it's me, Anna. I'm afraid I can't talk for long because I'm in a public phone box, but I wanted to know how you are.'

'Great, but busy. I've tried to call you but you're always out.'

Anna thought of her telephone which had been disconnected for nearly a month. 'When?'

'Last week, I think, but I can't remember. You know what it's like, life's so busy. What are you up to?'

She'd planned to confide in Delia about the baby, but now she decided not to, at least not yet. 'I haven't been very well and things aren't easy, but I'd love to see you. Why don't you come over?'

'To the house?' Delia didn't sound very enthusiastic. 'I'll try, Anna. Look, I must dash, Russell's just arrived. Call me soon and let's lunch.'

Anna replaced the receiver. Delia hadn't even asked her why she was in a phone box.

On her return to the house, she told Mr Marilyn, 'I don't think I'm very interesting to Delia any more now that I'm not part of her world.'

She tried to pretend that she didn't mind, but she did, and several days later she telephoned again, telling herself that perhaps she'd been over-sensitive. This time Delia was out, so she left her name. She heard nothing.

Decorating the first floor took longer than the attic because the rooms were bigger and the ceilings were higher. Mr Marilyn continued to bring Anna her daily cup of Earl Grey tea and her vitamin pill and, when they knew each other better, he told her of his childhood.

'I was born in Soho,' he said. 'An only child; my father died when I was a baby, I was brought up alone by Mother. She made clothes for the theatrical productions, beautiful clothes, chiffon dresses with pearl-encrusted headbands and crushed velvet coats with great, draped sleeves. When I grew tall enough to carry the dresses without dragging them in the mud, Mother allowed me to deliver them to the theatres. Sometimes the doormen let me in to watch a dress rehearsal. That's when I fell in love with the theatre, Miss Tobias.'

'Mr Marilyn, I wish you'd call me Anna.'
'My mother's name was Anna.'
'Then I quite understand if you'd rather not.'
'No,' he said very emphatically, 'I'd be pleased to call you Anna.'
One morning Mr Marilyn didn't appear and, worried in case he was ill, Anna went down to look for him. She found him in the basement, watering his busy lizzies. 'You're mother rang this morning,' he said, keeping his back to Anna. 'She knows you've lost your job.'
'Did you tell her about the baby?'
He nodded miserably. 'I'm sorry, I didn't realise you hadn't told her and when she asked how you were, I confessed that I was worried in case you were overdoing things. Then she started to question me.'
Anna gave him a quick hug. 'Don't worry, I'd have had to tell her sooner or later.' She started back up the steps, calling, 'When Mother arrives she'll find me on the first floor.'
'She didn't say she was coming.'
'She'll be here, I know my mother.'
Anna was painting a skirting-board when she heard her mother's footsteps on the stairs.
'I'm in here,' she called out.
Her mother stepped into the room. She wore a smart linen dress, which Anna recognised as formerly belonging to Jacynthia Peabody, and her silver-blonde hair was swept up into a velvet bow. 'Why didn't you tell me about the baby?' she asked in a small, hurt voice.
Anna lowered her paint brush. 'I didn't want to worry you.'
'But I'm your mother, the baby will be my grandchild.'
'I'm sorry.' Anna could see that she'd made a bad mistake and she felt very guilty. 'I did what I thought was best.'
'I wouldn't even know now if Tom hadn't let slip about Charlie leaving,' her mother went on. 'Of course, Tom refused to tell me any more but I sensed something was wrong so I phoned you at work and . . . well . . . Why did you give me that silly story about a business trip?'
'Because of . . . Father,' Anna said reluctantly. 'If I'd told you I'd been made redundant and had no money you'd have been so anxious, so I decided to wait until I found other work. Then I

discovered I was pregnant and Charlie left and . . . well . . . at first I wasn't planning to keep the baby, so what was the point of distressing you? I wasn't trying to exclude you, Mum, honestly.' Anna was almost in tears from guilt.

'Oh, now I've upset you too. Don't cry, Anna, please. You know, it might have been more logical to have an abortion. Babies are hard work. That peculiar old man in your basement told me it's due in November. Have you seen a good doctor? Are you booked in to a hospital?'

'Yes, and Mr Marilyn makes sure I eat the correct vitamins and do the right things. He may be odd, but he's very kind.'

Her mother glanced around the bare room. 'I'm so sorry about Charlie, I hate to see you hurt. I hope he's sending you regular money.'

'He thinks I've got rid of it.'

'But, darling, he must support the child.'

'No, Mum, I want nothing to do with him. I'd rather survive on my own than see that man again.'

'Anna, you must be sensible. Charlie's parents may not be rich, but they're comfortable and they could set up a trust for the child, whereas I can only help when I can, and I can't afford much.'

'Mum, I'll manage.'

Her mother sighed. 'You look so tired, darling. You're always welcome to move in with us if things become too difficult. I'd offer to come here and look after you, but Granny needs me.'

Anna stumbled to her feet and hugged her mother. 'Thanks for coming, thanks for offering the money, I'm so sorry I hurt your feelings.'

Gently, her mother eased her away and flicked dry specks of lemon from her dress. 'You're covering me in paint, darling.'

'Sorry.' Anna jumped back. 'Come down and I'll make you some tea. You must be tired after your drive.'

They started down the stairs and on the landing her mother said, 'Do you want me to tell Granny Tobias? I think I'll have to, but not this evening. I'd like a bit of time to think about it by myself.' She squeezed Anna's hand. 'It's at times like this I desperately miss Jeffrey.'

'To share the burden of your daughter's problems?' asked Anna, ruefully.

‘Oh, no, to share the joy.’ Her mother’s face lit up. ‘After all, I’m going to be a grandmother again.’

Very carefully, so as not to cover her in dried paint, Anna kissed her mother on the cheek.

19

ON A STIFLING weekend in August, Anna finished painting the house and on the following Monday, she invited Mr Hyde from East Metro to tea. That morning she had received a letter from a solicitor in Melbourne stating that Charlie wished to write over to her his interest in the house.

Mr Hyde arrived with a similar letter. 'Mr Blythely is most irresponsible,' he spluttered angrily as she led him through the hall. 'He wouldn't be gifting you anything, Miss Tobias, just his share of the debt. That's what you'd be agreeing to take on.'

'But since you'll never get a penny out of Charlie and I'm bearing all the expenses, I want the house in my name alone.' Anna ushered him into the sunlit drawing-room.

By the time Mr Hyde left, she'd persuaded him to advance her a further thousand pounds to cover the cheapest carpet she could find.

For furniture, Anna scanned the 'For Sale' column in the local paper and, with fifty pounds sent by her mother and much haggling, she acquired four beds and four sofas from a bankrupt hotel, and four gruesome but useful claw-footed tables from a refurbished funeral parlour. When the items were delivered, she stuck out her stomach to emphasise her pregnancy and the driver and his mate took pity on her and carried the furniture upstairs. Between the ground floor and the attic she let drop that her boyfriend had left her, so that when she bravely offered them a tip they handed it back, saying, 'Keep it luv, you're going to need it.'

Two elderly sisters, friends of Mr Marilyn, who'd once run a boarding-house in Hove, sold her a roll of blue and white ticking material for fifty pence a yard. The jolly, broad stripes reminded Anna of a canopy surrounding an Edwardian bathing hut. When her mother came to visit, she brought Granny Tobias's ancient, manual sewing machine and Anna spent all week making curtains, feeding the stiff material under the needle.

In the first half of her pregnancy she'd put on little weight compared to the other women she met during her monthly check-ups, but at six months she ballooned – at least she felt that way. Unable to fit into her shorts, even with the zip undone and the waist tied with string, she resorted to long, baggy T-shirts or Roz's old maternity dresses in faded floral prints which made her look like an inhabitant of a Victorian workhouse.

It was one of the hottest summers that Anna could recall, and she suffered. By day the streets were stifling and pedestrians fought to walk in the shade, the leaves barely moved and the air was laden with petrol fumes; a dirty yellow haze hung over the roof-tops of Portobello. At night she was often too hot and uncomfortable to sleep, and she took to wandering around the darkened streets. Where once she would have been afraid of being mugged, now she had the bravado of someone with little to lose. When a drunk stopped and demanded money, she informed him, 'I'm broke too,' and walked away.

On these nightly ramblings she sometimes thought of Charlie with a mixture of rage and bitterness, as she pictured him in the safety of his parents' home. One evening she passed the spot where he'd suggested that they steal a car. She remembered arguing that they weren't that desperate, and she wondered how much more desperate she would have to be before she would commit a crime, and what tipped people into taking such an irreversible step.

Another night she met Dominic meandering down the Portobello Road, peering into the shuttered antique shops.

'Hi, there,' he said, then he noticed her bulging waistline and blushed. 'Good heavens!'

'It's only a baby.' She was surprised how pleased she was to see him.

He stepped in to walk beside her, protectively taking her arm so that he was on the gutter side. 'Gerry was wrong to sack you,' he said. 'If Mr Marilyn had still disliked you, he wouldn't have come to the pub to say you were ill.'

Anna stopped dead. 'Dominic, if you thought that, why didn't you speak up for me?'

'Oh, I never get involved in other people's lives.'

'That's pathetic!' Anna stepped away from him. 'You have to stand up for what's right.'

'I never fight. I'm a musician, a dreamer, a poet.'

'Not so unworldly that you refused my five pounds!'

For a moment Dominic looked nonplussed, then he replied, 'If you didn't want me to have the money, you shouldn't have offered it to me.'

'You shouldn't have accepted it, no normal person would have.' She walked away from him.

He caught up with her. 'That's what I mean, Anna, I'm not like others, I'm not of this world.'

She marched on, ignoring him. He followed, and when they reached the house, he gasped. 'Do you live *here*? Oh, I've always loved this house.' He gazed in wonder at the white façade which gleamed ghostly against the indigo sky. 'Anna!' He reached for her hand. 'May I come in, may I live here for the rest of my life?'

Anna couldn't be angry with someone who loved Ladbroke Hill. 'No,' she replied, 'but you can come back tomorrow and help me hang curtains.'

To her surprise Dominic arrived punctually next morning and when not talking of his inner being, he was quick and practical. Over the following days, he put up the curtain poles, hung the curtains, and adapted the electricity to give each flatlet a separate system.

Before Anna could advertise the house, she had to pay the outstanding telephone bill. With nothing left to sell, she turned reluctantly to Roz, who lent her three hundred pounds. From the moment that the newspapers hit the streets her phone didn't stop ringing. The first applicant, a preppy American trainee banker, arrived at lunchtime. He was a blond giant, with a contented babyish face and an ingenuous smile.

'Hi there, I'm Macdonald Bradley.' He crunched Anna's fingers in his enormous hand.

She stepped back. 'Er . . . do come in.'

He charged past her into the hall, saying, 'My grandpa and grandma have a place like this out on Long Island. Is it a family home or did you buy it to rent out?'

'Neither,' she replied stiffly, leading the way upstairs.

He didn't seem to notice that Anna was not forthcoming and he followed happily, talking so fast that she could scarcely catch his words. 'I'm over here for a year . . . always wanted to live in London, it's so cute . . . couldn't stay here for ever, I'd miss home, but I guess in a year I should know the place pretty well – determined to meet British people, learn the culture, expand my experience.'

Anna showed him the master bedroom, renamed the Master Flat. He opened all the cupboards one by one, pushing his large head inside like a sniffer dog seeking drugs. 'When was the place painted?' he asked.

'Just now.' Anna bristled. 'Can't you tell?'

He smiled, unaware of her anger. 'Are the sheets cotton? I only like cotton.'

Deciding that any other tenant would be preferable, Anna said, 'You provide your own linen, plates and cutlery, so I think it won't be worth your while, Mr Bradley.'

'Call me Mac!' He ran his finger along the surface of the table to check for dust.

'It's very noisy at the weekends,' Anna went on. 'There's a street market directly below.'

'Good. I like people.'

'It's a high-crime area. You must have read of the arrests at the carnival this year.'

'I'm accustomed to New York.'

'You have to share the kitchen with the other first-floor tenant, and there will only be a pay phone.'

'I eat out and I'll have my own mobile.' A guileless smile dimpled his chubby cheeks. 'I appreciate you warning me of the drawbacks.'

Anna was about to spell out clearly that she didn't want him in her house when the doorbell rang. She hurried down to find a tall, pale man in a grey suit standing to attention on her top step. He was Colin from the Ministry of Defence, the ideal tenant, who had a wife in the country and would be away every weekend.

As Anna ushered him up the stairs, the American came out of the Master Flat. 'Macdonald Bradley.' He shook Colin by the hand. 'I'll be living here too.'

Anna was furious but she could hardly order him off the premises or Colin would think her a harridan. 'Call me later, Mr Bradley,' she said crisply.

'No need, my mind's made up.' He handed her a wodge of twenty-pound notes. 'Here's a month's rent in advance, the deposit, and my boss as my reference – just as you told me when I called. I'll move in on Saturday morning. You can give me my receipt then.' He pounded down the stairs, whilst Anna hovered between throwing his money after him and taking it, triumphantly, to Mr Hyde.

'Americans are very decisive, aren't they?' said Colin in a soft voice.

Anna nodded. She'd been outmanoeuvred by a big baby.

Colin took one of the attic flatlets and a very earnest Polish law graduate named Grażyna rented the other. She looked barely out of school, with short brown hair and a meek childlike figure, although she informed an astonished Anna that she was nearly thirty. Eight further prospective tenants viewed the remaining first-floor flatlet, but they all turned it down because they didn't want to share a kitchen. By ten o'clock Anna was worn out; her ankles were swollen and her back ached. She switched on the answering machine, poured herself a mug of milk and flopped into an armchair. No sooner had she sat down than a woman shouted through the letterbox, 'Hello!'

In her exhausted state Anna assumed it was Delia, and she staggered to the front door, pleased to think that she hadn't been mistaken about their friendship, but when she opened it she found a statuesque red-head, who seemed vaguely familiar, hopping up and down like an excited bird. Her face was hawkish, with irregular features, a wild burst of freckles and very fine orange hair whose ends curled like singed tobacco. Her clothes were an operatic costume: a swirling burgundy dress and a black shawl draped over one shoulder, the end of it trailing carelessly on the ground.

'I'm Louise,' she said. 'I phoned earlier. Sorry I'm late.'

'You'll have to come back tomorrow.' Anna was barely able to stand up.

'Oh please, it's not my fault, I left the van lights on and the battery went flat.' Louise waved towards a bright purple van which was blocking Anna's drive. 'You know how it is when you're in a hurry, something always goes wrong, but I'm not *that* late. I mean, it is only ten o'clock.'

'I'm too tired.' Anna leaned against the wall.

'Let me in, I'll look quickly, I promise.' Louise stepped past her into the hall. 'We've met before.' She examined Anna in the electric light. 'God knows where, I have a memory like a sieve, I'm probably developing Alzheimer's but I don't know it yet. How young can you get it?'

'I've no idea,' wailed Anna, wishing that Louise would stop babbling.

'Did we meet at art school? Yes, that's right. The Royal College? No? Then was it rep? Did you act?'

'I can't act and I can't draw.' Almost in tears Anna sank down on to the bottom stair. 'If you want to see the flatlet, it's on the first floor, to the left, but I can't walk upstairs again.'

'Don't worry.' Louise bounded up the stairs, the swirling, uneven hem of her dress catching between her long legs. She clattered through the rooms, then shouted over the banisters. 'Who do I share the kitchen with?'

'An American banker.'

'Fanciable?'

'Heavens no! Look, do you want the room? Because if not I have to go to bed.'

'I'll take it.' Louise came down the stairs two at a time. When she saw Anna slumped on the stairs she said, 'Hey, you're very pregnant.'

'Why the hell do you think I'm so exhausted?'

Louise flushed. 'I'm sorry to have come so late but I'm desperate. I bought a flat two years ago, but the interest rate is now so high that I can't afford my mortgage and my flat is being repossessed on Monday. Of course, I should have found somewhere else to live earlier but I always do everything at the last minute. I've looked at ten places today, all contestants for the Slum of the Year Award. I know you're thinking – why didn't I come to you first? Well, the truth is that I didn't want to share a kitchen because I'm a vegetarian and I'd hate to see meat in my fridge, but now I've seen your house I'd like to move in.' She paused. 'Could you reduce the rent?'

Anna was too weary to be affronted, she merely shook her head. 'I'm letting this place to stave off eviction and I need every penny I can make – not just for me, for the baby.'

Louise held up her hand. 'Forget I said it. I'm sorry, I should never have asked you.' She reached down and took Anna by the arm. 'Let me help you up, let me make you a cup of tea. God, I feel so crass having asked you for a discount. Look at you, pregnant and destitute.'

'Shut up!' Anna shouted, half-irritated, half-laughing.

'I'm trying to make you feel better.'

'By reminding me how bad things are?'

'You're right. I'm tactless, I've always been that way. Come on, where's that tea?'

Louise settled Anna into an armchair and bustled into the kitchen. A few minutes later she emerged with a pot of tea and a plate of cress sandwiches, almost as exquisite as Mr Marilyn made them.

'Now I know where I've seen you,' Anna told her. 'You have a clothes stall in the market.'

'I called your boyfriend an ignorant arsehole. Does that mean I can't move in?'

'He was an arsehole, but I didn't know it then.'

They looked at each other and laughed, and Anna was very glad that she hadn't sent Louise away. In spite of her fondness for Mr Marilyn she'd missed the company of her own generation and of other women.

The tenants moved in on Saturday. Mac had a set of matching luggage, Colin delivered five grey suits, Grażyna had one old leather suitcase. They met each other in the hall and on the stairs and shook hands awkwardly – except for Louise, who rushed in, shouted 'Hello', dumped an armful of clothes in her room, collected a key, and raced back to the market: Saturday was her busiest day.

It seemed strange to Anna to have people in her house, so that she could no longer pad half-clothed through the bare rooms, or watch the to and fro in the market from the attic windows. When noises happened they weren't her noises, when the phone rang on the first-floor landing it wasn't for her.

In the late afternoon there was a sharp tap on her door and she opened it to find Grażyna outside, white with anger, 'I cannot live in a noisy house,' she complained in her stiff English, pointing at Macdonald Bradley's room from which the booming voice of a football commentator was clearly audible in spite of his door being closed. 'I have to work. I won a scholarship to study international law in London and I owe it to those who selected me.'

'I'll ask him to turn it down,' said Anna, hoping there wasn't going to be an argument already. She went upstairs, followed by Grażyna, and tapped on the American's door. There was no answer. She was about to knock harder when she heard the front door open and Macdonald Bradley came in carrying a bottle of champagne and a six-pack of beer.

He smiled when he saw Anna and Grażyna outside his door. 'Can I help?'

'You must stop that noise,' snapped Grażyna.

He turned bright pink.

'It's disturbing my other tenants,' Anna explained. 'Can you lower the volume, please?'

'Sure. No problem.' He started up the stairs.

'He has to switch it off completely.' Grażyna clenched her fists. 'I must concentrate.'

'That's unreasonable.' Anna wondered how she could have mistaken Grażyna for meek. 'Mr Bradley has a right to watch his television. This is not a noisy house, but it is not a morgue either.' She marched downstairs, pushing past the American, and went into her flat, closing the door firmly behind her.

Upstairs there was silence. Anna expected Grażyna to announce that she was leaving and demand her money back, and since Anna had no way of repaying it, she avoided the issue by going out. She went down to Ceres to buy some fresh, crunchy bread, then wandered back through the market, hoping that peace would have prevailed by the time she reached home. Walking back up the lane she saw Louise trying to sell a sumptuous black velvet cape to a hesitating German woman.

Without a flicker of recognition to Louise, Anna crossed to the stall. 'This is nice,' she said, stroking the black velvet. 'How much is it?'

'Eighty,' Louise replied, straight-faced. 'It was a hundred but I've just reduced it.'

Anna turned to the German woman. 'If you're not going to buy it I'd like to try it on.'

'No! I buy.' The German scuffled in her hand-bag and brought out her purse.

Whilst the woman paid Louise, Anna pretended to consider the other clothes hanging from a rail beside the stall. They were mainly from the Twenties or Thirties, or of that style, and made of crushed velvet or crêpe de Chine, with drop waists and elaborate cuffs. At Louise's end of the table there was a row of antique brocade or beaded evening bags and a dozen pairs of buckled satin shoes with sculpted heels. The rest of the stall sold prints of old London.

When the German walked away Louise hissed at Anna, 'You were brilliant. Here's five pounds' commission.'

'No! I did it for fun.'

'Then we'll spend it on a drink. I'll pack up.' Louise lifted the clothes straight on to a rail in the back of the purple van which was parked nearby. Then she opened a large, battered leather suitcase and slotted the bags into it. 'The prints belong to Lionel. He lets me share his stall because he likes to bet on horses and needs someone to mind the shop,' Louise explained as she packed. 'I knew his daughter Karen at art school. She used to sell clothes here but she moved to New York and now she deals in old costume jewellery in a market on the Upper West Side. Lionel says she's doing well, which is a relief because if she comes back I'll be out of a pitch. You wouldn't believe how hard it is to rent space in the market. Most stall-holders have been here for years, so it was my good luck to come by at the right time.' Louise closed the suitcase and started to roll the shoes in strips of material, each one separate so that the satin did not scuff.

A grey-haired man with a neat goatee beard came striding up to the stall. 'I had two out of three in the triple forecast but the last damned horse got stuck in the starting stalls,' he lamented to Louise. Then he looked at Anna, smiled and said, 'Hello, Blondie, when's the baby due?'

Anna blushed. 'November.'

'Her name's Anna not Blondie, you chauvinist!' Louise elbowed him in the ribs. 'We're off to the pub. Coming?'

Lionel shook his head. 'It's the wife's birthday.'

Anna and Louise walked down the road to the nearest pub. It was crowded and the only spare table was in a corner near the window. 'Grab it,' said Louise, pushing her way towards the bar.

Anna sat down, with her bag of French bread on her lap. She looked around at all the people talking and laughing and it seemed incredible that this existed within sight of the house where she had lived in solitude and isolation.

A man touched her arm and she jumped with surprise.

'Haven't seen you in here before,' he said with a cheery smile.

'I . . . er . . . haven't been.' She moved the bread off her lap.

His eyes fell to her thickening waist and he turned scarlet.

Louise interrupted them with two long glasses of ice-cold white wine and soda water, and the man fled. 'Really, Anna! Picking men up in your condition!' she joked.

Anna giggled. 'He was so embarrassed.' She paused. 'Thanks for bringing me here. I haven't been out since Charlie left. I've been living in an oasis, me and the baby, us against the world, I dread to think how I'll get on when . . . if . . . I ever meet another man. I won't know what to say or do.'

Louise rested her elbows on their round table. 'I know what you mean. Freddie and I lived together for five years, we even worked for the same graphic design studio, but when I gave up my job to deal in antique clothes, which till then had been just a hobby, everything changed. Freddie liked to talk about his work in the studio but I was no longer interested; he hated the market and the fact that I was busy on Saturdays, and one evening he told me he'd had enough.'

'Were you upset?'

'Oh yes, I was devastated. I couldn't think straight. That's when I bought the flat – the one which was repossessed. It was expensive even at the beginning, but I had to move out of Freddie's house, so I went ahead. I don't blame Freddie, he was just as miserable, he'd lost the woman he'd loved because I'd changed. Or rather, I had in his eyes. Now I go out with a friend of Lionel's. Robert's a picture-restorer and he spends half his time in Italy, so we only meet every month or so. He's fun, he's ten years younger than me, and there are no expectations, no heartache. I don't want more, not at the moment, not so soon after Freddie.' Louise jumped up. 'Let's have another drink.'

Anna shook her head. 'Babies and alcohol don't mix.'

'Then I'll drive you home.'

'Seeing the picture-restorer tonight?'

Louise giggled and nodded. Then she linked her arm through Anna's, and they went out into the gloaming.

20

SIX WEEKS BEFORE the baby was due Anna attended her first antenatal class, where a graphic description of the birth left her more apprehensive than ever. Of the thirty women in her class, half brought their partners; at least she wasn't the only one on her own.

Arriving home she found Macdonald Bradley pacing the hall. 'The water pressure in my shower is not as forceful as it could be and I've discovered the reason,' he told her triumphantly. 'The unit should have a custom-made triple head, not a production-line single.'

Anna had no intention of explaining about Xavier and the unpaid bill. 'I know,' she replied, 'but the triples cost twenty times as much.'

'But a triple is the correct head.'

'I can't afford it. Does the shower work?'

'Yes, but . . .'

'Then please stop fussing! If you don't like my house, move out.' She went into her room and closed the door.

A moment later Louise appeared. 'What have you said to Big Mac, he slunk upstairs with his tail between his legs?'

'Big Mac! That's a good name.' Anna sank on to her bed. 'I told him to stop fussing or get out. Yesterday he complained about the cold, last week he wanted the heating on all night, and today it's the damned water pressure.'

Louise sat down beside her. 'You look exhausted. I'm going to buy a pizza. Share it with me?'

'I won't be good company. I feel fat, boring and clumsy.' Anna picked at her dress, one of Roz's faded cotton smocks. 'Look at my swollen ankles, even my fingers are swollen, surely God could have devised a better method of reproduction than this.'

Louise chuckled, and left. She returned after a short while, carrying a giant pizza which they ate, sitting out on the balcony, where the smell of autumn was encroaching on the last of the summer.

After that occasion they frequently ate together, sitting at the long refectory table in Anna's drawing-room, and when the evenings grew colder they lit the fire. It made the room cosy and welcoming and they lingered late, their shadows leaping up the walls as they talked. They took it in turns to cook. Louise was vegetarian. Always in a rush, she bought her meals from Marks and Spencer and decanted them into her own dishes. When it was Anna's night to cook, she went down to the market early and purchased the least expensive vegetables, making two casseroles, one with meat and one without. With a hand resting on her stomach, bouncing up and down as the baby kicked, she'd spend all afternoon waddling around the kitchen. She'd never liked cooking before because she never had enough time, but now she enjoyed experimenting with spices and herbs. Often they invited guests, such as Mr Marilyn, Lionel and his wife, Dominic, and occasionally Grażyna, though she usually preferred to work. The only person they never included was Big Mac.

Roz came to stay for a night, and slept on the sofabed. She brought bags of baby clothes, a cot and a pram, which Mr Marilyn stored in his flat against bad luck. Anna hadn't seen Roz since May, since the morning she'd left Lower Gossip to tell Charlie she was pregnant, which seemed like a lifetime away. They had a great deal to catch up on.

A week before the baby was due, Anna had a sudden urge to spring-clean. She wiped the shelves in the kitchen, scrubbed the cooker, washed the floor, and threw all the curtains into the washing machine.

Just as she finished, Roz telephoned. 'The ambulances are on go-slow. What are you going to do?' she asked in her bossy headgirl voice.

Anna yawned. 'I didn't know anything about it.'

'For goodness' sake! Don't you listen to the news?'

'Oh, Roz, don't be cross. You know what it's like when you're very pregnant, nothing enters your cocoon.'

'But this affects you. How are you going to get to the hospital if you have no car, no ambulance and, I hate to say, no husband?'

Anna thought for a minute. 'I suppose I'll have to ask Louise.' She didn't want to trouble Louise, who worked long hours in her various markets scattered around London, but she couldn't think of anyone else. To her relief, Louise seemed pleased.

'Of course I'll take you,' she said. 'I'll stay with you for the birth as well, if you like. I've never seen a baby born. Are you scared, Anna? I would be.'

'Petrified.' Anna gave a nervous giggle. 'But I'm also excited.'

Her first twinge came on a freezing November afternoon, three days before the baby was due. Apprehensive because Louise was out, Anna hovered beside her packed suitcase, wondering whether to telephone the hospital but not wanting to be labelled an alarmist. The next twinge didn't happen for two hours, by which time she'd begun to wonder if she'd imagined the first, but when Louise came home they had increased to hourly contractions. At midnight they were no more frequent, so Anna lay down on her bed, with Louise on the sofa nearby, the van keys ready.

'I wonder what babies think of the world when they first arrive?' said Anna, laying her hands on her stomach. 'I wish I could remember what I thought. It must be very frightening to be suddenly thrust among lights and people and noise. I'm sure they must wish they were back inside.'

'You do say the funniest things,' Louise murmured sleepily.

By three o'clock the contractions were every fifteen minutes and Anna telephoned the hospital. Then she woke Louise who shot to her feet, crying, 'Oh God! Is the baby here?'

'No, but it will be soon.'

With Anna gritting her teeth against the contractions, and both of them giggling from nerves, they staggered out into the freezing night. As their feet crunched across the gravel to the van, Mr Marilyn came running up from his basement. 'Is it time?' he asked.

'Not yet, but soon.' Anna gripped Louise's hand to stop herself from crying out as she climbed up into the van.

It was a nightmare drive for Anna as the old van jolted along the streets. She was terrified that the baby would be born in the van; Louise was equally frightened at the prospect of having to deliver it. Finally they reached the hospital and hands helped her down, along the brightly-lit corridor to the maternity unit.

Half an hour later she was lying on a bed in the labour room, dressed in a white cotton gown, with her hair scraped back, and the midwife saying, 'Oh, you've still got a while to go. I'll send in your friend to keep you company.' She opened the door and beckoned to Louise.

'Mr Marilyn's outside,' said Louise, pulling up a chair. 'I told the nurses he is the baby's father.'

'You beast!' Anna started to laugh, but her laughter was cut short by the next fierce contraction.

Daisy was born at six o'clock in the morning. Anna had carried the name in the secret recesses of her mind since that May morning when she'd seen the puppy playing amid the blossom and the daisies.

She felt sore and battered, and when Daisy was put into her arms she wished she could say that she was suffused by mother love, but she wasn't. Daisy looked like a baby bird which had fallen out of its nest. She was wrinkly, bright red and had wet slicks of blonde hair. Whilst Mr Marilyn and Louise cooed around Daisy, marvelling at her tiny fingers, Anna felt mean and horrible because all she wanted to do was sleep. She was relieved when they went home and she was taken to a large airy ward where five mothers were contentedly breast-feeding their babies.

'You'll want baby beside you,' said the nurse, parking Daisy's cot next to Anna's bed.

Anna was too tired to care. She flopped into bed and closed her eyes.

In what seemed no time at all she was woken by a mewling sound from the cot, followed by another nurse saying, 'Time to feed baby.'

Stiff and weary, Anna took Daisy from the nurse, gripping her tightly, terrified of dropping her. Trying to remember all she'd learned in antenatal classes, she held Daisy to her left breast but Daisy's mewls became wails. Anna tried to force the baby to suck, but that made matters worse and Daisy screamed even louder. The other mothers in the ward called out advice, but nothing made any difference, and by the time the midwife arrived to help, Anna was in despair, with tears of exhaustion and inadequacy rolling down her cheeks.

Feeding seemed to take for ever, after which Anna sank into the bliss of a warm bath. Returning to her bed she settled down to sleep but almost immediately she was woken by Daisy's mewling. It was time to change her, wash her and feed her. Anna had only just finished when her mother and Roz walked in. They gathered admiringly around the cot, whilst Anna wondered if there was something wrong with her because she felt no maternal love.

'She has your blonde hair.' Roz smiled down at Daisy.

'Or that wretched Charlie's,' said their mother, as usual oblivious to how tactless she was being. 'Darling, I do hope you've changed your mind about telling him. He must pay maintenance. You're going to need it.'

'Mother, not now!' said Roz.

'Oh, I'm sorry. Anna, I don't mean to interfere but . . .'

'Mum, please!' Anna held up her hand. 'I won't change.'

Roz patted her on the shoulder. 'You'll manage, Anna, you always have. Once this damned recession is over, Marinecover will be begging you to go back.'

Anna tried to smile, but she couldn't imagine ever having the energy to hold down a job again.

Over the next days Anna began to get the hang of the feeding. Compared to many babies Daisy didn't cry much, just for a couple of hours each evening; for the rest of the time she slept or ate or made funny kitten noises.

Five days after the birth Anna went home. Daisy's looks had improved and she was less red and wrinkly. Mr Marilyn was waiting on the front doorstep, clutching a large bouquet of white lilies, with a card inscribed to the 'two girls in my life'. In her flat Anna found the cot ready, the fridge stocked, the pram in place, a card from Grazyna, and flowers from Colin. There was also a bottle of champagne.

'I don't know how to thank you,' she told Louise and Mr Marilyn.

'The champagne is from Big Mac,' said Louise.

'How embarrassing.' She put the bottle to one side, planning to return it to him.

Alone, Anna settled Daisy into the cot, made herself some tea, and organised the baby clothes into what had been Charlie's side of the cupboard. At midday Daisy was still quiet and, worried in case she'd stopped breathing, Anna felt for her pulse. That woke

Daisy, who wailed. Anna picked her up, changed her nappy and fed her – at least she tried to, but Daisy refused to suck. She was restless and angry in her new surroundings and she began to scream. It took Anna hours to feed her and even then she fed fitfully. Afterwards Daisy, who had always brought up wind with ease, now either couldn't or wouldn't, Anna didn't know which.

When Mr Marilyn returned from his *thé dansant* Daisy was still crying and Anna was grey with exhaustion. 'Let me take her.' He held out his arms.

Thankfully, Anna handed him the baby. Daisy gave an enormous belch, spewed milk down Mr Marilyn's green velvet jacket and fell asleep on his shoulder.

'I feel hopeless,' said Anna, cleaning Mr Marilyn's jacket. 'I'm her mother and I couldn't stop her crying.'

'Oh, it was just chance that I took her at that moment. Now you eat something and go to sleep, you need your strength.'

Two hours later, as Anna was snuggling under her duvet, Daisy began to cry. She cried all night and when she wasn't crying she was tugging at Anna's tender nipples. In the morning, when the health visitor arrived, Anna was a wreck and Daisy had been neither bathed nor changed. The health visitor exuded calm and Daisy sensed it. She fed, she burped, she slept, but within a short while of the woman leaving, as Anna was eating her lunch, Daisy woke and started to scream again. She cried all afternoon and by the evening Anna was in floods of tears.

There was a knock on her door and she opened it to find Big Mac dressed in his office suit. 'I'm sorry about the baby,' she said, forestalling his complaint.

'Oh, it isn't that. I came to tell you that one of the light bulbs on the landing has gone.'

With Daisy in her arms, still crying, Anna fetched a bulb from the kitchen. 'Here you are.'

'Oh . . . er . . . have I to put it in?'

Anna exploded. 'For God's sake! I can't do it now. If you want another bulb, stick it in yourself.'

Big Mac took the bulb and fled.

For the next three weeks Anna lived a nightmare. If anyone had offered to take Daisy away she would have gladly let her go. Some days Daisy slept for an hour, sometimes it was three hours, sometimes she refused to sleep at all. When she was awake, if she wasn't feeding or being bathed, she screamed. The health visitor talked of 'getting into a routine', but it was all Anna could do not to hit her child.

Often she had no time to drink a cup of tea between one feed and the next scream. Kindly Mr Marilyn did her shopping, Louise popped in each evening, Roz telephoned with advice, her mother telephoned with more advice, but frequently Anna was so tired she could barely speak. Once, she found a message from Isaac on the answering machine, asking how she was and she was so befuddled with exhaustion that for a moment she couldn't even remember his surname.

One morning when she hadn't slept a wink and was trying unsuccessfully to bring up Daisy's wind, Big Mac knocked on her door. 'Would you have time to check my radiators?' he asked politely. 'They aren't as hot as they should be and they may need bleeding.'

'Time!' Anna shouted at him. 'Can't you see I haven't got a second to do anything?'

'I thought that . . . er . . . whilst the baby was asleep . . .'

'She doesn't sleep, you idiot!'

Big Mac flushed and backed away.

'I'm giving you a month's notice,' said Anna, her voice trembling with exhaustion and rage. 'You never stop whingeing and I can't stand it any longer.' She slammed the door in his face.

The noise startled Daisy who gave an enormous burp, stared at Anna in surprise, and slowly began to smile – or so it seemed to Anna in spite of the baby books saying that at Daisy's age it was only wind. Anna drew the tiny bundle to her, kissed the soft skin on Daisy's forehead – and from that moment onwards she would not have parted with her.

21

DAISY DIDN'T STOP crying just because Anna started to love her, but because Anna loved her she found the noise and the tiredness easier to cope with, just as when she decided not to have an abortion she'd found the sickness easier to withstand. Gradually she managed to get into the routine beloved by the health visitor and even started her exercises; to her distress she still couldn't fit into her clothes.

Tom and Roz had invited the whole family to spend Christmas at Lower Gossip Fen and Anna was much looking forward to the break, but a week beforehand, when her mother and grandmother were already there, Roz telephoned to say that their mother had flu and Phoebe had measles, and she expected Oliver to develop it too. Although Anna knew that Daisy ought still to benefit from her immunity system, she couldn't risk it. She was intensely disappointed.

Faced with Christmas on her own, she stood in the middle of the room, biting back tears. Then she gritted her teeth, and went downstairs to Mr Marilyn, who was sitting at his kitchen table making cards for his old ladies. 'What are you doing on Christmas Day?' she asked.

'Well, I . . .' He looked embarrassed. 'I usually spend it on my own.'

'Would you like to join Daisy and me? We could have a Christmas lunch upstairs on my long table.'

'Oh, Anna, I'd love to.' His face shone with pleasure. Then, he hesitated. 'But . . . aren't you going to your sister?'

'One of her children has measles, so I can't take Daisy there, and I thought that instead of moping around upstairs alone, I'd invite all the people in the house who are on their own and we could have a party.'

He smiled. 'That's a wonderful idea. I'll bring the pudding and the mince pies. No, Anna, don't argue. You can't afford to feed everyone, especially now you have Daisy.'

'Very well.' She didn't resist, because he spoke the truth.

They spent the afternoon making invitations. Anna wrote the words, whilst Mr Marilyn decorated the cards with intricate drawings of holly leaves and mistletoe. Then they posted one under each flatlet door, except for Big Mac's.

When Louise read hers she rushed down to Anna, shouting, 'Yes, please, I'd love to come. I hate going to my father and stepmother, I always feel an intruder, and Robert will be away, skiing. I'll contribute all the vegetables.'

Grazyna also accepted, which surprised Anna. 'May I invite an American colleague?' she enquired, formally. 'She will be alone on Christmas Day.'

'The more the merrier – especially if they're male and gorgeous,' said Louise. She turned to Anna, who was hoping Grazyna's colleague wasn't also very serious. 'What about Big Mac?'

'He'll have left by then, thank God!'

'Poor old Mac, he's a pain, but he means well.' Louise gave Anna a suggestive wink. 'And he likes you.'

'Balls!' Anna threw one of Daisy's bootees at her.

Louise caught the bootee with one hand. 'He told me so.'

'You could do worse, Anna,' said Grazyna, with cool logic. 'You are on your own, with a child, and Mac is a nuisance but he has money.'

Anna wailed in horror. 'That's the kind of thing my mother would say!'

On Saturday they bought a Christmas tree in the market. One of the lower branches was broken, so they got it for half-price. Dominic carried it home for them, so they invited him to the party. That evening they decorated the drawing-room by pinning their cards on long, red ribbons, strategically draped to hide the unpainted walls underneath. Anna was reminded of the magic of Christmases at Cliff Cottage, when her father would stand on the window seat whilst she and Roz handed up paper chains for him to loop along the pelmet. She could see him now, hammering in drawing pins, dropping more than he used: pins which would hide in the cushions of the window seat until – to Anna's fits of giggles – a visitor would sit on them.

Anna sent cards to Isaac and Sybil, Miss Thin, Elaine and, after some hesitation, to Delia. Only Miss Thin and the Finesteins responded. She was philosophical about Delia's silence but she was surprised not to hear from Elaine. But this contact with her former life reminded her that in the spring she would have to start looking for work and already she dreaded it, although she wasn't sure if it was the prospect of leaving Daisy or fear of failure in a world which had once rejected her.

On the day Big Mac was due to move out Anna waited for him to return his key. She expected him to leave by noon, but he didn't appear, so she hung around for a further hour. Then, fearing he might refuse to leave, she marched upstairs to confront him.

He was sitting on the end of the bed, surrounded by his matching luggage, his big shoulders drooping, his face in his hands. When he heard Anna's footsteps, he looked up. 'I apologise for being slow but I have flu,' he croaked.

'I'll . . . umm . . . call you a cab.'

'I can manage. Please don't trouble yourself.' He rose shakily.

'It's no bother.'

He looked at her with sad eyes. 'I regret it if I've angered you, Anna, I truly didn't mean to.'

'Mac, you never stopped complaining.'

'I wanted us to be friends, but each time I came down to talk to you I lost my nerve and . . . the only reason I could think of for disturbing you was to speak of the house.'

'A complaint.'

'Yeah, you're right, I ballsed up.' He picked up a suitcase.

He was like a big, sick baby and Anna already had a baby downstairs and she didn't want another responsibility, but she knew what it was like to be sick and alone. 'You needn't move out when you're ill,' she told him.

He picked up a second case. 'No! You wanted me out, so I'm leaving.'

'Mac, go back to bed before you die.'

He dropped the cases, slumped down on to the bed, closed his eyes and whispered, 'Thank you. I'll never be a pain in the ass again.'

That evening, when Louise and Mr Marilyn arrived to put the finishing touches to the Christmas tree, Anna told them why she'd allowed Big Mac to stay. 'I vote we invite him to Christmas.' She looked at their doubtful faces. 'He has nowhere else to go.'

There was silence, then Louise said, 'No wonder he's in love with you.'

Anna wrote out an invitation for Mac and posted it under his door. Early next morning he came down in his dressing-gown but she sent him back upstairs because she didn't want Daisy to catch flu. 'My contribution will be to provide and cook the turkey,' he shouted over the banister, waking up the whole house.

Anna gestured to him to keep his voice down. 'Thank you but . . . are you sure you know how?' She had visions of irate guests waiting all day to eat.

Mac straightened his shoulders. 'We always have Thanksgiving at my grandparents' house and I've helped with the turkey since I was a kid. It's the only dish I can cook but, hell, I do it well.'

'Okay. Thank you. Now go back to bed. You're ill.'

He gave her a mock salute. 'Yes, ma'am.'

Everyone dressed up for the party. Mac wore a dinner jacket, Mr Marilyn came in his velvet smoking jacket and even Dominic wore a suit. Grażyna had few clothes, and certainly nothing frivolous – Anna suspected that she had little money – and she wore one of her work suits. Victoria, Grażyna's American colleague, a pretty girl with glossy brown hair, came in a demure floral smock which reminded Anna of Roz's maternity clothes but it suited her quiet manner. Victoria soon discovered that her Long Island aunt had once lived opposite Mac's grandparents.

Anna borrowed one of Louise's market dresses because she still couldn't fit into her own evening clothes, not that she had many left since off-loading the best through the second-hand shop. The garment she chose was of midnight-blue crushed velvet. It had a deep 'V' in the front and was cut on the cross, which made it swirl around her hips to end in a six-pointed hem.

'It makes me look as if I'm still pregnant,' she lamented despondently to Louise, who was slinking around in a long gold shift which accentuated her beautiful, hollow collarbones.

'It looks fine.' Louise pulled Anna's hand away from the neck line. 'But you need to keep doing your exercises.'

'I'm going on a diet next month when I stop feeding Daisy.'

Anna had another attempt at making the dress cover her bosom, then she gave up and went to join the party.

They didn't begin eating until late and remained at the table talking long after they had finished.

'It's funny that in some years nothing seems to happen,' said Louise, 'but in others, like this last one for me, your whole life turns upside down.'

'I know what you mean.' Anna gave a rueful smile. 'Last year I was in Melbourne, expecting to become engaged. Now I have Daisy.'

Grażyna, who had said very little throughout the meal, spoke up. 'Last year I was delivering illegal pamphlets for Solidarity. I was cold, and afraid, and I had a hole in my boots.' She smiled, and her face lost its sharpness. 'Now Solidarity is in the Government and I am in London.'

'Oh, I was on my own last year,' said Mr Marilyn. 'I'd have been on my own again, if it wasn't for you, Anna.' He gave her his brightest, pixiest smile and raised his glass. 'To you and Daisy.'

Louise lifted her glass. 'I second that. To Anna and Daisy.'

As they toasted her, Anna's eyes filled with tears.

'Hey, don't cry!' said Louise.

'I can't help it, I'm so touched. After . . . Charlie walked out, I felt no one would ever . . . like me again.' Anna pulled a face and tried to laugh, but she knew that Mr Marilyn understood because he reached out and squeezed her hand.

Since Anna had been unable to be with her family at Christmas, her mother brought her grandmother down to London to see Daisy and in March, Anna went up to Lower Gossip. She'd forgotten how beautiful springtime was in the fenland, with the steep banks on the drains carpeted in primroses and the new-born lambs chasing each other through the bright green, succulent grass.

She remained there for a fortnight, relishing her long walks with Roz when they pushed Daisy in her pram, with Augustus ambling beside them, and the sun and the wind in their faces, and the salty smell of the Wash in their nostrils.

On her last day Anna weighed herself on the farm scales, which were normally used for sheep. 'Another ten pounds to lose.' She groaned at the prospect of more self-denial. 'Mind you, I'm bound to lose it once I start work.'

Roz looked surprised. 'Surely having all those tenants gives you an income?'

Anna pulled a piece of straw from a nearby bale and broke it in two. 'Their rent doesn't even cover the mortgage – and I still have to eat and pay my bills. There's a monthly shortfall accumulating at the bank which I have to repay.'

'But I thought the DSS was helping you,' Roz said as they walked across the farmyard towards the kitchen.

'Not now that I have tenants.'

'Then you'll have to be practical, Anna. Sell the house and buy something cheaper.'

'Don't, Roz, please! That's what Charlie used to say. Sometimes I think I drove him over the edge because I wouldn't part with the house, but I can't, you see. There would be little left to buy another. We have a huge mortgage and the house is worth less than what we paid for it. In any case, I couldn't bear to sell. Ladbroke Hill is my Cliff Cottage, my safe haven, my security. And it's not just my home, it's Daisy's. I don't want her to suffer from my terrible rootlessness.'

'I know what you mean,' said Roz, quietly. 'Lower Gossip Fen is my oasis. The house is too big for us and we can barely afford to run the farm, but it's ours. I was so lucky to be here when Father . . . died. It was much worse for you, being bundled off again, another house, another school.'

'I didn't realise you knew how I hated it.' Anna was touched by the sympathy in Roz's voice.

It was an effort for her to leave the safety of the farm, where nothing was her responsibility, and face the endless battle to make ends meet, but once she reached Ladbroke Hill, she was glad to be home. Louise and Mr Marilyn welcomed her with the news of the house: Mac had gone home for his grandfather's funeral, Grażyna had passed her first exam, and Errol Flynn had been in a fight and torn his ear.

That weekend Anna offered to look after the stall because Louise's boyfriend, Robert, was in London: Mr Marilyn minded Daisy. In keeping with the merchandise, Anna wore a wrap-over tea-dress with big puffed sleeves. At first she was afraid that she'd sell the clothes for the wrong price or lose the lot to shoplifters, but as she became more confident she enjoyed the stall. There was a camaraderie in the market which she'd always envied and the bearded Lionel spent the day regaling her with affectionate and amusing stories about the other stall-holders.

By the evening Anna had sold a hundred pounds' worth of goods which was not nearly as much as Louise usually sold, but at least nothing had been stolen. As she was packing the clothes into the purple van, Mac appeared. 'I'm sorry about your grandfather,' Anna told him.

'Thanks. I'm glad I went home for the funeral; it was sad but kind of nice, and there were cousins I haven't seen for years. It's strange, but those I used to like I now find pompous and the two who always called me boring have invited me to meet up with them in Paris. I guess I must have changed.'

From the back of Louise's van Anna called, 'You have, Mac, and please don't change back!'

'Do you really mean that?'

'Of course.'

He smiled, hesitantly. 'You're beautiful in that dress, Anna, it makes you look so feminine and soft and . . .' He turned pink and stopped.

'Thank you.' Anna straightened up. 'Hey, Mac, what have you done to yourself? You've lost weight. We'll have to call you Lean Mac.'

'I went on a diet.'

'You look much better.' Anna closed the shoes into their suitcase and bent to lift it into the van.

Mac helped her. 'I missed you, Anna,' he said quietly, his face very close to hers.

Embarrassed, Anna jumped away, swooped up the last of the dresses from the rail and stepped up into the van.

'Will you have dinner with me?' he asked.

She swallowed hard. 'I . . . umm . . . I'm very glad you didn't leave at Christmas, Mac, but . . .'

He held up his hand. 'Say no more!' and he turned on his heel, and walked back up the lane to the house.

Anna watched him go. She was reminded of the day when he

was due to move out and he'd picked up the second suitcase even though she'd told him he could stay, and she felt great admiration for the way he kept his pride in the face of rejection.

He stayed out of her way for a few weeks, after which he returned to being the same friendly, jolly Mac. It was as if he'd never spoken, but Anna remained disturbed because he'd reminded her that there was more to life than Daisy and Ladbroke Hill. He'd raised a hunger in her for romance, for love, for sex, and for intimacy.

Daisy was growing up. She couldn't crawl yet but she could wriggle sideways across the floor, gurgling like a baby seal. She liked music, and when Mr Marilyn put on his record player, she tapped on the floor. She liked the television and spent hours staring at the set from every angle, even when it wasn't on, until Anna came to the conclusion that she was looking for the people inside it.

To give herself some privacy, Anna separated her bedroom from Daisy's by closing the central double doors. She placed Daisy in the front section, which was quieter, and herself in the back, with the balcony and access to the kitchen and bathroom. It was a luxury to be able to read in bed again.

She'd intended to look for work once Daisy was six months old – the rents did not cover the mortgage and she was all too aware of the deficit accruing against her – but she kept putting off the search. The weather was particularly warm and the prospect of being cooped up in a stuffy office was unbearable – if she managed to find a job, which according to the news was becoming increasingly difficult. So she enjoyed the summer, and tried not to worry, and whenever Mr Marilyn offered to look after Daisy, she helped Louise in the market and, at Louise's insistence, she received a percentage of their takings. Earnings on the stall were erratic. One day they made less than thirty pounds, another they made five hundred. Anna's share was just enough to cover her food and bills, if she was very careful, but it could not pay East Metro. She dreaded their next communication.

Mac built a barbecue in the garden and on warm Sundays they ate outside, lying on rugs and reading the newspapers. Victoria was a frequent guest and they all liked her.

One evening, after she'd gone home, Grazyna told Mac, 'Victoria needs a partner for a ball and she is shy of inviting you in case you refuse.'

He flushed and glanced at Anna who was playing with Daisy. 'Oh, I'm not much of a dancer.'

'Go on, Mac.' Louise raised her head from the *News of the World*. 'Don't be a coward!'

'My dinner-suit is too big now I've lost weight.'

'That's no excuse, you can hire one.'

He gave them a look of desperation, like a reluctant groom at a shotgun wedding, but they laughed and chivvied until he sighed, 'Okay, you win.'

A week later he accompanied Victoria to the ball and the following morning Louise caught him creeping up the stairs, still wearing his evening clothes. 'Mac!' she gasped. 'It's eleven o'clock!'

He grinned sheepishly and hurried into his flat.

Louise rushed to tell Anna, who had returned to bed, Daisy cuddled up beside her. 'Mac's been out all night,' she spluttered.

'Victoria spent the night with Mac on their first date?' Anna sat up straight. 'She seems such a mouse!'

'It's always the quiet ones.' Louise rolled her eyes in mock disapproval. 'People expect that of a woman like me, who looks kind of wild, and even you.' She grinned at Anna. 'With your hotted-up-glacier look. But Victoria! And Mac! I mean, you wouldn't think he'd dare to try on their first date.' Louise opened the balcony doors and stepped outside.

Anna lay back against her pillows and looked out at the garden, where the morning sunlight poured through the branches of the old apple tree. She wondered if she would ever love again, if she would sleep again in someone's arms and share her life, her hopes, her fears – and suddenly she ached to be held.

22

ON THE MORNING when Iraq invaded Kuwait, Anna received a letter from Mr Hyde saying that he was to be promoted to head office and that a new manager, Mr Flatbush, would be taking his place. He warned that Mr Flatbush operated by the rules and would take immediate steps to repossess the property if she did not repay the shortfall in her monthly payments. This precipitated Anna's job-hunting.

She confided in Louise that the house was under threat, but she didn't tell Mr Marilyn because she didn't want to upset him, she merely said that she planned to start work. After bleak mutterings about ambitious modern mothers, so unlike his own dear mother, he offered to mind Daisy when Anna needed to attend interviews. Without his help, she could not have afforded to look for work.

Before her first appointment, with a marine insurance company near Aldgate East, Anna did her best to smarten up. Louise cut her hair to a neat bob and Victoria lent her a briefcase. She'd sold most of her smart clothes when she was pregnant and her only summer business outfit was a black linen suit. It had a short, straight skirt and a sculpted jacket, but the skirt was far tighter than before she'd had Daisy, and when she travelled by Underground to the interview she didn't dare sit down in case it creased across her hips.

When she reached the insurance company she found thirty other applicants. It was three hours before she was interviewed, by which time she was tired and hungry and her linen suit looked like a rag.

'Why haven't you worked for the past two years?' asked the personnel manager after glancing at her CV.

'I had a baby.'

'You're not married?'

Anna shook her head.

'Do you have a live-in nanny?'

'No, but . . .'

'Thank you, Miss Tobias. We'll be in touch.'

Anna recollected what Elaine had said.

Anna continued to look for work but there was something horribly *déjà vu* about the process, which took her back to Charlie, and she found herself missing him in a way which surprised her. She was reminded of him when she studied the *Lloyd's List*, recalling how they'd encouraged each other to chase every vacancy. It had been arduous when there were two of them; it was far harder on her own. Charlie, for all his faults, had at least shared her crippling sense of rejection.

Luckily Mac's bank wanted him to remain in London for a further year and Grażyna was extending her course until after Christmas, so she didn't have to worry about finding new tenants. In any case, she'd have been sorry to see them leave, particularly Mac. He'd become a kind of surrogate brother and, as Louise often said, it seemed unbelievable that they had once disliked him.

After two months of unsuccessful job-hunting, panic forced Anna to swallow her pride and telephone Gordon.

Miss Thin answered his telephone. 'Anna! What a nice surprise. You want to speak to the boss? Well . . . er . . . I'm afraid he's in a departmental meeting.'

'Please tell him I called.' Anna longed to enquire after everyone at Marinecover, but the hesitation in Miss Thin's voice made her feel awkward, so she said goodbye and hung up.

She waited all day for Gordon to ring back, but he didn't. Nor did he telephone the next day, or the next. Anna wished she hadn't contacted him. She became convinced that Miss Thin's hesitation was due to Gordon's presence beside her, gesticulating not to put Anna through. She imagined him telling her former colleagues, 'Anna Tobias still doesn't realise that she was fired for incompetence.'

When the telephone finally rang it was Isaac Finestein. 'So?' he said. 'You don't come to dinner with us any more, you don't telephone us, what have we done wrong?'

'Oh, Isaac, I'm sorry but . . .' She glanced at Daisy who was playing with a rag doll. 'I've been very busy.'

'And you're looking for work?'

'How did you know?'

'Gordon told me you'd phoned him.'

'Yes.' She dreaded to think what else Gordon had said.

'Come to us for lunch on Sunday?' said Isaac. 'We're having the family and a few close friends.'

'I'd love to, but . . . umm . . . I'd have to bring someone who's a secret as far as our working world is concerned.'

'You have an unsuitable lover whom you wish to bring to our home?' He was offended.

'No, Isaac, I have a little daughter called Daisy.'

'You have a child!'

'She was born last winter. That's why I've been out of contact.'

'Of course you must bring her on Sunday. Wait till I tell Sybil, she'll be thrilled. We love children.' He paused. 'You are not with the father, I assume?'

'He doesn't feature in our lives.'

'But why the secret?'

'Because I can't get a job, Isaac. No one wants to employ a single mother.'

'Your news will be safe with us, but I'd better warn you that we may have another guest, one whom you know. If you ask him, I'm sure he won't say anything about your little girl.'

'Who is it?'

'Sybil says I mustn't tell you or you might refuse to come. I'm afraid she's matchmaking again.'

'Isaac, I need a job, not a man.'

'There's nothing wrong in having both.'

'Men bring me nothing but trouble – at least the ones I get involved with.'

He chuckled and said goodbye.

The only men Anna could think of whom the Finesteins knew that she knew were Gordon and Paul Sheldon, and she couldn't believe that Isaac and Sybil would invite her with either of them: certainly not Gordon. That left Paul. She recalled the brief moment of intimacy which they'd shared on the balcony when they talked about sailing and he told her of the house in Rhode Island which he loved. What was the place called? She couldn't remember.

For the Finestein's lunch Anna wore a simple red wool dress which, although a little tight, enhanced her colouring. When she left home her hair was softly curled and her dress was clean, but by the time she'd journeyed to Highgate on the Underground with Daisy, the buggy and Daisy's paraphernalia of nappies, talc, spare clean dress and bib, she felt a wreck. Her shoes pinched, her arms ached, and Daisy had dribbled on to the shoulder of her dress.

Sybil was shocked when she realised that Anna had come all the way by public transport and she greeted her with added warmth, distressed to see how tired and pale she looked. 'What a sweet little girl,' she said, bending her kindly face to Daisy and adding in a jokey voice, 'but I'm cross with you, Anna, you never told me about your baby and I love babies.' She lowered her voice. 'Your beau isn't here yet.'

'Sybil, who is he?'

'You had a baby without telling me, now I have a secret from you.' Sybil unbuckled the straps which held Daisy in the buggy and lifted her out, saying, 'Come along, sweetheart.'

Before Anna joined the family she slipped upstairs to wash her hands, clean up her dress, retouch her make-up and comb her hair. When she came down she found Daisy sitting on the rug in the centre of the drawing-room surrounded by the entire Finestein family. She was playing hide-and-seek from behind the skirt of her red check dress with Gideon, the Finestein's eldest son, a usually solemn intellectual.

'Your daughter is enchanting,' Isaac told Anna as he poured a glass of white wine. 'Would it be wrong to ask if the Australian is her father?'

'Yes, Isaac, it would.' Anna didn't mean to sound so abrupt and was about to apologise when Isaac's attention was caught by a new arrival.

'Our last guest,' he said, smiling.

Anna looked, and saw Paul Sheldon being embraced by Sybil in the doorway. He saw her, and astonishment came into his face. When Sybil had told him that she'd invited someone special, he'd nearly refused to come because he disliked being set up, but that morning, driving up from Chelsea, he couldn't help wondering who the someone would be. It had never occurred to him to expect Anna Tobias.

Anna was embarrassed. She had an unwelcome suspicion that Paul thought she'd asked Sybil to engineer this meeting and she hurriedly turned her back on him, giving her attention to Rebecca Finestein although, out of the corner of her eye, she was aware of Paul circulating around the room, greeting everyone by name, kissing the women on the cheek and clasping the men by the hand.

When he reached Anna, he smiled and said, 'What a surprise. How are you?' but by then she had retreated behind a barrier of self-defence and could think of nothing to say, other than a mumbled greeting, so he moved on to talk to Gideon.

This confirmed Anna's fears that he assumed she'd asked to meet him, but there was nothing she could do to put him straight with everyone nearby able to listen, so she crossed to the far side of the room to talk to Sybil. But at lunch she was placed next to Paul, with Daisy on her other side. Feeling awkward she spent an unnecessary amount of time adjusting Daisy's bib.

Paul was astonished when he realised that Anna was the mother of the little girl with the blonde ringlets who'd been sitting on the rug. Apart from the night when he'd taken her home, drunk, and the morning when she'd punched Vince Ellerby-Creswell, in the six or seven years since he'd first noticed her, sashaying through Lloyd's in a short black skirt, she'd seemed very much in control of her life. Isaac often said that she was worth two of Charlie, and that Gordon only hadn't got rid of Charlie earlier because he couldn't risk losing Anna Tobias. Even on the balcony, in the middle of her party when she'd suddenly seemed very lonely in spite of all the people swarming around her, she'd talked of the past – but pulled herself back to the present with a bravado which he recognised, because he often did the same.

Now, as he watched her, he saw the tenderness with which she lifted Daisy's hair so that it didn't tangle in the ribbon of the bib, and he noticed how her face softened as she spoke to her child. He noted too that she'd varnished the nails of one hand but forgotten to do the other, and he found that strangely endearing.

When Anna had settled Daisy, Paul turned towards her. 'I didn't know you had a child,' he said.

She was still defensive. 'You mean, Isaac hasn't explained?'

He looked puzzled. 'Explained what?'

'That I don't wish anyone at Lloyd's to know about Daisy,

because it could ruin my chances of finding a job. Employers don't need to employ single mothers when they have hundreds of other applicants, without responsibilities, chasing every vacancy.' She stopped speaking, suddenly realising that she was attacking Paul as if it were all his fault.

Before she could add something more harmonious, he said, very gently, 'It must be hard, being on your own with a child.'

'Yes.' Both sadness and courage came into her face, and he saw them.

'I've misunderstood you.' Paul spoke softly so that no one else could hear.

Anna wasn't sure if he referred to now or to the whole of their spasmodic acquaintanceship, but something in his voice and in his face made her think he meant more than just today. 'You're a brave lady,' he went on.

She thought of her debts. 'It's a question of necessity.'

'I was remembering how you thumped Ellerby-Creswell.'

She gave a light laugh which brought colour to her cheeks. 'Vince deserved it, the rogue!'

He was about to say he hoped that by bringing Gordon's attention to her visit to Creswell he hadn't contributed to her losing her job, but she was smiling now and he wanted to defend her fleeting happiness. Filling her glass with white wine, he asked, 'Do you still live in that beautiful house?'

Her smile widened. 'Ladbroke Hill's my oasis, my rock. My biggest dread is that I'll lose my home.'

He was silent whilst around them the Finesteins argued about whether Saddam Hussein would retreat from Kuwait or he'd have to be driven out. When Paul spoke to Anna again, he chose his words carefully. 'Doesn't . . . Daisy's father help you?'

She shook her head. 'No.'

Before he could probe further, Sybil called down the table, 'Paul, you must invite Anna to see your boat. She loves to sail. You two have such a lot in common.'

Anna had almost forgotten her earlier embarrassment, but now she blushed and turned away from Paul to speak to Gideon, whilst Paul began a complicated discussion with Rebecca. As Anna listened to Gideon's views on the Gulf Crisis, she wondered if it would be easier to go home on the bus than by Underground.

After lunch Anna hurried Daisy upstairs to change her nappy. When she came down again, coffee was being served. 'I must go,' she told Sybil, thinking of the long journey home.

'Paul has offered to drive you home. I told him you had no car. And don't pretend you have, Anna! I saw you pushing the buggy along the pavement.'

Paul smiled at Anna. 'Would you like a lift?'

'Yes, thank you.' She thought he probably felt sorry for her, but she didn't care, she was just relieved not to have to struggle on public transport.

Because Paul had no child seat, she sat in the back holding Daisy on her lap. 'Is it true you don't have a car?' he asked as they set off.

She nodded.

'That can't be easy with a child.'

'It isn't.' She sank into silence, with Daisy sleeping on her lap. She didn't mean to be rude, but the prospect of tomorrow, another day of searching for work, brought her to the verge of tears.

Paul would have liked to talk more, to find out about her life which seemed so very different from the Anna Tobias he had known. He wondered what she did in the evenings, and if she was free to go out. If she had no car, he couldn't imagine that she had a nanny. He pictured her living in the beautiful rooms of her house, battling alone for her child. Or maybe she wasn't alone? He wanted to ask Sybil, but she was such a gossip she'd be bound to tell Anna. He glanced in the mirror, and saw that she was slumped into the corner of the back seat, cuddling Daisy, her face etched with anxiety. She looked so vulnerable, and yet so courageous.

When they reached Ladbroke Hill, he helped her up the steps with the buggy and her bag. 'I'd invite you in but Daisy's tired,' she said, fumbling in her pocket for her keys.

'Here, let me help.' He took the keys from her and their hands touched, just for an instant, then he unlocked the door. He would have liked to help her inside, to make sure she was all right, he didn't want to abandon her on the doorstep, but he sensed that she wished to be alone.

'Thank you for the lift,' she said, sorry now that she hadn't got round to asking him about his boat.

'It was my pleasure. Goodbye.' He walked down the steps to his car then turned, intending to say more, but Anna had already disappeared into the house.

23

GORDON TELEPHONED NEXT morning as Anna was stacking vegetables in the fridge. 'You never returned my calls,' he said abruptly.

'I know, I'm sorry.'

'And now you telephone because you need a job?'

Before Anna had time to elaborate, Daisy caught her hand in the pedal bin and let out an ear-piercing shriek. Dropping the telephone, Anna raced to rescue her. When she returned she found that Gordon had gone and Miss Thin was on the line. 'The boss wants to have lunch with you,' she told Anna. 'How about next Tuesday, at the Savoy? Are you free?'

Anna nearly replied 'If I can find a baby-sitter', but she kept quiet about Daisy. 'That would be lovely,' she replied, and because Miss Thin sounded friendly she went on, 'How are you? Oh good. No, I haven't seen Delia for months. She moved to Merchant & Leisure? What about Elaine? She's married and lives in the States? That explains why I haven't heard for some time. Yes, I'd like her address.' When Anna replaced the receiver she felt happy. Miss Thin had been friendly, Elaine had not ignored her, and Gordon had invited her to lunch, which with him meant only one thing: he intended to offer her a job.

She was digging through her wardrobe in the vain hope of finding something smarter than her black linen suit when the telephone rang. She answered it, steeling herself against disappointment if Gordon had changed his mind.

'Anna, this is Paul Sheldon.'

Sheer relief that Gordon wasn't cancelling her made Anna chatter uncontrollably. 'I think I have a job, it's not definite yet but Gordon Routlish invited me to lunch and we all know he never does anything except for work. Of course, before I had Daisy I'd never have gone back to Marinecover, but now I can't afford to be choosy. You can't imagine how near I've come to losing this house. When I was a child we moved continually because my father was in the army and later, well . . . he was often unemployed. I longed for my own home, for somewhere which was mine, which could never be taken away from me, and now I've been so frightened that I'd lose Ladbroke Hill.' She stopped talking, then added, 'I'm sorry, I'm babbling, I don't usually talk about my problems.'

'But you should; if you don't, they grow beyond redress, they get so that no one can help you.' He spoke with a vehemence which made her wonder what raw wound she had inadvertently touched. 'How is Daisy?' he asked.

'She's fine, thanks. In fact, she's in her high chair, waiting for her lunch. Why did you ring me? Oh, sorry I shouldn't ask that.' She gave an embarrassed laugh. 'I should wait for you to tell me, but that shows you how out of practice I am with this . . . kind of thing.'

He liked her honesty, it made a refreshing change, and it amused him, in a nice way, to pretend not to understand her. 'What kind of thing?'

'Oh . . . umm . . . you know.' She was blushing.

'No, I don't,' he teased.

'Well, you'll have to hurry up and say your piece because Daisy will start yelling for her lunch any minute.'

He chuckled at her mixture of embarrassment and orderliness. 'Come to lunch on my boat next Sunday.'

'I'd love to! I meant to ask you about her.'

'She's called *The Goshawk* and she's a forty-foot Bermuda-rigged ketch, hand-built in the Fifties by Laurent Giles of Portsmouth, and she's down near there now, being refitted. I bought her last year, in need of almost total rebuilding.'

'She sounds wonderful,' said Anna, enthusiastically. 'But I'll have to bring Daisy, I'm afraid. My basement tenant looks after her whilst I attend interviews, but I can't ask him to take her at the weekends as well.'

'The invitation was for both of you.'

'Then we accept. I just hope she doesn't fall in.'

'Don't worry, we'll watch her. I'll pick you up at eleven.' He said goodbye.

The prospect of Gordon's job offer and Paul's invitations put Anna in a buoyant mood, so that she allowed herself to think ahead, to a time when she had a life outside the house, when she had fun again. But before the week was through, her fragile optimism was shattered by another letter from East Metro demanding to know why she'd failed to repay her deficit. Anna was so worried that she nearly cancelled her lunch with Paul, only Louise stopped her from making the telephone call.

She didn't dress up but wore her old jeans, a baggy navy jumper and the trainers she'd bought before she went to Australia.

When Louise saw her, she groaned. 'Can't you wear some prettier shoes?' she asked.

'I'm going on a boat.'

'At least put on some nail varnish. I have a wonderful new colour, called "Magenta Temptress".' Louise waved her fingernails in front of Anna who couldn't help laughing as she imagined herself hoisting the mainsail with a pair of purple talons.

Paul arrived, looking handsome and relaxed. He sauntered across the gravel, his brown hair ruffled by the breeze, his grey eyes almost blue against his tanned skin.

'He's gorgeous!' exclaimed Louise, peeping out of the window from behind Anna's curtains. 'I like men with unruly hair, I love to run my fingers through it. Anna, if you don't want him, introduce me.'

'You have Robert.' Anna scooped up Daisy and her bag and jacket, and hurried out of the house before Paul reached the steps.

'Hello,' he said, drawing close, smiling, 'I was hoping you wouldn't be ready so that I could see inside again.'

'Oh, it's changed, it's mainly let to tenants.'

'I only ever saw the ground floor.' He was puzzled by her abrupt manner.

Anna knew that she'd sounded unfriendly, and she was sorry, but she couldn't explain that Ladbroke Hill was her haven and, if things were going to go wrong again, she felt too vulnerable to allow him inside, because he was both a stranger and yet he was not.

Throughout the drive to Portsmouth, he chatted whilst Anna answered in monosyllables, wondering how long she had before East Metro started legal proceedings.

When they reached the marina, Paul stopped the car and turned to her. 'If you'd rather go home, I'll take you,' he said. 'But I refuse to spend all day with someone who'd clearly prefer to be elsewhere.'

She flushed. 'I'm sorry, I didn't mean to be rude, it's just that . . .'

He softened when he saw the anxiety in her face. 'Anna, tell me.'

'I've had another letter from the bank about my mortgage and I feel guilty because I should be out looking for work.'

He look her gently by the shoulders. 'On Sunday? Who's going to interview you today, Anna? You're meeting Gordon next week; he wouldn't see you if he didn't have a vacancy, you told me that yourself. Today, you need to relax.'

She smiled tentatively. 'You're right. I just lose my nerve sometimes.'

He touched her cheek, briefly. 'I'm not surprised.'

They stepped out of the car, into the sunshine. Out in the marina, rows of expensive yachts were moored alongside slatted wooden pontoons. They bobbed on the dark-blue water, their halyards slapping against their masts, the light reflecting off the water in rippling patterns on their hulls.

'Which one is yours?' Anna asked, relishing the smell of the sea.

'The one with the dog.' He pointed at a two-masted wooden ketch, where a large black, woolly mongrel with bright tan socks and a curled feathery tail was bouncing joyfully on the beautifully varnished bow.

Paul steadied Anna as she carried Daisy along the pontoon. When he reached *The Goshawk* he swung himself aboard and patted the dog, saying, 'Good boy, Bobby, did you frighten away all the thieves? Of course you did. Bobby's my guard dog.' He held out his hands for Daisy.

Anna hesitated.

'Trust me,' said Paul. 'I won't drop her.'

She nodded and passed Daisy to him.

He set the child down in the centre of the boat and turned to help Anna, but she had already jumped aboard. 'I have something for Daisy,' he said, producing a tiny red life-jacket. 'I borrowed it from my sister, Harriet. Her son used to wear it.'

Anna was astonished that a man who had no children would think of such a thing.

Paul bent down to slip the life-jacket on to Daisy. 'You never mention her father,' he said, trying to push Daisy's arms through the arm-holes. 'Is it . . . what was his name . . . the Australian?'

'Daisy doesn't have a father – I mean, he doesn't feature in our lives.' She knelt to help him with Daisy, saying, 'You have to put her hands through first and hold on to them or she'll keep bending them back. That's right. Now close the jacket quickly.' She laughed. 'It's obvious you have no experience of dressing children or you'd know that they always play you up.'

He stood back. 'We didn't have children.'

'Oh, I'm so sorry, I didn't mean to be flippant.' Her words trailed away and she wondered if he regretted not having a memento of his wife in the form of a shared child.

'Let me show you the boat,' he said, walking ahead of her along the deck. From the stiff way he carried his shoulders, Anna was convinced that he grieved deeply and she wished again that she hadn't made that remark about children.

The Goshawk had an aged, mellow charm combined with the latest in electronic equipment. Her hull was mahogany and the deck and panels were teak. She was being beautifully rebuilt, her timbers recently varnished and the brightwork and fittings polished like new. Only the cockpit was a mess of loose wires and gaping holes awaiting new equipment.

'She can't be moved yet because there's no engine and all the sails are shot to pieces,' Paul explained. 'But I have to leave Bobby on guard, because I have an office in one of the cabins. Michael, an ex-policeman, mans it for me during the week and he sleeps on board if I'm not here.' He led the way down some steps into a surprisingly spacious saloon whose wooden panels had been stripped down to the bare wood but not yet revarnished, while the cabin seats had no cushions.

There was a fixed oval table with a curved bench on the starboard side. Anna rested Daisy on the table. 'This is beautiful,' she said, thinking how much her father would have loved to own *The Goshawk*.

Paul smiled proudly. 'She will be one day, when I have time to complete the fitting-out, but I have to run a business and I'm often away, not just in London but overseas. Tomorrow morning I leave for the States.'

Anna felt strangely deflated, simply because he hadn't told her this earlier.

'I'm going to Whaler's Rock, the house on Rhode Island which I told you about,' Paul continued. 'Steven, my godfather's son, who inherited the place, is one of my closest friends and we have a pact that I visit him there each fall. Every year I think of a hundred reasons why I shouldn't take time off work – not that I stop completely, I direct operations from there – but once I arrive at Whaler's Rock I'm always so glad I went.' He smiled. 'I remember you telling me you had a house you loved, where you learned to sail. Where was it?'

'Dorset, overlooking Belworth Cove. It was just a grey stone cottage, nothing spectacular, but the view was magnificent. I loved it.'

'Do you go back?' he asked, gently.

'Only to look, and each time it's more dilapidated. You see, Cliff Cottage was the only house we owned, the rest were never ours, and my father had to sell it when he . . . lost his job.' She didn't want to think about what drove her father to kill himself, not today, and she took a deep breath, and asked overbrightly, 'Tell me more about Whaler's Rock.'

Paul had seen the sudden sadness come into Anna's face, and he wondered why, but he sensed that she'd revealed as much as she wanted to for the time being. 'Whaler's Rock's a mansion,' he said. 'It's similar to the Breakers and the Marble House, those Newport mansions along Cliff Walk which were built for the Vanderbilts, only it's wilder and more remote. It's situated on a headland, with a rocky bay on one side and a sandy cove on the other. I'll never forget my first visit, stepping from the chauffeur-driven Cadillac after my long flight to Boston – my first flight alone – and seeing a palace. I'd never been anywhere so impressive, although I was too proud to admit that to Steven.'

Anna smiled. 'That must have annoyed him.'

'Oh, it did. We fought continuously, punching and kicking until we were covered in bruises. I was a gregarious little tough, away from home for the first time, trying to pretend that I wasn't scared and Steven was used to having his own way. My godfather had become a recluse since his wife had died and didn't allow Steven to invite friends to the house. He made an exception with me, out of friendship for my father. They'd met during the war. My father had been sent to blow up a bridge in Normandy and he got pinned down overnight, in the same foxhole as my godfather.'

'You must have been very sad when he died,' said Anna, thinking of the emptiness and disbelief her own father's death had left behind.

Paul leaned against the table. 'I hate to say so, but it meant little to me. Young boys are incredibly callous, and I hardly knew him. He was a geologist and he spent all his time abroad, working in places where we couldn't join him. He was killed in an accident with dynamite. I only missed him later, when people talked of his exploits and said that I reminded them of him. Then I missed not knowing him.' He paused. 'What about you? Do you come from a big family?'

Anna shook her head. 'Just an elder sister married to a farmer, and a mother who looks after my grandmother.' She bent to adjust the ribbon in Daisy's hair. 'My father's . . . dead.'

'I'm sorry,' said Paul, quickly. 'How tactless of me to talk in that way, I haven't done so for a long time.'

'I don't mind at all. Talking keeps them . . . alive.'

'Felicity used to hate it.' His face closed in. 'Now let me show you the rest of the boat.'

Anna followed him, past the galley to the cabins, and whilst he expanded on his plans, she realised that for the first time he had used his wife's name.

The boat had three cabins. The owner's had not yet been refurbished; it had a bunk in one corner and an upturned tea chest served as a table. The second, much smaller cabin was used by Michael, the ex-policeman, when Paul was away. The third had external video camera security and a burglar alarm connected to the nearest police station. Inside was a compact office, large enough for two people, with a fax, six telephones, a computer and a battery of screens and electronic equipment. All the notepaper carried the Sheldon Investigations logo of a ship crossed by an anchor.

'My main office is in London but I keep enough here so I can work at weekends – though not enough for anyone to understand if they broke in.' Paul pressed a button and the five small screens in front of Anna lit up instantly. She could see all approaches to *The*

Goshawk and even the interior of the saloon via a camera that she had assumed to be a spotlight.

'You must be afraid of burglars,' she said, setting Daisy down on a chair.

'I have to be careful. In my job I have information about a lot of people, some of them criminals or potential criminals, like your Ellerby-Creswell.' He pressed another button next to a larger screen and the image of a luxury cruiser appeared with its details listed alongside. 'This vessel is insured for two hundred and fifty thousand pounds and the owner claims that it sank in the Adriatic. On Wednesday I interviewed him in Cannes. I am sure, though I can't yet prove it, that he's lying.'

'What will you do?' Anna was fascinated. She'd only ever dealt with the client's side of a claim.

'Try to trap him with his own words.'

'And if you can't?'

'I won't accuse him outright, I never do. I merely keep suggesting that he might like to rethink this story. Eventually, unless he's an idiot, he'll back off and retract his claim.'

'What then? Will you report him to the police?'

'With this man, definitely.' Paul switched off the screen. 'Whether he withdraws his claim or not, he's attempted to commit a considerable fraud. What makes me furious is that there are so many people who love sailing and who economise to afford a boat, then this crook makes a false claim – and everyone's premiums are increased. A quarter of a million may not sound a lot in insurance claim terms, but it's over a pound a head from every inhabitant of a city the size of Derby.'

Anna laid a calming hand on his arm. 'Paul, I wasn't criticising you. I think you're right.'

'You do?' He looked pleased. Then he shook his head and laughed at himself. 'I was on my soapbox; I tend to climb on it when faced with injustice.'

'Oh, I have my causes too.' Anna was always relieved to find she wasn't alone. 'My current issue is the lack of affordable childcare, but don't get me going on it!'

He smiled at her. 'I won't, not today, you're meant to be relaxing.'

She was suddenly aware that her hand still rested on his arm and she removed it quickly, saying, 'Daisy will want her lunch soon or she'll begin to wail.'

She returned to the saloon, where she entertained Daisy whilst Paul went into the galley to prepare lunch. 'I'm afraid I can only offer fast-food service,' he called, as he placed a large shepherd's pie in the microwave. 'But the claret is excellent.' He poured her a glass.

They lunched at the oval table, with Bobby watching Daisy's every move, longing for her to drop food on to the floor. Paul talked of his plans for the boat, of how one day he'd sail around the world. 'That's why I bought a Bermuda-rigged ketch,' he said. 'Having two masts rather than one makes her easier to handle in strong winds. I'll be able to drop the mainsail, and still be left with a headsail and the mizzen to balance her.'

'And put less of a load on the rudder and the helm,' said Anna, sipping her wine.

'I'd forgotten you're an expert.'

She blushed. 'Oh, no, I'm out of practice, I haven't sailed for years, not since my father had to sell his boat. He moved her up to Bosham after we left Cliff Cottage but he couldn't afford the mooring fees, so she had to go too.'

Paul watched her eyelids flicker when she mentioned her father and he wanted to put his arm around her, but he did not wish to intrude in what he knew to be a very personal loss.

They drove back to London, with the *Enigma Variations* playing softly on the radio and Daisy asleep in the back, but it was not the rigid silence that they had encountered on their journey down, more a sensuous, companionable quiet, with the haunting crescendo of the music, the misty autumnal countryside, and the approach of night. At one point, when Paul changed gear, the back of his hand brushed Anna's hand and she did not move it away as she had done on the boat.

When they reached her house, Paul carried Daisy up to the front door. Anna hoped that he wouldn't invite himself inside, it was too soon, but at the same time she was sorry that they had to part. 'Thank you for lunch,' she said. 'I had a lovely day, one of the best for a long time.'

'I enjoyed it too.' He touched Daisy's cheek, and smiled at Anna. She looked so vulnerable, hugging her child in the darkened porch, the light from the hall making her face seem even paler. He wanted to reassure her, to offer his help, but now they were back on her territory she was even more guarded. 'Good luck with Gordon,' he said. 'I'll phone to see how you get on.' And he hurried down the steps and drove away.

Later that evening, when Daisy was in bed, Anna slotted some cassettes into her old tape deck. As she drifted around the house, tidying away Daisy's toys, she became aware that once again she was listening to the *Enigma Variations*.

24

IT TOOK ANNA all of Tuesday morning to smarten up for her lunch with Gordon. She pressed her black suit and cleaned her shoes, whilst Louise trimmed her hair. She studied the *Financial Times* so that she was up to date with the prices of shares and currency and not just disposable nappies.

She decided to treat herself to a taxi to the Savoy because she didn't want to arrive looking creased and hot from the Underground. As she walked into the River Restaurant, with its creamy décor, pillars and glittering chandeliers, she had to pinch herself to believe that this was really happening and that the scrimping and saving was finally over.

She smiled confidently as the restaurant manager approached her. 'I'm meeting Mr Routlish.'

'Ah, you must be Miss Tobias. I'm afraid he's running late; his secretary just telephoned.'

Anna tried to appear unconcerned but the slightest setback made her anxious. She bumped into one of the pillars as the manager ushered her across the dining-room, and when they reached Gordon's reserved table, which overlooked the gardens to the river, she knocked into a chair. Blushing and apologising, she sat down and ordered a glass of mineral water; she was afraid to ask for something more expensive in case some disaster kept Gordon and she was forced to settle her own bill.

Ten minutes later he marched into the dining-room, looked across at her and hesitated, so that Anna feared he'd expected to meet someone else. Then he came striding over, hand outstretched, the light from the chandeliers emphasising his burned-off, featureless face. 'Anna.' He clasped her hand firmly. 'It's good to see you, I'm glad you got in touch, but you look so different that I almost didn't recognise you.'

She sucked in her stomach. 'I've put on a little weight.'

'It suits you. You look more . . . womanly, which is a word I'm sure you feminists hate, but I mean it as a compliment.'

Anna smiled. 'Thank you.' She'd never particularly thought of herself as a feminist, although of course she wanted equal rights, but the way in which Gordon spoke the word suggested a woman who sought more than equal, whereas she just wanted an even break – but it wasn't the moment to argue.

Gordon ordered a bottle of dry white burgundy and launched into an update on Marinecover.

Anna listened closely, knowing that he never wasted time on small talk. 'I'm sorry we had to let you go,' he said. 'Had nothing to do with Creswell, although I know you believed it had. I gather your rogue client is still free as a bird, drinking pink gin on the Costa del Crime. Ah, good, you have a menu. Let's order, then we can relax.'

She chose smoked salmon with crab meat, followed by lamb.

'So? What have you been doing?' he asked, as the waiter retreated.

'Helping a friend run a stall in the Portobello market.'

'You're joking!'

'Quite serious, but now I need to earn a proper salary.'

'You'll have to take a cut. We're in deep recession.'

'I realise that.' She quoted the lead article from the *Financial Times*.

Gordon nodded in agreement and carried on talking about Marinecover and Lloyd's, telling her which syndicates were in trouble and which Names had lost a fortune. 'Some of them will have to sell their homes.' He lowered his voice. 'They'll forfeit everything. Of course they were warned, but greed makes people deaf to warnings.'

Anna thought of Ladbroke Hill and wondered if she'd been greedy to want to live in such a beautiful house.

'I just wish we had something to offer you, Anna,' he said as their coffee arrived.

'You mean . . . you don't have?'

'I'm afraid not – but it's been good to see you again.'

She was so crushed with disappointment that she could barely swallow. It was an effort not to break down in tears and scream, 'You raised my hopes; I took a taxi here – I wasted money.'

They parted outside the Savoy. She thanked him politely for lunch and insisted that he took the only waiting taxi, saying, 'You're in a hurry, I'll take the next.'

He called out a cheerful 'Goodbye' and he was whisked back to the City.

Anna smiled and waved, and waited until he was out of sight before she headed for the bus stop, pushing through the groups of tourists who meandered down the Strand. When her bus arrived she climbed wearily aboard and collapsed into the nearest seat, longing for the moment when she reached Ladbroke Hill and could shut the door on the hostile world. But before they reached the first stop she straightened up, she wasn't going to find a job by giving in and going home. 'I've made a mistake,' she told the conductor, ignoring his outstretched hand, 'I meant to go the other way.' She jumped off, ran across the road and took another bus, to the City.

She visited the five main headhunters in her field, none of whom had a vacancy, but it was good to show them her face, especially since she was dressed so smartly. Her last call was at the offices of Keifer & Bell. They seemed shabbier than Anna recalled, and the two smiling receptionists she'd seen before had been reduced to one sullen girl. She waved Anna towards Mr Keifer's office, saying, 'Go on in. He's free.'

Mr Keifer was at his desk, doing a jumbo crossword. He looked up, and struggled to remember Anna's name.

'Miss Tobias,' she said. 'I registered last year and I telephoned you a few weeks ago.'

'Oh dear! I'm afraid it's hopeless, I haven't one vacancy. It's this bloody recession. In fact, I'm closing the office on Friday. Sorry to be so pessimistic.'

Anna backed out of his room. 'Goodbye and good luck,' she said, hurrying from the bitter smell of failure.

She returned home feeling utterly defeated. Out in the garden she could hear Mr Marilyn talking to Daisy, and she decided to leave her with him for a little longer, to give herself time to recover. Her telephone rang but she didn't answer it, she felt too crushed. She flopped on to her bed, closed her eyes and let the machine cut in.

There was a series of clicks, then, 'Anna, it's Paul,' followed by silence whilst he waited for her to answer. But she didn't, she was too disheartened to speak. 'I was wondering how you got on today,' he continued. 'I hope the fact you're out means that you're celebrating.' He rang off, and the machine rewound. Afterwards she wished she'd talked to him, she remembered what he'd said about not bottling things up.

When Louise and Mac came home, they took one look at Anna's face and asked no questions. To cheer her up they ordered a take-away from her favourite Indian restaurant and refused to let her pay her share. For their sake, almost as much as for Daisy's, she put on a brave face.

Two days later Paul telephoned again. Anna was at home, at her desk, calculating how much extra rent money she'd make if she let out her drawing-room as a bedroom. This time she hurried to answer.

'You're there at last,' he said, relieved. 'How was the lunch?'

'Not so good.' She sank on to her bed. 'Gordon didn't offer me a job, it was just . . . lunch, that's all.' She couldn't prevent the tremor in her voice.

'Oh, Anna, I'm so sorry. Are you all right? I wish I was in England, then I could come round and take you out for dinner.'

She couldn't remember the last time someone had been so concerned about her welfare, and it was an effort not to cry 'Help me, I can't cope,' but she was afraid to depend on anyone after Charlie, so she said, with a confidence she didn't feel, 'I'll just have to battle on.'

'That's what I admire. You dust yourself down and try again.'

'Oh, I'm not brave underneath.'

'But you don't give up.' He paused. 'Anna, I want you to call me if there's anything I can do, if you get really . . . desperate. You just need to say your name and I'll ring you straight back.' He gave her his number at Whaler's Rock, then she asked about his holiday and if he'd been sailing yet. When they said goodbye, he repeated again that she should call him. She didn't tell him that she couldn't afford to telephone America, she barely had enough money to feed Daisy.

Gordon rang a week later, when Anna had just arrived home from another fruitless day. 'I have a job for you,' he said. 'Nothing glamorous, just a marine insurance saleswoman with Eurohull, one of the subsidiaries we partly own. Starting salary, fifteen thousand plus commission.'

Anna did a quick calculation. The increased mortgage payment to cover last year's shortfall would eat up five thousand and child care would take at least another four. 'Fifteen thousand isn't very much,' she ventured.

'Can't pay more, but we pay good commission.'

'All right, I'll take it. Thank you.'

'You'll have to travel, up to a couple of days a week, but only in Europe.'

Anna could hear Daisy giggling. How could she leave her when she was so little?

'Travelling isn't a problem, surely?' said Gordon, puzzled by her silence.

'No, of course not.' Daisy would be worse off if they lost their home.

Gordon dictated Eurohull's address, adding, 'Start on Monday. You'll be on a month's trial. You've no need to go for an interview, I've recommended you myself. In any case, you already know your boss, he's Stuart Porterill.'

'The Cobra! Are you sure he wants me?'

'He says you'll be an asset to his team.'

'I thought he despised women in the City.'

'He did, but he's mellowed. We had to lay him off, he was unemployed for a year till we took him on at Eurohull. There's nothing like a spell out of work to make employees less demanding.'

'You mean like me?' She tried not to sound as outraged as she felt in case Gordon retracted his offer.

'You said it, Anna.'

'How calculating! Nevertheless, I'm grateful for the job.'

He rang off without further talk.

Anna hurried into the drawing-room where Louise was playing with Daisy. 'I have a job,' she said. 'I can't believe it, someone wants me!' She scooped up Daisy and hugged her fiercely. 'Now I have to sort you out. I wish I didn't have to leave you, but I have no option.'

Paul telephoned that evening and she told him her good news.

He congratulated her, and said, 'I'll be back next weekend, before I go to Australia. Will you have dinner with me?'

'I'd love to.'

'I'm so looking forward to seeing you again, Anna,' he said softly.

She felt as though she were melting into his voice and mumbled a reply, and afterwards she wasn't sure what she'd said, but suddenly everything seemed to be going all right.

She hardly dared believe that her disasters were behind her, that she'd be able to open an East Metro envelope without feeling sick with fear that she was about to lose the house, that she had someone who cared and shared her problems, someone who she could trust, perhaps, if she could ever dare to trust anyone again.

It took Anna every waking moment to find suitable childcare for Daisy. She couldn't afford a live-in nanny, in any case she didn't have room, and a daily nanny would be too expensive and left the problem of her overnight business trips, so her only solution was a flexible child-minder. After a couple of false starts, she went to see one recommended by Lionel's wife.

Heather was a homely Scotswoman married to a gregarious Jamaican saxophonist. They lived in a large ground-floor flat with a secure garden a brisk fifteen minutes' walk from Ladbroke Hill. Aided by her daughter, Heather looked after four babies and if they were restless, Walter, her husband, would line up the infants and entertain them with Dixie music. Heather quoted Anna seventy pounds a week to keep Daisy from eight in the morning until seven at night, with extra if she had her at the weekends or for the night. This would take a large bite out of Anna's salary, but she had no alternative.

On the morning she was due to start at Eurohull, Anna rushed between the shower, her clothes, her breakfast and her make-up whilst Daisy sat in her high chair, refusing her breakfast, her big blue eyes deep with suspicion at the change in her routine. When Anna lifted Daisy into her pushchair she began to cry, kicking furiously as the straps were tightened. Her cries turned to shrieks as Anna hurried her out of the warm house and down the dark, cold street.

'Oh dear, we are a wee cross-patch,' said Heather, smiling

broadly as she opened her flat door. 'Hello, Daisy. Now, say goodbye to Mummy. And Mummy, you say it quick and leave. That's right. Go! Don't hang around, you'll only make her worse. We'll be fine, won't we, Daisy?'

Fraught with guilt, Anna kissed Daisy's tear-drenched cheek and fled.

Eurohull occupied the top floor of a large functional office block on the unsmart side of Blackfriars Bridge. Gordon had been right when he'd said it wasn't glamorous. There was just one large, unpartitioned room containing rows of plywood desks, telephones, and a dozen anxious, commission-driven salesmen.

It took Anna a moment to recognise the man waiting beside the reception desk as Stuart Porterill, because his hair had turned completely grey. He held out his hand. 'Glad you're joining us, Anna, you're looking well.'

'So are you.'

'No, I look like shit.' He greeted the seven other people who'd shared Anna's lift in a manner which made her realise that they too were new. He led them to his desk at the far end of the office, told them to find chairs and, as soon as they sat down, made them stand up, one by one, to say their names. Apart from Anna there was one other woman, a pleasant brunette called Sophie.

With little more than a preliminary welcome, Stuart launched into his spiel, telling them about Marinecover, Eurohull and their position in the insurance market. 'We're small and pushy, and your job is to grab as much as possible of the European shipping market so that we become big and pushy. You'll spend Mondays fixing appointments, some in the UK, some in Europe, Tuesdays through Thursdays you'll be on the road, Fridays you report back to me – unless you have a client meeting. A client always takes precedence, even over your grandmother's funeral. If you get behind with your paperwork, you do it at home. It's a tough job, but if you perform well the rewards are high. If you don't, you're out. The survival rate's twenty per cent.'

'Do you mean we cold call?' asked Sophie.

'That's the job.'

'I . . . er . . . don't think it's for me.' She gathered up her belongings and left.

Stuart looked at the others. 'Anyone else?'

An older man with a slight squint shuffled from the room. Watching him go Anna wondered how much notice she'd have to give Heather if she lost her job.

Stuart appeared unperturbed by the departures. 'Our business is placed in Lloyd's by the brokers at our parent company, Marinecover,' he continued. 'It's no secret that Lloyd's has had recent adverse publicity. You'll be questioned about it, and your response is that Lloyd's have never failed to pay a genuine claim. The publicity only concerns a few Names who have made a loss. Understood?'

They all nodded.

Stuart gave them each a potted history of Marinecover, a glossy Eurohull brochure, a list of shipping companies with their contact names, and he told them to choose a desk.

Anna selected a place beside the window, so as to have some privacy.

Stuart followed her. 'This is a dog-eat-dog job, Anna, you deserve better.'

'There isn't much choice, with so many out of work.'

'Don't I know it!' He touched his grey hair. 'I've lost my house, my Porsche, my yacht and my wife. Now I share a flat with my sister. What have you been doing since you left Marinecover? Someone told me that you and Charlie split up.'

'Charlie went back to Australia and I took a career break,' she replied, casually, trying not to giggle at the idea that mashing up potato for Daisy's lunch could be described as a career break.

Two hours passed and not one of the newcomers made a telephone call. They were anxiously studying the Eurohull brochure. Anna looked up to find Stuart evaluating them from beneath his hooded, cobra eyelids. Taking a deep breath to quell her nerve, she lined up her pen and note-pad and reached for the telephone to call the first name on her contact sheet: Mr Bernard van Rooyen of Van Rooyen Rotterdam, a family shipping line. Instantly, the others gazed at her with admiration and, more importantly, Stuart nodded his approval.

To Anna's amazement she was put straight through to Mr van Rooyen. 'This is Anna Tobias from Eurohull,' she began. 'I'd like to fix an appointment to discuss your insurance needs. We at Eurohull believe that we can . . .'

'Who are you?' demanded an irritated, guttural voice.

'Anna Tobias from Eurohull.'

'But I was expecting Merchant & Leisure. My telephonist must have become confused and put you through by mistake.'

Anna almost lost her nerve but she ploughed on. 'This is providence, Mr van Rooyen. You were waiting to hear from an insurance broker and I am speaking from another company who can offer you a much better package – better coverage and lower rates. I'll be in Rotterdam next week. When can I see you?'

'It's out of the question. We've used Merchant & Leisure for five years. In any case I shall be in London next week.'

'Better still. Will you have lunch with me?'

'Miss . . . er . . . you're wasting your time. I admit we are concerned about Merchant & Leisure's high rates, but . . .'

'Next Tuesday at the Savoy's River Restaurant?'

Stuart was on his feet, waving at Anna and hissing, 'Too expensive!'

But she took no notice. 'Would one o'clock suit you, Mr van Rooyen?'

'Oh very well, fax me your figures and I'll examine them, but I can't promise we'll move to Eurohull. This is just a preliminary talk, Miss . . . er . . .'

'Tobias. I look forward to meeting you.'

As she came off the line Stuart exploded. 'Anna, you can't afford to take clients to the Savoy on your expenses.'

'I can't afford not to, Stuart. I need to impress van Rooyen and it's the only expensive restaurant in London where the manager will remember me. You see, I went there last week with Gordon.'

'Did you? Good heavens! Well . . . er . . . okay, but if you don't get the business you pay for the lunch yourself.'

Anna nearly backed down but she didn't, she went with her instinct.

She spent the afternoon preparing the package for van Rooyen, faxing it to him just before she went home. That first small success had pumped her with energy and adrenaline, but once she'd fought her way home on the Underground she was exhausted. She longed for a bath, a meal, and sleep, but first she had to collect Daisy, who was tired and grumpy after her first day in a strange place and with other children. She cried all the way home, wouldn't eat her supper, and took hours to settle, screaming when Louise came in. When Anna finally crawled into bed it seemed no time at all before her alarm sounded and she was rushing Daisy through her breakfast and back to Heather.

On Friday night, as she was leaving work, Stuart called to her, 'Coming for a drink, Anna?'

'I'd love to but I can't.' She said good night and hurried home to Daisy.

Paul had hoped to return to England that weekend but a valuable yacht belonging to Steven's cousin had been stolen off Newport and Steven had asked Paul to use his expertise to find it. As he explained regretfully to Anna, it was impossible to refuse. So he heard the story about Mr van Rooyen on the telephone and laughed at her outwitting the Cobra.

For her lunch with Mr van Rooyen, Anna wore her grey suit with an elegant and feminine cream silk camisole. She arrived at the Savoy ahead of her guest and, in case the restaurant manager didn't remember her, she gave him her name and asked if she could have the same table she'd shared with Gordon the previous week. Instead of waiting at the table she purposely took a seat in the lounge from where she could watch the entrance to the restaurant. At one o'clock precisely a portly, sandy-haired man with a neat beard approached the dining-room. Taking a gamble that this was van Rooyen, Anna followed him.

'I'm meeting a Miss Tobias,' he informed the manager in a deep guttural voice.

'She's right behind you, sir. Ah, Miss Tobias, your favourite table is ready.'

Mr van Rooyen looked suitably impressed.

Like Gordon he was a man of few interests apart from work. From the moment they sat down he launched into a history of Van Rooyen Rotterdam, his family firm, droning on throughout the entire meal without a mention of insurance, until Anna feared that he had no intention of giving her any business. He ate two rich chocolate puddings, one after the other, and when he raised his napkin to wipe his fleshy lips, he said, 'Delicious. Very well, Miss Tobias, I've studied your package and I am persuaded to allow you to insure the hulls of our three medium-sized tankers. If your back-up service is as good as your promise, in January you will come to Rotterdam to discuss our new supertanker.'

Anna beamed. 'Thank you, Mr van Rooyen.'

'You're a clever young lady.' He rose abruptly and left her to settle the bill.

Anna couldn't wait to reach Eurohull. Stuart was as his desk when she sashayed across the office, waving the Savoy bill. 'Lunch is on you!' she told him triumphantly.

He was astonished. 'You did it! You won van Rooyen!'

'Three tankers this year, one giant in January.' Laughing, she dropped the bill in his lap, crossed to her desk, picked up her client contact sheet, and telephoned five more names. Her sheer confidence persuaded them all to see her.

That evening Stuart said, 'How about celebrating?'

'I'd love to, but not tonight.'

'That's what you always say. Have you a secret lover, Anna, is that why you rush off?'

She laughed and walked out of the office, calling 'Good night' over her shoulder. One day she might tell Stuart about Daisy, but not yet.

On the way home she bought a bottle of wine to celebrate her van Rooyen victory, but when she arrived at Ladbroke Hill she found the place in darkness. There was a message from Louise on the answering machine saying she'd gone to a party, and a note from Mac to say he was in Zürich on business. Deflated, Anna put Daisy to bed. Then she opened the wine, poured herself a glass and sat down in front of the television. But she couldn't concentrate on the programmes, she wanted someone with whom she could share her good news.

She telephoned Roz but she was out, taking Luke to a concert and, although Tom congratulated Anna, her world meant little to him. She phoned her mother who was pleased, but because she'd never wished for a career herself, she had little concept of the satisfaction it could bring. Anna sat by the telephone, drumming her fingers and frowning. She wished Paul would phone, but he was on his way to Miami where he'd tracked the stolen yacht. He'd understand, he knew how anxious she'd been and how much she'd need this victory, not just for the money but for her battered, fragile confidence.

*

She flew to Rotterdam, leaving Daisy with Heather all night for the first time. She'd never been to Rotterdam before and her first sight of it didn't particularly appeal to her. She preferred old cities and this was modern, most of the old buildings having been destroyed by bombs during the Second World War. But it was a good place for business, being a highly industrialised transit port.

Although Eurohull representatives weren't usually allowed to use five-star hotels, Stuart had agreed that Anna should stay at the Hilton in order to impress Mr van Rooyen, for whom these details were clearly important. The hotel was in the centre of the city, on the Weena, a wide street running between the Stationplein and the Hofplein, and within an hour of landing at the airport Anna was in her room, telephoning Heather to check on Daisy.

Making that call left her barely enough time to brush her hair before she hurried to the restaurant to meet a prospective client, a distant cousin of Mr van Rooyen's wife. By the end of lunch he'd agreed to consider her quote on one of his three supertankers: Anna was elated. She went straight to her second appointment with the financial director of a small shipping line whose offices were on the south side of the Nieuwe Maas, the wide, tidal, northern branch of the river Rhine on whose banks Rotterdam was built. Within ten minutes of arriving Anna sensed that he was merely comparing her quotation with that of his present insurer, with no intention of moving to Eurohull. Had she been more experienced she'd have wrapped it up quickly. As it was, she was there for two hours.

She raced back to the Hilton for an early dinner with Mr van Rooyen. Throughout the meal he repeated his family history whilst she gritted her teeth to stop herself from yawning. As soon as he left Anna hurried up to her room to telephone Heather. 'Is Daisy all right?' she asked anxiously.

'She's fast asleep. Stop worrying.'

'I can't help it!'

'I understand,' said Heather gently, 'I'd be the same.'

It was too early for Anna to go to bed and too late for her to go out. In no mood to write up her reports she stood by the window, looking out over the lights of the city. She wasn't so much lonely as isolated and she wished there was someone whom she could ring up and chat to. From the stationery provided by the hotel she wrote a postcard to her mother and grandmother and another to Roz. Then she took the remaining card, and wrote, 'I wish you were here, I really do, Love, Anna.' She addressed it to Paul at *The Goshawk*, because she couldn't remember the street number of his London studio, but when she read it back, she was afraid of being too open and, unsure whether to send it, she propped it on her dressing-table and left that decision until the morning.

An early phone call from another of Mr van Rooyen's contacts requesting a breakfast meeting meant that she had to dress and pack in a rush. She was on the plane flying back to London before she remembered the postcard.

She arrived home to find a message from Paul saying that the stolen yacht had taken so much of his time he'd had to fly direct to Australia, but would be back in two weeks. She hadn't realised that he travelled so much and she felt disheartened and disillusioned, wondering when they would ever see each other and if, perhaps, she should forget the whole thing rather than risk depending on someone who was never there. It seemed doomed before they even began – and yet, she wasn't sure.

Anna didn't enjoy her job at Eurohull as much as she had enjoyed Marinecover, but she was the star of the newcomers and success made her feel good. Her commission figures were high, but at Mr Flatbush's insistence all the extra money she earned was paid into her account at East Metro. After deductions for the mortgage and an extra charge to repay last year's deficit, she had barely enough to pay her bills, Heather, and all the expenses which accumulated now that she worked: smart suits for the office, a regular hair cut, a new briefcase, and taxis when she'd worked late and was too tired to struggle home on public transport.

She longed to escape for a whole weekend, to walk in the countryside, to sleep, to relax, but at the weekends she had paperwork to catch up with, so the most she could manage was a Sunday lunch with her mother and grandmother – a long drive for one day.

On Daisy's first birthday Anna had to be in Rotterdam. Although she felt guilty about it, she couldn't cancel her meeting so they celebrated with a tea party the following Sunday. Everyone in the house was invited.

Anna was in the kitchen, decorating the birthday cake, when there was a ring on the front bell and Mac went to answer. Anna heard him talking but she didn't pay much attention. Then she heard Mac say, 'She's in there.'

'Hello, Anna.' Paul stood in the doorway looking darkly tanned and foreign, especially compared to Mac who was so blond and pink. 'I'm sorry to drop in uninvited,' he said, 'but I got back today and I'm only in London this afternoon and . . .' He smiled. 'I wanted to see you.'

She blushed, not knowing what to say to him now that he was here. 'It's Daisy's birthday.' She waved the sugar-coated palette knife towards the cake, forgetting that she didn't like her home invaded.

'Thank you for the postcard,' he said softly. 'It was a lovely surprise.'

She remembered what she'd written and went scarlet. 'Did you get it?'

'Of course.'

'But I never sent it, I left it on the hotel dressing-table.'

'Then whoever found it must have realised it was meant to be posted.'

Anna busied herself planting the candleholder in the centre of the cake. On the telephone they talked with ease, but now that Paul was here she found it hard to look at him. She tried to twist the candle into its holder, but it was too large and wouldn't fit.

'Let me do that,' he offered, picking up a sharp knife and deftly whittling the end.

'If you'd come earlier you could have made the cake too,' she joked, to keep the conversation humorous, because she was still unsettled by his unexpected arrival.

He handed her the cake on the plate, saying, 'Don't make fun of me or your hair will curl.'

'But I've always longed for curly hair,' she replied truthfully as she led the way into the drawing-room where Daisy was seated in her high chair, with Mr Marilyn on one side and Louise on the other. Setting the cake on the table in front of her, Anna helped her blow out the candle, whilst everyone sang *Happy Birthday*.

Paul left shortly afterwards. 'I wish I'd brought Daisy a present,' he told Anna when she accompanied him to the front door.

'Her birthday was really on Friday but I was away on business.' She pulled a face. 'I feel guilty about it, but I couldn't take a day off, especially not when I've only just started; and certainly not for Daisy's birthday when the Cobra doesn't know I have a child.'

'Daisy doesn't realise her birthday isn't today,' said Paul to reassure her.

'I know, but she will next year and if not then, the one after. But what can I do? I have to work.' She didn't mean to reveal all her uncertainties.

Paul took her hands in his. 'Stop berating yourself; you're doing your best.'

She looked at him and, suddenly, she laughed. 'You're right, I do berate myself. I get up on my soapbox and . . . tell myself I'm hopeless at everything.'

'Well, I shall push you off it because you're doing fine.' He smiled, although his clear grey eyes grew pensive. 'I'll be back on Friday. Have dinner with me.'

Anna hesitated, not because she didn't want to see him, but she remembered how she'd longed to talk to him when he was on his way to Australia, and she was afraid of becoming dependent on his presence and his support.

When she didn't reply, he answered for her in an exaggerated imitation of her voice. 'Yes, thank you, Paul, I'd like that.'

She couldn't refuse a man who made her laugh.

25

ANNA ARRIVED AT work on Monday morning to find that one of the senior salesmen had walked out after a row with Stuart and, since her figures were the highest of her intake, she qualified for his company car. That evening she drove it home, in the pouring rain, and collected Daisy in it, instead of wheeling her through the cold, wet streets.

Paul telephoned that night. He asked after her day and she told him about the car. She thought he was in Jamaica, but he'd flown on to Colombia. When he told her, she said, 'You travel more than anyone I've ever known.'

'It was the perfect way to escape, and there was a time when I wanted to.' He paused, then added in a softer voice. 'But now I'd prefer to be at home.'

She wondered if he'd wanted to escape from his wife, or her death, and hoped he'd elaborate, but he went on, 'I'm organising a worldwide network of contacts with whom I'll pool information. Once this is up and running, I'll travel less.'

'Then you'll have time to enjoy *The Goshawk*.'

'And other things!' He spoke with such intimacy that his words were like a caress on her skin.

She relished the frisson of excitement which his voice sent through her, but it also made her nervous. 'You mean, you want to spend more time with Bobby?' she joked, retreating to the safety of their teasing.

He chuckled. 'I'll see you on Friday. I'm looking forward to it – very much.'

Anna put Daisy to bed and read her a little story, but her mind wasn't on the pictures in the book, it kept drifting back to Paul. She found him so attractive and, on reflection, she realised that she always had. If she hadn't, she wouldn't have gone home with him, however drunk. He was an intriguing combination of unruly boyishness and sophisticated charm, and she enjoyed their banter which counteracted the awkwardness of their one unsuccessful fling – not that Paul seemed remotely embarrassed by it, which meant that she wasn't either.

Since Anna had started work, the social life in the house had ground to a halt because she was too busy to gossip around the dining-table. In any case, the surface of the table was frequently covered with her work reports. She wasn't aware how much the others regretted this change until, on the morning after she received the car, Mr Marilyn stopped her in the drive. 'I suppose we won't be having a Christmas party this year?' he said, sorrowfully.

Anna had intended to invite herself to Lower Gossip Fen, because she hadn't seen Roz since she'd started at Eurohull, but Mr Marilyn looked so sad. She hadn't forgotten what a good friend he'd been to her and how often he'd looked after Daisy whilst she was job-hunting. 'Of course we'll have the party,' she said, buckling Daisy into the child-seat and hoping that her mother would forgive her.

His eyes brightened. 'Do you mean that?'

'Certainly. After all, Grażyna is going back to Poland soon and we should give her a good send off.' Anna gave him a quick kiss on the cheek and jumped into the car.

As she drove away, she wondered what she was going to tell her mother, who was not a woman who had close friendships, even with Jacynthia, and would not understand that to Anna, her friends were just as much her family.

All week Anna thought about Paul. He was in her thoughts when she flew to Rotterdam on Wednesday; he was beside her in the back of a taxi as it whisked her from one appointment to the next; and he held her in his arms at night, when she drifted into sleep. She alternated between the fear that she would be hurt again and the desire to have him in her life and in her bed.

She purposely arranged to fly home early on Friday, but at the last minute Stuart faxed her a lunchtime meeting with a new client, so by the time she climbed aboard her flight from Rotterdam, it was late afternoon. Then a fault on the instrument panel caused the pilot to abort take-off, and she was transferred to another flight. After collecting Daisy, she reached Ladbroke Hill with only half an hour to spare before Paul arrived. She was exhausted, but she couldn't bring herself to cancel dinner when she saw so little of him.

Louise returned to babysit and found Anna slumped in a chair, reading Daisy a story. 'You looked whacked,' she said. 'What's happened?'

'I've had a bad day and I've only just got home.'

'I'll finish Daisy.' Louise pulled Anna to her feet. 'Pour yourself a brandy and have a bath. It'll make you feel better.'

Anna was dozing in scented water when Paul rang the doorbell. She shot out of the bath as Louise went to answer, drying herself rapidly whilst Louise and Paul chatted in the drawing-room.

She'd intended to wear a slinky black crêpe dress, but after searching through her cupboard she remembered it was still at the dry cleaners, so she pulled out a black leather skirt, one she'd bought in her early days with Charlie and not worn since because she associated it with him. Now, she was too tired to worry.

Working at Eurohull, she'd lost all the weight she'd put on with Daisy, but she didn't look better for it, at least she felt she didn't. Her face was drawn and her eyes had dark, hollow rings. She could have camouflaged them if she'd had time to make up carefully but she was in a hurry. She slapped on some moisturiser, followed by some rouge, touched her eyelashes with mascara and glossed her mouth. Finally, she put on a pair of pumps, which were comfortable, although high heels would have been sexier.

As she walked through to the drawing-room she could hear Paul speaking to Louise, and she remembered how his voice had brought a frisson of excitement to her. Now all she could think about was how long would it be before she could sleep.

Paul turned, smiling, as Anna entered the room. He was looking very smart in a dark suit although his hair had its endearing unruliness. 'Hello.' He kissed her on the cheek. 'I told you I'd be here. She didn't believe me, Louise, she thought I'd cancel from the other side of the world again, didn't you?'

She nodded and tried to appear animated. She felt guilty because he'd come all this way to have dinner with a zombie.

'I've booked a table at L'Artiste Assoiffé,' he said. 'I hope you like it.'

'I do.' She didn't tell him that it had been one of Charlie's haunts.

He helped her on with her coat and they went out into the night. She showed him her car and then stepped into his, where the warmth made her even sleepier.

'I saw there was fog over the Netherlands,' he said, concerned to see that she looked even paler than usual. 'Did you have a bad journey?'

'Just an aborted take-off.' Her eyes began to close.

'How's boring Mr van Rooyen?'

'He's . . . dull.' She tried to pull herself together. 'Tell me about Colombia.'

'It's a dangerous place – beautiful and very dangerous.' He paused, then added in an attempt to make her smile, 'Just like a woman!' To his surprise Anna didn't bounce back with some jokey response, and he remembered that a few minutes earlier she'd deflected him from the subject of herself by asking about Colombia, and he wondered why.

When they reached the restaurant he took her by the arm and ushered her inside, not into the bar where the voices of the parrots were vying with those of the guests, but straight to their table. To her relief it was not up beside the carousel, where Charlie had preferred, but in a secluded corner, next to a mural of a clown.

The waiter brought the wine list and whilst Paul studied it, Anna drifted. He made a suggestion and she nodded, although she hadn't heard a word he'd said, but when the waiter returned with a bottle of Château Laroze, she was pleased, except that the wine made her even sleepier.

'How is Daisy?' Paul asked, thinking that was the problem.

'She's fine. Heather's very good. I'm lucky to have found her. And having the car is such a relief.' The wine had gone straight to her head and she leaned her elbows on the table to steady herself. 'Tell me more about your cases in South America,' she said.

He responded, encouraged by her interest, but he was too experienced an investigator not to realise that once again she was deflecting him. 'I found two of the three I was tracking. The other one, the most expensive . . . God knows where it is. Most large cruisers which disappear in Europe end up in the Caribbean to be sold to drug runners. I fear this boat has suffered the same fate.'

She woke from her doze and remembered the car bomb in Medellin. 'Aren't you afraid?'

'I'd be a liar if I said I wasn't, but I'm careful, and I remind myself that it is not worth losing my life just to recover a yacht or to disprove an insurance claim.'

The waiter took their order, although when he'd gone Anna had no idea what she had chosen. She placed one elbow on the arm of her chair and her chin in the palm of her hand. From somewhere far away she heard the rich cadences of Paul's voice. It acted like a lullaby, and slowly her eyes closed and her head dropped sideways, against the mural of the clown.

Paul stopped talking and stared at the sleeping woman in front of him. Then he leaned across the table and gently shook her by the shoulder, saying, 'Anna, are you ill?'

She woke with a start. 'What's happened?'

'You fell asleep.'

'Oh no! I'm so sorry!'

'I didn't realise I was that boring.' He was more amused than offended.

'Oh, you're not! It's just that . . . I'm so exhausted. I got home less than an hour before you arrived and it's not only the job, it's the constant juggle. I rush Daisy to Heather, hurry to work, battle all day to make my target figures, then race back to collect Daisy.' She took a deep breath. 'Oh, I'm sorry, I don't mean to moan.'

He reached across the table and took her hand in his. 'Anna, why didn't you postpone tonight?'

'Because I wanted to see you and you're going away again tomorrow, and heaven knows when you'll be back.' She was too sleepy to be anything but honest.

He linked his fingers through hers. 'I wanted to see you too – very much.'

'And you came all the way across the Atlantic and you're not tired, whereas I just crossed from Holland.'

'Anna, I don't have Daisy.' He beckoned to the waiter. 'The lady isn't well. May we have our bill?'

'Oh, no, you must finish your dinner,' Anna protested. 'I'm all right, I can wait.'

'You're going home to bed.' Paul handed over his credit card.

Too tired to argue, Anna allowed herself to be ushered out to the car. Now that she no longer had to pretend to be awake, she fell asleep in the front seat, her head resting on Paul's shoulder.

When they reached the house, he half-carried her up the steps, took the key from her fingers and unlocked her front door. Then he smoothed her hair back from her forehead and cupped her face in his hands.

'I'm sorry,' she repeated. 'Thank you for being . . . so nice about it.'

'Sleep well.' He brushed her mouth with his, very softly, and whispered. 'I'll phone you tomorrow, before I leave. Now, go to bed.' Gently, he pushed her inside the house.

Louise was sprawled on the sofa, watching the television. She looked up in amazement as Anna walked in, alone. 'What happened? You've only been gone an hour.'

'I fell asleep.' Anna started to laugh.

'On your first date – and after all that anticipation!' She gave a wail of horror which ended in a giggle. 'What did he say?'

'He was very nice about it, incredibly nice. If I'd behaved like that with Charlie he'd never have forgiven me.'

'Well, I hope that's not your one and only date.'

'Definitely not.' Anna tottered through into her room, kicked off her shoes, pulled off her clothes, and flopped into bed, too tired even to remove her make-up.

Louise came to the door. 'I like Paul and I'm glad he's asked you out again.'

'He didn't.' Anna closed her eyes. 'I'm going to invite him to the Christmas party.'

Paul telephoned Anna next morning and accepted her invitation. They talked for over an hour, until his taxi arrived to take him to the airport. She felt very deflated when he'd gone; he wouldn't be back before Christmas Eve. In the two months since the Finesteins' lunch, they'd only met three times and yet, somehow, he was becoming such an important part of her life. The following morning Anna received a postcard, a picture of a dormouse fast asleep. It had been posted at Heathrow. Like so many things he did, it made her smile.

To reassure everyone in the house that the party was definitely going ahead, Anna ordered a Christmas tree. This year she could afford an undamaged one but she couldn't spare the time to decorate it – Mr Marilyn and Louise did that while she was away on business. As with the previous year, everyone provided a dish. Anna was to supply the pudding, only she didn't make it, she bought it; she had no time to cook. But she did treat herself to a gorgeous new dress. It was made of dark green velvet, full length, with a seductive slit up one thigh.

She got round the problem of her mother by saying that she had to work late on Christmas Eve, but promised to visit Lower Gossip Fen during the week before the new year. She didn't like to lie, but it seemed the only way not to injure her mother's feelings.

In the weeks before Christmas, Eurohull was particularly busy and Anna was away most of the time. It was always a wrench to leave Daisy, but when Anna reached Eurohull she slotted into a work mode as if she were two people, and that somewhere between Holland Park and Blackfriars she metamorphosed from mother to career woman. Nevertheless, she nearly cried when she returned from Holland on Christmas Eve to discover that Daisy had hauled herself upright in the middle of Heather's playroom. Whilst she'd been discussing insurance, her daughter had taken her first faltering step, and she'd missed it.

At noon on Christmas day Anna stood in front of her long mirror, wearing her new dress, and suddenly she was beset with nerves. It was several weeks since she'd seen Paul, although they spoke on the phone often enough, but he was the first man whom she'd invited to the house and she so wanted her Ladbroke Hill family to like him – and he them.

The doorbell rang as she was painting her nails. She strained to hear as Grazyna answered, relaxing only when she caught Dominic's voice.

'Happy Christmas, Anna,' he called to her. 'What's this I hear about a new boyfriend?'

'He's *just* a friend!' She hoped that Dominic wouldn't say anything embarrassing in front of Paul.

They congregated in the drawing-room, where Mac was in charge of drinks and Mr Marilyn handed round the minuscule vol-au-vents which had taken him all week to make. A few minutes before Paul was due to arrive, Anna slipped into the kitchen, not because she was needed there – Victoria and Mac were in charge – but because she was so nervous that she couldn't keep still. She found Louise leaning against the fridge, looking sad.

'What's wrong?' she asked.

'Robert promised to call me yesterday.'

'He'll phone, he always does – eventually.'

'Yes, but this is the fifth time he's phoned late.' Louise sighed. 'Has Paul arrived?'

Anna shook her head. 'I hope he hasn't forgotten.'

'Now who's being pessimistic?'

The bell rang again and Anna clutched Louise's arm. 'Oh no! He's here!'

'Of course he is, you invited him,' said Mac.

'I know, but I'm scared.' Anna ran her fingers through her soft blonde hair. 'I feel like a teenager on my first date. Do I look all right?'

'Yes. Go on, answer the door!' Louise gave her a gentle shove.

Paul was standing on the top step holding a luscious bouquet of golden lilies in one hand and a life-sized walkie-talkie doll in the other. He stared at Anna in silence.

She smiled shyly. 'Is something wrong?'

'You're beautiful.' He took a step towards her and kissed her on the cheek. 'Happy Christmas, Anna,' he whispered into her hair.

'Happy Christmas, Paul.' She didn't move away from him.

They were interrupted by Daisy who toddled out of the drawing-room. When she saw Paul so close to her mother, her eyes filled with deep and instinctive suspicion.

'Hello, Daisy. I've brought you a present.' Paul bent to hand it to her.

Daisy put her hands firmly behind her back.

'Oh dear.' He glanced up at Anna.

'She'll be all right,' said Anna. 'She isn't used to seeing me . . .' Her words trailed away and she blushed.

Paul touched her hand and gave her a smile which told her that he understood her fears and reservations.

She led him into the drawing-room and introduced him to those he hadn't already met. Mr Marilyn and Mac made no secret that they were sizing Paul up. Their concern touched and amused Anna, and she was relieved to see that Paul took it in good spirit.

He was charming without being obsequious and Anna was pleased that he made a special point of speaking to Mr Marilyn. At lunch he sat next to her, with Daisy on her far side, and he paid her quiet attention, which she enjoyed, although every time he spoke, Daisy gave him a suspicious stare.

When Mac finished carving the turkey and every plate was piled high, he beamed down the table. 'Victoria and I have an announcement,' he said. 'We're getting married in September and we hope you'll all come to our wedding.'

Everybody cheered and raised their glasses. Anna watched Louise put on a brave face and knew that she was trying to forget about Robert.

Lunch lasted all afternoon, and when they left the table they sprawled in front of the fire. Paul sat on the sofa next to Anna, with Daisy on the far side. 'I see that a certain small person is playing with my present,' he whispered, watching Daisy stroke the doll's yellow curls.

Anna smiled. 'She likes to take her time; she's not a girl who gives her affection to just anyone.'

He touched her hand. 'Like her mother?'

Anna felt the frisson of his skin on hers and their eyes locked. In that moment it was as though there was no one else in the room; all she knew was Paul. Eventually the voices of the other guests drew them back to reality, but even then they did not relinquish their new-found intimacy.

Paul had to leave for the Isle of Wight before the party ended because his sister was expecting him that night. He had warned Anna, but nevertheless she was disappointed. 'Don't think I want to go,' he said, reaching for her hand, 'but Harriet's having a party tomorrow and I promised to help. Justin – her husband – fell off a ladder and broke his back a few years ago and he can hardly walk.'

'I understand,' said Anna, thinking how unselfish he was, how unlike Charlie.

She accompanied him to the front door, and in the half light of the hall he took her by both shoulders, drawing her so close that she could feel her heart thudding against him.

'I'll be back the day after tomorrow.' He kissed her gently. 'Will you be here?'

'Yes, but I have to visit my mother this week.'

'So we'll have one day.' He drew her closer. 'Then I leave for South America.'

'Again?' she asked dejectedly.

'For two weeks. It's my last trip, I promise.' He smiled. 'After that I'll be around so much that you'll get bored with me.'

She laughed because she couldn't imagine it, and they clung together, their mouths touching and no more, their bodies pressed together but immobile. She felt his breath caress her skin and his hands on her shoulders and she relished the strength and determination in him. He made her feel safe, he made her feel cherished and wanted, and no longer alone. She longed to share her thoughts and herself with him, to melt into him and become a part of him, and to feel him a part of her. She was gripped by the power of her desire for him, and she shuddered against him.

'I want you,' he murmured in the corner of her mouth.

'Yes.' Her voice was hoarse and her desire for him so fierce that if they'd been alone she couldn't have resisted him. Yet she was glad that, because of Daisy and everyone milling around the house, they were forced to wait.

26

PAUL COULDN'T COME back to London as planned, because an urgent case on the Costa del Sol meant that he had to drive straight from the Isle of Wight to catch a plane to Malaga, but he asked Anna to meet him for breakfast at the airport.

Leaving Daisy with Mr Marilyn, she drove out to Heathrow, arriving in good time to comb her hair and gloss her lips, but in her excitement at the prospect of seeing Paul she discovered that she'd gone to the wrong terminal. By the time she reached the correct place she was very late. She ran up the escalator, cheeks flushed, to find him pacing up and down in front of the information desk, looking worried.

'I'm sorry,' she gasped. 'I went to terminal four.'

He smiled, relieved, and kissed her on the corner of her mouth. 'I thought I'd been stood up. Come on!' He took her by the arm. 'My flight will be boarding soon.'

The restaurant was packed and they had to wait for a table. To her surprise Paul, who was used to travelling around the world at breakneck speed, waited good-humouredly, but the babble of voices speaking every known language, and the Tannoy relentlessly calling for people with unpronounceable names, made conversation between them impossible.

'At least I'm not asleep,' she joked to him during a lull in the noise.

He put an arm around her and drew her very close, so that she could not possibly escape. 'Or being sick on the carpet . . .'

It was the first time either of them had referred to the night in his studio, and Anna blushed furiously. 'That was unkind, Paul,' she said, trying to pull away.

But he refused to release her. 'We've been pussy-footing around the matter of what happened that night, with neither of us mentioning it, and now it's in the open. We can't have forbidden subjects.'

She thought of her mother's continued pretence that her father's death had been an accident. 'You're right.'

He kissed her on the cheek. 'See it this way: things can only get better.'

She laughed and linked her fingers through his. 'Life's looking up already. The manager is beckoning – we have a table.'

They ordered coffee and toast, and Paul charmed the waitress into bringing their breakfast ahead of everyone else's. Suddenly, everything was all right and Anna was no longer embarrassed that he'd mentioned her drunken débâcle; he'd been right to clear the air. She smiled at him across the table and thought how barren her life had been before he'd come striding into it.

'I think I've found an assistant,' he told her, pouring the coffee whilst she buttered the toast. 'He's an ex marine and he has no ties.'

She smiled. 'Or he's escaping from those he *does* have?'

'I'm not escaping any more, Anna.' Paul reached for her hand across the table and squeezed the tips of her fingers. 'Tell me,' he said, watching her closely, 'what happened to the Australian?'

'He walked out when the going got tough.' She pulled a face to mask her lingering anger.

'You never mention him.'

'There's nothing to say.'

'And Daisy?'

'She's mine and mine alone.' Anna raised her chin and met his gaze. 'You never talk about . . . your wife.'

He frowned. 'What would you like to know?'

'Did you . . . love her?'

'Very much.'

She felt deflated. 'How did you meet?'

'At Steven and Georgina's wedding, when I was twenty-one. Felicity had been at school with Georgina.' He paused. 'But later they became less close.'

'And you . . . separated and then got back together?' Anna was aware that she was being intrusive but she had to know how deeply he mourned Felicity and what feelings he could have left over for her.

'Yes, but it was a mistake.'

Anna wanted to ask him if separation had been the mistake – or getting back together. But he was looking out of the window at the aeroplanes being manoeuvred up to the jetways, and there was a terrifying bleakness in his face – but also rage. She reached across the table and stroked the skin on the back of his hand. 'Sorry to question you, but I needed to know.'

He covered her hands with his, and said in a hoarse voice, 'One day I'll tell you everything.' Then he glanced at the monitor to check his departure time, and shot to his feet. 'My flight's finished boarding. I must run. I'll call you later.' He leaned across the table and kissed her on the mouth, and was gone before Anna remembered to tell him that she was going to Lower Gossip Fen that afternoon.

Granny Tobias made a tremendous fuss of Daisy; and Anna received a slightly cool reception from her mother.

'She's upset that you didn't come for Christmas,' Roz told her as they walked around the desolate wintry garden.

'I didn't finish work till late on Christmas Eve and . . .' Anna thought of Paul and turned pink.

'You've met a new man!' Roz laughed at Anna's confusion and gave her a teasing hug. 'I know you're up to something, because you have a gleam in your eye, but I won't interrogate. I just hope he's nice.'

'Oh, he is!' Anna thought of Paul and her whole body tingled with anticipation of his touch.

Arriving back in London, she was met in the hall by Louise. 'Just look what's been delivered for you,' she said, opening the drawing-room door.

In the centre of the refectory table there was a vase brimming with red rosebuds. Anna didn't need to read the card to know that they were from Paul, and she hugged herself.

After the freedom of the holidays, it was an effort for Anna to return to work. As she steered her way through the traffic along the Embankment, she envied Paul his self-employed freedom, but by the time she reached Blackfriars Bridge she was looking forward to the challenge of work.

She arrived at Eurohull to find an atmosphere of despondency. Half the sales force had just been made redundant and she was now the only survivor from her intake. Watching the shock waves hit her departing colleagues, Anna felt sick with fear. The memory of her last day at Marinecover was as vivid as though it had happened yesterday.

Stuart called the remaining staff to a meeting and announced that in future they would have monthly target sales figures. If they failed to make them, they too would lose their jobs. Anna's target was the highest. 'This isn't fair,' she protested to him.

'You made more than that one month.'

'Because I had a one-off brilliant deal with van Rooyen.'

'You'd make more good deals if you socialised after work. You need to show your face, Anna. That's part of the job, remember. I'm meeting a couple of brokers for a drink tonight and you should be there.'

It wasn't the moment to tell Stuart that she had a child. 'All right,' she said, giving him a breezy smile, 'I'll come.'

They went to the wine bar where she'd often met Delia, and she couldn't help searching for Delia's dark, gamine head amongst the crowd at the bar, but there was no sign of her. The brokers whom Stuart had arranged to meet had known Anna at Marinecover. They enquired after Charlie and she repied that she thought he was in Australia, speaking casually as if she'd almost forgotten his existence. The group was joined by Kevin Kitterick who regaled her with stories of his latest golfing holiday, until Bridget arrived and Anna caught up on the Lloyd's gossip. She enjoyed herself so much that she didn't leave until late.

Arriving home she found a card from Elaine. It was full of her new life in the States, her new husband, and Danny. Anna was very pleased to hear from her at last. Next to the card was a note from Colin, giving in his notice to leave – Anna had hardly been aware of his presence since he moved in – and another note from Louise offering to move up to the attic so that Mac and Victoria could have the whole of the first floor. Finally, Anna played her answering machine. On the tape was a message from Paul, wondering how she was, wanting to talk. She played it twice, just to hear his voice.

At the end of the week, Gordon took Anna out to lunch to

congratulate her on her making a success of Eurohull. 'It's a tough job and I take my hat off to you for sticking at it,' he told her.

'I have commitments which don't allow for unemployment.' She decided not to mention Daisy yet.

'I know what you mean. The interest rates are killing us all.'

Gordon went on to talk of further cutbacks at Marinecover, and Anna was glad that she hadn't elaborated.

They parted on the pavement outside Lloyd's. He went inside, she walked down to Leadenhall Street to find a taxi. As she hailed one, there was a shriek from the far side of the road and Delia darted through the traffic, looking like an escaping giraffe.

'Anna!' she squealed. 'Someone told me you were back, but I didn't believe them because I said I'd be the first person you'd call. Why didn't you ring me? I'm most offended.'

'You could have contacted *me*.' Anna beckoned the taxi closer. 'I was at home for months.'

'Oh, I know I should have called you.' Delia was irritated by the criticism. 'But I'm hopeless with people who are ill or depressed, and you know what life's like – one's so busy that time flies. But now you're back, let's meet one evening.'

'I can't.' Anna opened the taxi door and stepped inside.

'What about the weekend?'

'Delia, there's no point. We weren't real friends: if we were you'd have come to see me after Charlie left, when I was unemployed. Ours was never a proper friendship; we only had work and men in common.'

Delia bristled. 'What else is there?'

Anna thought of Daisy, and all the people in the house on Ladbroke Hill. 'Many things, but it would take too long to explain.' She closed the taxi door and called to the driver to take her to Eurohull.

She'd hoped that Paul would manage to come back before the weekend, but he was detained in Morocco informing a distraught couple that the boat which they'd bought a month earlier had been stolen the previous winter and would now have to be returned to its rightful owner. Since he couldn't be with her, he sent her a long letter. It was warm, humorous and romantic. Curled up on her bed, Anna read and reread his words until the paper they were written on became as soft as fabric. The telephone rang, and because Paul had said he would ring she assumed it would be him, and she answered with a soft, 'Hello?'

A woman's voice, which was familiar but which she couldn't place, said, 'May I speak to Anna Tobias?'

'You're speaking to her.'

'This is Phyllis Blythely, Charlie's mother.'

Anna was so surprised that she couldn't think of anything to say. It had never occurred to her that the Blythelys would contact her, and she reached out a hand to Daisy, wondering fearfully if somehow they knew of her existence.

'We did enjoy meeting you,' Phyllis went on. 'And we were sorry when things didn't . . . work out between you and Charlie. As we're in England we decided to call, because we'd love to see you, Anna – if you'd like to meet us. We'll be here for another week.'

They didn't know that she'd kept Daisy, unless they were very devious, but she decided to take no chances. 'I'll be abroad on a business trip,' she said.

'We understand.' Phyllis sounded genuinely disappointed. 'I hope you didn't mind me getting in touch.'

Anna felt guilty, although she told herself she had no reason. 'Of course not, it was nice to hear from you.'

'Then I'll call you again before we leave and hope to catch you between trips. Have a good journey, dear. Donald sends his love.'

Anna dropped the receiver and ran upstairs to Louise's flat. 'If a woman called Phyllis Blythely telephones or comes here, I'm always away,' she said, her voice trembling with agitation.

With a puzzled smile, Louise looked up from her market ledger. 'Why?'

'Because she's Charlie's mother and I don't want her to find out about Daisy.'

Now Anna was thankful that Paul had not come back early.

27

HEARING FROM PHYLLIS BLYTHELY greatly disturbed Anna. It brought back all the unfinished – and unfinishable – business with Charlie, forcing her to confront the unpalatable fact that Daisy not only had a father, but she had other grandparents and another aunt, and one day she would want to meet them. Anna was sure that Phyllis wouldn't call at the house uninvited. Nevertheless, she was glad to get away to Rotterdam for the week. Returning to the Rotterdam Hilton on Wednesday, after an exhausting but fruitful day, Anna was handed a message from Paul to say that he would be in The Hague the following evening and hoped she was free for dinner.

She had meetings until late and was due to fly back to London at dawn the next day, but she managed to reschedule her appointments and alter her flight home to a mid-morning one.

All the next day Anna could think of nothing but Paul, longing for the moment when they would be together again. During her meetings she'd suddenly imagined him holding her, loving her, and a softness came into her eyes, so that every prospective client she met eagerly placed his business with Eurohull.

Her last appointment was over by five and she hurried back to the Hilton, cutting through a pedestrian-only shopping street to the south of the hotel. As she passed a smart boutique she noticed a beautiful dress in the window. It was made of the finest Italian silk jersey in a deep, dark red – the colour of the roses which Paul had sent her on New Year's Eve – and the wrap-over tulip skirt gave a tantalising glimpse of leg, sensuous but not vulgar. Anna hesitated, but only for a moment, before she entered the shop. The dress fitted as though it had been made for her.

Back at the hotel she had time to soak in a hot scented bath, to brush her hair until it felt like silk, to paint her nails and apply her make-up at leisure instead of slapping it on in a hurry. She had just slipped on her new dress when the porter rang to inform her that Mr Sheldon was in reception. Giving herself a final spray of scent, Anna slung her coat over her shoulders and left.

Paul was glancing through the tourist leaflets on the table near the front desk. He looked very sophisticated, and yet not quite tamed, in spite of his immaculate dark suit. He smiled when he saw Anna. 'You look wonderful.' He turned to her and kissed her on the cheek and held her very close. 'I can't believe we're finally together. How insane that we have to come all the way to Holland to meet.'

She leaned against him. 'My answering machine will feel abandoned without your frequent calls.'

'I'll ring her in the morning, I wouldn't want to offend her.'

'Or she might refuse to register your messages.'

He laughed and helped her on with her coat.

Outside the hotel the porter was waiting with Paul's car, the motor already running and the heater on.

'I've booked at a small Italian restaurant which has a wonderful reputation,' said Paul as they set off. 'I've never been there but it's not far away.'

Anna wondered if he'd chosen to dine nearby so that they could come back to her room afterwards. She'd never taken a man into her hotel bedroom before and didn't know the procedure, but whatever it was she would brave it to be with Paul.

The restaurant was in a narrow street in what looked like an old quarter, but Paul said it had been rebuilt after the war. It was small and welcoming, and the table he'd reserved was in a separate alcove near an open fire. They ordered immediately so as to be left in peace.

'I saw Isaac yesterday,' said Paul, taking Anna's hand in his. 'They've invited us to one of their Friday night dinners.'

'Do they know we're . . . together . . . here . . . tonight?'

'No, but just think how pleased Sybil would be.'

'I haven't been set up like that, on a blind date, for years,' said Anna, 'except with a widowed farmer produced by my sister Roz.'

'Ah, so that's who you went to visit in the fenland. My rival. I shall call him out for a duel. Pitchforks at dawn.'

Anna giggled. 'He grows water lilies.'

Paul drew her closer. 'I refuse to fight over you in a pond.'

She leaned against him, her mouth just below his, and said with mock offence, 'That's not very flattering.'

'I have my limits.' He bit the lobe of her ear – not hard, but enough to send a shiver of desire rippling through her body, down her arms, under her skin.

There was a discreet cough from the waiter and they parted whilst he served their hors d'oeuvres of prosciutto and mixed fruits.

'Have there been any more redundancies at Eurohull?' Paul asked her when the waiter withdrew.

Anna shook her head. 'No – thank goodness.'

'Did you tell Gordon about Daisy?'

'I didn't dare. It would get back to the Cobra and next time he had to cut staff, he'd choose me.' She ate a slice of melon. 'Not that he'd say it was to do with Daisy, he's far too clever for that, he'd claim that outside interests took my attention from my work.'

'Which is why you have to work so hard – in case he does find out.'

She nodded. 'Exactly. My high figures are my only insurance.'

Paul raised her hand to his lips and kissed the soft skin between her fingers. 'I wish my mother was still alive, I'd have liked her to meet you. She also struggled to bring up children on her own, though it's only now, knowing you, that I realise quite how tough it must have been for her.'

'I'd like to have met her too,' Anna said softly.

He kissed her gently on the mouth and she parted her lips beneath his.

The waiter gave another discreet cough and removed their plates, served their main courses, and refilled their glasses. The wine was warm and mellow, and they sat close in the private world of their alcove, with the glow from the fire lighting their faces.

'You still haven't told me what you're doing in Holland,' said Anna, breaking a piece of bread.

'I'm showing Ginger, my new assistant, how to carry out an investigation in foreign waters. There's a suspect yacht in Scheveningen and I left him on the dock watching her.'

Anna remembered poor Mr Cargill who had come under suspicion at Marinecover. 'What makes you think she's stolen?'

'She's an expensive boat but her paintwork is sloppy. A genuine owner doesn't spend ninety grand on a vessel then paint her in a hurry. At present she's called *Magnolia II* but I'm convinced she's really *The Lady Jane*, which was taken from Poole Harbour.'

'How are you going to prove it?'

'By getting close enough to see her real number, which has probably been covered by a false number, then checking the original against her name in the *Small Ships Registry*. At the moment this suspicion is only based on my instinct and, although the police are interested, they want something more concrete than my vague hunch before they impound the boat. So she could be moved any time – except that she's fifty foot long and only one man remains on board. He wouldn't dare take her out alone, not into the North Sea, and I've instructed Ginger to warn me if his accomplice returns.'

'You're not going to board her?' she asked, horrified at the risk.

'Not at night, but I need to photograph her registration number, and since I'm sure it's been tampered with, that's better done in daylight. Until now, there has been someone on deck all day. This is a game of endless patience. Ginger is watching from a parked car and he can't even turn on the heater in case the sound alerts someone to his presence.'

Anna kissed Paul on the chin. 'But if it wasn't for Ginger, you'd be there – and not here with me, so I'm very grateful to him.'

They raised their glasses to Ginger, whose arrival would enable Paul to have more free time, with the unspoken implication that they would spend that time together.

As they reached the end of their meal, there was a very faint hum from Paul's jacket pocket and he took out a mobile telephone, far smaller than any which Anna had seen before. 'That'll be Ginger,' he said, giving her a quick kiss on the tip of her nose before he answered. 'Yes . . . When? . . . Stay right there.'

Whilst Paul talked in monosyllables Anna watched the flickering flames curl around a log of wood in the open grate. She felt loved and cherished and deeply happy.

He replaced the phone. 'I'm sorry,' he said to Anna.

'Don't worry.' She thought he referred to the interruption, and turned to him with a smile, but faltered when she saw his expression. 'What's wrong?'

'The accomplice has returned. I can't believe his timing! After being away for fifteen hours, he chooses this moment to come back. Anna, if Ginger was experienced he could handle it, but this is his first job and I'll have to go.'

'I understand.' She stood up.

Paul hugged her. 'Thanks for not making it harder for me. I'm sorry, I really am. You know I am.'

'So am I.' She gave him an impish grin.

The waiter brought her coat whilst Paul settled the bill. 'I'll drop you at the hotel,' he said as they walked out into the cold damp night.

'No, Paul, I'm coming with you. I want to see what happens.'

'You can't, it might be dangerous. He could be armed.'

'I'll keep well back.'

'You'll be cold and bored. We might be there for hours.'

'I have a warm coat.' She linked her arm through his 'It's no good, Paul, you can't get rid of me so easily.'

'Oh, all right, but don't blame me if you regret it.' He unlocked her side of the car, adding, 'This is not the evening which I'd hoped for.'

She slipped into her seat. 'I agree.'

The drove out through the north-eastern suburbs of Rotterdam, past the airport and up the motorway towards The Hague, an orderly city of decorous tree-lined suburbs which reminded Anna of Melbourne. Scheveningen was on the coast. It had once been a small fishing village but was now a sprawling commercial resort, with a long, wide sandy beach, a pier and a promenade. In summer it was packed with holiday-makers; on a cold damp evening in January it was desolate.

The harbour was at the south end of the promenade. It had an inner and outer basin, a yacht haven, and a terminus where the ferry to England docked. The area was well lit and the lamp light glistened on the damp tarmac and bounced on the dark, oily water of the sea. Most of the yachts were battened down and the port was deserted, except for the occasional person walking briskly along the edge of the quay.

Paul tapped out a number on his phone. There was a crackle, then a deep guttural voice answered, '*Politie*.'

'Hendrik, this is Paul Sheldon.'

'Aaah, Paul, so you work again tonight?'

'I'm still checking out that boat, so please don't let your boys arrest me.'

Hendrik laughed. 'I won't. *Goedenacht.*'

Paul slipped the phone into his pocket. 'Hendrik's an old friend. My brief is merely to locate the boat and inform the underwriter, nothing more, but I always keep the local police informed. After all, this is their country and if things turn nasty I may need their help.'

He eased the car quietly along the side of the port until he came to a stop behind another vehicle which was parked in the shadow of a wall. Anna could just make out the shape of a man sitting low down and motionless in the front seat. As she watched he disappeared from view, and a moment later he slid along the wall and into the back of their car.

He was a stocky man with short, red hair and a very round face, and he was clearly surprised to find a woman in the car, although he didn't say so.

'Anna, this is Ginger,' whispered Paul, then by way of an explanation to Ginger, 'Anna's in marine insurance.'

'Hello, Ginger.'

He grinned. 'Hi, Anna. Good to meet you.'

'Any movement?' Paul asked, nodding at the large white yacht which was moored some thirty yards head.

'The big man left ten minutes ago and he hasn't come back.'

'And the other man, the one with a limp?'

'Still on board.'

They all stared at the boat as it bobbed on its mooring, the harsh glare from a nearby street light creating eerie patterns on the white-painted deck. The only sound was the distant murmur of traffic and the lap of the water against the harbour wall. Suddenly, a light came on in one of the cabins, but although they could see the shadow as a person moved backwards and forwards across the beam, they were too far away to see what he was doing.

'Shall I move up?' asked Ginger.

Paul thought for a moment. 'No, I'll go.' He looked at Anna. 'Do you really want to help?'

She nodded enthusiastically.

'A man on his own looks more suspicious than a courting

couple, so if you haven't changed your mind open the door and step out, but don't make any noise until we're well away from the car.'

'I'm with you.' Anna slipped out, to be joined by Paul. It was freezing cold and damp, but she was too exhilarated to care.

'We'll wander past the boat,' said Paul, putting his arm around her shoulder. 'No, don't look at it. You're meant to have eyes only for me, remember?'

She giggled as much from nerves and cold as from amusement.

As they drew level with the yacht, Paul suddenly pulled her round and kissed her fiercely. His passion made Anna gasp – until she saw that his eyes were looking straight over her shoulder into the lighted cabin. For a moment she felt not exactly offended, but something along those lines.

Then Paul winked at her and whispered against her mouth, 'If I took you on all my jobs I'd never get any work done.'

'You call this work?' She found the whole thing – the night, the stake-out, him – wildly exciting.

They walked on arm in arm until they were far enough away for Paul to call Ginger without being overheard. 'He's packing a case,' he whispered. 'I couldn't see what was inside, so we'll go back and try again.'

Arms wrapped around each other, they idled along the quay. 'We could sit there,' Anna said, pointing to a low wall directly opposite the port-hole.

He nuzzled her neck. 'If you ever need a job, let me know.'

They sat down and pretended to be engrossed in each other whilst taking time to watch the cabin where a small, hunched man sat writing at a table. Paul held Anna close. 'You're cold, but we'll soon be back in the car,' he said.

'I'm all right.' She tried not to shiver. 'Is this how you spend many evenings?'

'Not now I have Ginger. I used to have another assistant, who was freelance, but then when . . . my marriage was in trouble, I had a lot of . . . unexpected expenses, and I couldn't afford to keep him, so I started doing all the stake-outs myself.' He paused. 'Or maybe I wanted an excuse to be away.' He smiled and kissed her on the cheek. 'It's easy to delude oneself from the real reasons one does things. I'm sure the thieves delude themselves that the owners are happy to collect the insurance money, which in some cases is true, but not in all, and not with this boat. Her owner is devoted to her.'

'Where would they sell her?' Anna asked, wondering what he meant by 'unexpected expenses', but sensing he would tell her in his own time.

'A boat this size?' he said. 'Probably in the Med, whilst a smaller vessel would be advertised in one of the yachting magazines under a box number.'

'But my father took weeks to sell the *Little Auk*.' She remembered the anxiety when they received no response to their ad and how, eventually, they'd anchored the *Little Auk* in an overgrown creek when they could no longer afford the Bosham mooring fees.

'That's because your father wanted a good price,' said Paul. 'Stolen boats sell quickly because the thieves advertise them below market value – though not so low that it's too obvious. People ask why the police don't check all the ads with box numbers, but how can they? There are hundreds. And buyers are so unsuspecting. The thieves often have the logbook and papers because careless owners leave them on board. It's as easy to get rid of a stolen boat as a stolen car, if you know how.'

Anna thought of Charlie. Would he really have stolen that car if she hadn't objected? She wasn't sure.

Paul took a very small video camera from his pocket and laid it on her thigh, its lens pointed at the port-hole. 'This is infra-red,' he explained. 'It'll be better than nothing, if they move the boat before I can check the registration number.' He rested his hand on the camcorder to steady it, but to anyone glancing at them he appeared to have his hand on Anna's thigh.

She kept as still as she could, but the wall was damp and hard, and the cold came through her coat. Her legs, encased in silk stockings, had no protection against the night and her toes had turned to ice inside her dainty shoes.

Seeing her grit her teeth against their chattering, Paul blew warm air down her neck. 'One more minute,' he said.

His mobile phone light flicked on and he answered with a whisper. 'The second man? Damn!' He murmured in Anna's ear, 'The accomplice is coming back. We'll have to wait till he's aboard.'

She nodded, but she was suddenly frightened. She thought of Daisy, and berated herself for taking this risk.

They listened. They could hear heavy, distant footsteps. Paul held her tightly. 'Don't look at him! Oh, I shouldn't have let you come with me, it was madness; this could be dangerous.'

'I wanted to come.' She slid her hand inside his coat and shivered with cold and nerves.

'You're freezing.' He did his best to wrap her in both their coats, as if they were their bed-covers.

The footsteps grew closer, Anna trembled.

'I won't let him hurt you,' said Paul, sheltering her body with his own.

The man on the boat opened the hatch and looked out. He frowned when he saw the courting couple opposite, but was relieved that they had eyes for no one but each other. Paul cupped Anna's face in his hands and kissed her. She parted her lips beneath his, wanting him more than she had ever desired any man, her longing for him overwhelming her fear. In his arms she forgot the hard wall, the cold, and the dangerous boat thief. Beneath their coverlet of coats the tulip skirt of her dress fell open, exposing her leg right up to her thigh.

'What's happened to the camera?' whispered Paul.

'I don't know.'

He slid his hand up her leg and chuckled. 'It's here, and it's very comfortable.'

In his arms again, she watched the occupants of the cabin over his shoulder.

'The big man's standing. He looks angry. The little one is pleading.'

'Anything else?' He slid his hand inside her coat and stroked her neck.

'The big man is taking off his coat and jacket. Now he's left the cabin, he's gone next door, he's lying down on a bunk, he's turned out the light. The little man is clearing away his writing things. He looks worried, he's opening the cabin door, he's closed it again. He's making up a bed on the sofa. Paul, if you caress me, I can't concentrate.'

He didn't withdraw his hand. 'I want to touch you so much – I keep stopping myself, then I'm tempted all over again. I haven't brought a woman on a stake-out before. It never occurred to me, but sitting here on this wall with you, however uncomfortable, is one of the most erotic experiences of my life. The combination of the night, the danger, and you makes me want to make love to you here and now, and damn the risk! The only reason I won't is that I wouldn't want to endanger you more than I already have.'

The light went out in the cabin and there was silence from the boat. Paul switched off the camcorder and they waited for a few minutes until he considered it safe to leave. Then they walked slowly back towards the car, idling like lovers who dread the imminent parting, although every nerve in Anna's body cried out to run.

It was nearly dawn before Paul deemed it safe to leave Ginger whilst he drove Anna back to Rotterdam. They kissed a sleepy goodbye in the car outside the hotel, with the porter pretending not to notice. 'Are you free on Saturday?' he asked her.

Anna nodded.

'And Sunday?'

She smiled. 'That too.'

'What about Daisy?'

'I'll ask Heather to have her.'

He kissed her again. 'It's not that I don't like Daisy, but I want to spend time with you alone.'

'I want it too,' she replied. 'I want that very much.'

28

WHILST ANNA AND Paul had been staking out the boat, the allied forces had bombed Baghdad. Over breakfast in her room Anna watched the CNN news, on the aeroplane she read the newspapers, at Ladbroke Hill she found Louise and Mac barely on speaking terms; Louise was a pacifist, Mac was gripped by military fever. At night the sound of gunfire on their separate televisions echoed through the house, interrupted from time to time by Mac opening his door to sing the words of *The Marine's Hymn*, and Louise retaliating with *Give Peace A Chance*. Anna listened to their arguments with half an ear. She was walking on air, and not even the threat of World War III could compete with her anticipation of Saturday.

She had come back to a message on her answering machine from Phyllis: 'We leave on Sunday. Call us if you can.' Anna erased it. She was no longer anxious about the Blythelys; in two days they'd be on the far side of the world.

Heather agreed to take Daisy on Saturday night and, although Anna didn't tell her why, the jolly childminder rewarded her with a broad wink.

Paul telephoned her at midday to say that he'd caught an earlier plane. 'Is it too early if I come at five?' he asked.

'Not for me, but I've arranged to drop off Daisy about then.'

'We can take her together. Then I thought we'd drive out along the Thames and have dinner in a restaurant by the river. I know it's not the sea but . . .'

'Oh, I love rivers too. Anywhere which has open water.' She pictured them in a low-beamed dining-room, with lattice windows overlooking a weir, and Paul holding her hand across the white damask table-cloth.

Anna decided to wear something elegant but simple, a straight black dress with a sweetheart neckline which she'd bought before Christmas to take on business trips, then decided the skirt was too short. As the hour of Paul's arrival approached, her excitement turned to nerves and she jittered around the house, wishing that Louise was home from the market so that they could talk.

The doorbell rang, and with her heart thudding in her ears Anna answered it. When she saw Paul she was suddenly so shy that she could barely muster a smile, but he wrapped her in his arms and hugged her fiercely. 'I missed you,' he said.

'I missed you too.' She melted against him.

She led the way into her bedroom, where Daisy was sitting in the centre of her bed trying to unpack the overnight bag Anna had prepared for her. When she saw Paul, she gave him a suspicious look.

'Hello, Daisy,' he said gently. 'Shall I help you put your coat on?'

To Anna's surprise, Daisy allowed Paul to dress her, giving him a haughty stare as if she were an empress and he her slave. Anna slipped on her own coat and picked up Daisy's possessions and her own bag. 'Can you carry her for me?' she asked Paul.

'If she'll let me.' He bent to pick Daisy up. She condescended, although she refused to smile at him.

Anna led the way to the front door, but as she opened it a movement near the gate caught her eye. Standing in the drive were Phyllis and Donald Blythely. They saw her and waved.

'Stay in the house!' Anna hissed at Paul, pushing him and Daisy back into the hall.

'Why? What's wrong?'

'Don't ask me! Get inside!'

She closed the front door as the Blythelys walked eagerly towards her, calling out, 'Anna, what luck to find you home! We were in the Portobello market and decided that we just had to see the house where Charlie used to live.'

Through the door Anna could hear Daisy whimper and Paul say, 'It's all right, Mummy's just coming.'

To keep the Blythelys away from the house and out of earshot, Anna raced down the steps and across the drive to greet them.

Interpreting this action as friendliness, a broad smile came to Phyllis's weathered face and she opened her arms wide to embrace

Anna, clasping her to her broad bosom. 'Oh Anna, we're glad to see you. We were sorry about you and Charlie, though of course we shouldn't say that. It's none of our business.'

Embarrassed, Anna freed herself. 'I'm afraid I'm just leaving for the country.'

'What a shame! We'd love to see the house; Charlie's sure to ask us about it.'

'Though of course we know he has no stake in it any more,' Donald added hurriedly, in case Anna misunderstood their interest.

Anna took her car keys from her bag. 'I'm sorry, I'm late as it is.' Out of the corner of her eye she could see Paul standing at the drawing-room window holding Daisy in his arms, looking puzzled.

Suddenly, Phyllis seemed to realize that Anna was not pleased to see them, and she stepped away. 'It was tactless of us to come,' she said, 'but we liked you and you were good for Charlie, you stood up to him.'

'Now then, Phyllis,' Donald said, tucking his wife's hand under his arm. 'Anna doesn't want to hear all that, she's in a hurry.'

'Yes, how silly of me. Goodbye, dear.' They walked away, arm in arm, out of the drive and down the hill.

Anna slumped against the side of her car. She was weak with relief that they hadn't discovered about Daisy. She hoped never to see them again, but at the same time she was extremely sorry that it had to be this way, because she liked them.

Paul came out of the house without Daisy. 'What was all that about?'

'Oh, they're just some people I used to know but I didn't want them to come inside because . . . they'd never have left.'

'They were Australian. I recognised their accent.'

'Yes, Australians.' She didn't look at him.

'Like your ex-boyfriend?'

'Yes.' She ran up the front steps, suddenly, desperate to reach Daisy and reassure herself that she had not been snatched away. Although Anna knew such fears were irrational, the Blythelys had reminded her of all the insecurities in her life – of dreams which foundered, of being abandoned.

Paul caught up with her. 'They were Charlie's parents, weren't they?'

'What does it matter?' Anna went into the drawing-room where Daisy was heading determinedly towards the bookcase. 'You're mine. Mine!' She scooped her up and hugged her fiercely as though someone were trying to separate them.

Paul watched. 'Charlie is Daisy's father.'

She shrugged. 'You know he is.'

'And you don't want them to see their granddaughter?'

'Daisy is my child. I told you before, her father doesn't feature.'

'Does he know of her existence?'

'No, he doesn't, and that's how I want it. Charlie walked out and left me destitute, he took what little money we had – money I'd earned working in a pub – and when I told him that I was pregnant, he whimpered that he couldn't afford to come back. I've provided every mouthful Daisy has eaten, I decorated this house single-handed to let it and give us a roof, I work twelve hours a day to keep us, Daisy's my daughter and I'm not sharing her with him.'

Paul held up his hands. 'I'm sorry, I didn't mean to upset you.'

'Then stop questioning me,' she shouted, almost in tears.

Paul walked over to the window and looked down on the bare, wintry garden. 'Anna,' he said, quietly, 'we have to talk.'

'What is there to say?' She rounded on him, distressed not only by seeing the Blythelys but by the ruined evening.

He looked at her sadly. 'You reacted so strongly to seeing Charlie's parents that it makes me wonder if . . . perhaps you still care for him.'

'I don't love Charlie. I feel nothing. I never want to see him again. I was just upset at the shock of seeing them, because of Daisy and . . .' She stopped. She hadn't told him yet about her father and her terror of being deserted.

Paul took her by the shoulders and looked deep into her eyes. 'I want to believe you, Anna, but I think you need time to sort things out. You see, I could fall deeply in love with you – maybe I am already – but I don't want to go any further with a woman who loves another man.'

'What about your wife?' she asked angrily. 'How do you think I feel, knowing that you'll always love her?'

His fingers dug into her shoulders. 'I didn't love Felicity at the end. Too much had . . . gone wrong between us. I don't think she loved me either. If we'd each been honest, we would have remained separated, but neither of us said what we really meant.' His eyes took on a dark, haunted look, and he added, in little more than a whisper, 'If I had been stronger . . . she would not have died.'

Anna didn't try to stop him leaving, she knew he wouldn't stay, not today. She wished now that she'd told him about her father. It might have helped convince him that it was not Charlie but all her other secret nightmares that made her react so strongly. She knew it wasn't going to be easy, for the more she saw of Paul the more she realised that he too carried suitcases from his past.

29

ANNA DECIDED TO write to Paul, because she often found it easier to express herself in a letter, but she had no time to do so that night because Daisy was sick, and the following day Daisy was tearful and slightly feverish, crying whenever Anna was out of sight. She was still unwell when Anna set off for Holland on Monday morning.

Anna felt very guilty leaving Daisy but she couldn't cancel her trip. To make matters worse, she arrived at Heathrow to find that the incoming flight had been delayed by fog in Rotterdam, and she had to hang around the airport for two hours, hoping that she wouldn't run into Paul – and at the same time hoping that she would.

Before boarding she telephoned Heather. 'How's Daisy?' she asked.

'Very sleepy and she seems cold, so I've put her to bed. Now don't worry, I'm sure it's nothing serious.'

Over the Tannoy came the final call for Anna's flight, so she shouted her love to Daisy and hurried to the jetway.

Her delayed flight departure meant that she reached the Hilton with no time to settle in before her lunchtime meeting. She raced up to her room, dropped her suitcase on her bed and, whilst she tapped out Heather's number, opened her briefcase to check the day's schedule.

Walter answered the phone and put her on to Heather, who said, 'Daisy has a slight temperature. If it gets worse, I'll call the doctor.'

'And you'll let me know?'

'Of course I will, Anna; but children often run slight fevers, I told you that last time she had one.'

'I know. I'm sorry to fuss.'

Anna's first appointment was lunch with a new client, another of Mr van Rooyen's contacts. From the restaurant she had to go straight to her second meeting, at a small shipping line on the far side of the Nieuwe Maas. She'd done business with them before, so this was more of a courtesy call, but whilst her clients talked insurance, she fretted about Daisy, picturing her subdued little face. Her next appointment was an early dinner with Mr van Rooyen at the Rotisserie, at the top of the Euromast tower, and she had just enough time to return to the Hilton, telephone Heather to check on Daisy, bathe and change.

Relaxing into the back seat of a taxi, Anna watched the first bank of evening fog roll up the Nieuwe Maas and listened to the fog horns as the great ships moved up and down the river. She thought of Paul, and decided to telephone him the following evening; a letter would take too long. She rehearsed what she'd say: about her father, Leatherbridge, and how Charlie meant nothing, not any more.

Suddenly, she became aware that her taxi had ground to a halt on the approach to the Maas Tunnel.

'Accident,' shouted her driver.

She leaned forward to speak to him. 'I'm in a hurry. Is there a way round it?'

He shook his head. 'Only if you swim the river.'

For an hour Anna fumed and fretted in the stationary taxi. By the time the road was clear, it was too late for her to return to the hotel, so she went straight to the restaurant.

Mr van Rooyen had reserved his usual table, near the window, which had a panoramic view of the city and the port – when not blanketed by fog. To Anna's surprise he was with two other people, a homely middle-aged blonde and a good-looking younger man of about Anna's age who wore the kind of wire-rimmed spectacles fashionable in the sixties, and whose tidy features reminded her of Charlie.

Mr van Rooyen rose to greet her. 'It's my wife's birthday, so I invited her to join us,' he explained as he introduced his companions. 'And this is my nephew, Nicolaas, who has just returned from America.'

Anna wished Mrs van Rooyen a happy birthday. She was delighted not to dine alone with Mr van Rooyen.

Whilst Mr van Rooyen and his wife painstakingly discussed every dish on the menu, Nicolaas caught Anna's eye and grinned. 'Don't talk to me about shipping, Miss Tobias.' He spoke with a strong American accent. 'I'm the black sheep, as you say.'

Mr van Rooyen gave an impatient sigh. 'Miss Tobias, my nephew threw away a wonderful opportunity to head the next generation of Van Rooyen Rotterdam.'

'Uncle, an opportunity isn't wonderful if you don't want it.'

'Shipping is in our blood.'

'Not in mine, but I'd have been more interested if the port was full of pretty women like Miss Tobias.'

'Nephew, please don't be frivolous!'

Anna recognised long-term family friction and she turned to Mrs van Rooyen to enquire after her children, listening politely as each child's attributes were detailed. But her mind was on Daisy, and whether she could reach a telephone before it was too late to disturb Heather.

Mr van Rooyen usually ate quickly and hurried from the restaurant as soon as he had finished, but tonight he lingered over his coffee and repeated one of his many stories about the van Rooyen shipping line, whilst Mrs van Rooyen patted his hand indulgently as if he were a small boy recounting his day at school. Controlling her impatience, Anna watched the clock hands move well beyond the hour at which she could decently incommode Heather. Finally, Mr van Rooyen called for the bill and insisted for once that he, not Eurohull, should pay.

They shared the lift down to the foyer, where they said good night, and Mr van Rooyen asked Nicolaas to find Anna a taxi. As he and his wife headed for the car park, Anna noticed that they were holding hands and she felt a wave of affection for Mr van Rooyen, boring though he was.

'Do you like jazz?' asked Nicolaas.

'Some jazz. Why?'

'You'll like this.' He seized her by the hand. 'Come on! Let's go to a club.'

'I must go back to my hotel.'

'What for?'

She nearly told him about Daisy, but there was nothing she could do for her daughter at that moment which warranted the risk of Stuart hearing that she had a child, so she replied, 'I have a breakfast meeting.'

'So do I. We won't be late. Just one hour.' He beckoned to a taxi and ushered her into the back seat before she could think of a better reason not to go.

'My aunt and uncle are so boring,' he said, slipping his arm along the back of the seat behind Anna's head.

'They're very nice.' She wasn't about to criticise her best client.

He laughed – 'How diplomatic!' – and leaned forward to clarify directions with the driver, whilst she wondered what Paul was doing and if he would be jealous to see her with another man.

The jazz club was in the basement of an old building in a narrow street somewhere near the centre, although Anna had no idea where. It was dark and smoky, and the clientele was monied bohemian. In one corner a large black man was playing the piano, his dark fingers caressing the ivory keys. From time to time he glanced around the room, then smiled at some private joke. He didn't seem to notice the people; he played exquisitely, but for himself.

Nicolaas appeared to be well known at the club, and they joined a table of smart young people, most of whom were very drunk. They all spoke English and Anna noticed that when Nicolaas introduced her, he omitted to say that she was a business acquaintance.

'Rum?' he asked.

'Well . . . er . . . all right, thanks – but just one.'

He draped his arm across the back of Anna's chair. 'Don't be so nervous.'

'I'm not, I'm just not used to socialising in Rotterdam, except on business.' She wasn't going to tell him about her dinner with Paul in the Italian restaurant.

The rum arrived in tall glasses. It was much stronger than any she had tasted before, and the combination of the alcohol, the heat and the music made her light-headed. She leaned back against Nicolaas's arm and immediately his fingers began to stroke the nape of her neck.

'I want to know all about you,' he said. 'Is there a Mr Tobias?'

She shook her head.

'Do you live with a man?'

'Not any more.'

'Nor do I, not any more. I mean, I don't live with a woman any more. I split up with my girlfriend before Christmas and I missed her a lot – but now I'm ready to live again.'

Anna nodded without meaning to, and Nicolaas interpreted this as encouragement, whereas it was the rum which had gone straight to her head. She knew that she should move away from him – he was a business contact and a stranger – but Paul had raised a hunger in her for love, for romance, sex and intimacy.

Nicolaas ran his finger along her jaw line. 'I want to kiss you,' he said.

She turned her face to him and his lips brushed hers, gently, barely touching. 'I . . . umm . . . must go back to the hotel,' she stammered.

He touched her mouth with the tip of one finger. 'Very well, I'll call a taxi.'

She was surprised that he didn't argue, until she realised that he'd assumed she would invite him to her room. In the taxi he took her in his arms and kissed her hard, pulling her on top of him, her skirt sliding up her thighs as his knee separated her legs. For a moment she was too befuddled to stop him. Then she pulled sharply away, saying, 'Nicolaas, please, I hardly know you, and . . .'

He patted his breast pocket. 'Don't worry. I too believe in safe sex.'

'I didn't mean that.' She held him at arm's length. 'Look, I'm sorry if I seemed to lead you on but . . . the rum was stronger than I thought.'

The taxi stopped in front of the hotel. Anna straightened her clothes and stepped out. She hoped that Nicolaas would say goodbye there, but he accompanied her into the foyer and she realised that she had been too obscure. Nicolaas spoke good English, but he hadn't picked up on her imprecise message.

The receptionists looked at her and she blushed furiously as if they could read her dilemma. 'Miss Tobias, you have an urgent message.' One of them held out a piece of paper. 'The caller has been trying to reach you all evening.'

Anna hurried to the desk and read the message: 'Daisy in hospital. Possible meningitis. Phone me. Heather.' The words swam before her eyes and the floor seemed to buckle beneath her feet. 'It's my daughter,' she cried, clutching at Nicolaas to stop herself from falling. 'She's ill.'

'I didn't know you had a child.' He looked bewildered.

'Daisy. I must use the phone. I should never have left London. I'll never forgive myself if . . .'

Whilst the porter checked on flights to London, Anna dialled Heather's number. Walter answered sleepily. 'Heather's at the hospital, she's been trying to reach you.' He gave Anna the number.

Blaming herself for being so frivolous as to go to a jazz club when Daisy was ill, Anna telephoned the ward. She was put through to the sister. 'How's my daughter?' She almost screamed with panic.

'She's very ill, Mrs Tobias. We suspect meningitis. We've carried out a lumbar puncture so that the nature of the infection can be determined. In the meantime, we've started to treat your daughter with penicillin because it is too dangerous to wait for the results of the test.'

Anna was so bludgeoned by shock that all she could do was to stutter. 'She's . . . going to be all right, isn't she?'

'We are doing our best, but I suggest you come quickly.'

She passed Anna to Heather who said, 'Oh, thank God you've called. I've been so worried. An hour after we spoke Daisy's temperature went right up and she was sick. Then I noticed that the light hurt her eyes – photophobia, the doctor calls it – and I remembered reading about meningitis when I was at the hairdresser's last month, so I rushed her to the hospital. I tried to phone you.'

'I know, it's my fault. I should have checked with the hotel. You've been wonderful, Heather. I'm sorry I left you to cope, but I'll be on the next flight back. Tell Daisy that Mummy's coming.' Tears filled Anna's eyes. 'Tell her that Mummy loves her.'

Anna came off the line to find Nicolaas holding out a glass of brandy. 'Drink it,' he said. 'You're going to need it. Fog has closed the airports and they won't be open until mid-morning.'

She declined the brandy; she'd drunk enough already. 'But I have to go home. Daisy's ill; she may be dying.'

'There are no flights, Anna.'

'I'll take the boat.'

'The ferry from The Hoek to Harwich lasts seven hours. The plane is quicker.'

'Not if it can't fly. Nicolaas, I have to get home. My daughter needs me.' Anna's voice rose with anxiety. 'If I have to, I'll steal a boat and sail across to England.' She remembered what Charlie had said, and added, 'I'm that desperate.' She was shocked to realise that she meant it.

'I'll drive you to Ostend,' said Nicolaas. 'There's a ferry at five which arrives at Dover before nine. The boats sail even when the planes are grounded.'

'Oh, I couldn't let you take me; it's a three-hour drive. I'll rent a car.'

'You can't drive – you're too upset, you'd have an accident. Pack your bag whilst I fetch my car. It's only seven minutes away.'

Anna hesitated, then she said, 'I accept. Thank you.'

He squeezed her hand. 'It is not exactly the evening I had hoped for.'

As Anna headed for the lift, she recalled that Paul had once said the same thing, here, in Rotterdam. The difference was that she'd felt that way too.

By the time Anna reached London she'd been travelling for thirty hours and she was exhausted. On the ferry she'd taken a cabin but she'd been too worried to sleep or even stay inside it for more than a short while, preferring to pace the deck with the cold salty wind in her face. Even in her direst moments the sea helped her. In the sounds of the waves she called to Daisy not to die.

At Dover she telephoned Roz and asked her to warn their mother: she had no time to say more because her train was leaving. From Victoria she went straight to St Kathryn's Children's Hospital, where Daisy was in the intensive care unit. In spite of the serious condition of the patients, the ward tried to be cheerful, with stencilled Peter Rabbits on the brightly-coloured cots and jolly teddy bears picnicking on the walls.

Anna hurried to the nurses' desk, crying, 'I'm Daisy Tobias's mother. How is she?'

'Oh, Mrs Tobias. Sister wants to see you.'

Anna let her bags fall to the ground. 'Daisy's dead, isn't she?'

'No! Really!' The nurse pressed the intercom. 'Here comes Sister.'

A smart, grey-haired woman with thick, dark Stalinesque eyebrows came striding up the ward. Anna rushed up to her. 'How's my daughter? How's Daisy? Is she . . . ?' Tears filled her eyes and the words stuck in her throat.

'Daisy is very ill, Mrs Tobias.'

'What about the test?'

'We're still waiting for the diagnosis. Meningitis is an inflammation of the membranes around the brain and the spinal cord. From the CSF – cerebro-spinal fluid – we'll be able to tell if she has meningoccocal meningitis, where the penicillin will be effective, or viral meningitis, for which we have no treatment but it is less severe.'

Anna tried to follow the medical details but all she could think of was that Daisy was dying and she, her mother, had deserted her. 'Can I see her?' she asked, her voice shaking.

'Only if you calm down. You won't help her if you're upset.'

'Yes, of course. I'm sorry.'

The sister gave her a firm but not unsympathetic smile. 'Naturally you're worried, but you mustn't let Daisy see that, she has to be kept quiet.'

'I understand.'

Anna was ushered into a small darkened side room where Daisy lay, deathly pale, in a padded cot to prevent her from thrashing about. In the vein of her arm, hidden by a bandage, was an intravenous drip carrying penicillin and liquids. Besidc the cot sat a nurse with a chart on her knee and a pen poised to record any changes. When she saw the sister she sat up even straighter and held her pen so tightly that it nearly snapped in two.

Daisy was drowsy but restless, as though she were having a bad dream. Biting back tears, Anna reached down into the cot and held her tiny hand. 'Daisy,' she whispered, 'Mummy's here.'

Daisy opened her eyes and tried to focus on Anna, but even the faintest light made her wince, and she closed them again.

'Is there anything I can do?' Anna turned to the sister, feeling desperate but utterly helpless.

'Nothing.' The sister took Anna by the arm to lead her from the room.

'No, please, I want to stay with Daisy. I won't make a noise, I promise, but I can't bear to leave her, even if I can't help.'

'Very well.' The sister kept her voice low. 'I'll ask someone to bring you a cup of coffee. You must be tired if you've been travelling all night.'

'I am, but I couldn't sleep.' Anna pulled a face to hide her emotion. 'I should never have left Daisy, but it's so difficult to take time off. I have a job and we need the money.'

'Stop blaming yourself.' The sister pushed Anna gently into a chair. 'Life's a juggle for a working mother. I know, I've been through it.'

'Thank you for saying that,' Anna whispered. 'You've made me feel less guilty.' She turned to the nurse. 'Thank you for looking after my daughter.'

'Oh, it's a pleasure. We all hope she gets better, she's such a dear little girl.'

'I know.' Anna bit her upper lip to stop herself from crying.

She sat for hours, leaning forward, her chin resting on her hands as she watched Daisy. She wanted to pray to God not to let Daisy die, but was afraid that He – if 'He' existed, and she still wasn't sure – would think her a hypocrite for only turning to Him when she was in need.

She realised that she must have dozed off when she awoke to find Daisy's nurses were changing shift, and the previous nurse was beckoning her into the corridor, where Louise, Mr Marilyn and Mac were waiting. As soon as Anna joined them and they enveloped her with their concern and affection, she started to cry whilst they huddled around her, holding her upright and telling her to stop blaming herself.

'I brought your track suit and trainers,' Louise said, producing a plastic bag full of clothes.

'Oh, thank you. I can't wait to change out of my suit.'

'Sybil Finestein called,' said Mac. 'I told her about Daisy and she sent her love. And Stuart has left two messages on your machine. Shall I explain the situation to him?'

'Yes, please. I can't bear to speak to him today. I might break down in tears, and he's such a bully that I can't afford to let him see me so vulnerable.'

'What about Paul?' Louise asked. 'Shall we tell him?'

Anna hesitated, then shook her head. 'He'll hear soon enough from the Finesteins, and if he wants to get in touch he can. I don't want him coming here because he feels obliged to.'

They only stayed for a few minutes, sensing that Anna was anxious to return to Daisy, and she appreciated them as much for knowing when to leave her as for coming.

Not long afterwards Heather arrived, and whilst she remained with Daisy, Anna searched the lino'd corridors for an unoccupied bathroom. Being a children's hospital there was no lock on the door, so she had to jam a chair under the handle whilst she quickly soaped the grime of two days' travelling from her body. Obliged to dry herself on hand towels, she was still wet when she pulled on her track suit.

On her return to the intensive care unit, she found her mother talking to Heather in the corridor outside Daisy's room.

'Oh, darling, I'm so sorry about Daisy.' Her mother came towards her, arms outstretched, her sympathy making Anna dissolve into tears yet again. She cried on her mother's shoulder in a way which she hadn't done since she was a small child.

Her mother could only stay for an hour, because she couldn't leave Granny Tobias alone after dark, but Anna treasured the effort she had made in driving over a hundred miles on a freezing, wintry night.

An hour or so later, the sister called Anna out of Daisy's room. 'We've had a result,' she said, smiling, 'Daisy has meningococcal meningitis, so the penicillin should start to have effect very soon.'

Anna felt faint with relief. 'So she's going to be all right?'

'It's too early to be definite, but at least we know what's wrong with her.'

'What about her mind? Will she be . . . handicapped?

'She's reacting to stimuli, so we hope not. Now run along home and get a good night's sleep. You're going to need your strength, my dear.'

'Oh, Sister, I couldn't leave her, not till she's in the clear.'

'Then I'll send you in a supper tray and ask a porter to find a trestle bed. We can't have you becoming ill as well.'

Anna went home two days later, by which time Daisy was declared to be over the worst. Her temperature was down, she was fully conscious, and her reactions confirmed that she had suffered no lasting brain damage. Barely glancing at her mail, and not bothering with the messages on her answerphone, Anna went straight to bed and slept. She was woken by the telephone ringing on her bedside table and, terrified that Daisy had worsened, she grabbed the receiver, screaming, 'Yes? Yes!'

'Anna, it's Stuart. What the hell's going on? I had a garbled message about looking after a sick child.'

'My daughter, Stuart.' Anna sat up in bed. 'She's in hospital with meningitis and she's only just off the danger list.'

He was silent for a moment, then he said, 'I'm sorry to hear about your kid but you can't expect me to be very sympathetic when you didn't even tell Personnel that you had a child.'

It was pointless to deny her subterfuge. 'I didn't tell you about Daisy because I know your opinion of working mothers,' she said.

'I see. Well, what can I say except when are you coming back to work?'

'Not for another week – at least.'

'A week! Anna, what about your clients? Van Rooyen's expecting you to quote on his new tanker.'

She wanted to say that she didn't give a damn about work when Daisy was ill, but she couldn't afford to, so she replied, 'Van Rooyen knows the situation, his nephew drove me to the ferry and cancelled my remaining appointments, so don't hassle me, Stuart. It's all under control.'

Like most bullies, he retreated when attacked. 'Van Rooyen's nephew! I always said you were an ace at networking. Okay, take another week, but it'll have to count as holiday. Hope the kid gets better.'

'Thanks.' She replaced the receiver and recalled the many reasons why she'd never liked Stuart.

Daisy improved rapidly. By the weekend the drip was removed and she was eating and drinking normally. Restless and easily bored in her darkened room, it took all of Anna's imagination to keep her entertained so that she didn't become agitated. Anna received many messages of good will, including a note from Gordon who had heard about Daisy from Isaac, and a telephone call from Nicolaas van Rooyen. But she did not hear from Paul, although she was sure the Finesteins must have told him about Daisy, and his silence hurt her.

Daisy came home from hospital in the middle of a snowstorm, three days before Anna was due back at work, and although she was much improved she was still pale and clinging, dissolving easily into tears.

Anna telephoned Stuart. 'I need another week,' she told him. 'I'll take it as unpaid leave.'

'Annie, you're needed here.'

She resented his use of her pet name. 'Stuart, I can't leave Daisy yet.'

'And you can't neglect your job any longer. You may be my star saleswoman, but you're not my only star, and there are thousands of hungry people out there looking for work.'

She felt her temper rise. 'I'm perfectly aware of that.'

'Have you forgotten what it's like to be unemployed?'

'No, I haven't, but I cannot abandon my child when she's ill. I've told you, I'll take unpaid holiday, so stop threatening me.'

'Annie, if you aren't here on Monday morning you'll be on a permanent vacation. Think about that! No salary. No car. Who's going to pay for the kid then?'

Anna was silent.

'Good. You've understood – at last. I'll see ya Monday. You'll be leaving for Rotterdam in the afternoon, so bring your bags. I'll rebook your appointments. And remember, the kid doesn't interfere with your work. I want to hear no more of this mumsy crap.' He cut the line without saying goodbye.

Anna looked at Daisy whose face was puckered with misery and uncertainty, and she tapped out the number of Stuart's second phone line, the one that was switched permanently to the loud speaker. 'Stuart.' She could hear her voice echoing around the office at Eurohull. 'I've seen sense.'

'Good girl, Annie. I knew you would.'

'Stuart, you're a wanker. I always thought so, and my intuition was right; and you know what you can do with your job? You can stuff it!' As Anna replaced the receiver, she could hear the stifled laughter of the entire browbeaten sales force.

She laughed too, punching the air with elation, and instantly

Daisy began to smile. 'It's going to be no joke,' said Anna, scooping her up and kissing her. 'No new clothes. No new toys. No car. I'll have to find some sort of job. You must understand that, Daisy. We have to live. We have to eat. But whatever happens, I won't leave you all day, every day, not until you're older. That I promise.'

30

THE MORNING AFTER Anna told Stuart to stuff Eurohull, when the snow lay thick on the ground and icicles hung from the trees, the boiler broke down, and the old familiar terrors gripped her so tightly that she nearly screamed. But she took a deep breath and told Mac calmly, 'Thanks for letting me know. I'll have it mended.'

She sat down at her desk and told herself not to panic. Eurohull owed her a month's salary and nearly seven thousand pounds in commission, thanks to her recent business with Van Rooyen Rotterdam. That was sufficient to pay off Heather and to clear the final excess mortgage supplement, after which the rents would almost cover her monthly payments. Anna planned to look for part time work as soon as Daisy had recovered. When she had been made redundant by Marinecover, she'd felt cut adrift and helpless. Now she was more in control, because she knew how to adapt – she'd done so before.

She hadn't forgotten about Paul, of course she hadn't, but she was wounded by his silence. Logically, though, she knew it was up to her to get in touch with him. But the situation when they had last seen each other, the letter she'd planned to write, the phone call she'd rehearsed, had been superseded by her fears for Daisy. She'd been so anxious, so frightened, that there had been no room in her thoughts for anyone else. And now, somehow, it seemed too late.

Daisy's health improved rapidly and soon she was well enough to go into the garden, where Mr Marilyn showed her how to make a snowman. Watching them from the warmth of the drawing-room, Anna was greatly relieved not to have to battle through the cold to work.

The postman delivered a registered letter from East Metro.

Surprised that they'd gone to such expense just to send her a normal monthly statement, she opened it and read: 'This unexpected reduction in your monthly income means that we have been unable to recover the five thousand pound excess mortgage charge which you agreed to pay in order to clear your earlier deficit.'

Irritated, she telephoned Mr Flatbush. 'I don't understand your letter. Apart from my salary you should have received just under seven thousand pounds of my commission.'

'Miss Tobias, when I took over this branch I warned you that if you defaulted again we would start proceedings to repossess the property.'

'But I've just told you, I'm due commission. My employer must have made a mistake.' It wasn't the moment to tell him that she'd left Eurohull.

'Then I expect to see it credited to your account within seven working days.'

'It will be.' She thumped down the phone, wishing that nice owly Mr Hyde was back.

She phoned Eurohull and was put through to the wages department. 'You've omitted my commission,' she told the clerk politely.

'I'm sorry, Miss Tobias, but the figures were sanctioned by Mr Porterill.'

'Well, he's made a mistake. Could you rectify it, please? I have to pay my mortgage.'

'I'll look into it and ring you back.'

Anna expected him to take at least an hour, so she was agreeably surprised when Stuart himself telephoned a few minutes later. 'What's the problem?' he asked.

'Thanks for calling me back promptly,' she said, pleasantly, deciding that that was the best approach. 'There seems to have been an error in my final payment.'

'No mistake, Annie. If you walk out on your job without giving notice, you forfeit a month's commission.'

'Come on, Stuart, that's not true and you know it.'

'Who are you to tell me what the rules are?'

'Stuart, don't play games; I need that money.'

'Now I bet you're sorry that you made a fool of me on the squawk-box. You shouldn't have told me to stuff the job,

Annie!' He gave a cruel snigger. 'Well, you're the one who's stuffed now.'

She tried to keep calm. 'Stuart, if you don't pay me what I'm owed I shall take you to court.'

'Annie, my sweet, didn't you read the small print in your contract?'

She hesitated.

'Of course you didn't. You were desperate for work. But now you have another job – as a nanny.' He was laughing as he cut her off.

Anna hurried to her desk, opened the top drawer and took out her letter of employment. The second page dealt with an employee's resignation. She'd skimmed it when she'd signed, but now she read each line carefully: 'An employee who fails to give one month's notice may be liable to forfeit thirty days' commission.' Stuart didn't have to withhold her commission, he'd chosen to – and there was nothing she could do about it. A swell of fear rose up inside her, bringing bitter bile to her mouth. She ran into the bathroom, and was violently sick.

When she came out, Daisy was standing in the middle of the kitchen, holding the doll which Paul had given to her as if it were another child to whom she was clinging for support. 'Mummy ill?' she whispered, tears welling in her eyes.

'No, darling.' Anna knelt down beside her. 'Mummy's fine. Don't worry.'

'Mummy work?' Daisy's voice quavered.

'Of course not. Didn't I promise you that I wouldn't go back until you're big enough to go to school all day? And Mummy always keeps her word.' Anna enfolded Daisy and the doll in her arms. She didn't know how she was going to pay East Metro but she had to think of a solution. She'd counted on the commission, not just to pay the excess mortgage, but to live.

Louise was the only person from whom she felt comfortable borrowing money, and when she heard her return earlier than usual, she opened her door and began tentatively, 'Have you . . . umm . . . time to talk?'

'I've time for a drink!'

Louise turned to face her and even in the dim light of the hall, Anna could see that she'd been crying. 'What's wrong?' she asked.

'Half my stock has been stolen.' Louise slumped against the wall. 'I left the van door unlocked and some bastard's walked off with a thousand quid's worth of clothes.'

'Oh, no! How awful.' Anna forced her own troubles to the back of her mind as she ushered Louise into the drawing-room and settled her into one of the armchairs in front of the fire. 'Can I help? Did you tell the police?'

'Yes, but what can they do? It's my fault for not securing the van.' Louise pushed her tobacco hair back off her face. 'What did you want to ask me?'

'It's not important.'

'Come on, it must have been, you had that worried look in your eyes. Is it . . . the house again?'

Anna hesitated. 'Well . . . I have a problem, you see . . .'

'You need to work on the stall? Oh, Anna, I wish I could say yes, but what with the recession and being robbed, I'm barely making enough to keep myself.' Louise paused. 'It was that, wasn't it?'

Anna nodded. There was no point in worrying Louise over the five thousand pounds if she couldn't help, but Anna did wonder about the mentality of the thief, who'd stolen clothes from someone who could clearly ill afford the loss. However desperate, she knew she could never stoop to that.

Anna tried every avenue to raise the money for East Metro. She contacted the DSS, but since she'd given up her job voluntarily she couldn't claim unemployment benefits, not that they would have given her anything like the sum she needed to save the house. She turned the drawing-room into a bedsit and prepared to live with Daisy in two rooms, but so many other houseowners were trying to let spare rooms that her advertisement brought forth only three replies, none of whom turned up. She priced her wardrobe, but even if she sold every item of clothing she wouldn't raise more than a couple of hundred pounds. She scoured the papers for highly-paid part-time work, and all she found were adverts for escort agencies.

In desperation she telephoned one. 'How much would I earn?' she asked the smoky-voiced woman who answered.

'That depends what you do, luv, but as far as the agency is

concerned you're only booked for your companionship, for which we charge you an introduction fee. What you charge the client is up to you.'

'How much could I earn by just going out to dinner, nothing more?' Anna persisted.

'Not a lot, and your bookings would be limited. Most clients want . . . a little extra.'

Anna's flesh crept at the prospect. 'I see.'

'You haven't done this work before, have you?'

'No, of course not. I mean no, I haven't.'

'You sound classy. If you're pretty, well dressed and imaginative – if you know what I mean, dear – you could make two hundred an hour, maybe three hundred, maybe more. Men pay extra for something . . . special. Shall I send you an application form, luvvie?'

'Er . . . I don't think so.' Anna rang off.

No house, not even Ladbroke Hill, was worth that.

31

AS THE DAYS passed Anna became more frantic, so much so that she couldn't sleep; and when she did sleep, she had terrifying dreams from which she woke shaking and crying. In one recurrent nightmare she was homeless, with Daisy in her arms and all their possessions piled in the pram. They wandered through the streets of London – Anna knew it was London although she did not recognise any landmark. It was freezing cold, bitter, and Daisy was running a temperature, but Anna couldn't call a doctor because she didn't have a home. She woke to find her face wet with tears and turned on the bedside light, comforted by the safety of her familiar surroundings, but although she knew she'd been dreaming, the fear did not go away.

More than ever, she sympathised with her father. She would not kill herself, she could never do that to Daisy, but she understood what it meant to teeter on the brink – and she knew exactly why he'd been unable to confide in her mother, or in any member of the family. She also was too ashamed to worry them.

Increasingly, she thought of what Charlie had said about being desperate, and she knew that she was reaching that point. She recalled both Paul and Kevin saying how easy it was to steal a yacht from the swinging moorings, and how sometimes the owners were relieved to lose their vessel and claim the insurance money. She would not have considered stealing money or jewels, but when she thought of taking a car – or a boat – occasionally she could nearly persuade herself that it would be a victimless crime, because the owner would be compensated. But as soon as she'd almost convinced herself, she'd remember what Paul had said about a pound for every inhabitant of Derby, and she knew that there was no such thing as a victimless crime; someone somewhere suffered.

She alternated between disbelief that she could even contemplate committing a crime and terror of what would happen to Daisy if she were caught; but as the days passed that fear was slowly negated by her dread of losing her home.

When she received another demand from East Metro, panic propelled her to find the sea charts which her father had given to her to soften the loss of the *Little Auk*. Scarcely able to believe what she was seriously considering, she smoothed out the English Channel section and ran her finger up the Solent to Chichester Harbour and Bosham.

Abruptly, she refolded the chart. What was she doing, even thinking of stealing a boat? How would she face her family, her friends, Daisy – and most of all herself? What about the owners? She had no guarantee that they'd be glad to collect the insurance. And supposing she was caught and went to gaol, what then of Daisy?

From the basement came the sound of music, and she pictured dear old Mr Marilyn being turned out to live in a tower block. Ladbroke Hill wasn't only Daisy's haven, it was home to all of them and her friends in the house had been as much Daisy's family as her blood relations, if not more so. She thought of the escort agency, which seemed to be her only alternative, but she knew that to have sex for money would invade not just her body but her mind.

In the afternoon, when the house was deserted, she unfolded the chart again and studied it more thoroughly, locating the unnamed creek near the entrance to a small river where she and her father had hidden the *Little Auk* when he couldn't afford Bosham's charges. Then she retrieved her old black wetsuit from the cupboard under the stairs and examined it for holes by submerging it in a bath full of water. Finally, she checked her padded waistcoat buoyancy and located her hand-bearing compass and bought a battery for the torch. Even after these preparations, she could not really believe that she would go through with it.

Before Louise and Mac came home, Anna packed everything away. She longed to say to Louise, 'If something goes wrong, make sure Daisy understands I did it for her,' but Louise would demand an explanation, and Anna felt that it wasn't fair to involve her.

That night she opened her old sailing books and reminded

herself of the idiosyncrasies of each type of boat, and of the dangerous shoals and currents in the Solent – so much more difficult to navigate in the dark. From her charts she worked out that on the following day low tide would be at lunchtime – a neap tide, because it was half moon and the pull of gravity would be at its lowest. Next week there would be a full moon and, accordingly, a powerful spring tide.

As the night hours passed Anna became more nervous. She'd have to find the money another way. What good would she be to Daisy if she was swept out to sea and drowned? But in the morning, as she was finishing breakfast, the postman brought a card from Roz asking if she'd found a job yet, and a final warning from East Metro informing her that 'the matter was to be placed into the hands of their solicitors'. Anna was backed into a corner, with only one chance of escape. She telephoned Heather and asked her to look after Daisy for the night, then she packed a waterproof sailing bag with her wetsuit, the buoyancy aid, the charts, the torch, a second pair of trainers and an extra sweater. When she left Daisy with Heather, she felt so guilty at the risk she was about to take that she could scarcely look her daughter in the face.

At Waterloo she boarded a train to Portsmouth. Sitting in the almost empty carriage, she looked out at the verdant fields of Hampshire and wondered if this was really happening. At Portsmouth she changed trains for Sailham, an ugly, recently developed resort. Unlike Bosham and Belworth, and many of the older fishing villages, it had no centre but consisted of rows of dreary bungalows overlooking a large marina, with a fairground on one side and fast-food shops and a garish pub on the other.

It was a glorious, crisp morning, the first warm day that spring, and the tide was on the ebb. The sea glittered on the emerging mudflats and a light onshore breeze created small wavelets along the recently dredged channel, the only exit from Sailham at all states of the tide. A number of people wandered around the marina, looking at the boats, whilst on board some owners were already repainting the decks in preparation for the summer. No one gave Anna more than a glance. In her track suit and trainers she looked like any other sailor.

She ascertained that the yachts moored alongside the slatted wooden pontoons in the marina were safeguarded by an exit card system, whereas those outside were not – and the boats on the swinging moorings, out in the Sailham channel, were even less protected.

Walking along the water's edge, she came to an area of rough ground where dozens of upturned dinghies lay in haphazard rows. She didn't need to look closer to see that some had their oars tucked underneath. She followed a path leading up to a small, rounded headland. It was only about twenty feet above the mudflats, but from it Anna had a clear view of the boats on the swinging moorings. They all had their mainsails furled around their booms, and in a few cases the jibs had been left untidily in the cockpit. She imagined what her father would have said to see a sail unstowed, and she was nearly able to convince herself that owners like these deserved to lose their boats.

She still wasn't certain if, when the moment came, she could actually bring herself to steal, but in any case she would need high water and the cover of darkness. To kill time, and to postpone the moment of decision, she caught a bus into Portsmouth and spent the afternoon in the public library, studying all their books on the Solent. When the library closed she wandered through the town until she found a fast-food joint where she had a hamburger and a cup of coffee, and bought a sandwich which she tucked into her sailing bag.

Feeling remarkably in control, she took a train to the station before Sailham – a busier stop where the other passengers would be less likely to remember her later. From there she walked, with the traffic whisking past her.

Dusk fell and from the countryside, which during daylight had seemed friendly and pastoral, strange animal noises emanated. The darkness made Anna nervous. Suddenly she was terrified. She stopped in a gateway to steady her nerves but her teeth were chattering. She had to force herself onwards.

In a public lavatory on the outskirts of Sailham she pulled on her wetsuit under her track suit. She was going to need it: the sea was at its coldest after the long winter. Then she walked down the slip road to the marina. It appeared deserted, with just a light at the end of each pontoon, and the only sound – apart from the sea – came from a rowdy party in the furthest mobile home, where the marina staff lived.

In the pale glimmer of the half moon, Anna picked her way across the rough ground to the dinghies. During the afternoon several more had been added to the erratic lines. One had been left the right way up and only just short of the water, with its oars tossed carelessly inside. She felt the wind on her cheek. It was now offshore and had strengthened to a fresh breeze. The tide was high but on the turn, and if she was going to steal a boat she had to do it now – at slack water, before the ebb gathered speed and she couldn't control the dinghy.

She stepped away – she couldn't do it, she was too frightened. She imagined herself lost in the darkness, fighting the waves in a strange boat, being knocked overboard with no one knowing that she was missing, until her body was washed up along the shore. She started walking back, towards the road, but when she reached the shops, she stopped. She pictured Ladbroke Hill with a 'For Sale' board outside, and heard Daisy cry, as she herself had cried for Cliff Cottage.

Returning to the water's edge, she checked the upright dinghy for holes and examined the oars. Then she stripped down to her wetsuit, put on her buoyancy aid – she might be a thief but she wasn't a fool – and rolled her clothes into her sailing bag which she placed in the boat. As quietly as she could she eased the craft down the slope into the water, wading out after it, up to her knees, trying not to gasp as the freezing water seeped into her trainers. Once clear of the mud, she climbed aboard, keeping her face down so that it did not catch the light from the marina.

She rowed towards the swinging moorings, the ebbing tide helping her on the way. After a short distance the darkness blurred the coast and anyone watching would have had difficulty in seeing Anna. As she suddenly approached the yacht she thought of Vince Ellerby-Creswell. How he would laugh to see her now.

The first boat was at least thirty-seven feet long, which even at her most practised would have been too large for her to handle on her own. The next couple were also too big, but further down the channel she singled out an ancient wooden sloop. When she drew closer she saw that the sails had been beautifully furled. Whoever owned her possessed little money but was a true sailor, and Anna couldn't bring herself to steal a much-loved boat.

She rowed on until she came to a twenty-four footer called *The*

Blonde Bimbo. Even in a crisis, the name irritated her and she drew nearer. This yacht was quite new and the reinforced plastic hull appeared in good condition, although it was streaked with grime and the paintwork was sloppy. Afraid that someone might be asleep on board, Anna circled *The Blonde Bimbo* before daring to draw alongside, terrified when her dinghy banged against the hull. She froze, nauseous with fright, but no one appeared, no light came on, no one shouted – so she forced herself onwards, tied up the dinghy, and very cautiously climbed on board the yacht.

The Blonde Bimbo rocked under her. Crouching low, she listened for the roar of a motor boat and shouts of 'Stop, thief!', but the only sounds were of the sea: the thud of the waves, the slap of the halyards against the mast, and the knocking of the dinghy. Gingerly, she tried the hatch. It was unlocked and led down to a cabin in which there were three bare bunks, a cooker, and a black plastic sack full of empty beer cans. Even in the faint light Anna could see that this boat was unloved, with the jib unstowed and the ropes thrown in untidy piles instead of coiled, as her father had taught her.

Taking out her torch and hiding the glare with her body, she examined the floor for ominous signs of water. Once satisfied that the boat was seaworthy, she picked up the jib and returned to the deck, where she scrutinised the mainsail, partially unfurling it to make sure that it wasn't torn before she clipped it on to the main halyard. Then she checked the rudder and the tiller to ensure they weren't broken, acutely aware that there would be no one to come to her rescue if something went wrong.

Keeping her head down, Anna worked quickly to clip the jib to the forestay, but she didn't hoist the sail yet, she had to prepare the boat. She fed the jib sheets through the fairleads and jammed them in the cleats, her fingers fumbling with fear as she tied the knots. When all was ready, she took a series of deep breaths to calm her nerves and, reminding herself that she had no alternative, she transferred the dinghy to the mooring buoy, let slip *The Blonde Bimbo*, and quickly hoisted the jib.

The wind filled the sail and the yacht swung round, gathering headway downstream. Instinctively, Anna eased out the sheet and the boat picked up speed, cutting through the darkness, and the icy black waves which slapped at her badly-painted hull threw salty spray up into Anna's face. She laughed aloud from terror and relief and from excitement, for in spite of the circumstances Anna was exhilarated to be sailing again.

There was just enough light for her to see the mouth of the harbour and the looming land mass on either side. She remembered that there was a sand bank near the exit, not navigable at low tide, and she couldn't recall its exact location, so she turned the boat head to the wind, allowing *The Blonde Bimbo* to drift whilst she studied her chart in the light of her torch. It was nearly an hour since she'd left the shore and she wondered if the theft had been discovered already. She didn't imagine so, but the prospect of arrest was terrifying. Quickly she hoisted the mainsail and with both sails drawing well, *The Blonde Bimbo* skimmed through the water, over the submerged sand bank and down the narrow channel to the Solent.

With no lights to warn another boat of her presence, Anna fought to keep safely to the starboard side, but the pull of the tide in the channel was fierce and it kept dragging her to port. She gybed, turning the boat with the wind behind her. Unlike tacking, there was no moment of stability as the boat went through the wind. Instead, Anna had to change sides quickly, ducking under the boom when it swung across the vessel, whilst the incoming waves of the open sea crashed over the bow, the white horses drenching her in spray.

She was cold. Her wetsuit had perished along the seams and let in too much water; her face was wet and her eyes stung from the salt; her hands were freezing and her feet in her sodden trainers had turned to ice. The exhilaration she'd initially felt had long since disappeared. It had been replaced by exhausted nerves and sheer physical tiredness.

The creek was a short distance up the coast, but with the wind offshore and the tide still ebbing she could not get there. She needed one or the other in her favour. It was an hour until low water and a further two hours before the incoming tide would gather enough strength to help her to sail against a head wind. To kill time, she tacked around, backwards and forwards, afraid to heave to in case she fell asleep and, without an anchor, drifted into the path of one of the huge container vessels whose lights winked at her through the darkness as they progressed up the East Solent towards Southampton.

Shivering with cold, Anna ate the sandwich she'd bought in Portsmouth and wondered if she'd die of pneumonia, and if she did – would that be her punishment? Now she had time to consider the owner of *The Blonde Bimbo* and she hoped he or she wouldn't be too distressed. Every ten minutes or so she used her compass to take a bearing on the distant Chichester Bar beacon which flashed white/red at five-second intervals, then she took another on the red-flashing Fairway buoy outside the entrance to Langstone harbour. So long as the two readings remained constant, she hadn't drifted.

As dawn approached the tide turned, and by continual tacking Anna was able to ease the boat slowly up the coast to the unmarked creek which her father, when a small boy, and his father, Grandpa Tobias, had discovered during a sailing holiday the summer before the war broke out.

Anna hadn't been there for fifteen years and she found it far more overgrown than she remembered, with the trees on both banks meeting above the water to form a dark green tunnel. She lowered the sails and lifted the rudder to manoeuvre the boat well into the creek, but it had become so filled with silt that the keel stuck, and she had no alternative than to drop anchor in the entrance. Now, in the early morning light, she could see the boat properly. It wasn't in bad condition, it was just badly maintained. She remembered how much paint, varnish and love she and her father had lavished on the *Little Auk*, a far less expensive craft than this.

She was so cold that her teeth chattered and her hands and feet ached. She longed for a mug of coffee, food, a hot bath and home – but to walk through the countryside so early would draw attention to her presence. In any case, she had work to do. With what looked like someone's forgotten face flannel she cleaned the hull as best she could, dipping the flannel into the freezing, muddy water, then wiping the surfaces. She furled the sails and coiled the various sheets and halyards, stowing everything neatly. As she was hiding the sack of beer cans under one of the bunks, she noticed a key tucked behind a ledge. It fitted the locker beneath the other bunk. Inside it she found some suprisingly new-looking registration papers belonging to *The Blonde Bimbo*. She was owned by a company in Essex and, according to the logbook whose entries were patchy and written in different hands, she'd arrived at Sailham two months earlier. The last entry read: 'Motor buggered up. Get it mended by summer.' This was not a boat which was loved, and Anna felt increasingly less guilty about taking her.

Tucking the logbook into her sailing bag, Anna dropped a rope over the side, lowered herself into the cold murky water, and swam ashore with the bag balanced on her shoulders. On reaching the bank she had to scramble up it, cutting her palms on the brambles and jabbing her collarbone on the lower branch of an old oak tree. With no means of drying herself, she struggled out of her wetsuit and straight into her track suit, with her body still slippery from the sea and her trainers squelching with mud.

Then she set off to walk the two miles along the river bank to the busy crossroads where the bus for Portsmouth stopped. An hour after leaving the boat, she boarded a fast commuter train to London. The only spare seat was next to an arrogant man who made a fuss about moving his coat to let Anna sit. Half-way through their journey she noticed that the water from her wetsuit was seeping through the sailing bag, which was on the rack above him, and dripping slowly on to his precious coat. He didn't notice, and she said nothing.

From Waterloo, Anna took the Underground to Notting Hill. As she stepped from the train, Mac entered her carriage.

'Anna!' He stared at her. 'What are you doing out so early?'

She flushed. 'Oh . . . I . . . er . . . went to visit a friend.'

He grinned. 'I didn't mean to pry. See ya later.' The doors closed and he was gone, to his office near Moorgate.

Anna smiled wryly at what Mac imagined she'd been doing the night before. If he knew the truth, she doubted if he'd ever speak to her again, if any of them would, and she could not blame them. She was a thief, and the enormity of what she had done hit her as she trudged home.

Ladbroke Hill was very quiet. It slumbered in the morning sunshine, the only sign of movement being Errol Flynn, who walked purposefully along the wall towards the dustbins where the alley cats gathered. Anna couldn't believe that the house looked the same, whereas her life had changed so irreversibly. She made a mug of coffee and opened the balcony doors. The balcony reminded her of Paul and she was swept by acute sadness as she realised that she had now jeopardised any possibility of a future for them, not that there'd been much chance beforehand – but last night she'd crossed to the other side; she had become the poacher, whereas he was still the gamekeeper.

32

ANNA DIDN'T WISH to profit from the sale of *The Blonde Bimbo*, she only wanted to make enough money to prevent East Metro from repossessing the house. Although she knew it sounded irrational, she felt less dishonest if she did not keep any money for herself, but because any purchaser would expect to beat her price down, she advertised the boat for £5,400 o.n.o. To safeguard her identity, she used a box number.

In the first week she only received one reply, and when she telephoned the respondent he'd already bought another boat. In a panic, she re-advertised at £5,200. This time she received three replies: one wanted to swap a larger boat, another lived in Ireland, the third was a typed note: 'Cash buyer, can view any time. Derek.' Anna recognised the prefix of the telephone number as that of the Southampton area.

She didn't telephone him from the house in case she was overheard, but asked Mr Marilyn to mind Daisy for ten minutes whilst she hurried down the hill to the public phone box.

A man answered. His voice was curt and wary, and Anna was so nervous that she stammered. 'I'm . . . er . . . ringing up about your reply to my advertisement.'

'Which boat?'

'The sloop in *The Yachting Exchange*.'

'I've got you.' He relaxed and became more friendly. 'Where's she moored? When can I see her?'

Suddenly Anna realised how unwise she'd been to choose an isolated creek. Even a fool would guess that *The Blonde Bimbo* was stolen. 'She's . . . umm . . . in the Solent, on a private mooring.'

'Are you the owner?'

'She belongs to my brother who's working abroad.'

'Do you have her logbook?' He sounded suspicious, and that frightened her even more.

'Oh, yes, of course, and the registration papers; and the key to the locker. I have everything. If you're interested, I'll bring her into one of the harbours then you can see her for yourself.' She was babbling with nerves but she couldn't help it.

He said, immediately, 'How about Cobbleford? There's a pub called the Cobble Keys, beside the river, beyond the disused church. You can moor along the towpath and ring me from the bar.'

Cobbleford was on the far side of Southampton Water from the creek. Anna knew it vaguely; she and her father had once stopped there for lunch. 'That's fine,' she said. 'Subject to the tide and the weather, I'll be there tomorrow morning.'

'Give me your number in case I need to call back.'

'I . . . umm . . . don't have a telephone.' She lied to protect herself.

'Do you have a name?'

'Yes, it's Caroline.'

'I'll see you in the Cobble Keys, Caroline. I know your boat's just what I'm after. I'll have the cash waitin'.'

'Thank you.' The receiver slithered from her sweating hands.

She calculated that high water would be just after dawn. If she caught the morning tide it would lift her out of the muddy creek, and with a reasonable wind she'd be in Cobbleford for breakfast. Late that afternoon she exchanged her pale grey leggings for black ones and her white sweatshirt for navy, purposely selecting dark colours. Then she made three rounds of sandwiches and a Thermos of strong, sweet coffee, packed her wetsuit and her charts and delivered Daisy to Heather, who raised a suggestive eyebrow when she saw the bag again, but made no comment.

Anna caught a commuter train to Portsmouth, mingling easily with the other travellers in her unobtrusive clothes. From the station she took a bus to the crossroads, from where she walked.

It was dusk when she reached the creek. She approached carefully, keeping to the shadows whilst her eyes searched the nearby trees for signs of life, but there were none. Beside the oak tree she stopped to pull on her wetsuit, rolling her clothes into her bag, but as she stepped towards the water, she heard a noise in the undergrowth and froze, terrified that the police were waiting to arrest her. A minute passed and nothing happened. Anna started to relax. Then a twig broke, and she bit her lip with fright.

A vixen stepped from the bushes opposite. Raising her pointed nose, she sniffed the damp evening air, cautious but not suspicious because Anna was downwind. Ears pricked, the vixen listened for unfamiliar sounds, her brown eyes combing the undergrowth before, with a swish of her white-tipped brush, she set off to hunt for food. Anna watched her go, sensing – although she couldn't see them – that somewhere not too far away were the vixen's cubs. Then she slid down the bank, into the water, and swam out to *The Blonde Bimbo*, the bag across her shoulders. With the help of the rope she climbed aboard, dropping swiftly to her knees so as not to stand silhouetted against the twilight sky. Like the vixen, she was cautious.

Once inside the cabin she settled down to eat half her sandwiches and drink a cup of coffee. Beyond the creek the countryside came alive with rustling and squeaks as little animals came out to feed – or to be fed upon. She huddled on one of the bunks and tried to sleep.

At dawn it was drizzling and there was a light onshore breeze. Stiff with cold, Anna devoured the remainder of the sandwiches and drank all the coffee. Then she put on her wetsuit, rolled her clothes into her sail bag to wear later and began to rig up the boat. Within a short while she was underway.

The shipping lanes seemed particularly busy that morning, with monster tankers pounding up and down to Southampton, and car ferries criss-crossing to the Isle of Wight and to France. Several times Anna was drenched with spray as the waves in their wake tossed *The Blonde Bimbo* around. It took her until noon to reach Cobbleford. At the far end of the village, a dead-end lane led past the church to the Cobble Keys, a dilapidated pub whose roughly-cut lawn ran down to the towpath. Anna moored beyond it, where *The Blonde Bimbo* would be hidden by the lower branches of a willow tree.

There was no one around, just a couple of boats battened down against the drizzle and the damp. Since leaving the creek, Anna hadn't dared let go of the tiller for a second in case of catastrophe and now, freezing cold, she was longing to go to the loo, but she could hardly run into the pub in her wetsuit. In the privacy of the cabin she struggled out of the wet rubber, pulled on her clothes and ran up the path, her trainers squelching with sea-water.

The pub had a scruffy warmth, not unlike The Admiral Vernon. A couple of people were talking at the bar, but they took no notice of Anna as she scuttled into the ladies'. Until she saw herself in the mirror she hadn't realised quite how bedraggled she looked, with her tired face, her dark-circled eyes and her wet hair hanging in rat-tails. Instinct warned her not to meet Derek when she appeared so vulnerable, and she forced a comb through her tangled hair, pinched her cheeks to give them colour, painted her lips, and removed her trainers to squeeze the water from them so that they didn't squelch when she walked.

Returning to the bar, Anna ordered a cup of tomato soup and a cheese roll. Whilst they were being prepared she used the telephone.

Derek answered, again with caution.

'It's Caroline,' she told him. 'I'm at the Cobble Keys.'

'I'll see you in ten minutes.'

She took her soup and her roll to a corner table near the window from where she had a clear view along the dead-end lane to the bus stop on the Southampton route. The nightmare was so nearly over that she could almost touch the moment when she stepped aboard the bus.

Five minutes passed – then ten, fifteen, twenty – but no one came down the track towards the pub. She started to panic, afraid that Derek had changed his mind. Then the back door of the pub opened, and a whippet-thin man in a camel-hair jacket slipped into the bar.

'Your usual, Derek?' called the barman.

'Make it a double.' Derek turned his pale eyes to Anna. 'What are you drinking, Caroline?'

She smiled politely. 'Nothing, thank you.'

'I hope you don't mind if I do.' He sat down and she saw that although his skin was weather-beaten he had a neat face with delicate features and smartly cut, greying hair. 'Let me see the logbook,' he said. 'Punters always like a nice logbook.'

Anna laid the papers on the table before him. 'Wouldn't you be buying her for yourself?'

'For my daughter.' He checked the papers quickly but carefully. 'And the key?'

She held it out in the palm of her hand.

'Everything seems in order.' He finished his drink and stood up. 'Let's have a look at her.'

He walked fast, down to the towpath, hissing his breath through his front teeth. Anna had to run to keep up with him. When they reached the boats he didn't ask which was hers, but stepped confidently aboard *The Blonde Bimbo* in a way which made her suspect that he'd already looked the yacht over whilst she'd been waiting in the pub. 'Got an outboard motor?' he asked.

She shook her head.

Anna expected him to check the sails, but he didn't bother. 'I'll buy her,' he said, putting his hand in his jacket pocket and bringing out a wad of notes. 'Fifty-two hundred.'

Anna was astonished that he didn't try to beat her price down. 'Oh . . . er . . . my brother only wants five thousand,' she said. 'I made a mistake.'

'Take the extra for your trouble.'

'No! Really! I don't want it.'

His eyes became shrewd. 'Why not? You deserve it, girl. You must be a bloody good little sailor to bring this boat up here single-handed.'

To allay his suspicions, Anna agreed. 'You're right, I have earned it.' She took the envelope and, to show him that she wasn't naive, she counted the contents. Then she handed him the key, the logbook and the boat's papers. 'Thank you,' she said, picking up her sailing bag and stepping briskly ashore. 'Goodbye.'

He didn't reply, and there was something malevolent in his silence.

Anna set off along the towpath towards the bus stop. When she'd gone about twenty yards he shouted, 'Caroline!'

It took her a couple of paces to remember her name, and answer, 'Yes?'

'I'll buy your brother's next boat too.'

'He only had this yacht.'

He gave a disbelieving laugh. 'This boat's worth twice what you asked. I'm not complainin', mind, but only a fool or a thief sells cheap – and you ain't no fool.'

'My brother wanted a quick sale.'

He laughed again. 'And I have lots of daughters!'

Anna didn't reply. She walked on, fighting a desire to run.

She reached London in the middle of the afternoon and went straight to East Metro to rid herself of Derek's dirty money. As she was standing at the counter, feeding the last few notes under the grill to the cashier, Mr Flatbush came out of his office. 'Miss Tobias, you haven't replied to my letters,' he said sternly.

'Mr Flatbush, I've cleared my debt. In fact, I've paid in a little extra.' With a triumphant wave she sashayed out of the bank.

Daisy was happily stacking plastic bricks with the other children when Anna arrived at Heather's. She scooped her up and hugged her fiercely, only now allowing herself to confront the appalling risk she'd taken. She felt sick with despair for what she had done, not solely in case she was caught but, more important, because she had acted against her own, inner honesty.

33

THE SEA HAD awakened a yearning in Anna for the sound of the waves and the salt wind, and on the next sunny morning she dressed Daisy in her springtime yellow jumpsuit, and herself in jeans with a cotton sweater, T-shirt and thin jacket, made a picnic lunch, and took the train to Chichester from where they caught a local bus to the old fishing village of Bosham.

Within a few minutes of their arrival a wall of cloud appeared in the west and a cold wind whipped up the Bosham channel, at the top of the much larger Chichester harbour. She'd brought an anorak for Daisy, but she blamed herself for not packing more warm clothes, and as Daisy's face quivered she considered ordering a taxi instead of waiting for the next bus, but she'd already spent more than she'd expected on the rail fare. So she strapped Daisy into her buggy, saying, 'It'll be warmer if we keep moving.'

Bending her face against the wind and the odd spot of rain, Anna hurried the buggy down a street of old cottages to the tidal Shore Road where a couple of cars were parked in front of the pub. At high tide they would have been submerged. A couple of ducks approached them, cackling for food, and to cheer Daisy up Anna sacrificed a sandwich to feed them. In spite of the cold she could still find pleasure in the magic beauty of Bosham, where the light reflecting off the windows of the Georgian houses along the sea front bounced down on to the mudflats, creating dark mirrors between the swans and ducks who fed on the plankton.

She carried on walking along the shore, past the watermill which housed the Sailing Club, to the quay. At the far end, protruding out into the channel, there was an old wooden barn called the 'Raptackle'. *The Little Auk* had been moored directly north of this spot.

With half an hour to wait before the next bus, Anna sat down on a bench in front of the ancient Saxon stone church and unbuckled Daisy from her buggy and gave her a Marmite sandwich. Then she sat back and looked out at the boats in the harbour, and although she tried to block it from her mind, she kept thinking back to the night when she'd stolen *The Blonde Bimbo*. She rose abruptly – she shouldn't have come, not that Sailham was Bosham, but they weren't so far apart. As she lifted Daisy into the buggy a large drop of rain fell on her head, and within seconds it was coming down like stair-rods. With Daisy crying under one arm, and the picnic and the buggy under the other, Anna raced towards the nearest shelter, the old Saxon church.

It was empty and quiet, although the flowers on the altar were fresh. Anna dried Daisy's hair as best she could, relieved to find her warm and dry in her anorak, although she herself was freezing and her cotton sweater was sodden. 'This was not Mummy's most brilliant idea,' she said, holding Daisy tight and longing for the fire at Ladbroke Hill.

She was too cold to sit still for long, so she rose and, carrying Daisy, walked around the little church, leaving wet footprints on the flagstone floor. In one corner, flush to the ground, she found a stone tablet on which there was a black raven, the insignia of the royal house of Denmark, and the words: 'In memory of a Daughter of King Canute, who died early in the fifth century, aged about eight years.' She was bending to have a closer look when the church door creaked. Expecting a church warden, Anna was on the point of saying, 'I'm sorry about my wet feet.' But she stopped.

'Hello, Anna.' Paul was standing in the gloom at the far end of the aisle. He was wearing an oilskin from which rainwater ran in rivulets, and his dark hair was so wet that it stuck to his head. He could hardly have looked more different from the sophisticated loss adjuster whom she'd first met in her Marinecover days.

Anna was so surprised to see him that she nearly dropped Daisy. 'What . . . what are you doing here?' she asked in a tight voice.

'I was having a drink with some friends in the Sailing Club, when I saw a woman and child sitting on the bench eating a picnic in the rain. She looked like you, and I couldn't believe such a coincidence, but I had to come and see.' Paul walked down the aisle towards her. 'I was so sorry to hear about Daisy's illness,' he said. 'Is she all right now?'

'Yes but . . .' Anna gave him an unforgiving look. 'She became ill six weeks ago, Paul.'

'I only heard last night, from Sybil. I've been in South America.' He drew closer. 'This morning, driving down here, I was wondering if I should write or telephone you, that's why I couldn't believe it when I saw you on that bench.'

'Oh, I'm sorry. I thought . . .' She was full of remorse and her voice trailed away.

'That I didn't care?' He touched Daisy's soft cheek. 'Anna, of course I would have telephoned. How can you doubt that?' He held out his hands as though about to take her by the shoulders, then he let them drop. 'You've had a terrible time.'

She nodded, too choked to speak, wondering what he would say if he knew about *The Blonde Bimbo*.

He saw the bleakness come into her face, and said, 'I wish I'd been there to help.'

'Thank you.' Her voice was little more than a whisper. They both fell silent as they recalled their last meeting.

'You were wrong about Charlie,' she said, eventually. 'I feel nothing for him now, but you were right that he doesn't know of Daisy's existence. He thinks that I had an abortion, because that's what I planned to do – until the last minute. But seeing his parents brought back all the memories of when he . . . walked out – of when he left me. And not just those memories – the others. You see, what I didn't tell you was that my father . . .' she swallowed hard. '. . . that my father killed himself.'

'Oh, God!' Oblivious of the fact that they had not spoken for six weeks, and that they might never have met again, Paul wrapped her and Daisy in his arms. 'I'm so sorry.'

'He stepped under a train, after he'd been made redundant – yet again.' Anna's voice was muffled by Paul's shoulder. 'I felt so deserted, so angry, so helpless. It happened sixteen years ago, but I can remember it like yesterday.'

Paul stroked Daisy's hair. 'Believe me, I know how hard it is to escape the past.'

'Because you still mourn Felicity, even though things . . . went wrong?'

'Anna, if you only knew!' He had his hands on her shoulders and suddenly realised that her cotton jumper was soaking. 'You must be freezing,' he said. 'Here, take my sweater.' He slipped off his oilskin and then his navy, oiled-wool jumper. When she tried to protest, because he would be cold, he insisted. 'No, you're shivering, you'll get pneumonia. Look, why don't you come to my boathouse, get dry, and have something hot to drink? I want to hear all about it, everything. Isaac told me you've left Eurohull.' He paused. 'I told you of my boathouse, didn't I?'

Their hands did not touch as he handed her his jumper. 'No, Paul. You didn't.'

He laughed aloud, then stopped. 'I forgot we're in a church,' he whispered. 'You're right, I was keeping it a secret. I wanted to surprise you because it's only a few miles away, at Black Swan Bay, and I knew that you had memories of Bosham.' His eyes became very serious. 'You see, I forget nothing.'

She thought of *The Blonde Bimbo*. 'Nor do I, though sometimes I wish I could.' When she pulled his sweater over her head and rolled back the cuffs because the sleeves were far too long, she could feel his warmth in the wool and smell him, masculine with a hint of lemon, so that, standing there, she had the sensation that his arms were around her.

'Better?' he asked.

She smiled. 'Much warmer.'

'Now come and admire my boathouse.' He hooked the buggy over one arm, and Anna collected the picnic bag. Together they went out into the freshly washed air, where the clouds were giving way to tentative rays of sunshine.

Black Swan Bay was one of the few harbours which Anna had never visited. It was a fishing hamlet a few miles along the coast, and it resembled Bosham, but on a smaller scale. The handful of attractive old cottages clustered around a tiny tidal bay and a dramatic headland on which stood the ruins of a monastery, and the even older ruins of a stone crypt in which a hermit and a black swan were said to have lived during the seventh century.

The shore road was untarmacked and Paul's Land-Rover bounced through the puddles, passing a tiny newsagents which doubled as a grocery, and an ancient beamed pub, renowned for its seafood restaurant. It was called The Hungry Pirate and it never closed, except when the landlord, an amusing rogue, went to court to face charges of breaking the licensing laws.

On the far side of the bay the smoothly gliding Black Creek met the faster flowing Swan River and on a handkerchief of land, where the waters joined, there was an old boathouse hidden from the village by a large oak tree. It was built of a mixture of warm, rounded Sussex flint and dark, weathered wood. Part of it was on land, the rest straddled the Black Creek, which was deep enough to moor a reasonable sized boat.

Anna gasped at its beauty. 'This is the kind of magical place my father always dreamed of buying.'

He touched her hand. 'I hope that doesn't make you sad.'

She smiled. 'Not as it used to.'

Paul stepped from the vehicle, put two fingers to his lips and gave a piercing whistle like a hotel doorman calling up a taxi. Instantly, Bobby appeared in the field on the far side of the creek. He raced through the long lush grass, his dark head bobbing up and down, until he reached the creek where, with no hesitation, he launched himself into the water, sending a family of moorhens paddling for cover. A moment later he bounced up the bank, shaking the water from his long wet coat. Daisy squealed with delight.

Paul ushered them into the boathouse. It consisted of a large white cavernous room, with big, comfortable sofas in front of an open fireplace, a beamed kitchen at the far end, and a large glass plate in the floor through which the Black Creek could be seen gliding past underneath. The whole place reeked of paint and white spirit, odours Anna knew well.

'You should have seen the mess it was in when I bought it,' he said, heating up some milk for Daisy.

Anna laughed. 'But Paul, everything you buy needs restoring.'

He chuckled. 'Yes, I like to save. I'm probably descended from missionaries, though I don't know it.'

Anna tucked her damp hair behind her ears and looked away. He hadn't been around to save her, and she wondered just how quickly he'd throw her out if he knew about *The Blonde Bimbo*.

Paul made coffee and sandwiches, then they settled down on the sofa in front of the fire. 'Tell me about Daisy's illness,' he said.

Anna looked down at her hands. 'I've never been so frightened. I really thought she was going to die. I was in Holland when she became ill, and I felt so helpless, so guilty for being away, for leaving her. I almost believed that I deserved to lose her for being such a bad mother.'

'Anna that's certainly not true; but is that . . . fear what made you leave Eurohull?'

'I'd intended to go back, but Stuart began hounding me. He wouldn't even allow me to take an extra week to be with Daisy, even as unpaid leave, so I told him what he could do with his job – on the squawk-box when everyone could hear.'

He laughed. 'I wish I could have seen his face.'

'He got his revenge.' Anna couldn't mask her bitterness. 'He kept my commission in lieu of notice.'

'That's so unjust. Look . . .' He paused. 'Anna, I don't want to intrude, but if I can help . . .'

If he'd offered a week earlier, she'd have swallowed her pride and accepted, but now it was too late. 'I can manage, thank you,' she said, forcing a smile. 'I'm just sorry that I let Gordon down. He gave me a break.'

'Oh, he'll survive, but what are you going to do?'

'Tighten my belt.'

'Are you going to work?'

'Not full-time until Daisy is at school. I'll try to pick up little jobs, like assisting Louise and helping Lionel in his frame shop. I won't earn much, but I'll get by. And at least I won't be abandoning Daisy for nights on end.'

He reached across to her and ran his finger down the soft skin on the back of her hand. 'As I've said before, you have great courage.'

The bleak look returned to her face, which puzzled him, and she asked, 'What are your plans for the boathouse?'

Once again, Paul knew that he had been deflected but he decided to bide his time, and he talked enthusiastically about the boathouse. 'I'm going to bring *The Goshawk* here,' he told her. 'The creek is deep enough, even at low tide, and I plan to have another office linked to the one in London. I'll show you where.' He led the way up a flight of open wooden steps to space above, where a carpenter was panelling a dividing wall between a spacious bedroom with a view of the bay, and a functional study with many wooden shelves, looking down on to the approach road.

They stood, side by side, looking out. The tide had turned and it was creeping slowly up the mudflats to where a couple of yachts were marooned, left high and dry on their sides when the water had receded. On the far side, the ruined monastery rose up into the pale sky. Its image reflected like a moving mirror on the incoming flow. Anna was very conscious of Paul next to her, of his warmth and his breath, of his arm touching hers.

'I missed you,' he said softly.

'I've missed you too.' She felt every nerve of her body sharpen, as though she were naked and he were caressing her skin.

He stroked her sleeve and she was as conscious of his touch as though his fingers had met bare flesh, instead of the thick wool of his sweater.

Then she remembered the morning when she'd stood on the balcony after she'd stolen *The Blonde Bimbo*, and known that she'd jeopardised any future with Paul. Suddenly she felt utterly deflated. Their relationship was doomed, and there seemed no point in going any further. 'I must take Daisy home,' she said abruptly, stepping away from him.

'I'll run you to the station.' Her sudden mood swing resurrected dark memories of Felicity, and he wondered if he'd been mistaken about Anna. Did that mixture of bravery and vulnerability which he found so endearing really exist, or was he merely seeing what he wanted to see; was he deluding himself again?

She started to take off his sweater.

'Keep it or you'll freeze,' he said.

She hesitated. 'No, thanks. I'll be fine.' There was a clip in her voice and, picking up Daisy, she hurried downstairs before she could change her mind, collected her jacket and her bag, and went out to the Land-Rover.

They drove to the station in silence. Anna wanted to explain that she'd backed away because she was afraid, but the right words wouldn't come. They always seemed to fail her when she needed them.

The London train was waiting and they had to run on to the platform. Paul lifted Daisy into the carriage and found them a window seat. Then he turned to Anna. 'You left your wet sweater in the boathouse, and you know what they say about people who leave things behind?'

'No. Tell me.'

'It means you want to come back.'

Her resolution dissolved, and she smiled, helpless to refuse him. 'I do.'

Before she could say more, the guard blew his whistle, the carriage doors slammed, and the train gave an ominous shunt. Paul gave her a quick kiss on the mouth. 'Have dinner with me on Saturday,' he shouted as he jumped down on to the platform.

Anna sank into her corner, with Daisy on her lap, and laughed. She knew that she was playing with fire; that one day she'd tell him about *The Blonde Bimbo* because it weighed on her too much to keep it secret, and he might reject her because of it. But for Paul, she was prepared to take that risk.

34

PAUL TELEPHONED ANNA during the week. 'I have a suggestion,' he said. 'Instead of just dinner on Saturday, if you're free for the day, we could sail *The Goshawk* round to the boathouse and eat at The Hungry Pirate.'

'I'd love to,' she said, eagerly. 'Let me see if I can get Heather to take Daisy.'

He hesitated, then added, 'Will you let me pay the childminder?'

'No, absolutely not. In any case, Heather still owes me a couple of days.'

Paul collected Anna early on Saturday. They dropped Daisy at Heather's before heading out of town. Anna was dressed warmly in a thick yellow sweater, with her jeans tucked into her yellow sailing boots. She had a waterproof bag with her buoyancy aid and a change of clothes – a short red dress – to wear for dinner. As they drove out of London they listened to the shipping forecast: 'Wind force four to five, moderate to fresh.'

At the marina they were met by Michael, the ex-policeman, looking gloomy. 'There's a problem with the engine, Paul. The same as you had before. She runs for a bit, then cuts out as soon as you slow down.'

'It's probably a speck of dirt.' Paul turned to Anna. 'By the time the oil is changed I'm afraid we'll have missed the tide. That doesn't matter here, but Black Swan Bay is tidal.'

'We don't need the engine, we can sail her.' Anna looked at the ketch rocking on the small, choppy waves. 'The wind's offshore.'

'I would if I were alone, but . . .'

She gave him a mutinous glare.

He squeezed her hand. 'If you're game, so am I. Let's rig her up and be on our way. I'll check the spares and the generator. Michael, could you see that we have water, coffee, sandwiches and flares. We should only be at sea for a couple of hours, but with no engine we need to be well-stocked for emergencies.'

They hurried along the slatted pontoon to *The Goshawk*. Paul swung himself aboard, then held out a hand to help Anna. Whilst he checked the instruments and charts, she prepared the sails, trying not to think about the last time she'd done so. The ketch was a two-mast boat, with three sails, which made her easier to handle in a storm, because if the mainsail had to be lowered in a high wind, the jib and the mizzen balanced the craft.

She'd just finished knotting the ends of the ropes to prevent them sliding back through the cleats and falling into the sea when Paul appeared. He studied her handiwork and smiled. 'I had no idea that my crew was so expert.'

'I told you that I used to sail.'

'Thousands of people say they sail, but they're useless.'

She raised an eyebrow. 'I am not one of them!'

He laughed. 'So I see.'

They were soon ready to cast off. The stiff offshore breeze took them downriver with just the two smaller sails. Paul took the helm, Anna beside him, her sweater pulled well down against the cold, her blonde hair continually blown across her face.

'Glad you came?' he asked.

She nodded. 'How much did you say the crew is paid?'

He looked shocked.

She laughed, and walked away to check the ropes.

As they reached the Solent, they hoisted the mainsail to make up over the tide, sailing close to the wind, skimming the waves. It began to rain. They pulled on their oilskins and attached their safety harnesses to the boat in case one of them slipped and fell into the sea.

The rain showed no sign of abating. Anna went down into the galley to make coffee, closing the hatch door firmly after her so that water didn't pour into the cabins. It wasn't easy to boil the water, with it slopping each time the boat was buffeted, but she succeeded, and she returned to the deck with a mug each.

Paul took it from her. 'Thanks.' He had to shout to make himself heard above the sound of the wind and the waves slapping against the hull.

She smiled and gave him the thumbs up.

'Still glad you came?' he shouted again.

'This counts as double time.' The wind caught her salty hair, wrapping it around her face.

He reached out to free her from its strands, his fingers icy on her cheek. She smiled her helplessness to reject him. He held out his arm, and she went to him, nestling against him, her wet oilskin rubbing against him. A huge wave hit the side of the boat and covered them with spray. They looked at each other and laughed, relishing the sea, the danger and each other. She was so engrossed in him that she did not notice when they passed the entrance to the unmarked creek or the mouth of Sailham harbour. Paul drew her closer and kissed the salty water from her lips, and they stayed together, wrapped in each other, until the need to change course sent Anna back to the sails.

It took them less time than they'd expected to reach the Chichester Bar buoy, half a mile out from the harbour.

'We have to keep to the port of it,' Paul shouted to Anna.

She nodded. 'I remember from my father.'

The tide had turned and the wind had shifted. *The Goshawk* was carried so fast towards the narrow entrance that they almost missed the green flashing West Winner buoy, but at the last minute Paul managed to pull her round and they shot through into the more sheltered waters beyond. Once inside they had to gybe quickly to starboard so as not to miss the Bosham channel. Within a short while they caught sight of the ruined monastery at Black Swan Bay. The tide was racing now, submerging the mudflats, righting all the yachts left high and dry, and swamping the shore road.

Anna was freezing. She began to wish she'd worn her wetsuit, whatever its adverse memories.

'We'll have to take her in on the jib and the mizzen,' said Paul. 'The entrance to the creek is narrow and the water runs strongly there. It can make for a choppy ride.'

She smiled. 'You don't scare me.'

'So I realise.'

They tacked into the wind, and in the brief moment of calm they lowered the mainsail. With less sail area, they moved sedately, bumping slowly over the tide.

'Almost home.' Paul placed the fenders over the side of *The Goshawk* to protect the hull from the jetty.

Anna took the bow rope and jumped ashore. With a quick turn of the rope around the post, she held the boat whilst Paul secured it with the mooring lines.

'I couldn't have managed without you,' he said, joining her on land and hugging her.

Her teeth were chattering. 'I enjoyed it.'

'You must have a hot bath.' He ushered her towards the boathouse where Bobby was leaping up and down, barking excitedly.

'What about you? Aren't you cold?'

'Freezing – but I want to attach the burglar alarm. I'd look pretty foolish if I had my own boat stolen.'

The building enveloped them in its warmth. The lights and heating had been left on, and the fire was laid. Paul put a match to it, and it crackled into life.

'May I phone Heather?' said Anna, not adding that she intended to ask the childminder to keep Daisy for the night.

'Of course. There's a phone on the landing. Do you like lobster?'

'I love it, but don't tell me you're going back to catch one now.'

He laughed. 'Hardly! One of the advantages of Black Swan Bay is that it has The Hungry Pirate, the most wonderful seafood restaurant – and they deliver inside the village.'

It took Anna some time to thaw out. She dozed in the warm water, with her hair spread out around her. Outside she could hear Paul talking to Bobby, then Paul walking up the stairs, then the sound of a car drawing up outside. Realising that the lobster had arrived she shot out of the bath, wrapped a towel around her wet hair, and then discovered that she'd left her bag downstairs. There was a blue towelling dressing-gown on the hook behind the door. She slipped it on and hurried down, her bare feet light on the wooden steps.

In the grate the flames were licking up the chimney. There was no sign of Paul. She scampered across the room, but her bag wasn't where she'd left it. She searched, but she couldn't find it, so she sat down on a large cushion in front of the fire, unwound the towel from her head, and proceeded to dry her hair.

The front door opened and Bobby bounded in, followed by Paul. He smiled when he saw Anna in his dressing-gown, kneeling in the glow of the fire, her wet hair hanging around her like a tousled curtain.

She looked up at him. 'I couldn't find my clothes.'

'They're in the spare room.'

She made as though to stand, but he said, 'No, don't! You look beautiful as you are.'

She sank back on to the cushion. Paul went into the kitchen and returned, carrying a tray on which there was a bottle of white wine, two glasses, some crusty French bread, and a plate of hot asparagus dipped in melted butter, which he laid on the floor in front of them.

'I love to eat in front of the fire,' he said, pulling all the cushions off the sofa so as to make them a seat. 'Bobby too, so I've closed him in the kitchen.'

'Poor Bobby.'

He handed her a glass of wine. 'You wouldn't say that if he was here. He doesn't steal food, he just sits in front of you, dribbling and pleading.'

She chuckled and leaned back against the cushions, sipping her wine through a gap in her hair, very conscious of Paul next to her, his long legs stretched out, his handsome face glowing in the light of the flames. She knew that he was equally aware of her, and that fact, and the warmth, and his proximity, conquered her usual caution. She glanced at him under her eyelashes and found him watching her. She didn't blush and look away, but met his gaze, challenging him, craving him. He broke off a piece of bread, dipped it in the melted butter and held it out to her. She ate it, then broke a piece for him. He held her wrist and at his touch she felt as if she'd been electrified. They took it in turns to feed each other, not talking, not touching except when they licked the butter from each other's fingers.

The sensation of his skin on hers sent ripples of desire through Anna. Even if she'd been told that tonight was to be their only night, she would not have walked away. She craved Paul with an obsession which fired her whole body, which made her incapable of resisting him.

Paul refilled their glasses. 'Your hair is drying in knots,' he said. 'I'll comb them out with my fingers.'

Her scalp rippled to his touch. He stroked her hair, then her neck, cupped her face in his hands and brushed her mouth with his lips, gently, slowly. He held her closer and kissed her more urgently. She parted her lips beneath his, drawing him to her.

They fell back among the cushions. He covered her neck and her shoulders with light butterfly kisses which she could scarcely feel but which made her long for more. Her dressing-gown fell open, and he slid it from her as he moved down between her breasts. Her body glowed warm and golden in the firelight. For the first time in her life she did not feel awkward at being naked. Paul made her feel beautiful and desirable.

She knelt to undo the buttons of his shirt, kissing his chest as she unfastened them one by one. He seized her and rolled her over, kissing the soft backs of her knees. She responded, wanting him and wanting to do with him things which even with Charlie she had sometimes found embarrassing, but with Paul she had no inhibitions. In the glow of the fire they made love – at first slowly, rhythmically, kissing and looking deep into each other's eyes, then fiercely, urgently, their limbs entwined. She wrapped her legs around him, drawing him into her, crying out for him. He responded, taking her with him as the waves of acute pleasure rolled over her and out of her, until she was left weak and soft and sated.

Anna knew now why she'd been afraid of Paul. She could fall deeply in love with this man, and for that reason he was dangerous.

He turned his face to her, then saw her expression. 'Don't think like that!' he said determinedly.

'How do you know what I'm thinking?'

He kissed her. 'I just do.'

She snuggled up to him, and with her fingers in the light of the fire she made shadow rabbits hop up his bare chest. He whispered, 'Can I tell you something very personal?'

She nodded and, as always, feared the worst.

'I'm absolutely starving.'

She laughed with relief. 'So am I.'

They wolfed the lobster and finished the wine, ignoring Bobby who snuffled under the closed kitchen door.

'He can't understand why he's banned,' said Paul. 'It's never happened here before.'

He was telling her that she was the only woman he'd brought to the boathouse, and she felt pleased and very special.

They loved again, slowly, tenderly, and afterwards they drifted off to sleep. Anna woke to find the fire had died and Paul was awake and holding out the dressing-gown for her. 'Come up to bed,' he said.

She stumbled upstairs and fell into a deep sleep.

In the early morning Anna was woken by loud snores. She looked at Paul, but he was sleeping quietly on the pillow beside her, so she peeped over the edge of the bed. Bobby was stretched out on the rug, fast asleep, snoring. Anna blocked her ears.

When she woke again it was to feel Paul caressing her back. 'Do you think Heather would keep Daisy for another night?' he murmured.

'I'll ask her. Do you think Bobby could wear an anti-snoring device?'

He nuzzled her neck. 'I'll ask him.'

They stayed in bed till noon, talking and making love – and sometimes not talking at all, just lying side by side in contented silence. Eventually hunger drove them downstairs. Whilst Anna telephoned Heather, Paul cooked an enormous breakfast of bacon, eggs, mushrooms, tomatoes and thick brown granary bread covered with lashings of butter.

In the afternoon they went for a walk around the harbour to the ruined monastery. The wind and rain had died down and warm sunshine pushed its way between the fluffy clouds. The tide was out and the ducks and gulls foraged for food on the mudflats. Out in the channel a boat, not unlike Paul's, was making its way down towards the Solent.

She was still curious about his past. 'Where did you live when you were married?' she asked.

'In the Cotswolds.'

She was surprised. 'Miles from the sea.'

'Yes.' He tightened his hold on her. 'How I missed it.'

She leaned against him. 'Instead, you had all those dry stone walls.'

His arms stiffened and he didn't reply.

Anxiously, she turned to him. 'Paul, did I say something wrong?'

'Felicity was killed when her car hit a wall.' Sorrow flooded his grey eyes. 'She skidded across the road, she'd . . . had too much to drink.'

'Oh, I'm so sorry.'

He smoothed her hair back from her face. 'Anna, you weren't to know, I should have told you before, but . . . I find it impossible to talk about . . . her death. I feel so disloyal when I say she'd . . . been drinking, even if it's true.'

'But you mustn't blame yourself,' she said.

'Oh, yes I should.' Paul held Anna so tight that she could hardly breathe, but she didn't ask him to release her. Although she willed him to elaborate, she sensed that he'd talked of Felicity's death more perhaps than he would have wanted for one day. But the fact that he'd bared his anguish to her, as she had to him, brought them closer, so that on the following morning, when she returned to London and he had to leave for Spain, they clung together, missing each other even before they had parted.

35

PAUL HAD OFFERED to drive Anna back to London, but knowing how much work he had to do before he left for Spain, she assured him that she could easily take the train.

It was a glorious spring morning and, after collecting Daisy from Heather, Anna walked home, the fallen petals of cherry blossom sticking to the buggy's wheels. Recalling that other May morning, Anna leaned forward to stroke Daisy's blonde head. As she straightened up, she became aware of someone standing behind the storm-damaged yew tree by the entrance to the drive. She stopped and stared into the shadows.

Derek stepped into the sunlight. 'Hello, Caroline.'

She gasped with fright. 'What . . . what are you doing here?'

'You don't sound pleased to see me.' He sauntered towards her, a controlled smile touching his neat, delicate features.

'How did you know my address?' Anna demanded, agitated.

'Oh, I have a . . . good friend at *The Yachting Exchange*.'

'You mean they gave you my details after I'd paid for a box number?' She was furious. 'What do you want?'

'I thought we might have a little chat.'

'What about?'

'You were good, Caroline. Very good. I reckon you and I could make big money.'

'I don't know what you mean,' she said, uneasily.

He looked her up and down and laughed. 'Who'd guess that you were a fucking boat thief?'

She knew that she mustn't let him see she was afraid. 'The sloop belonged to my brother, as I've already told you.' She walked purposefully up the drive, lifted Daisy from the buggy, and marched up the steps and into the house.

To her surprise and relief Derek didn't follow, and when she peered out from behind the safety of the drawing-room curtains he'd disappeared. Nevertheless, she was unnerved. Her hands trembled as she undid the fastening of Daisy's jacket and when the telephone rang, she nearly screamed in fright. Convinced that it was Derek, she didn't answer; there weren't so many Tobiases in the London directory that he couldn't guess which was her number. So she hovered beside the answering machine as it ran through the familiar series of clicks. Then Paul spoke. 'I'm about to board my flight and I wanted to check that you got home safely.' He paused. 'No, that's not strictly true. I wanted to hear your voice.'

She clenched her fists together as he talked, longing to cut in and speak to him, but afraid to do so. This was her own private hell and it was not fair to involve Paul, because in this purgatory he was also her enemy.

The appearance of Derek so terrified Anna that she dared not leave the house in case he was waiting for her. She became convinced that justice had taken control of her fate, and in her mind she was already arrested, tried and facing a lengthy prison sentence. She wished she could confide in Louise, but that was impossible without revealing how she had met Derek. When Paul telephoned from Spain, she still didn't speak to him in case he heard the guilt in her voice. And yet, when she looked at Daisy, secure in her familiar world, she recalled the reasons which had driven her to steal *The Blonde Bimbo*.

Eventually, she was obliged to leave the house because she'd promised to help Lionel in his framing shop. Leaving Daisy with Mr Marilyn, she checked the drive before opening the front door. Then she ran.

Lionel had already cut the mounts. It was to be Anna's task to assemble them, slot them into the frames, and polish the glass. In between that, she answered the telephone and tried to instil a semblance of order to his accounts. He paid her thirty pounds for the day, and booked her for the following week, saying, 'You'll do well, you have a steady eye.'

She returned to Ladbroke Hill, approaching the house very cautiously, scanning the overgrown bushes which surrounded the drive, but there was no sign of Derek and she came to the conclusion that he'd merely been trying to intimidate her; thinking he'd failed, he wouldn't bother to come back.

Paul telephoned again that evening and this time she responded eagerly.

'Where have you been?' he asked. 'I've been worried about you.'

She settled into an armchair. 'I'm sorry. I . . . umm . . . turned off the telephone bell by mistake.'

'What – for three days?'

'I know, it was silly of me.' She hated to lie but she could think of no other reason for not having answered his call.

They talked of the following Saturday. She told him that Mac and Victoria had offered to look after Daisy for the night, and he told her that he'd switched flights so as to arrive at Gatwick. 'Ginger's leaving the Land-Rover there,' he said. 'Would you meet me? Then we can drive straight down to Black Swan Bay – to our boathouse.' His voice became softer, deeper. 'I can't wait to see you, to kiss you, to make love to you. When I couldn't get hold of you I kept imagining . . . that you were ill or had had an accident or that Daisy was ill.'

She realised now that she'd been selfish, but at the time silence had seemed her best solution. 'We're perfectly safe,' she said, relishing his concern and his words, and all the sensations which the prospect of being with him again brought forth in her.

She decided to tell Paul about Derek that weekend because she wanted everything between them to be open and honest. On the train to Gatwick she rehearsed her lines, telling herself that if he rejected her because of what she'd done, then she preferred to know now, before she cared too much. But when she saw him enter the arrivals hall, her heart turned over and she knew that already she loved him deeply. She raced across to him and he opened his arms to embrace her, and she experienced that wonderful feeling of safety.

They spent the afternoon in bed, making love, rising only to have dinner in The Hungry Pirate, where they sat in a quiet corner and shared a dish of mixed seafood. Anna kept thinking of what she planned to tell Paul, but the right moment didn't present itself.

In the morning they overslept and had to hurry breakfast. Driving up to London to collect Daisy, they listened to *La Traviata*, and Anna was loathe to break the magic of the music. On their return they had Daisy chattering in the back seat, and during the afternoon there was never an appropriate time, so she decided to wait until the evening. Whilst she settled an excited Daisy in the spare room, Paul cooked *spaghetti alle vongole*. They ate in front of the fire, lolling over the Sunday papers which they'd had no chance to read. As they finished supper, she took a deep breath.

But before she had a chance to speak Paul said, 'Oh, look! One of my favourite films is on the television tonight: *To Have and to Have Not* with Humphrey Bogart and Lauren Bacall. Have you seen it?'

She shook her head and wondered if she should tell him now, quickly.

'Then you must, you'll love it. It's one of those sizzling wartime intrigues. We can watch it in bed. Come on! It starts in ten minutes.'

She decided to tell him after the film.

Anna couldn't concentrate on the story because she kept running over her speech. She was still practising her first line when the film ended, and Lauren Bacall sashayed out of the piano bar and into Humphrey Bogart's life.

'Did you enjoy it?' asked Paul, nuzzling up to her.

'Yes . . . very much.' She took a deep breath and marshalled her thoughts.

'I knew you would.' He flicked off the television. 'The only angle I find a little far-fetched is when she takes the wallet.'

'Why?' Anna's voice was strained.

He drew her to him and kissed the tip of her nose. 'Because most people would find it hard to love someone whom they caught stealing.'

She stared out at the dark night beyond the window. She couldn't tell him now.

Anna fell in love with Paul – and with Black Swan Bay. She and Daisy remained at the boathouse for most of that week. The weather was glorious, with clear blue skies and warm sunshine. During the day, whilst Paul worked, Anna took Daisy to a nearby sandy cove, where she dozed on a rug, built sand castles, and pondered her love affair with Paul. It was both exciting and yet so comfortably familiar. It seemed incredible to Anna that she could go from barely knowing Paul to spending all her time with him and suffer none of the insecurities of her early days with Charlie.

Because of Daisy they couldn't go out in the evenings, so they ordered off The Hungry Pirate menu and ate sprawled before the fire, for in spite of the warm days the nights were chilly.

They talked of their childhoods and their families. She told him about Cliff Cottage and her father's failed inventions. She spoke of the *Little Auk* and her delight when her father took command – if only at sea.

She talked of the cheap little house in Leatherbridge where her bedroom walls were so damp that fungus grew along the top of the skirting board. She lay in his arms and relived the moment when the police had said, 'Mrs Tobias, we have some bad news for you.' She told him how much she'd resented her mother for manipulating their father – and her rage at him for being weak. She recalled the sudden uprooting to her grandmother's house and the change of school in her last year. She talked of Roz, who was so reassuringly bossy, and Lower Gossip Fen where she slept in the attic and could see the spire of Ely cathedral on a clear day. She told him of the Christmas when her father had tried to save the sheep from slaughter – but in all these recollections of childhood there never seemed to be the right moment to tell him of her own, more recent past.

In return, Paul talked of his boyhood, growing up in a small, steep village on the edge of the Forest of Dean. He'd identified with a father whom he seldom saw, a man who appeared every couple of months and took them on exciting outings to Cardiff or Gloucester or for long walks in the forest, where he taught Paul country tricks, such as how to call up a fox by making a noise like an injured rabbit.

'When Father was killed, my mother had just discovered she was pregnant, and the shock gave her a miscarriage,' he said. 'I didn't realise that at the time, but it's partly why I was sent to Whaler's Rock.'

'What about your sister?' asked Anna.

'Poor Harry had to stay at home. My godfather wouldn't allow a woman in the house – even a fourteen-year-old girl – after his wife died.'

'Did your mother never remarry?'

He shook his head. 'She met another man just before she had her final stroke, which was a shame, because she deserved happiness. My father was an optimist, he thought he'd live for years and he left little money and no provisions, so my mother had to go to work full time for a local sawmill.'

'And Harriet's husband? How does he manage now he can't walk?'

'They make the best of it – Harry's like that. They have a yacht especially adapted for Justin. Harry's a good sailor – though not as expert as you, although you must never tell her I said so.' He kissed Anna on the neck, and added, 'Unfortunately they had to leave the boat in Yugoslavia at the end of last summer because Rupert, their eldest son, broke a leg water-skiing, and now the conflict has escalated into war they can't get her out.'

'And their insurance won't cover them against acts of war,' Anna said knowledgeably.

He nodded. 'Sadly, if this boat is blown up, they could never afford another.'

Anna watched the fiery embers in the grate. Her skin glowed from the sun, the sea and from their lovemaking. It felt taut across her cheekbones and her lips were bruised from the fierceness of Paul's kisses. Every day that she was with him took her one small step nearer to believing that this happiness would not be snatched away. Even the little things helped – Paul asking Anna not tell his sister that he said she was a better sailor made her feel part of his life, not just now but in the future.

It was an effort to leave the beauty of Black Swan Bay and return to the muggy heat of London, but the Finesteins had invited them to dinner that evening and Paul had business in Lloyd's during the day.

He left Anna and Daisy at Ladbroke Hill on his way to the City. 'You look so smart,' she told him, leaning in through the car window to kiss him goodbye. 'Very Lloyd's and very un-Black Swan Bay – except for this.' She removed one of Bobby's hairs from the sleeve of his pin-striped suit.

'It's all just camouflage.' He touched her cheek. 'I should be here by six. Please don't turn the telephone off, it might be dangerous.'

She raised an eyebrow. 'Why?'

'Because I'm not sure I can survive all day without speaking to you.'

He drove away, and she danced up the steps and into the house.

Louise came downstairs, swathed in a black silk dressing-gown with a rampant gold dragon embroidered on each bosom. 'Won the pools?' she enquired on seeing Anna's radiant smile.

Anna laughed. 'No, I'm in love. Madly, passionately, desperately in love.' With Daisy in her arms, she waltzed around the sunfilled rooms.

There was a sharp ring on the doorbell and Anna stopped dead. 'Don't answer it!' she hissed.

Louise looked nonplussed. 'Why not?'

'A man has been . . . er . . . following me.'

'Don't worry, I'll get rid of him.' Louise marched to the front window, threw it open, and shouted, 'Piss off!' Then she pulled back sharply and said to Anna, 'He doesn't look like a molester. He's tall, blond and not unattractive.'

'Not Charlie?' Anna asked, horrified.

'Definitely not. Charlie was an arsehole. This guy looks like a trendy intellectual.' She leaned out of the window again. 'Hey! You! What's your name?'

'I am Nicolaas van Rooyen, and I am looking for Miss Tobias.'

Anna turned pink. 'He's the man from Rotterdam, the one I told you about.'

'The one in the taxi?' Louise giggled. 'Well, you can't leave him on the doorstep.'

Nicolaas was half-way down the drive by the time Anna opened the door. She apologised for keeping him waiting, and invited him inside, saying, 'Thank you again for driving me to Ostend.'

He laid a hand on her shoulder. 'It was my pleasure. How is your daughter?'

'Oh, fully recovered, thank you.' Anna stepped aside, wondering how she could apprise him of Paul's existence without sounding laborious.

'I was afraid I had come to the wrong house,' said Nicholaas. 'A very strange woman shouted at me to whizz off.'

Anna had to bite her lip to prevent herself from laughing as she ushered Nicolaas into the drawing-room, where Louise was sprawled on the sofa in her dragon dressing-gown. When he saw her, he stammered, 'I . . . didn't mean to be rude about your friend.'

n to pry.' He looked ashamed. 'But I can't help know it's selfish of me, only you're all the family I nd I couldn't bear to die among strangers.'

na reached across to squeeze his hand. 'You won't. I nise.'

He smiled and closed his eyes, but did not release Anna's hand, d when he did it was only because he had fallen asleep.

Paul's business was expanding and he decided to move his entire office down to Black Swan Bay, leaving just a telephone and a fax at his Chelsea studio. He transformed the old workshops into offices and hired more staff, including a good-humoured legal secretary named Virginia, and a cheerful accounts clerk called Jackie. Michael, the ex-policeman, had moved to Chichester. He did much of the local investigations, and also slept at the boathouse when Paul was away. Ginger spent his time overseas, but he used the office for checking data on future jobs and writing reports on completed assignments. All this activity meant that Paul and Anna had little privacy during the weekdays, and there were moments when she caught his warm look and knew that he – as much as she – wished that they were alone.

Nevertheless, Anna enjoyed the bustling office, which reminded her of her department at Marinecover, and she helped wherever she could. She researched information for Ginger when he telephoned from abroad, sent faxes for Virginia, stocked up on supplies from the supermarket, and made sandwiches for lunch when everyone was usy. She would have liked to do more, to use her expertise to work or Paul, but he did not suggest it and Sheldon Investigations was too uch his creation for her to intrude uninvited.

One morning, afer Paul had dropped Anna at Ladbroke Hill on way to Lloyd's, and she was tidying the house after an absence nearly a week, the telephone rang.

he answered, and her blood froze. 'Hello, Caroline,' said ek. 'Where have you been? Anyone would think you didn't t to speak to me.'

er hands were clammy on the receiver and her voice quavered ugh she tried to prevent it. 'You're right, I don't.'

t I'd like to do business. I told you, we could make good . No one would suspect a classy-looking bird like you.'

'Oh no, I was rude.' Louise gave him her big, friendly, freckly smile. 'But Anna has been pestered by a flasher and we thought you might be him.'

Anna blushed. 'Louise, you exaggerator! I never said he flashed.' She retired to the kitchen to make coffee whilst Louise launched into a graphic explanation of a flasher.

Nicolaas invited Anna and Daisy and Louise out to lunch, at the Italian restaurant where Anna and Charlie had once celebrated the jobs they thought – mistakenly – they were to be offered. Afterwards, they took Daisy for a walk in Kensington Gardens. On their return to Ladbroke Hill, Nicolaas showed no sign of leaving, but settled happily into an armchair with a copy of *Time Out*, marking the plays he seemed to assume that Anna would see with him whilst he was in London.

Eventually Anna beckoned Louise to the kitchen and whispered, 'Paul's arriving soon.'

'What are you going to do about . . . ?' Louise nodded her head towards Nicolaas.

'Would you want to go to the theatre with him, if he needs company?'

'So long as it's not to see some naff musical.' Louise rolled her eyes in horror.

To Anna's surprise Paul didn't mention Nicolaas. All the way up to Highgate, she kept expecting him to ask who the Dutchman was, but instead he entertained her with the latest Lloyd's gossip. At the Finesteins' they were engulfed by good-natured teasing, as Sybil joked that she'd be sending Paul her bill for the introduction, and he argued that since he'd already known Anna he'd expect a hefty discount.

'I always knew you two were suited,' Sybil beamed at Anna when she took her upstairs after dinner. 'Paul seems happier than he has been for years and it's all due to you, dear.'

Anna turned pink with pleasure. 'Thank you.' She adjusted her dress in the long mirror in Sybil's bedroom. 'How long have you known Paul?'

'Oh, twelve years at least.' Sybil lowered her voice. 'It was a shame about Felicity. She was charming and such a pretty girl, quite exquisite, but when she drank . . . well . . . she was embarrassing. Not that she consumed much in public – it was what she had beforehand, at home, in secret. I felt so sorry for Paul; he did try to help her.' Sybil patted Anna's hand. 'We'd better go down, dear, or the men will know we're gossiping.'

As Anna followed her hostess down the stairs, she recalled her first, drunken night with Paul. No wonder he'd been cool on the telephone.

It was late when they left for home, and no sooner were they underway than Paul asked, 'How do you know Nicolaas?'

'He's Mr van Rooyen's nephew.'

'So he's a friend of yours, not of Louise?'

'Yes, Detective Inspector Sheldon, but he didn't know about you . . . about us . . . when he turned up today, because when I met him you and I were not . . . a "we".' She leaned across and kissed the side of his face. 'Satisfied?'

He smiled at her. 'It's my job to suspect.'

She thought of Derek, and was heartily relieved that Paul had not caught sight of him.

36

ANNA DRIFTED THROUGH that summer, playing with and making love with Paul. She didn't tell him about *Blonde Bimbo* although she kept intending to, and for most of the time she managed to put it behind her – until something happened to bring it all back, like the day she overheard Paul telling Ginger that an expensive yacht had been stolen from Sailham. Then she crept away, shaking with terror, haunted by her crime and the fear of homelessness which had driven her to commit it.

Now that her excess mortgage charge had been paid off, the rents nearly covered her monthly payments. By working for Lio and Louise, she earned sufficient to make up the shortfall, pay bills, and feed herself and Daisy. For once she was not fr about her precarious existence, and she realised that much inner calmness came from being with Paul.

Often in these limbo days she wondered how she'd cope working for Eurohull, when her life had been a constant match with never a moment to herself. At the same time that she appreciated this lazy summer because of the t had gone before, and that eventually she would Mostly, when she wasn't working, she stayed with boathouse, but there were also days when she cou there but didn't, because she still feared to depend him in case things suddenly went wrong and he sometimes she stayed at Ladbroke Hill, in her own much she would have preferred to be with Paul

One warm afternoon, when she was having with Mr Marilyn, he asked nervously, 'What house if you marry Paul?'

She turned slightly pink. 'Oh, really, Mr M . . . got to know him.'

'I don't know what you're talking about,' she said, stiffly.

He gave an unpleasant laugh. 'I take me hat off to you, Caroline, you've got guts. But who the hell do you think you're kidding? I know you stole that boat, because you took her from a friend of ours – and he'd stolen her from someone else.' He laughed again. 'That's the problem, you see. When we sold her, we had to give him half the money, so we're now out of pocket. You owe us, Caroline.'

She was furious with him for bullying her and with herself for allowing him to do so. 'Now you listen to me.' She spoke with icy clarity. 'You are not to telephone me again. Ever!'

'Or what? You'll call the police?'

'Yes I will.'

'And what do you think they'll say when they hear about *The Blonde Bimbo*?'

'Nothing. They'll be too delighted to capture you.' She put the phone down.

She was no longer cowed, she was furious, but most of her anger stemmed from fear. Now, she had to tell Paul.

He returned in the middle of the afternoon, earlier than she expected, and because she was so agitated about Derek she irrationally assumed that he had discovered about *The Blonde Bimbo* and she rushed to him, crying, 'I know why you're back, I was going to tell you.'

He looked nonplussed. 'How did you hear about Yugoslavia?'

She stared at him. 'Yugoslavia?'

'Yes.' He took her by the shoulders. 'I came back to tell you that I'm going to Dubrovnik tomorrow morning.'

Her relief that he didn't know about her crime was surpassed by her fears for his safety. 'Paul, it's dangerous. They've just announced that all tourists are being evacuated.'

'I'm not a tourist, Anna.' He cupped her face in his hands. 'I'm going to get Harriet and Justin's boat out.'

She had a frightening premonition that he would be killed. She felt as though she were standing on the edge of an abyss and that until now her feet had been, if not firmly on the ground, then at least partially. Even in her most passionate moments with Paul, she had kept her reason. The past had prevented her from completely letting go; fears dictated that she retain a little of herself, enough pieces to stick together if things went wrong. Now the abyss opened up beneath her feet, and her defences melted away.

'Don't go, Paul!' She dug her fingers into his arm. 'It's not worth dying for a boat.'

'I have to try; the yacht is Justin's greatest pleasure.' He attempted to soothe Anna's anxiety by adding, 'I'll be quite safe. I know the place well, she's moored in a resort called Cavtat, an old fishing town twelve miles south of Dubrovnik.'

'But they said on the news that the Serbs are in the hills behind Dubrovnik.'

'They haven't started shooting yet, at least not there, the unrest is mainly further north, near Slovenia, so now is the time for me to go.' He stroked her cheek. 'Don't worry. There's a high, wooded peninsula on the Dubrovnik side of Cavtat, with an ancient mausoleum, all hidden by gnarled pine trees. From there I'll be able to see what's happening in the harbour and if it doesn't look safe, I can wait till nightfall. The boat is moored on that side of town, along the quay, in front of what used to be the smartest restaurant – although I doubt it has many customers now.'

'Supposing the boat isn't seaworthy,' she said, trying to think of more reasons why he shouldn't face such danger.

'Then I'll come back – somehow. The airport's still open. I'm flying in tomorrow, and that's only three miles from Cavtat. If I can't find a taxi or the main road is blocked, I can walk. You see, I have it all worked out.'

Anna dreaded being separated from Paul, left to fight Derek alone. 'Take me with you,' she pleaded.

'Not to a country on the brink of civil war.'

'I'm not scared – and I'm a good sailor.'

He drew her closer. 'I'd be frightened for you, and that would cloud my judgement.'

Outside, in the garden, they could hear Daisy babbling to Mr Marilyn. 'I suppose you're right,' she said, resignedly. 'I have to consider Daisy, I'm all she has.'

They stood looking into each other's eyes. Anna felt a rush of desire for him. It ran through her body, her veins, to the tips of her fingers. Paul pushed her backwards against the wall, kissing her hungrily. He slipped the straps of her sun-dress from her shoulders and kissed her neck beneath her hair. He lifted up her skirt and ran his hand up the inside of her thigh. She unfastened the buckle of his belt, and caressed him. He seized her with his strong hands, his fingers digging into her, hurting her, but she wanted him to. He lifted her on to him, and she gasped with pleasure, sinking her teeth into his shoulder to muffle her cries as he took her urgently against the wall of her bedroom.

Afterwards they clung together, shaking with the ferocity of their passion. They had needed the danger of his forthcoming mission to confront their feelings, and now they could not bear to separate. The intensity of their coupling had not been the easy lovemaking at the boathouse, with all its ample opportunities, but an admission by each of them of how much they needed each other.

He kissed her cheek and smiled into her eyes, and she responded, rubbing her face against his shoulder. Then he straightened her dress, whilst she rebuckled his belt – just in time, before Mr Marilyn came up the steps with Daisy.

That night, as they lay close in bed, Paul said, 'When I arrived you seemed upset. What had happened?'

'I . . . It doesn't matter.' She couldn't send him away on a dangerous mission worried for her safety.

'No, tell me! What was it?' He took her in his arms and kissed the corner of her eyebrow.

'It was nothing . . . really.'

'Anna, please tell me?'

She was not to know that her reticence brought back painful memories of the times when Felicity had refused to admit she needed help; she merely thought he was being Paul, the investigator, who would not give up until satisfied, and she said, 'I feel guilty because it's months since I've visited my mother and grandmother.'

'Is that all?'

She nodded. 'Of course.'

He smiled with relief. 'I'll leave you my car so you can drive up. That'll make it easier for you to travel with Daisy.'

She thanked him and pretended to fall asleep, but her thoughts kept returning to Derek. She could no longer delude herself that he would leave her alone.

*

Anna missed Paul, not with the misty tenderness of before but with a raw hurt, as though he had been extracted from her without an anaesthetic. She listened avidly to the latest reports from Yugoslavia, as if they enabled her to touch him. Her concern for Paul drove Derek to the back of her mind. If she barely left the house, it was not only because she was afraid of meeting Derek, but because she wanted to be home if Paul managed to telephone. When she spent a night at Lower Gossip Fen she could hardly control her impatience because Melissa was on the phone for most of the evening, and when she visited her mother and grandmother she was on tenterhooks because their telephone was out of order.

Louise had gone to the West Country to attend the house contents sale of an old lady who had once been the mistress of a wealthy French industrialist. She returned laden with satin peignoirs and silk camisoles, to find Anna hunched over the television news, and she had barely begun to recount that Nicolaas had invited her to visit him in Holland but she'd decided not to go, when the phone rang.

Anna grabbed it. There was a crackle on the line, then Paul said, 'Is that you or your damned answering machine?'

At the sound of his voice, Anna felt quite giddy. 'It's me!' She laughed with excitement. 'How are you? Where are you?'

'I'm in Cavtat. How are you? How's Daisy?'

'We're fine. Are you all right? Are you safe?'

'Yes, but the place is very tense. I'm staying at the Croatia hotel. Last time I was here it was full, now I'm almost the only guest.'

'So I could have come with you,' she teased.

He laughed. 'I couldn't hear that.'

She chuckled, 'Oh, yes, you could! Tell me, how is the boat? Is she seaworthy?'

'One of the engine mountings was cracked and it's had to be soldered because there are no parts available, but I hope to leave tomorrow.' There was a strange echo and his voice grew faint. 'I miss you,' he shouted, and the line went dead.

Anna put down the receiver and turned to Louise. 'He's all right. He's alive.' She put her hands up to her face and cried from sheer relief.

*

Now that Anna had heard from Paul she was less anxious, although she continued to follow the news from Yugoslavia.

On Saturday, as the market closed, she met Dominic whilst she was buying roses for Mr Marilyn, who'd been looking after Daisy.

'Still with the same boyfriend?' he asked.

She smiled proudly. 'Very definitely.'

'Lucky man!' Dominic picked up her shopping and helped her carry it home, but for once he refused her offer of a drink.

She went down to the basement to collect Daisy and found Mr Marilyn beaming with pleasure. 'Mac and Victoria have invited me to their wedding.' He pointed to a large white invitation which had pride of place on his mantelpiece.

'Will you go?' asked Anna, bending to give Daisy a hug.

He shook his head. 'I couldn't afford it. And to tell you the truth, I wouldn't want to fly all that way, to a strange place, to be with people I don't know. I'm just thrilled to have been asked.'

'I can't afford to go either,' Anna said regretfully.

Upstairs, she found the house quiet. Everyone seemed to be out. On the hall table were two neat piles of mail, one for herself, the other for Louise, and on top of each there was a large white envelope addressed in Mac's sloping handwriting. Anna's pile also contained an invitation for Paul, and she felt a warm glow of pleasure that he had been included with her, even if she couldn't go.

She opened the rest of her post: her monthly statement from East Metro, a card from Roz to say that Luke had passed another music exam, a magazine article about potty-training from her mother, and a plain typed buff envelope. At first she thought it was empty, then she tipped it upside-down and a snapshot fell into her hand. It was a picture of Daisy in the garden, playing with Errol Flynn, and across the top was scratched, 'You owe us.'

Anna bit into her hand to stifle her terror. The message was unmistakable. She rushed into the kitchen where Daisy was sitting on the floor, pretending to give her dolls their supper, and dragged her away from the back door. Then she drew all the curtains, hiding behind them as she scanned the drive and the garden.

Keeping Daisy by her side, she searched frantically through the pockets of her sailing bag, trying to remember where she had left Derek's telephone number. Finally she found it, in an inner zip pocket.

Her hands shook as she tapped out the number, but they shook not only with fear but with rage.

He answered promptly.

'Derek?' she said.

'Hello, Caroline, I thought I'd hear from you. Glad you've come to your senses.'

'Derek, if you touch my child I'll kill you. Do you understand? I don't care if I go to prison, but I'll come after you and kill you.' She cut him off before he could reply.

Within seconds her phone rang. She grabbed it, screaming, 'Yes!'

'Anna, it's Paul. What's wrong? Why are you shouting?'

Her knees buckled and she sank to the floor. 'I don't know what to do, I'm so scared, I . . .'

'What do you mean? Darling, tell me, please. Is it Daisy?'

She didn't answer – she couldn't speak, she was shaking with fear.

He went on, gently. 'Anna, listen. I'm in Italy, I've got the boat out. I'll book you on a flight to Naples tomorrow and we can sail her back together. We'll have a wonderful time, on our own, just the two of us, and we can talk about whatever is upsetting you. I know something's wrong.'

'I can't leave Daisy!' she cried in anguish.

'I'll pay for Heather to have her.'

'No! Not now!'

'Anna, have Charlie's parents come back? Is that the reason you're distressed? Or is it Charlie? Has he reappeared? Darling, I can't help if you won't trust me.'

'I can't leave Daisy alone any more.' Anna's voice was trembling. 'I'm going to my sister.'

Since she seemed so reluctant to talk, Paul said a subdued goodbye. He wanted to help her, but it was impossible when she wouldn't confide in him. Again, her reticence reminded him of Felicity, although he kept assuring himself that they were completely different. Anna was gutsy and upfront, with endearing pockets of shyness. Felicity had been the life of every party, but terrified of being alone, which he hadn't realised until too late. He was sure Anna didn't drink – he had a second sense for that now – but she was distressed about something, and her secretiveness affected him deeply. It resurrected the nightmare in his past.

37

ANNA LEFT FOR Lower Gossip Fen within the hour. She didn't go because she was afraid for herself, but she was terrified for Daisy's safety. She felt bad about letting Lionel and Louise down, especially now the market was busier, but she couldn't help it.

Roz didn't question her sudden arrival; she assumed that Paul had proved to be yet another of Anna's unreliable men, and when Anna refused to leave the farm, even to shop in Ely, she presumed she was hoping that he'd telephone.

The calm of Lower Gossip Fen steadied Anna's nerves. When she looked out over the misty fenland, at the sheep grazing peacefully along the banks of the deep drainage ditches, and heard the soothing hum of a distant combine harvester, she could not believe that she had allowed herself to become involved in the seedy violence of Derek's world.

At Lower Gossip everything was simplified. She should have raised the money another way – there must have been an alternative, although she could not think what – but if she had committed a crime then she should have gone straight to the police, right at the start, when Derek reappeared, and accepted her punishment, for nothing could be as bad as this quagmire of fear and threat.

She considered walking into Lower Gossip and confessing her story to the elderly constable, but decided that would not be fair to Tom and Roz. This was a small community and they would be besmirched through no fault of their own. No, she had to tell Paul. He'd know what she should do.

She thought of him constantly, sailing up the coast of Italy, and wished that she'd been able to join him. She imagined his arms protecting her, his body close, his voice, his smile, his tender joking, his kisses.

He didn't telephone for several days, by which time Anna feared that she had driven him away, then he called her from Genoa as they were sitting down to supper.

'At last I've found you,' he said. 'Roz's number is at the studio and I don't know her surname, but luckily I remembered Mr Marilyn's, so I tracked him down through international directories.'

She felt weak with relief at hearing from him. 'I'm . . . sorry about the other day. I'll explain everything when you come back.'

'Can't you tell me now?' he asked, unable to forget how her distress had worried him.

'Not on the phone. It can wait.' Now that she was at Lower Gossip, she felt able to hold out until she saw him.

'Then you may have to tell me in New York.'

'I can do what?' she said with a laugh.

'Mr Marilyn told me we've been invited to Mac and Victoria's wedding. Don't you wish to go?'

She didn't want say that she couldn't afford it. 'Yes, but I'm . . . er . . . not sure if I can.'

He guessed that she alluded to the expense and he loved her for her pride, smiling ironically as he recalled how Felicity had always expected him to pay for her, even when he'd been a twenty-one-year-old impoverished student and she'd been living on a private income.

'Anna, I'm inviting you to the wedding and then on to Whaler's Rock. I want you to meet Steven and Georgina, and they're giving a ball to celebrate their twentieth wedding anniversary the following weekend – and before you tell me that you can't leave Daisy, Steven has already lined up his old nanny to look after her.'

'I'd love to go.' Anna laughed from sheer joy. 'I can't wait!'

'I wish I was with you now.' His voice grew tender. 'I want to see your smile, to hold you in my arms, to make love to you. The other day when you were so . . . agitated, I thought that Charlie had come back.'

'Paul, I keep telling you, he's in the past.'

'But the past can haunt you, even though you try to forget it.'

She knew that he referred to Felicity, and was on the point of saying something comforting when she became aware of Roz shouting 'Your supper is cold', and she said, 'My sister is getting impatient. I'd better go.'

They took several minutes to say goodbye, neither wanting to be the first to ring off, and even after Anna had replaced the receiver, she stood for a moment in the darkened hall, hugging herself with excitement. Being invited to Whaler's Rock was the greatest accolade. It was the magic place of Paul's childhood, as Belworth had been for her.

Roz and Tom were already on to their cheese course when Anna came dancing into the dining-room. 'I'm going to a ball.' She clapped her hands. 'In Newport.'

'In the Isle of Wight?' asked Tom.

'Rhode Island!' Anna dropped on to her chair. 'And a wedding in New York.'

Tom lowered his knife. 'This chap can't be so bad, Roz. I thought you said he was another wastrel.'

'I never said anything of the sort.' Roz gave Anna a flustered look. 'I was just . . . concerned for Anna. When she invites herself to stay, out of the blue, for the second time – not that I mind, Anna, I'm delighted to see you – but of course I think you must be in trouble. But I was wrong.'

Anna cut into a cold roast potato. 'Would you help me make a dress for the ball, Roz? Something gloriously romantic.'

'Of course.' Roz began to stack the plates. 'Hurry up and finish supper so we can spread the dress patterns on the table. Tomorrow we'll go to Cambridge to buy some fabric. I know just the shop.'

With Roz's expert help Anna made a beautiful midnight-blue ballgown and a simple but elegant dress in taupe crêpe-de-Chine for the wedding. In a second-hand shop in Ely they found a large, black cartwheel hat which, according to the assistant, had only been worn once, to Ascot. They trimmed it with taupe silk.

They were so busy during the daytime that Anna managed to control her terror of Derek, placing him at the back of her thoughts. She felt increasingly safe in the fenland. The farmhouse was isolated, but the land around it was so flat that no one could approach unseen. Even a bicycle passing along the lane brought Augustus racing out of the house, barking fiendishly. Only at night, listening to the creaks in the old house and the scuffle of little animals outside, did Anna feel uneasy and she would creep into Daisy's room and look at her little face on the pillow, sleeping peacefully and unaware.

To keep Daisy occupied, and out of the sewing-room, Melissa was allocated to play with her. She'd finally been allowed to leave boarding school and was waiting to go to college. She spent her time lying on her bed listening to music or clumping miserably around the house in heavy boots, baggy black trousers and a shapeless cardigan. With Roz she argued, with Anna she was shy, but with Daisy she was sweet and patient.

Whilst they sewed, Anna told Roz all about Paul. 'He makes me laugh,' she said. 'None of the men I've been with have done that.'

Roz gave her a mature, maternal smile. 'It's time you settled down. Oh, don't pull that face – I mean it nicely – you need someone to look after you . . . and Daisy. When you get back from the States you must bring Paul up to meet us.'

'I'm sure you'll like him.' Anna smiled fondly. Then a look of apprehension came into her face. 'I just hope that Steven and Georgina approve of me. He and Paul are such close friends and Felicity was Georgina's schoolfriend. They're bound to see me as an intruder, even if Paul's marriage had gone . . . sour.'

'Of course they'll like you,' Roz said reassuringly. 'And the dress is perfect.' She touched a remnant of blue silk, adding wistfully, 'I wish Melissa would let me make pretty clothes for her, instead of those shapeless widow's weeds.' She hesitated, then added, 'Would you do me a favour when you come back?'

Anna looked up from her sewing with a smile. 'Anything.'

'Have Melissa to stay before she starts college. She can help you with Daisy.' Roz went on quickly when Anna hesitated. 'She's good with children, you've seen that, and she thinks you're marvellous. I get so frustrated with her, I'm always shouting, and that makes her sulkier.'

Reminding herself of the many times when she'd used Roz as a bolt-hole, Anna said, 'Of course I'll have her. How about the week after I get back?'

Roz smiled. 'Thanks. She'll be so pleased.'

Paul could not come back to England before the wedding, he moored Justin's boat in Barcelona and flew straight to the States to complete an assignment. Anna didn't risk returning to Ladbroke Hill until the afternoon before her flight to New York. On the hall table she found her mail neatly stacked. The sight of it made her stomach lurch with fear, but there was nothing from Derek, no badly-typed buff envelope. Nor was there any message from him amongst those on her answering machine. Nevertheless, she was uneasy and she searched the rooms before she allowed Daisy out of her arms.

It was with great relief, early next morning, that she stepped into the minicab which Paul had thoughtfully ordered for her. She would never have believed that she'd be glad to leave Ladbroke Hill – but she couldn't wait to escape.

38

New York

PAUL WAS WAITING for Anna as she came through the immigration hall carrying an exhausted Daisy. He took her in his arms, hugging her fiercely, saying, 'I've missed you so much, you can't imagine.'

'I've missed you too.' She buried her face in his shoulder, relishing his special smell, and all the terrors of the past weeks receded as though they had happened to someone else – someone close, but not actually herself.

Paul kissed Daisy's sleepy face. 'Hello, poppet. I think we'd better get you to bed.' He took the luggage trolley from Anna and ushered them out of the air-conditioned terminal into the hustling heat of Kennedy airport.

'Mac's recommended a beautiful hotel on Long Island,' he told Anna once they were settled into the back of a taxi. 'It's within walking distance of the wedding. You'll love it.'

'Does our room overlook the sea?' she asked, thinking how dashing and debonair he looked in his open-neck cream shirt and casual beige trousers.

'Not just a room, but a suite!'

'It sounds perfect.' She gave him a suggestive little nudge, and his eyes grew warm and fond.

They took just over an hour to reach the small town on the north shore where Mac's grandmother lived and Victoria's aunt had once owned a house. In the Thirties this had been a fast-living, fashionable resort, but now it was serenely conservative. Built around a gentle bay, it was an attractive place, with wide, clean, tree-lined streets and well-maintained, white weatherboard houses, each with a veranda, spacious manicured lawns, and a surrounding picket fence.

Their hotel was formerly a large private house and the oldest building in the town. It nestled between a golf course and the glittering blue Long Island Sound. They went up to the suite, where Paul had slept the previous night, and stepped out on to the balcony, which ran the whole length of their sitting-room. Below them the bay curved like a crescent of white sand, lapped by the waves. There were few people on the beach, just a couple of families, and a dog racing up and down in the surf. A week earlier, on Labor Day, it would have been packed with holiday-makers, but most had now gone home, back to the cities, to jobs or school.

'Happy?' Paul kissed the back of Anna's neck.

'Very.' She leaned against him and, tired though she was from the journey, she tingled to his touch.

He held her close. 'Anna, what . . . were you so worried about?'

She almost told him, then stopped. Derek was two thousand miles away and there was no need to mar her reunion with Paul. 'Oh, it's not important, not now I'm here.'

Because she seemed so relaxed and happy, Paul decided not to persist.

After settling Daisy into the smaller bedroom Anna took a shower and slipped on a cool summer dress. When she came out of the bedroom she found Paul still on the balcony and he beckoned her to him.

Walking along the edge of the sea, with his shoes in one hand and his Panama firmly on his head, was a man who looked very similar to Mr Marilyn.

'Dear old Mr Marilyn,' said Anna, slipping her arms around Paul. 'He didn't want to come to the wedding, but he was so pleased to be invited.'

'I know.' Paul caressed her neck. 'He told me so, that day when I had to get Roz's number from him.' He paused. 'Why were you so distressed, Anna? What had happened?'

She pressed against him, wanting him. 'It doesn't matter, not tonight.'

He kissed her gently, his mouth barely touching hers, then, suddenly, he picked her up and carried her through to the bedroom.

In the morning Anna woke to sparkling sunshine and Paul's dark head on the pillow next to her. She lay very still, watching the light patterns dance on the ceiling of the unfamiliar room and listening to American voices calling to each other on the beach below.

With an ocean between herself and Derek, she couldn't bring herself to jeopardise the holiday by telling Paul about him yet. She'd tell him nearer the end, when they'd had a wonderful fortnight together, and she was as sure as she could ever be that he would not reject her. She'd pick the perfect moment, when they were alone, when she had time to make him understand her reasons. But even as she assured herself that she was right to wait, she knew the truth was that she was so in love with Paul she feared anything going wrong – in case everything crashed down in pieces, as it had when her father had lost his job and they'd been forced to sell Cliff Cottage.

Mac and Victoria married in the garden of his grandmother's house. They said their vows under an arch of roses, with the sea as their backdrop and the rolling green lawns as their surround. Some three hundred of their relatives and friends watched from the shade of a candy-striped canopy, whilst nearby a string quartet played selections by Mozart.

After the ceremony the guests mingled. Mac and Victoria had invited many relatives as well as their friends from college days, colleagues from Mac's bank, and family friends from the close-knit old-moneyed families which had inhabited the north shore for several generations. Paul and Anna knew few other guests but they did not mind. They were happy just to be together.

A kindly aunt of Victoria's offered to look after Daisy for a few hours. Initially, Anna was reluctant, her fear of Derek was so great, but Paul was eager for her to accept, and she could think of no reason to refuse without telling him the whole, sordid story – and now, in the middle of the wedding, was not the moment.

In the early evening, as the sun was setting, they strolled hand in hand through the garden, drinking in the scent of jasmine which grew over a wooden arbour.

'You look beautiful in that hat,' Paul told Anna. 'I love women in hats, they always seem so . . . mysterious.'

She smiled at him from underneath the brim, and knew that she'd been right to keep her secret and not ruin today.

*

Mac and Victoria departed for their honeymoon in the Galapagos Islands, but Anna and Paul remained on Long Island until the beginning of the week, when they headed north for Whaler's Rock. As they skirted New York, they saw signs to Brooklyn and Anna told Paul about Elaine, adding. 'I wish I'd brought her telephone number. She worked for me for less than a year, but she was such a support and it's strange how similar our lives turned out.'

After crossing the East River, they proceeded up through the Bronx and the choking urban sprawl of soulless high-rises and grafitti-covered playgrounds, fast-food joints and advertising hoardings, thankful when they finally reached the undulating wooded hills of Connecticut.

They stopped for lunch in New Haven, at a pizzeria popular with students from Yale, where Paul told her that he had often eaten when Steven was at the university.

'A walk down memory lane!' Anna teased him, though she was flattered to be included in his past.

It was hot, and even in the short walk between the restaurant and the car park Anna felt her arms and legs burning. She was wearing her pale pink sun-dress, and it had looked fresh and pretty when she'd left Long Island. Now it was crumpled from the journey.

'I hope I'm smart enough,' she said, nervously picturing herself judged by a wealthy, designer-clad Georgina.

'Of course you are.' Paul touched her cheek. 'They're very casual – in the daytime.'

Anna tried to look confident but she wished she'd brought more evening clothes.

Paul read her mind. 'Stop worrying! You'll be fine. Georgina buys her clothes with her eyes shut. It's part of her charm.'

Anna laughed, but she was still apprehensive. She couldn't forget that Felicity and Georgina had been friends since girlhood, or that Sybil had called Felicity exquisitely pretty.

It was late afternoon when they crossed the great steel suspension bridge over Narragansett Bay, from Jamestown to Newport, and Anna saw the harbour, full of expensive yachts, and the old town of brightly-painted weatherboard houses clustered behind it. Although the holiday season was officially over, the narrow streets still overflowed with sun-tanned shoppers in designer T-shirts, wandering in and out of fashionable boutiques or drinking coffee outside one of the many restaurants.

'Most of the mansions, like Cornelius Vanderbilt's The Breakers, are away from the quay, along Cliff Walk,' Paul told Anna as they left the harbour and headed up through wide streets of large colonial-style houses. 'They're mainly tourist attractions now. Whaler's Rock is one of the few still inhabited and by the same family.'

They were now in deep countryside and twisting along small wooded lanes, down a peaceful valley, and then up the other side, the car labouring until it reached the top – and there, in front of them, at the end of the headland, was Whaler's Rock, a magnificent, white marble palace with four Corinthian pillars holding up its portico and a circular, balustraded drive leading to an enormous studded front door.

Anna was speechless. She had expected it to be grand, but this was spectacular.

'Now you know how I felt on my first visit,' said Paul, smiling at her look of wonder.

'And you were only nine!'

The front door opened and a portly, smiling man stepped out. He was prematurely bald and wore heavy-rimmed spectacles behind which his eyes twinkled merrily. 'Paul!' he cried. 'At last you're here. I've been so looking forward to your arrival.' He clapped Paul on the back and grinned at Anna. 'So this is the lady who sails better than I do? Yes, I've been told you do.' He held out his hand. 'Steven Winslow. Welcome to Whaler's Rock. I hope this will be the first of many visits, though if it's true that you're a better sailor than me, I don't know how my ego will stand it.' He joked in much the same way Paul did.

Anna laughed. 'Don't worry, I won't show you up,' she said, instantly warming to Steven.

'Hi there.' A tall, angular woman, with shoulder-length brown hair and a loose cotton dress, came striding across the lawn. She had a pair of secateurs in her hand, a willow basket of cut roses in the other, and three huge Irish wolfhounds at her heels. She kissed Paul on the cheek, then turned her very direct gaze on Anna.

'I'm Georgina.' She held out a bony, grass-stained hand to Anna. 'We're glad to meet you at last.'

'Thank you.' Anna smiled nervously.

Georgina peered into the car. 'My God!' She stared at Daisy. 'She's a baby.'

Daisy's face puckered and Anna reached inside to comfort her. 'She isn't a baby, she's nearly two,' she said, springing to Daisy's defence.

Georgina patted Anna on the back, as though she were one of the wolfhounds. 'I didn't mean to offend her. I like children – though I do prefer dogs – but Paul, you should have warned me that the child was so young, then we'd have brought the cot down from the attic.'

'Georgey, I told you,' said Steven.

'Yes, but I thought you were exaggerating.' Georgina smiled at Anna. 'Men always exaggerate, don't they?'

'We do not,' protested her husband, laughing at what was clearly an ongoing but good-natured skirmish.

'Come on, Anna, let's leave the men,' said Georgina. 'I'll show you to your room.'

By the time Anna had unstrapped Daisy and lifted her out of the back seat, Georgina was already half-way up the magnificent gilded staircase and Anna had to hurry to catch up with her.

'I've put you and Paul in the west wing,' Georgina said as they started down the long, wide, mirrored corridor which ran the entire length of the house. 'I'll have the cot brought down before tonight.'

'Oh, please don't go to too much trouble.' Anna had to skip to keep up with Georgina's long strides.

'We can't have her falling out of bed. I'd really no idea she'd be so young. I'm sure Steven told me but I'm very forgetful. The charm of Whaler's Rock is that the days drift into each other, the down-side is that I can't recall if it's Monday or Friday.'

Anna smiled. 'I'm like that too – and I'm worse since having Daisy.'

'What happened to your husband?' Georgina asked with a directness Anna found unnerving.

'I . . . er . . . wasn't married.'

'Where's Daisy's father?'

'We have no contact.' Anna tried not to sound too irritated by her hostess's curiosity.

'That must be tough.' Georgina placated Anna with a smile of genuine sympathy, and led the way into a sun-filled blue and gold bedroom dominated by an enormous four-poster bed which was draped with blue and gold tassels. The same colour scheme was carried through into their private sitting-room and the dressing-room, where a single bed had been prepared for Daisy.

'Is that the cove where Paul and Steven learned to sail?' asked Anna, looking out from one of the floor-to-ceiling windows, all of which had stupendous views across the lawns to the sea.

'Yes, that's the path which leads to the jetty. They've been friends ever since that first year.' Georgina smiled again, and her hawkish features softened. 'We're so glad to meet you, Anna, and to see Paul happy again.'

Anna blushed with pleasure, and forgave Georgina her nosiness. 'Thank you. I'm delighted to be here. Paul's always talking about Whaler's Rock.'

They were interrupted by an elderly retainer slowly pushing Anna's luggage on a trolley. He was introduced as Bowson, Nanny's older brother. 'My sister's gonna just love that little girl,' he said, giving Daisy a broad grin.

'I'll leave you to settle in,' Georgina told Anna. 'I'm going to shoot into town and buy a rubber sheet for the cot. My two are long grown up, thank God, so we don't have anything like that.'

'Don't worry! I have everything.' Anna pointed at her luggage, which looked horribly scruffy against the glorious pale pink and blue Aubusson carpet.

'How well organised.' Georgina rewarded her with another pat. 'But you must get Daisy out of diapers. Dogs and kids are impossible until they're potty-trained.' There was a shout from the garden. Georgina leaned out of the window and called, 'I'll be right there.' Then she turned to Anna. 'Tea is in the yellow drawing-room, first left at the bottom of the stairs. Come down when you're ready. I just love tea. I caught the habit when I went to school in England.' She swished out of Anna's room and down the stairs, calling to her sons, her dogs, her servants and her husband.

Anna took Daisy to the bathroom, changed her nappy, washed her hands and face, and combed her hair. Then she tidied herself, changing from her sun-dress to a short, cream linen skirt and blouse.

'Come on.' She picked up Daisy. 'Time to be inspected.'

Outside their suite of rooms, at the head of the mirrored corridor, there was an alcove with a writing desk and a chair. On the wall behind were several black and white photographs. Anna gave them a quick glance as she passed. Then she stopped and walked back. The largest picture showed some thirty girls in three rows. Underneath was written '1967, Lower Sixth', and below that their names, in italic print. Anna found Georgina standing in the back row, with the tallest girls, looking very much as she did today. But it wasn't her hostess whom Anna sought. She ran her finger down the names until she came to Felicity Granger-Thompson, the only Felicity in the class. She knelt at the headmistress's feet, dainty and exquisite, her face framed by fair curly hair, by far the prettiest girl in the photograph. Having seen her, Anna wished that she hadn't stopped to look.

She took a deep breath and walked on, down the sweeping staircase to the circular pink marble hall and opened the door to the yellow drawing-room. It was such a large room that the others, seated at the far end, did not hear her. Watching them before they noticed her, she hovered shyly. At Whaler's Rock, she was aware of Felicity in a way that she had never been before. Felicity had been Georgina's schoolfriend and welcome in this family. She'd stayed in this house, shared a room with Paul – perhaps even the same bed. They'd met here, kissed here, made love and exchanged endearments. Anna took a step backwards.

Then Paul saw her. 'I didn't come up, I thought you'd find it easier to be alone with Daisy,' he said, hurrying to her, smiling, driving away her uncertainty.

Steven introduced his sons, two big, sporty teenagers named Eddie and David. 'Isn't your little girl pretty?' he said, smiling at Daisy. 'I always wanted a daughter.'

His sons laughed good-humouredly, and Georgina quipped, 'Well, I'm not having another baby, honey, not at my age. I've done my duty, so it's no good hoping. Do sit down, Anna, you mustn't stand on ceremony here.' She passed Anna a cup of tea, then offered Daisy a chocolate biscuit, but the little girl buried her face timidly in her mother's short skirt. To Anna's relief, Georgina didn't persist with Daisy and they turned the conversation elsewhere.

Anna admired Whaler's Rock, which delighted Steven who was extremely proud of his inheritance. 'My great-great-grandfather had it built as his summer residence,' he informed her. 'He kept a staff of thirty and only stayed here one month a year. We make do with six staff – all members of the Bowson family – which may sound a lot, but it isn't in a house this size.' He patted his wife's hand. 'And, of course, I have Georgey who organises everything. Now you must meet Nanny. Eddie, fetch Nanny.' He turned back to Anna. 'Nanny's a Bowson. Her son is our head gardener and his wife is our cook. Their grandfather taught Paul and me to sail. He was nearly seven feet tall, with a white beard and a booming voice. We used to call him Captain Ahab, after the character in *Moby Dick*, but only behind his back.'

'We were twelve when he died,' Paul continued the story. 'I'd just returned to England after my third summer at Whaler's Rock and I was at school, in the middle of a geography lesson, when I was summoned to the telephone. It was the first call I'd ever received from overseas, and my small country school wasn't used to transatlantic dealings. You cannot imagine how my star rose in the eyes of my friends.' He smiled at Steven. 'Dear old Captain Ahab; we were so in awe of him. We did miss him.'

'Nanny's not at all frightening,' Georgina hurried to reassure Anna. 'Daisy will love her.'

'I hope so.' Anna prayed that she was right. Daisy did not often take to strangers.

Eddie returned with a tiny, tubby woman who had a face like a cheerful chipmunk. She clasped Anna warmly by the hand, saying, 'I just love little girls.' Then she bent to Daisy's level. 'I have some delicious cookies in the kitchen. Would you like one?'

'A cookie is a biscuit,' Anna told Daisy. 'You like biscuits.'

Daisy hesitated, then slowly she held out her arms to Nanny, who picked her up, cuddled her, and carried her from the room.

'That's a relief!' said Anna, relaxing.

Paul reached for her hand. 'I want to show you the cove. Steven . . . Georgina, will you come?'

'No, you two go alone.' Steven smiled. 'Take the boat out, if you like.'

They hurried from the yellow drawing-room and out into the golden heat of the evening sun. Crossing the marble terrace, they ran down the steps to the beautifully-manicured lawn which stretched to the very edge of the headland where a steep path wound down through a secret garden of massive rocks and wine-red rugosa roses, waist-high grasses and trees bent by the wind.

The path led down into the private cove where the boathouse nestled against the undercliff, and the Winslows' motor launch was moored alongside the wooden jetty. It was beautiful and deserted, and the evening sun cast a deep gold light on the water.

They stood together, looking out at the sea where the waves crashed on the rocks at the foot of the headland, venting their anger before entering the secluded cove.

'This is magical,' she said, standing very close to him. 'I understand why it's your special childhood place; it would be mine too, had I come here.'

He put his arms around her. 'Does it remind you of Cliff Cottage?'

'Oh, no! This is a palace. And yet . . .' She studied the rocky coastline. 'There is a similarity. They're both wild and isolated, and open to the elements.'

He kissed the soft skin at the corner of her eyebrow, running his mouth down her cheek to her mouth, giving her tender butterfly kisses. Slowly his kisses grew more urgent until, suddenly, he drew back and, taking her by the hand, he led her along the edge of the sea to the far side of the boathouse, where the sand was soft as silk and hidden from view. They lay down side by side and kissed softly, tenderly, with the warm sun on their limbs and the cries of the seagulls above them. He caressed her body, his hands so gentle that they barely touched her. She unfastened the buttons of his shirt, licking his bare chest, giving him little kisses. He ran his hands down her thighs to the hem of her short skirt and lifted it, caressing her gently, touching her until she moaned with pleasure.

Suddenly there was a shout from Georgina. 'Paul, Ginger is on the phone. He says it's urgent.'

Paul sat up. 'Oh hell, I'll have to go. I need to talk to him.' He gave her a gentle squeeze. 'I'm sorry.'

'I'll get my own back later.' Anna kissed him and sent him on his way, but she didn't return to the house immediately; she walked in the surf, relishing the touch and the smell of the sea.

They had no chance to be alone again before dinner, because Paul was on the phone for nearly an hour, and when he'd finished, Anna and Nanny were bathing Daisy. By the time Anna had settled Daisy, Paul had showered and gone downstairs. She'd intended to ask him what she should wear – her choices were the taupe dress, a black and white silk pyjama suit, and a navy linen dress. She settled for the latter. It seemed the safest.

Dinner was a more formal affair than Anna had anticipated, with gleaming silver on a long mahogany table and Nanny's granddaughter, in a black dress and small white pinafore, waiting at table. From time to time Anna caught Paul's eye and exchanged a secret smile. Once, she found Steven watching her and she blushed furiously, but he laughed and patted her hand.

Anna was nearly asleep by the end of dinner. It had been a long day, and she was exhausted by the strain of being a guest, with a small child, in such a grand household, especially when she felt sure they must be comparing her to Felicity. By force of will she managed to keep awake through coffee, but when Steven suggested a game of cards, she braved Georgina and said, 'I'm very sorry but I must go to bed.'

'Oh, but of course, I want you to feel at home here,' Georgina said pleasantly.

Paul touched Anna's cheek. 'I'll be up in a minute.'

She said good night and slipped from the room. When Paul came up not much later, she was already half asleep, snuggled into the pillows. He threw his clothes in a heap on the chair and stretched out beside her, taking her in his arms, gently, stroking her hair. She raised her face to his and he kissed her eyes and her mouth. Tired though she was, Anna's body awakened to his touch – which was like no other man's touch for her. They made love gently and quietly, with the windows wide open on to the night, and the sea breezes which came off the Rhode Island Sound and across the darkened garden fanning their naked bodies as they found deep and fulfilling pleasure in each other.

Afterwards Anna lay with Paul's arm around her, holding her, and together they listened to the sea. She felt as if nothing could touch her; no one could hurt her. Derek inhabited another planet now.

On the following afternoon, whilst Daisy remained contentedly with Nanny, Steven took Paul and Anna around the coast to Newport harbour in his motor launch, pointing out all the mansions along Cliff Walk as they passed.

'Two hundred years ago this was the busiest harbour on the East Coast,' Steven told Anna as they drew into the quay alongside some brightly-painted weatherboard houses. 'Most of these buildings have been rebuilt, but at least they're in the old style.' He winked at her. 'Restoration is my passion, Anna.'

She laughed. 'Just like Paul.'

Steven was a fascinating guide to the town, where he'd spent all his life except for the years when he'd been at Yale. He knew the history of each building, and of most people, and every few yards he was stopped by friends, all of whom talked enthusiastically of the forthcoming ball.

'One day we'll sail *The Goshawk* over to Newport,' Paul told Anna, whilst Winthorp was talking to an old lady. 'Would you like that?'

'I'd love it.' She leaned against him, nuzzling his shoulder with her face. She loved him – not just for today, but for the fact that he said 'we' and talked of them as being together in the future.

There was a graceful timelessness about the days at Whaler's Rock which was utterly seductive. With Nanny looking after Daisy, Paul and Anna stayed in bed late, making love in the blue and gold four-poster, swam in the pool or the sea, and sailed with Georgina and Steven in their sloop.

One day, when the men went fishing, Anna accompanied Georgina to Boston to collect her ballgown. On the way home they stopped for lunch at a seafood restaurant and they each ordered a glass of white wine.

'It's so nice to be able to drink what one likes,' Georgina confided. 'We seldom drank alcohol in front of Felicity, so as not to tempt her. I'm sure Paul has told you everything.'

'Not in any detail, he's too loyal, but the friend who . . . brought us together told me that Felicity had . . . problems.'

Georgina waited whilst their seafood salads were placed before them, then said, in a lowered voice, 'Felicity was an alcoholic.'

Anna was surprised. 'I didn't realise it was that serious.'

'Alcohol killed her.' Sadness came into Georgina's angular face, and she looked drained and much older. 'We should have realised something was wrong, she had a couple of vodkas before even the smallest social gathering, but she was so clever at hiding it. She brought her own secret supply of bottles, in a locked suitcase, and since she had her own money, Paul couldn't know how much she spent on liquor.'

'Didn't she act . . . drunk?' asked Anna, breaking a piece of bread.

Georgina shook her head. 'Not till the last years. You see, Felicity had always been so bubbly. When I was sixteen my mother decided I needed polishing, so she sent me to an English boarding school. It was hell – except for Felicity. No one was more friendly and welcoming, though she wasn't popular, which I thought unfair. When Steven first met her, he said that she wanted to be liked too much. I was cross, because she was my friend and he'd criticised her, but later I had to admit that he was right. Felicity was afraid to be herself, so she mirrored the person she was with – their attitudes and opinions, likes and dislikes. I think this is why Paul fell out of love with her.'

'Is that . . . when she began to drink?' Anna asked, no longer threatened by the girl in the photograph. If anything, she felt sorry for her.

Georgina pushed her plate to one side. 'No, that's when she started to make . . . accusations. She didn't mean to, it was the vodka. But the poison in what she said was impossible to ignore, and those last years, before she died, Paul stayed away from Whaler's Rock.' She glanced at her watch. 'We'd better hurry. The marquee is being delivered this afternoon.'

They arrived at the house to find the marquee partially erected on the lawn and urns of flowering roses lined up along the drive. Whilst Georgina rushed off, issuing instructions, Anna retired upstairs, to snooze and think about Felicity, wondering what she'd said that had been serious enough to separate Paul from the people and house he loved so dearly.

On the morning of the ball Nanny removed Daisy to her own home, and Paul and Anna, after having their offers of help rejected, took the motor launch down to Brenton Point, the south-westerly tip of the island.

'In the early eighteen hundreds a Spanish brig was wrecked

here,' said Paul, steering the motor launch between the rocks. 'A ship called the *Minerva* went down on Christmas Eve. They buried the bodies on Castle Hill, but much of the merchandise was never recovered. Steven and I used to spend hours searching for artefacts.'

Anna knelt beside him and peered into the water. 'What you seek is gold bullion. Admit it!'

He ruffled her hair. 'What I want is you.'

They anchored in a deserted bay, stripped off their clothes and dived naked into the cold sea, splashing each other and laughing. Then they swam ashore and stretched out on the white sand, hidden by a large black rock from anyone walking along the cliff. They touched with their eyes and their finger tips, lying side by side with just an inch between them, until they reached such a pitch of desire that they made love on the sand with the surf rolling over their feet.

They arrived back at the house, flushed and sun-kissed, to be scolded good-naturedly by Georgina who was already dressed for the ball in a sumptuous silver gown, with her hair sleeked into a French roll and the famous Winslow emeralds around her neck.

'That dress is wonderful,' Anna told her, before racing upstairs to change, with Paul on her heels, shouting compliments to Georgina.

They shared a shower, laughing and giggling and telling each other they must be quick. Paul shampoo'd Anna's hair whilst she kissed his chest, then they rubbed each other dry. He was dressed long before she was and she begged him to go down ahead of her and leave her to finish her hair and her make-up or else she'd never be ready. She'd planned to curl her hair, but she had no time, so she smoothed it back into a high plait, leaving the sides free and curled around her finger.

Most of the guests had already arrived by the time Anna descended the stairs, swathed in midnight silk, with her bare shoulders lightly gilded by the sun and her eyes polished with love and laughter.

Paul extracted himself from a group of people and hurried to her. 'You look beautiful,' he said, taking her hand in his and admiring her dress. 'I'm the envy of every man in the room. They're all watching you and thinking how lucky I am.' Some deep memory darkened his grey eyes. 'And I am lucky, Anna,' he said fiercely. 'God, don't I know it!'

'I'm lucky too.' She thought of the lonely months at Ladbroke Hill, before Louise and Mac, before Daisy, before Paul.

He murmured, 'You were beautiful on the beach today as well.'

Her body tingled with the memory of his touch. He saw the light in her eyes and squeezed her hand as he led her around the room to introduce her.

The marquee had been set up on the lawn, but because the night was so warm the sides were open to the sea breeze and the dance floor was laid out beneath the stars. They drank champagne whilst a pianist played *Rhapsody in Blue*, then dined on clams and strawberries. Steven toasted Georgina and she toasted him, whilst their guests raised their glasses and called out their good wishes. The band started up, and Steven and Georgina took to the floor, just the two of them, whilst their friends clapped and cheered and, finally, joined in.

'Let's dance,' said Paul, taking Anna by the hand and leading her towards the floor, but just before they reached it he stopped and turned her to face Whaler's Rock, whose great, white marble exterior rose up into the night sky.

'Isn't it magnificent?' he whispered in her ear.

She nodded. 'Thank you for bringing me here.'

'I wanted to share it with you.' He slid his hand up her neck and stroked the soft hair under her plait. 'Have I told you that I love you?' he asked her in a quiet voice. 'Because I do, Anna. I never thought I'd love again, not after . . . what happened.' He held her close. 'When we go back to England, I want us to be together, not just for a couple of nights, with our own separate houses. Yes, I know that I'm to blame for being away so often but I plan to travel less. I want to share my home with you, Anna, to share our lives. I love to talk to you in bed, late at night, in the darkness. I love to wake up and see you next to me, snuggled into the pillows. I want to come home and know you'll be there.'

He took her in his arms and swung her on to the dance floor. Paul was a wonderful dancer, because he danced as he lived, as he made love: with rhythm, intimacy and humour; and although Anna was no expert at ballroom dancing, with Paul she could waltz. Her feet took the right steps, she didn't trip, she was graceful – but most of all, she looked radiantly happy.

39

ANNA HAD TEARS in her eyes as they drove away from Rhode Island. They'd been so happy there that she was afraid to leave. At Whaler's Rock she'd felt safe and untainted by her past, but now as they headed back towards New York her guilt and her fears returned, as if Derek were waiting for her at Heathrow airport, and no one could save Daisy from him.

She decided to tell Paul on the aeroplane. He'd reserved three seats in a row, next to the window, paying a child fare for Daisy, although it wasn't necessary, so she could have her own place. On the flight they'd have hours to talk, undisturbed, and she'd have time to explain the desperation which had driven her to steal, and to voice her deep regret.

Paul was on the car-phone, talking to Ginger. Anna watched the way the afternoon light caught his cheekbones and how he pushed back his dark hair, only to have it flop forward again. Their fortnight together had brought them so close that at times it seemed as if they inhabited the same skin. She laid a hand on his thigh.

He smiled at her, and mouthed, 'I'm sorry.'

She felt happier. By the time she reached England, Paul would know about Derek and *The Blonde Bimbo*, and the weight of her secret would be lifted. She would no longer fear him finding out and abandoning her.

From his telephone conversation, she gathered that a suspect cruiser, which Ginger was watching in Jamaica, looked as if she were about to be moved, but because they had no evidence the local police couldn't hold her. It was a similar story to Scheveningen, except that this was more perilous. The men aboard the cruiser were Colombians and suspected drug-runners.

Paul came off the phone. 'I'll have to go there,' he said. 'My contacts don't fully trust Ginger yet, not in such a tricky situation.' He covered Anna's hand with his own. 'Do you mind if I put you in a taxi at Heathrow?'

It took her a moment to realise that he planned to cross the Atlantic twice and, although she was anxious to talk to him she could not bear to force on him the added risk of confronting danger when he was exhausted.

'You must go straight to Jamaica and I'll go home alone,' she said bravely, wondering why she had to love a man who courted danger.

He glanced in the mirror at Daisy dozing in the back. 'I wouldn't leave you to travel on your own with a small child.'

She moved closer and kissed him. 'I want you safe; I'll be all right, Daisy was no trouble on the way out.' She saw him hesitate, and added, 'Paul, the flight attendants will assist me. They always allow small children to board first, and when I get to London I have Melissa coming to help me.'

He touched her cheek. 'If you're sure – it would save me a day.'

'Just come home quickly.' She thought of Derek and had to bite her lip to stop it trembling.

They made good time until they crossed the East River, where they caught the tail of the evening traffic. It snarled them up all the way to the airport. With not a minute to spare before the plane left for Kingston, Paul roared up to the British Airways terminal. He couldn't even wait to help Anna check in, because he still had to return the rented car and make his way to another terminal. Beckoning to a porter, he slipped him twenty dollars and asked him to look after Anna. 'I hate to abandon you like this,' he said, kissing her and then Daisy, with the traffic, the passengers, and the porters milling around them.

'We'll be all right.' She held Daisy tightly. 'Go! You'll miss your plane.'

He saw the white fear in her face. 'Darling, you're not afraid of flying, are you?'

She shook her head. 'Paul, you must hurry.'

Still, he hesitated. 'I'm being selfish; I should stay with you.'

'We'll be fine.' She forced a smile. 'Honestly.'

He kissed her again, and stepped into the car. 'I'll phone tonight, I mean tomorrow – your tomorrow.'

She waved goodbye. She was too choked to speak.

Daisy slept for most of the journey, curled up on her seat, her head on Anna's lap. Anna didn't sleep at all. She spent the whole flight worrying about Paul, picturing him cornered in a dark alleyway, murdered by drug-runners, disappearing – and she'd never know how or where.

She arrived home exhausted, both physically and mentally. The house was quiet – Louise was out, and Anna could tell that Mac and Victoria had not yet returned because all the post was scattered untidily over the hall table, instead of in neat piles. As she sorted through the letters, she steeled herself to find Derek's erratic typeface, but there was nothing. Giddy with relief, she opened the door to her bedroom and let her bags fall to the floor.

She felt terribly flat, coming back. The reality of being without Paul hit her as she looked around the room, the scene of her excited departure to New York. She opened the windows to dispel the dusty, slightly musty air, then pressed the 'Play' button on her answering machine, waiting as the tape rewound. There was a message from Roz, reminding her about Melissa; her mother wanting to know when she was going to meet Paul; a couple of clicks from people who'd left no word; and – finally – Paul: 'You're still on the plane, and when you get home I'll be on a boat, but I want you to have this message on your arrival. When I left you at the terminal, standing there, holding Daisy, trying to smile, I loved you more than ever.'

She replayed his message several times. She was still playing it when Roz rang. 'Did you have a nice time? How was the ball? Did the dress look nice?'

'Oh, it was magic – and the dress was beautiful. Paul loved it. Thanks for helping me.' Anna went on to decribe Whaler's Rock.

When she'd finished speaking, Roz enquired anxiously, 'You haven't changed your mind about Melissa?'

'No, of course not. Send her tomorrow, around tea-time. She'll have to sleep on the sofa-bed. I don't have a spare bedroom.'

'So long as you take her I don't mind where she sleeps. She's being so difficult.' Roz gave a groan of exasperation. 'Now, when are we going to meet Paul? Can you bring him to stay at Lower Gossip next month? Mother will be here, and she's dying to give him the once-over.'

Anna laughed. 'I bet she is! Yes, I'm sure he'd like to come – if he's in England.'

Melissa arrived an hour late, by which time Anna was on the point of telephoning Roz. She stomped up the drive carrying one small suitcase, and wearing her black boots, her shapeless black cardigan and her black leggings, with her dark hair parted in the centre, hanging like mourning curtains to hide her face. Anna recognised it as an act of self-protection and felt a wave of sympathy.

'Hello, Melissa,' she said pleasantly. 'I was worried about you. Roz told me you were coming by taxi.'

'I took the tube to save money.' Melissa clumped into the drawing-room and threw her bag down. Then she sank to the floor, took out a packet of cigarettes, lit one and inhaled deeply, letting the smoke drift slowly out through her nostrils.

Anna's sympathy dissolved as she wondered what she'd let herself in for. 'I don't want you smoking in front of Daisy,' she said. 'I know Roz never lets you smoke.'

Melissa's jaw set in a mutinous line. 'Mother doesn't let me do anything.'

The telephone interrupted them and Anna hurried to answer it in her bedroom, closing the door firmly behind her.

It was Paul, speaking from his hotel in Kingston, and she was so relieved to hear him safe.

'How was your journey?' he asked.

'Fine, no problems, just a bit tiring. What about you? I've been so worried. What's happened with the boat?'

'She's been temporarily impounded. Her papers appear genuine, though I'm sure they're forgeries, but if we can't prove it, the police will let her go.'

'How frustrating!'

'It is – and all the time I keep thinking I could be home with you.'

'So . . . when will you be back?' she asked, trying not to worry him by sounding too anxious.

'Within a day, if we have a breakthrough. If not, I could be here for a week or two. I'm sorry, darling, I really am. It seems so strange, so arid, to be alone, without you, after Whaler's Rock.' He paused, then said, 'You sounded flustered when you answered. Is something wrong?'

'It's my niece, she's testing me by smoking when I know that Roz doesn't allow it.

He chuckled, relieved that it was nothing more urgent. 'Tell her she can have the odd one in the garden.'

'Roz would never forgive me.'

'Harriet's son only smokes to rile her.'

She laughed. 'All right. I'll try it.'

They went on to talk, of everything and nothing, at the end of which she said, 'This call must be costing you a fortune.'

Her concern made him smile. 'It doesn't matter, I want to speak to you – though next time British Telecom float their shares we'd better buy some, we must be their best customers.'

Anna returned to the drawing-room to find Melissa lying on the floor, helping Daisy to make a house out of Lego. She told her what Paul had suggested, though she passed it off as her own idea.

Melissa looked surprised. 'Okay,' she mumbled, and she continued to make the Lego house. It was nearly two hours before she slipped outside to smoke.

Anna had invited Mr Marilyn to join them for supper. He came up, eager to hear about the wedding. As they were about to sit down, Louise swanned in, dressed in magenta chiffon. Melissa was fascinated by the occupants of the house.

On the following morning Anna left Melissa asleep and took Daisy shopping for food. On the way home she dropped in to see Heather, where she had a cup of coffee. It was after midday when she arrived at the house. The curtains were still closed and Melissa was in bed. As Anna surveyed the mess in the drawing-room – the girl sprawled across the sofa-bed, her clothes strewn around the room, her wet towel on the floor – her sympathies were entirely with Roz.

'A man telephoned,' mumbled Melissa without opening her eyes.

'Was it Paul?'

'Dunno.' She turned her back on Anna.

'You should have asked his name.' Irritated, Anna opened the curtains.

Melissa sat up. 'Why? He didn't want you, he asked for someone called Caroline.'

Anna stumbled. She gripped the sofa-bed to steady herself. 'You're not to touch my phone again!' she snapped.

'Why not? It might have been for me.'

'Because I say so!'

Melissa lay down again and pulled the duvet over her head.

Anna grabbed the end of the duvet and yanked it off, leaving the girl uncovered except for her childish pyjamas decorated with teddy bears. 'Get up!' she shouted. 'Tidy this room! You're meant to be here to help me, not lie around all day long; no wonder Roz is sick of you.' She marched out and slammed the door. If she'd been a smoker she'd have lit a cigarette. As it was she went to the fridge and poured herself a glass of wine, then she thought of Felicity and tossed it down the sink.

Once Anna calmed down, she was sorry about what she'd said to Melissa, but she'd been frightened and angry; she was still frightened. She lifted Daisy into her high chair, and was about to call Melissa to lunch, when the front door slammed and she heard footsteps hurry away from the house. Wondering if she could stand a whole week of this, Anna peered into the drawing-room. It was immaculate, with sofa-bed closed, the cushions in place, the duvet folded, and Melissa's belongings piled neatly in one corner. At least she hadn't run away.

Anna spent the afternoon pacing the house, wondering how to handle Derek. She knew that she ought to go to the police, even at this late stage, but she couldn't without admitting her earlier crime. In her Marinecover days she'd known many solicitors but she didn't know any well enough to seek free advice. She thought of ringing the Citizens' Advice Bureau, but she wasn't sure if they'd record her call. She wished she'd told Paul, but each time she'd been on the point of speaking, something had prevented her. More often than not, she admitted now, if had been her fear of losing him.

Several times the telephone rang but she didn't pick it up, she merely listened. There was a click but no one spoke – just breathing, then the receiver was replaced. She knew it was Derek and she felt him closing in on her, persecuting her – and more terrifying still, stalking Daisy.

Anna was so preoccupied that she forgot about Melissa until Louise came home at six and asked, 'What's happened to the widow?'

'The widow? Oh yes, she does look as though she's in mourning. I'm afraid I shouted at her and she stormed out.'

They chatted for a few minutes, then Louise went upstairs and Anna returned to her anxieties.

Melissa still wasn't home by eleven and Anna was becoming very worried. She searched the drawing-room to see if there was any clue as to where she'd gone. On the floor, next to her suitcase, was a leaflet from the Electric Cinema in the Portobello Road. There was a red cross next to *Rebel Without A Cause*.

She asked Louise to mind Daisy. She hated to leave her even for a short while, but she was afraid that Derek might intercept Melissa. 'Don't let any strangers into the house, whatever happens,' she urged Louise.

'I wouldn't dream of it.' Louise looked perplexed.

It started to drizzle as Anna hurried down the Portobello Road. She glanced fearfully over her shoulder, cursing Melissa for taking her away from Daisy, and herself for having shouted at the girl. The antique shops were closed, battened down for the night, but Anna was aware of every shadow in each doorway. There were few people around, just a couple of men outside a pub and two teenage boys sharing a bag of chips. She studied each face, searching for Derek.

The Electric Cinema had a small foyer, where they served proper coffee and carrot cake. Two girls were chatting behind the cash desk.

'I'm looking for my niece,' Anna explained. 'She's visiting me and we had an . . . er . . . argument, and I think she may be here.'

The girls smiled. 'The picture has just ended. See if she appears.'

Anna was desperate to get back to Daisy, and she waited impatiently as the audience streamed out, blinking in the fluorescent light. Melissa wasn't among them.

'I'll take you inside.' One of the girls ushered Anna into the auditorium.

It was empty, except for a hunched figure at the far end of the back row. Anna walked over to her. 'Melissa!' she said gently. 'I'm sorry I said . . . what I did about your mother.'

Melissa looked up. Her pale face was blotchy from crying. 'But she is sick of me; she's only interested in Luke.'

Anna found it hard to respond, torn between her loyalty to Roz and her sympathy for the distressed girl. She remembered the times in her childhood when Roz had seemed so much more acceptable to their mother. 'Luke is very talented,' she began, tentatively, 'but you also have your talents.'

'Like what?'

'Everyone is good at something. Come on! We'll talk about it on the way home.'

Melissa shuffled out of her seat and followed Anna from the auditorium, receiving a friendly smile from the girls in the foyer. Anna walked briskly, controlling an urge to run. Melissa trundled along behind, chewing gum.

'I hated school,' she said. 'I didn't make friends; I never do – I want to but . . . Mum says I try too hard, but I don't see how I can win people otherwise. I know if I had a boyfriend it would be different. All the other girls had boys writing to them, but I never did. If I try to talk to Mum she says I'm too young for all that, but I'm not, I'm nearly sixteen.'

'Roz wants you to concentrate on your education.' Anna walked even faster. She should never have left Daisy, not even with Louise.

'Mum should be pleased I've left school,' Melissa continued. 'College is free and she always complains that we're short of money – though there's enough for Luke's music lessons.' Melissa threw her chewing-gum paper on the ground, but before Anna could say anything, she bent guiltily to pick it up and put it in a nearby rubbish bin.

As they approached Ladbroke Hill, Anna scrutinised the trees for signs of movement, but there were none.

'Mum was so envious when you bought this house,' Melissa confided. 'She used to say that you had everything and I'd think, now you know how I feel about Luke.'

'I don't think she's jealous of me any more,' said Anna, unlocking the front door and calling, 'Louise, we're back.'

'Oh, no, not since Charlie left you pregnant.' Melissa gulped. 'Sorry. I shouldn't have said that.'

'I doesn't matter.' Anna opened Daisy's door and nearly wept with relief when she saw the dear little face, sleeping peacefully, snuggling into her pillow.

'Thanks for listening,' said Melissa from behind her. 'I'm sorry I didn't help you today.'

'You can give me a hand tomorrow. Now go to bed and don't

worry about the future. It'll all work out. I bet half those girls who claimed to have boys writing to them didn't. It was their brothers!'

Melissa giggled and disappeared into the drawing-room. Alone, Anna returned to her own fears. She lay on her bed, listening, frightened. She didn't know what to do, and until she'd made a decision she had to avoid Derek.

In the morning Melissa was up and dressed promptly, and whilst she gave Daisy her breakfast, Anna made a picnic, hurrying them all out of the house, saying that they needed fresh air. They spent the day in Kensington Gardens and didn't return to Ladbroke Hill until Anna was sure that Louise would be home.

That evening she invited Dominic and Mr Marilyn to supper again, partly to make the evening more fun for Melissa and partly because there was safety in numbers. It was a warm September night, and everyone wanted to eat in the garden, except for Anna, but she couldn't think of a valid reason to refuse. All through dinner she felt as if eyes were watching them, although when she looked around the garden, there was no one.

Dominic didn't leave till late – he never did – and when Anna accompanied him to the front door, he bent to pick up an envelope from the mat. 'For you.' He handed it to her. 'Thanks for supper. Good night.'

Anna didn't even notice him go, as she stared at the erratic typeface. With trembling fingers she opened the envelope. Inside was a photograph of Daisy, identical to the previous one, only this time it had been cut in half. She gave a stifled scream, hurried into her bedroom, and dialled Paul's hotel in Jamaica. She had to speak to him now, she couldn't wait to tell him face to face, it no longer mattered if she lost him – no, of course it was important because she loved him – but she was too frightened for Daisy to think of her own happiness.

She perched on the end of her bed, the receiver pressed to her ear, and when the hotel answered, she spoke so fast, that they couldn't understand her, and she was obliged to repeat Paul's name.

'Mr Sheldon? Oh, I'm afraid he checked out this morning,' the hotel receptionist informed her.

'This is terribly urgent. Did he leave a forwarding number?'

'No, ma'am, he didn't.'

Anna replaced the receiver. She felt as if Paul had deserted her, although she knew she was being irrational because he couldn't know how much she needed him.

It was well past midnight but she couldn't wait till morning, and she telephoned the boathouse, waking Michael. 'I'm sorry to ring so late, but I need to speak to Paul.'

'Oh . . . Anna?' She heard the bedclothes rustle as Michael sat up. 'Paul's out of contact.'

'But he always carries a mobile.' Her voice rose in panic.

'He's on one of the smaller islands and the reception is very bad. Anna, can I help? What's wrong?'

She nearly confided the whole, terrible story to Michael, but she stopped herself. She owed it to Paul to tell him first. She should have told him long ago, she shouldn't have been silenced by her fear of losing him. 'It's all right,' she replied.

'I'll tell him you rang. I'm sure he'll be in touch as soon as he can.'

'Thank you.' It was hard not to cry.

She'd barely replaced the receiver when the telephone rang. Hoping it was Paul, she grabbed it, shouting, 'Hello . . . hello?'

There was no answer, just breathing. She put down the receiver.

It rang again, and she answered, and the same thing happened.

Anna stood in the middle of the room, staring at the telephone. She felt as if an evil current were coming out of it, enveloping her in its web, sucking at her legs, dragging her backwards towards Derek; and that however hard she tried to fight against it, she could not do so because she had done wrong, and she deserved to be sucked under.

She barely slept that night and in the morning she came to the conclusion that by remaining at home she was drawing Derek towards Daisy, so the next time the telephone rang, and no one spoke, she said, 'I'll meet you at noon in the gardens in the centre of Ladbroke Hill.'

She hated to leave Daisy but it was too dangerous to take her, so she climbed down the old interior staircase, startling Mr Marilyn by appearing in his hall with Daisy in her arms. 'Could you look after her?' she whispered. 'Just for an hour. But don't let her in the garden.'

'Of course, but what's wrong, Anna? You look so pale.' Again, she lied because she could think of no other way. 'Charlie's in London.'

Mr Marilyn hurried to close the garden door. 'Don't you worry,' he said fiercely, 'I won't let him in the house.'

Anna gave Daisy an anguished hug and clambered back up the stairs.

She'd chosen the centre of the square because she could see it from the house, and therefore needn't leave home until Derek arrived. In this way he couldn't cross behind her – and reach Daisy.

Well before noon, she went up to the attic landing and stood by the window, watching. She didn't have to wait long before Derek sauntered into view. She raced downstairs and slipped on her jacket, then she hesitated. Supposing he was armed, supposing he attacked her and grabbed her house keys? She went into the kitchen, opened the drawer and stared at the row of knives. She couldn't imagine actually using one, but at least she might be able to hold him off for long enough to retreat to the house. She selected an evil-looking but not particularly sharp knife, put it in her pocket, and left.

Derek was seated on the bench smoking a dark Turkish cigarette. He looked up as Anna entered the gardens and gave her an amiable smile. 'Hello, Caroline, I knew you'd see reason.'

It seemed unbelievable that this slight, dapper man could be so menacing. 'I told you to stay away from me,' she said.

'You're not being very sensible. You owe some friends of mine, and they're getting impatient.'

'If you don't leave me alone, I'll go to the police.'

'I wouldn't do that,' he said quietly.

Her fingers curled around the handle of the knife. 'Don't you threaten me.'

'Caroline, all we want is our money. Just do one more job, and that's the end of it, we won't bother you any more.' He smiled. 'I promise.'

'I'm not that stupid. You'd never let me go.'

He took a photograph from his pocket and laid it on the bench. 'This is the boat we want. She's moored near the mouth of the Lymington river. The owners haven't been near her for weeks, bloody fools! The sails are in good condition, the engine's on board, and they leave the keys in the hatch on a hook just above it. You'd take her out with the jib, then hot-wire the engine. No, maybe not: I don't reckon a young lady like you would know how to do that. But you're a handy sailor, and a good westerly and a flowing tide would have you in Cobbleford within a couple of hours. You'll be in time to catch the last train to London – and you'd never hear from us again.'

Anna couldn't resist glancing at the picture. The yacht was called *The Ballard*, and she was beautiful. 'This boat's worth at least seventy grand,' she protested.

'Then we'll give you a present, enough to take your little girl on a nice holiday, by the seaside.'

'I don't need your money. I just want you to stay away from us.'

He gave her a sad smile. 'My friends don't like being kept waiting, Caroline. I haven't told them where you live – not yet – and I'd be sorry if you forced me to.' Leaving the photograph on the bench, he rose and sauntered away. When he reached the railing at the end of the garden, he said, 'I'll give you a few hours to come to your senses. I'm not a hard man, I like kiddies.'

Anna watched him go, her hand in her pocket, the knife loose between her fingers. She longed to stab him, to eradicate him, but it wouldn't help Daisy to have a mother on a murder charge. Leaving the photograph where Derek had placed it, she hurried back to the house.

Using the inside staircase, she went down to collect Daisy from Mr Marilyn. He was so concerned about Charlie that he'd drawn all the curtains. She returned to the main house by way of the inner staircase, which brought her out in the hall, near the table. She glanced at it – then gasped with fright. The photograph of the boat was placed right in the centre. Derek had not only been up to the house, but he'd gained entry. Anna felt the world closing in. There was no one to help her protect Daisy. By the time Paul came home, it would be too late.

That evening, after Melissa had gone to bed, she telephoned Derek. 'I'll do it,' she said. 'This once.'

'You're a bright girl, Caroline; I always thought so.' He gave her details of the boat, her mooring, the closest access, the weather, the tides and the nearest police launch.

When they finished speaking, Anna put her hands up to her face and cried. How could she have imagined that she could commit a crime and that it would not haunt her?

40

ON THE FOLLOWING afternoon Anna left Daisy with Melissa, saying that she was going to visit a friend and wouldn't be back till late. Before she went she checked that not only Mr Marilyn but Louise would be at home that night. She took the rush-hour train from Waterloo to Brockenhurst, in the New Forest, where she changed for Lymington and the Isle of Wight ferry. In her skirt and jacket she mingled easily with the commuters hurrying home on a cloudy September evening. Not even her sailing bag looked out of place.

At the ferry pier she changed in the ladies' loo, slipping out of her office-worker clothes and wriggling into her wetsuit, over which she pulled on a black track suit.

When she came out of her cubicle a peroxide blonde was combing her hair at the basin. 'Shame about the weather,' she said to Anna. 'It always rains for my holidays.'

'What a pity.' Anna hooked her sailing bag over her shoulder and walked out. She wondered what the woman would say if she knew that Anna planned to steal a boat.

She crossed the car park and turned sharp right, as Derek had instructed, branching off from the main road to follow a wooded country lane which snaked along the opposite side of the river from the town. It was verging on dusk and she walked briskly, passing several large houses, some private and others divided into flats. The lane narrowed and moisture dripped from the bordering trees which almost touched above her head. It was eerie in the half light, and when a branch fell to the ground Anna jumped with fright. She stopped and glanced back, towards the station, wondering if she should go home and forget the whole thing. Then she thought of Derek, and forced herself to keep walking.

At a certain point, where the lane widened and the houses gave way to rolling fields, Anna came to the path leading down to the river. She followed it, hurrying through the long, wet grass until she came out on the river bank, beyond the boom which lay part-way across the mouth of the harbour.

The walk had taken longer than she'd expected and the tide was now on the ebb. She could see the glisten of exposed mudflats where the water had retreated, revealing gullies and tall red reeds. The only area navigable at all states of the tide was the central channel, marked by red and green lights. The Wight ferry was on its outward journey, churning down the channel, making the yachts dance on their moorings. Anna stood in the shadow of a dripping elder bush until it had passed, then she proceeded along the river bank until she could identify *The Ballard*, on a swinging mooring, in a group of a dozen other vessels.

She found the fibreglass rowing boat pulled up under a bush at the head of a narrow channel, exactly where Derek had said it would be. Inside were the oars. Quickly, she slid the boat down the bank, into the water, and stepped aboard.

The outgoing tide was stronger than Anna had anticipated and it swiftly drew her level with *The Ballard*. She'd intended to circle the yacht from a distance to ensure that there was no one aboard, but that proved impossible because the tide kept dragging the dinghy out towards the sea. Forced to abandon the fight, she hoped for the best and tied up alongside *The Ballard*.

She waited for a minute before boarding, listening hard, her every nerve on edge, but the only sound was the slap of the waves and the rattle of the halyards. She rose very slowly and reached up to take hold of *The Ballard*, preparing to drop down in an instant. But no one challenged her, no lights came on in the cabin, and as she climbed swiftly aboard, it occurred to her that the rowing boat was undoubtedly also stolen.

Derek had said that *The Ballard* was thirty-six feet, but she was over forty – far larger than Anna had ever handled on her own, which made her even more nervous. But she was a beautiful, streamlined boat and to Anna it seemed so perverse that her owners, who clearly spent money on her maintenance, begrudged her the expense of a secure marina. She gave the yacht a quick check, found the hatch key, wondering briefly how Derek knew its hiding place, and located the jib which was stowed neatly inside the cabin.

Returning to the deck she discovered that even in this short while the water had retreated, leaving *The Ballard* less than ten yards from the nearest mudbank. Working quickly, she clipped the mainsail cover and attached the sail to the main halyard. Then she transferred the dinghy to the buoy and let slip the yacht, turning immediately to hoist the jib. But when it was half-way up, the halyard stuck. Trying not to panic, she loosened it and pulled again, but it was caught in the mast and she couldn't release it. As the yacht began to drift downstream, perilously close to the marshland, Anna suddenly noticed the other Wight ferry, pounding up the channel on its return journey. Quickly she hoisted the mainsail, but before she gained control of *The Ballard*, the wash from the ferry buffeted her sideways, its swell lifting her on to the mud, and when the water retreated, her keel was stuck fast.

Stranded aground, Anna was paralysed by fear. She couldn't think what to do. On the far bank of the river the lights from the old town of Lymington twinkled into the night. From the yacht club voices and laughter carried across the river. Then she became aware of the distant roar of a twin-engined vessel coming from the direction of the Isle of Wight. This was no ferry, it was a fast, powerful boat and she remembered Derek's warning about the Ashburton police launch.

Images of prison and Daisy's tearful face rose up before her and she started to climb over the side. Then she recalled what Derek had said about not leaving evidence, and she grabbed her sailing bag from under the foredeck before swinging herself down from the boat.

She sank straight into the mud, right up to her knees, and overbalanced. Grabbing at some reeds which cut the palms of her hands, she pulled herself upright and waded frantically through the glutinous muck which seemed determined to swallow her. With the launch fast approaching, she reached firmer ground. Slipping on wet plankton, her hands lacerated by brambles, she crawled up the bank and into the safety of the undergrowth. Glancing back, she saw that the launch was within yards of *The Ballard*.

At that moment, the searchlights swung into action, raking the choppy surface of the water, and voices shouted, 'Anyone there? Anyone hurt?'

She knew that it wouldn't be long before they suspected an attempted theft and widened their search, so she kept running, gasping with heat inside her wetsuit, until she reached the riverfront garden of the first house. Although her instinct was not to stop, she couldn't board the train covered in mud. With no time to remove her wetsuit, she cleaned up as best she could by rolling in the long, wet grass. Then she scraped her hair into a ponytail and put on her track suit. She felt hot and uncomfortable and revoltingly dirty, but she could have been any other fitness fanatic jogging in the rain. Derek had been right. She didn't look like a boat thief.

The last train to Brockenhurst was waiting at the platform when she raced into the station. She purchased a ticket with a damp twenty-pound note and jumped into the nearest carriage. She longed to take off her wetsuit but the journey was too short, so she stood near an open window, gasping for air, sweat rolling down her body inside the rubber.

As soon as Anna boarded the London connection she locked herself in the loo and struggled out of the wet rubber, with the movement of the train throwing her from side to side. Then she splashed her face, cleaned the cuts on her hands, and washed the front of her hair, alternately scalding and freezing in the spurts of water.

When she came out, her hair was slicked back behind her ears and her face was pink from scrubbing. She took a window seat, at one end of the only carriage where there were other women passengers, and clasped her hands in her lap to stop them from twisting nervously. She could hardly believe that just a week ago she was swathed in midnight silk, dancing in Paul's arms.

At Waterloo she half expected to find a cordon of policemen awaiting her, but the station was deserted except for the homeless, sleeping rough in dark corners. The Underground had closed, so she had to wait for a night bus, and it was nearly two o'clock when it dropped her near Holland Park. By now she was bitterly cold and her hair had dried into stiff, salty streaks. She was so tired that she could barely walk up the hill, and when she reached the house she cried with relief. She opened the front door and crept into her bedroom, lowered her sailing bag to the floor and collapsed, fully clothed, on her bed.

The far door opened and Paul walked in. 'Darling, why didn't you tell me you were in trouble?' he asked, hurrying to her side. Then he stared at her, horrified when he saw her dishevelled appearance. 'What's happened? Are you hurt?'

She shook her head, stunned that he already knew about Derek and *The Ballard*, but at the same time tremendously relieved. 'I . . . I was desperate. Oh, Paul, I didn't know what else to do.' Her whole body shook in the aftermath of terror.

He took her in his arms and held her tight, caressing her, comforting her. 'Why didn't you tell me on the phone that Charlie was hassling you?'

She couldn't understand what he was talking about. 'Charlie? He has nothing to do with it.'

'Anna, I know he's here – Mr Marilyn told me.'

'But you're wrong, Paul.'

He held her at arm's length. 'Then why did you leave Daisy downstairs this afternoon?'

She'd been caught in a web of her own making and she had no one to blame but herself. She'd been foolish to mislead Mr Marilyn, but as with so many things in her life, at the time it had seemed the best solution. Only afterwards did she realise her mistakes. But she was too fatigued now to disentangle the lies, to explain about Derek, to think of the right words. All she could do was mumble, 'Charlie isn't here.'

'If it isn't Charlie, then what is the matter?' he asked. 'I must know, Anna. Don't you trust me? I love you, but I can't continue in this secrecy.'

'I'll tell you tomorrow, I promise.' Her eyelids drooped and, unable to prevent herself, she slept.

Paul studied her drawn, white face, not knowing what to believe, except that he'd already lived one life of pretence, and however much he loved Anna, he would not live like that again.

41

ANNA WOKE NEXT morning knowing that she would lose Paul, perhaps not today – but eventually. Her secrecy had created a cancer, eating away at his belief in her, and as she lay in bed, reliving the previous night, she realised that it was too late to merely admit her part in *The Blonde Bimbo*. She had to repair the damage – not only for Paul's sake but, equally important, for her own.

She telephoned Derek early. 'The boat capsized,' she whispered, so that Melissa couldn't hear. 'I nearly drowned in the mud and the police launch came. I thought I was going to be caught; I was terrified.'

'I know. We had a bloke watching.'

She thought of the fibreglass dinghy which someone had positioned for her and *The Ballard*'s hatch keys whose hiding place had been known. 'If you have a man in Lymington, why did you need me?' she asked.

'Because no one would suspect you, Caroline.'

'You're wrong.' She lowered her voice further. 'There's a car parked in the street and I think the driver is watching the house.'

'Since when?' Derek sounded alarmed.

'Our last phone call.'

'And you're ringing me on your home phone?'

'Why not?'

'It's bugged, you stupid bitch!' He slammed down his receiver.

Anna felt a small surge of triumph. Derek had terrorised her, and now she'd frightened him. He wouldn't dare come near Ladbroke Hill, at least not for some time.

By the time Melissa rose, Anna had hidden her track suit and sailing bag in the cupboard under the stairs, thrown away her perforated wetsuit in one of the municipal dustbins near the

Portobello market, and disinfected the cuts in her hands. She sent Melissa shopping; she needed time to think. But as she was settling down with a mug of coffee, Mr Marilyn knocked on the garden door.

'Anna, I must talk to you,' he cried, twisting his fingers in anguish.

She opened the door. 'What's wrong?'

He had tears in his eyes. 'I'm so sorry about last night. I shouldn't have told Paul that Mr Blythely was here, it was none of my business.'

She sighed. 'Don't worry, it's not your fault. I'm to blame.' She drew him into the house. 'I've just made some coffee. Join me in a cup.'

'Well . . . a quick one.' He gave her a shy smile, and went on talking. 'It was silly of me to upset Paul. I know you wouldn't do anything behind his back, you're not that kind of girl, you're like my mother – honest and kind.'

Anna pictured herself wading through the mud as she escaped from the police launch. 'Mr Marilyn, you wouldn't say that if you knew the truth.'

'Rubbish! You're not capable of doing anything to be ashamed of.'

'Aren't I? Well, I'll let you into a secret, something I haven't even told Paul yet, but I can't allow you to go on believing I'm so perfect. Last spring, when I couldn't pay the mortgage, I . . . did something dishonest.' She didn't tell him exactly what, because she knew he'd be so distressed.

'Whatever you did, it was to save our home and I'm grateful.' He laid his wrinkled hand on Anna's. 'I also have a sin to confess. I've always told you how I danced with Marilyn Monroe. Well . . . it isn't true.' His eyes were stricken. 'You see, as I crossed the room to invite Miss Monroe to dance, another man cut in and whisked her away.'

Anna nearly blurted out that his small exaggeration was nothing compared to her crime, but she realised that for him it was very serious. 'I'm sure Marilyn Monroe would have preferred to dance with you,' she said to comfort him.

He leaned towards her and, very slowly, kissed her cheek. 'Thank you. I've never told anyone before, it's been such a weight on my mind. It's a mistake to bottle things up.'

She thought of Paul. 'You're right.'

It rained all afternoon, which pleased Anna, because she didn't have to think of a reason to keep Daisy inside. Whilst she believed that Derek wouldn't dare come to the house, she couldn't take the risk that he was in the streets nearby. So Melissa entertained Daisy in the drawing-room, and Anna rehearsed her conversation with Paul in her bedroom. She'd hoped that he might telephone, but he didn't, and when she rationalised it, she realised that he was waiting for her explanation. As the day drew to an end, and the light died, she stood by the balcony windows, looking out at the rain-soaked garden, and wondered how she had got herself into such a mess. She imagined her life without Paul – lonely, arid, desolate – and tears filled her eyes.

She brushed them away and called to Melissa. 'I have to go out tonight. I'm sorry to leave you again, but Mr Marilyn will be downstairs and there's plenty of food in the fridge.'

Melissa smiled. 'Don't worry. Louise said I can try on her market dresses.'

'Is she at home this evening?'

'She's updating her stockbook.'

Anna ran upstairs and knocked on Louise's door.

'Enter if you're male and virile,' Louise called out.

'It's only me.' Anna stepped inside.

'One can but hope!' Louise was sitting on the floor, surrounded by piles of recently acquired clothes. 'What did you get up to last night?' She asked in the same tone of disapproval she'd adopted when Victoria had let Mac stay the night on their first date. 'Mr Marilyn said you were with that arsehole Charlie. Honestly, Anna, you need a brain transplant.'

'I wasn't with Charlie.'

'So who were you with, you naughty girl?'

'Please don't ask me.'

Louise rocked back on to her heels. 'What's the matter? You look all hollowed out.'

Anna longed to confide, but she was afraid that once she began to talk, she'd break down and never regain the courage she needed for tonight. 'Oh . . . it's nothing,' she said, trying to sound unconcerned. 'But you could do me a favour, Louise. May I borrow the van?'

'Of course.' Louise dropped the keys into Anna's hand. 'You look so unhappy,' she said sympathetically. 'Won't you let me help? Is it the bank again?'

Anna shook her head. 'I can't tell you, maybe another day, but not tonight.' She pulled a face, a mixture of fear and bravado, and hurried downstairs before she weakened.

She dressed to mingle with the night, in a black body under black trousers and her black leather jacket and boots. She didn't take a bag, it might hinder her, but in the pocket of her jacket she carried her small camera, her keys and some cash. Before leaving she opened the door to Daisy's bedroom and stood looking at the small, sleeping figure. 'Good night, darling,' she whispered. 'If anything goes wrong . . .' She was too choked to finish.

Anna was frightened but very determined as she drove the purple van down the M3 motorway to the Rownhams Service Station, just west of Southampton. There she stopped to fill up with petrol before branching off, through the darkened outskirts of the city, to follow a small road which ran parallel to Southampton Water. She didn't have to go far before she came to a signpost to Cobbleford.

It was a mistake to use such a noticeable vehicle as the purple van, she realised that now, but it was too late to turn back. She drove slowly through the village, past the bus stop, parking the van behind the disused church, out of sight of the pub. Leaving one door unlocked in case she had to make a quick retreat, she slipped quietly across the car park towards the pub. Her heart was thudding in her ears and her hands were slippery with fear. The keys in her pocket clinked and she gripped them tightly.

The sky was clouded and the new moon produced little light, but the lane to the Cobble Keys was illuminated spasmodically and the glow and voices from the bar acted as a beacon. The towpath crossed in front of the pub, and Anna could see two boats tied up where she had moored *The Blonde Bimbo*, but there was another track, wide enough to take a lorry, which ran behind the building. At first Anna thought that it went no further than the back door, being solely for deliveries of liquor and food, but as her eyes grew more accustomed to the darkness she saw that this unmade road continued, curling behind an old corrugated iron shed.

She hesitated, standing in the shadows, listening, her ears straining to hear before she was heard. She didn't know exactly where Derek's boatyard was, but she felt sure that it was near. With her fingers clenched in her pockets, she crept along the track. It was rough, with deep tractor furrows, and on either side brambles and creepers grew in profusion. They reached and grabbed at Anna's legs as she passed.

After some fifty yards she came out into a clearing strewn with rusty trailers and discarded tyres. On the far side, visible in the feeble moonlight, she could just make out the dark silhouette of a large shed, like a small aircraft hangar. Next to it was a lean-to, and behind that a smaller hut with a sloping roof. She eased her way around the clearing, stopping every few yards to listen, but the only sounds were the distant laughter in the pub and the lapping of nearby water.

As she drew near to the shed she saw that it was situated beside a tributary of the River Cobble. Careful not to leave obvious signs of crushed grass, she picked her way across the bank and peered down into the water. There was a large boat moored in the shadows, well covered with tarpaulin. She took a few steps nearer and reached out to lift one corner. Underneath was the gleaming stern of a small but expensive yacht.

She started to retrace her steps, thinking only of the moment when she climbed thankfully in the van and drove away from Cobbleford forever. But she stopped herself – she hadn't come this far to turn tail. Clutching at the long grass so as not to fall in the river, she climbed back down to the yacht and eased her way along the bank, under the building, until she was level with the bow. Balancing between the bank and the boat, she removed the tarpaulin. There was no name on the boat. Gingerly she stepped aboard and, kneeling on the foredeck, she checked the other side. Nothing. Then she ran her hand along the exterior until her fingers came to the point where the *Small Ships Register* number should be. There was no indentation, but the surface was rough as though packed with cement filler which had yet to be sand-papered.

She climbed back on to the bank and listened again, but she could hear no one except the distant pub. Taking her camera from her pocket she clicked on the flashlight and pressed the button. There was an alarmingly bright glare as she took a close-up of the doctored registration number. She stepped away and took another picture from the right and another from the left, snapping quickly, knowing that if she were spotted, she'd have little chance of escape.

Replacing the tarpaulin, she scrambled up the bank, squashing the grass as fear overcame caution. She raced across the clearing, then stopped again. Braver now that she was in the open, she lined up the shed, the lean-to, the little hut and the tip of the yacht in her viewfinder and took one last picture.

An instant after the clearing was illuminated, a noise like a chain being drawn across a wooden floor came from the small hut and the door burst open. An enormous white mongrel raced out, barking furiously. Anna screamed as it bounded towards her. She lifted her hands to protect her face from the slavering, snarling jaws. She wanted to run but she was paralysed with fear, and in any case the dog would certainly catch her.

Then the dog stopped dead, slithering to a halt in the mud, yelping as the chain tightened around its neck. Anna fled back along the track towards the Cobble Keys, the dog barking furiously behind her, lumbering up and down at the end of its chain as it howled its anger into the night. As she reached the corrugated shed, the back door of the pub was flung open, lighting up the whole yard. Anna retreated into the shadows, biting on her hand to stifle her gasps for breath. She just managed to hide before Derek stepped out.

'Bloody animal never stops barking,' she heard him say.

'I thought you told me the dog was deaf,' said his companion.

'That's what the vet claims. Damned vets, cost you a fortune and know nothing.' Derek grumbled on down the track towards the boathouse.

Anna waited until both men were out of sight and then she ran as fast as she could, terrified in case Derek loosed the dog and it came after her. She was trembling so violently when she reached the van that she could hardly fit the key into the ignition, and as she drove out of the car park, she knocked over a tub of geraniums, but she didn't stop.

42

ANNA WAS STILL shaking when she reached Black Swan Bay. She drove slowly around the harbour, past the black-beamed Hungry Pirate whose lights blazed although it was after midnight. On the headland the ruined monastery stood out, pale and eerie. Opposite it the lights in Paul's boathouse twinkled behind the giant oak tree. She stopped to extract the film from her camera then paused, her chin on the steering wheel, drinking in the sights and sounds of the little fishing village. She'd been so happy here with Paul.

Bobby started to bark as she turned under the oak tree and she saw movement in an upper window, and knew that Paul was aware of her arrival. Running her fingers through her hair, she took a deep breath, and stepped from the van.

Paul had been about to go to bed, and he pulled on his jeans and a sweater, and hurried down. He opened the door before Anna reached it, and stood in the threshold, watching her approach, knowing how deeply he would miss her. He hadn't contacted her during the day, he'd decided it was up to her, and when he'd heard nothing, he'd resigned himself – at least, he'd attempted to.

Anna stopped just short of him, and they stared at each other in raw silence. She hadn't expected him to fall into her arms, but his detachment unnerved her. And yet he had seldom looked so attractive as he did then, with his ruffled dark hair and sleepy grey eyes.

'I promised you an explanation,' she said.

'I expected it earlier.'

'I couldn't get it until now.'

Puzzled, he stepped aside. 'Come in.'

She walked to the far side of the fireplace, keeping a distance between herself and Paul. 'Please sit down,' she said, 'I want to tell you . . . everything. I should have told you long ago.'

He turned a chair to face her and sat down, his long legs stretched out in front of him, the tips of his fingers touching in a point beneath his chin. 'I'm listening,' he said in a non-committal tone.

She'd forgotten the speech she'd rehearsed, so she clenched her fists and grappled for the words, pacing up and down in front of him. 'It started when I left Eurohull,' she began. 'No, it was long before, when Charlie and I bought the house on Ladbroke Hill. It was too expensive, really, but I fell in love with it – I've told you already that it reminded me of Cliff Cottage. When we were made redundant and lost our cheap mortgage, the only lender who'd consider us was East Metro.' She noted his expression. 'Yes, they're sharks, but we had no alternative. They agreed that we could use the house as collateral to run up a deficit until we started work – only we couldn't find jobs, then Charlie walked out – and I discovered I was pregnant. East Metro threatened repossession. Somehow – God knows how – I persuaded the manager to let me take in tenants and pay off the excess after Daisy was born. But the interest rates rose and the rents didn't cover the mortgage, so I continued to accumulate debt. By the time I started at Eurohull, I owed quite a sum. Nearly all my earnings went towards it. I was due to repay the last five thousand pounds when Daisy became ill, I could still have done it – if Stuart hadn't withheld my commission.'

She looked at Paul but he said nothing, neither judgmental nor sympathetic.

'As soon as I defaulted, East Metro started proceedings to repossess Ladbroke Hill,' she continued. 'I tried every means to raise the money . . . selling my clothes, offering to help Louise, the DSS, I even rang an escort agency.' She answered his questioning look. 'No, I didn't do that! But I was faced with being homeless, with a sick child. I was desperate.' She paused, then added very slowly, 'So I . . . stole a yacht.'

Paul stared at her in disbelief.

She went on quickly, not wanting him to interrupt her flow. 'I didn't want to do it, but could think of no alternative. I went to Sailham . . . yes, you will remember that you told me there'd been a number of thefts from that area. Well, mine was one of them. I rowed out, took a small yacht called *The Blonde Bimbo* and hid her in a creek, the one where my father kept the *Little Auk* when he couldn't afford mooring fees. Then I advertised her in a yachting magazine, using a box number. A man called Derek answered – I don't know his surname, but he lives at Cobbleford. I sailed the boat there. He liked her, and paid me cash. I only wanted five thousand pounds, just enough to clear my debt and no more. I didn't tell him my real name or give him my address, and I never expected to see him again. But I was wrong.'

She was speaking with barely a pause, purging herself of the nightmare. 'Derek had a contact at the magazine who released my details. He came to the house. 'He wanted me to continue. He said I was the perfect thief because I didn't look the part, and when I refused he started to threaten Daisy.' Her voice shook. 'He sent me a photograph of her, slashed. He came to the house; he threatened me on the telephone; he said that *The Blonde Bimbo* was already stolen and that I owed him and his friends the five thousand pounds they'd paid me.' Tears rolled down her cheeks but she did not try to stop them. 'He said that I had to steal another boat to clear my debt, and if I refused, they'd hurt Daisy. That's why I stayed with Roz whilst you were away, before we went to America, I was afraid to remain at Ladbroke Hill. If you'd been in England I'd have told you then.

'Within a day of my return from Whaler's Rock, Derek was threatening me again. That's why I rang Michael in the night – I was frantic to speak to you, I didn't know what to do, I was in too deep to go to the police, and in any case Derek was watching the house.' She took a deep breath. 'In the end, I agreed to do . . . one more job. That's where I was when you thought I'd been with Charlie, trying to steal a yacht on the Lymington river.'

Paul spoke for the first time. 'Do you mean *The Ballard*?'

She nodded, too miserable to be surprised that he knew the name.

'And you believed they'd leave you alone?' His tone was non-committal, almost as though she were a stranger.

'Yes . . . no . . . of course I didn't, but I was desperate.' She looked at him, but he was staring at the floor, frowning, and she was convinced that his love was dying, and she could not prevent it, she only had herself to blame. 'I know . . . this is the end for us. I realise that it's impossible for you to understand how I could have done such a thing – I ask myself the same question. But this film should enable you to catch Derek and when you do, hopefully, you won't think so badly of me.' She laid the reel on the coffee table and started for the door.

Paul wasn't aware of her movements, only of the torment she'd endured and the awful predicament it posed for him. Then suddenly he heard her open the front door, and he looked up. 'Wait,' he called.

She hesitated, wanting to stay with him but afraid to prolong the inevitable pain.

He rose. 'Anna, why didn't you confide in me?'

'I tried to, I wanted to from the beginning. I planned to that night when we watched *To Have and to Have Not*, but then you said you'd never trust a woman who stole.'

He couldn't believe how she'd been prevented by a casual remark. 'That was just a comment.'

'On the day you left for Yugoslavia, Derek had phoned before you arrived home. Don't you remember I told you I had something important to say?'

'Yes, but you said it concerned your mother.'

'I know. I was wrong to lie, but I didn't want to worry you with my problems when you were going away.'

'Anna, we were in the States for a fortnight, together every minute. Why didn't you tell me then?'

'Because I'd concealed the truth for so long that I became afraid that once you knew . . .'

'I'd walk out on you?'

She nodded. 'Yes.'

He nearly said that he wasn't like Charlie or her father, but he stopped himself because she didn't deserve to suffer any more. He saw the remorse in her eyes and heard the deep regret in her voice, and he took her in his arms gently, as though she were very fragile. 'Don't worry,' he said. 'We'll sort it out between us – somehow.'

She couldn't speak, she was crying so hard into his shoulder, all the terrors of the past weeks unleashed by the knowledge that he still cared, that he did not reject her. 'I'm sorry,' she whispered. 'So very sorry.'

He stroked her hair. 'It's all right, darling. You're safe. Derek can't hurt you, but we must think of a plan. What's in the film?'

'Night photos of Derek's boatyard, and of an expensive yacht moored underneath. I ran my hand along the side. The number has been filled in.'

'Where is this place?'

'At Cobbleford, behind the pub.'

'When did you take the film?'

'Tonight.'

He was both horrified at the risk she'd taken and full of admiration. 'You mean you went there alone, at night?'

'I had to.' She raised her chin. 'I wanted evidence for you – and for me.'

He released her and walked to the cupboard, took out a bottle of brandy, and poured them each a drink. 'This is a terrible coincidence,' he said, handing her a glass. 'I've been asked to investigate a claim for water damage to *The Ballard*. According to Michael, the police suspect that the thief was a woman. They found size six footprints in the mud along the shore.'

'Oh, God!' All her fears returned and she put down her glass, untouched. 'I'm sorry. I'll do anything to trap Derek. Paul, please let me help you.'

He took her face very firmly in both of his hands. 'Only if you promise to trust me.'

'I do. I will.'

He brushed her mouth with his. 'We need to act quickly. The police have to catch Derek actually tampering with the boat or else he'll claim he bought it in good faith from a man whose name he can't remember. If we approach them direct, they'll want to know your part in it and would try to persuade you to give evidence.'

'I couldn't do that,' she said, her voice rising in fear. 'Once Derek realised that I'd turned against him, Daisy would never be safe. He might go to prison for a year, even two, but sooner or later he'd be out, and he'd come after her.'

With his hands cupping her face, Paul forced her to look at him. 'Anna, it's all right, I wasn't suggesting that. Michael's our best bet. He used to work undercover, he has all the contacts, but he's no longer in the force. He'll know what we should do.' He released her gently and reached for the telephone.

She seized his arm. 'Paul! No! I'd risk myself to catch Derek, but not Daisy. I'll tell you all you need to find the boatyard, and you can pass it on to Michael, but no one must know the information came from me.'

He took her hands in his, wincing when he saw the lacerations in her palms, but he didn't ask how she'd cut herself. He knew that from the police report. 'I wouldn't dream of endangering you,' he said, 'but I'd trust Michael with my life.'

'I can't take the risk.' She stepped away from him. 'Please don't think I don't have confidence in your judgement, but I'm terrified for Daisy.'

Paul moved nearer, intending to reassure her that it didn't matter, they wouldn't call Michael, they'd do it her way, whatever made her feel safe, but she backed away from him, afraid that he'd persist. Before he could speak, she said, 'I can't expect you to understand what drove me to . . . steal. I realise that my . . . crime will always stand between us. It was naive of me to hope otherwise.' She was crying now, softly, tears sliding down her cheeks. 'I broke your code, Paul. I know you could never forgive that, because you wouldn't have done the same. You'd never do anything you're ashamed of, that you'd regret, you're not haunted by the past . . .' Her words trailed away when she saw the dark anguish in his eyes.

They looked at each other in silence, then he said, in a voice which shook with emotion. 'I understand only too well. You see, I . . . killed Felicity.'

She was so stunned that she didn't react.

'I don't mean that I murdered her,' he went on, 'but I let her take the car keys, knowing she was drunk.'

Forgetting her own predicament, Anna took a step towards him. 'Paul . . . that wasn't your fault.'

'Oh, yes it was.' He began to pace up and down, exactly as she had done when telling her story; and just as he had done, she allowed him to tell it uninterrupted. 'I went back to Felicity after our separation because I . . . still loved her – or maybe I loved the memory of what we'd once had – and when she told me she was booked into a clinic, I hoped that maybe we could start afresh.

After all, it was partly my fault that she . . . drank. She wasn't an alcoholic when we married, and I blame myself for being so blind to her distress. But it wasn't easy to help Felicity. She always maintained that nothing was wrong – like you did.' He gave her a wry smile. 'Anyhow, once I was back, she cancelled the clinic. We staggered on for a couple of weeks. She was drinking heavily, but always in secret. On the night she died, I told her I wanted a divorce. We had a terrible row. She started talking about Georgina again – we'd stopped going to Whaler's Rock because she'd accused Georgina and me of being lovers. I remember, I was walking upstairs, and she took her car keys from the brass plate where she always kept them, and shouted after me, "I'll kill myself." For the first time, I didn't try to prevent her. She went out of the house, and I let her go. It was only when I heard the car go down the drive that I realised she was serious. I ran after her. I know she saw me in her rearview mirror, because she speeded up. I think she wanted to give me a fright – but when she reached the road she lost control and skidded straight across it into a wall.'

Anna walked back to Paul and put her arms around him. 'You mustn't blame yourself,' she said.

He drew her close. 'I could have removed the car keys.'

'I could have sold Ladbroke Hill.'

'But you didn't – and that doesn't stop me loving you. I know what it means to be desperate.'

She whispered, 'We both do.'

Paul kissed her tenderly – and she knew that he was her oasis, her Cliff Cottage; but most of all, because he too had been through hell and back, she could be herself with him. She could be Anna Tobias, and he'd still love her.

OTHER TITLES AVAILABLE IN ARROW

☐ A Man	Oriana Fallaci	£5.99
☐ Bermuda	Vanessa Fox	£4.99
☐ The Rose Bowl	Judy Gardner	£4.99
☐ The Last Reunion	Sara Hylton	£4.99
☐ A Tracing of Angels	Mary Minton	£4.99
☐ Players	Nina Lambert	£4.99
☐ Sleeping With The Enemy	Nancy Price	£4.99
☐ A Heartbeat Away	Barbara Rogan	£4.99
☐ Fantasies	Beverly Sassoon	£4.99
☐ Acts of Faith	Erich Segal	£5.99
☐ The Shadow Players	Linda Sole	£4.99
☐ Friends and Other Enemies	Diana Stainforth	£4.50
☐ The Wilder Side of Life	Diana Stainforth	£4.99
☐ The Eden Inheritance	Janet Tanner	£4.99

ALL ARROW BOOK ARE AVAILABLE THROUGH MAIL ORDER OR FROM YOUR LOCAL BOOKSHOP AND NEWSAGENT.

PLEASE SEND CHEQUE/EUROCHEQUE/POSTAL ORDER (STERLING ONLY) ACCESS, VISA OR MASTERCARD

☐☐☐☐☐☐☐☐☐☐☐☐☐☐☐☐

EXPIRY DATE ....SIGNATURE ....

PLEASE ALLOW 75 PENCE PER BOOK FOR POST AND PACKING U.K.
OVERSEAS CUSTOMER PLEASE ALLOW £1.00 PER COPY FOR POST AND PACKING.

ALL ORDERS TO:
ARROW BOOKS, BOOK SERVICE BY POST, P.O. BOX 29, DOUGLAS, ISLE OF MAN, IM99 1BQ.
TEL: 01624 675 137 FAX: 01624 670 923

NAME ....

ADDRESS ....

....

Please allow 28 days for delivery. Please tick box if you do not wish to receive any additional information ☐

Prices and availability subject to change without notice.